DESPITE THE FALLING SNOW

YOU CAN BETRAY YOUR COUNTRY
BUT NOT YOUR HEART

SHAMIM SARIF

metro

Published by Metro Publishing
an imprint of John Blake Publishing Ltd,
3 Bramber Court, 2 Bramber Road,
London W14 9PB, England

www.johnblakebooks.com

www.facebook.com/johnblakebooks
twitter.com/jblakebooks

First published in 2010

This edition published in 2016

ISBN: 978 1 786061072

British Library Cataloguing-in-Publication Data:

A catalogue record for this book is available from the British Library.

Design by www.envydesign.co.uk

Printed in Great Britain by CPI Group (UK) Ltd

3 5 7 9 10 8 6 4 2

Papers used by John Blake Publishing are natural, recyclable products made
from wood grown in sustainable forests. The manufacturing processes conform
to the environmental regulations of the country of origin.

Every attempt has been made to contact the relevant copyright-holders,
but some were unobtainable. We would be grateful if the
appropriate people could contact us.

For Hanan, Ethan & Luca,
for the revelation you have bestowed –
that every moment of life can be wondrous and beautiful.

~

And in memory of David Pithlado,
who in life and death taught everyone he touched
that life is a gift.

ACKNOWLEDGEMENTS

The following people were invaluable during the process of researching this book:

My sister Anouchka who accompanied me to Moscow, and who introduced me to Nazim Walimohamed, who was so generous with his time and contacts. Marina Rabinskaya took on the role of guide and proved to be a superb interpreter. She also helped me to find people who remembered Khrushchev's leadership. Galina Dronova, Yuri Bychkov and Zinaida Gurevitch provided an overall sense of that time as well as much important nuance and detail in their recollections of the period. Michael Weinstein helped to consider the most probable plotlines over (not too much) vodka in Moscow. Thanks also to Yasmine Naber who introduced me to Varvara Underwood here in London and to Zinaida Chnitko, who took the time to answer the questions that arose later in the writing process.

Thanks to my agent Euan Thorneycroft for his excellent guiding comments and to Rosie de Courcy, for her delicate editing. Thanks also to David Pitblado and Katherine Priestley for an excellent final reading. And immense gratitude to my partner, Hanan Kattan, for everything, not least her brilliant, thorough, incisive close reading. It is a rare dream for a writer to have an involved, sensitive reader who knows what you wish to convey, and is unafraid to tell you if you have not quite managed it. It is a thankless task, but I thank her for it.

She tells her love while half asleep
In the dark hours,
With half-words whispered low:
As Earth stirs in her winter sleep
And puts out grass and flowers
Despite the snow,
Despite the falling snow.

Robert Graves

CHAPTER ONE

BOSTON – NOVEMBER 1998

S HE HAS BEEN SITTING ON A WOODEN BENCH in the courtyard of this office building for some time – about twenty minutes, she guesses – and she is briefly grateful that the large quadrant is enclosed from the ice-hard blasts of wind that seemed to burn through her as she walked here; only the soft purity of the blue sky above is caught between the tops of buildings. The space is explicitly welcoming, but she cannot help but feel oppressed by the ungainly height of the structures around it. The shiny, varnished seating, the eerily immaculate late autumn flower beds, the studied restfulness of the trickling fountain – all these lead her to regard this corporate resting place with subdued contempt. Resolving that she will not check her watch – not just yet – she turns her attention back to the novel. She is on page five (of seven hundred and forty three) and she decides to begin the page again, since she has read it through without absorbing a single word.

1

It is hardly more gripping the second time around, and she wonders whether, at the age of sixty one, she might not be excused from reading things that don't grab her at once, taking into account that even in the best of circumstances, she can't have *that* much time left in this world. Her husband has gruffly advised her to read Proust, to revel in his refinement of thought, to admire his delicacy of phrase. She is intelligent enough and perceptive enough to recognise both of those things, even within the small portion she has read, but something is lacking *here*. Unconsciously, she touches her heart. Perhaps it will come later, if she will but give the novel a chance. She eyes her handbag with a sidelong, slightly guilty gaze, like a child trying not to stare at a forbidden toy. The bag contains two slim volumes; one, a Hemingway novel, the other a book of stories by Salinger. Her husband is unimpressed by both, but holds a particularly sarcastic contempt for the Salinger. Nevertheless, she likes it, admires the direct simplicity of the sentences. She had been hesitant to read the stories again after Professor Johnson's vehement assertion that they possessed no real merit, but she found to her pleasure that they had come through unscathed, and were as poignant and relaxed and cleanly written as she had first thought them.

Her eyes are drawn back to the looming building before her. The endless squares of darkened glass and polished steel are uninviting, inscrutable, protective of the activity going on behind them. She is rarely in the business district. It is a section of the city that is unfamiliar to her, that has no relation to the Boston she loves. Hers, rather, is a world of red brick houses and streets lined with trees that are coolly shady in summer and starkly proud in winter. The calm, broad sparkle of the Charles River, and the sweeping energy of the Back Bay. The small specialist shops of Newbury Street, the cobbled streets of old Beacon Hill, and the faint rumble of traffic that counterpoints the delicate quiet of the public gardens. The coffee houses around the many university campuses where you might stumble upon a reading or some music. Still self-consciously avoiding the book in her hands, she glances away from the structure before her, and looks for comfort to the solitary tree that soars up from the concrete. It is half-stripped of leaves, but those that remain still show deep, burnished reds and darkening browns; the fading colours of a New England autumn that has come late this year, and is now almost at its end.

She becomes aware that something is buzzing. She glances around seeking the source of the noise, but there is no one in the courtyard but herself. Then she feels a vibration against her feet. Inside her handbag. Reaching in, she pulls out her mobile phone, and slams shut the Proust. The handset shudders in her hand like a thing in pain. She focuses on it – none of the buttons appear clearly marked. She pushes a black one, then a green one, then holds it to her ear. Nothing.

"You're not used to it, are you?" says a voice.

She turns her head. Beside her, watching her, stands Alexander Ivanov. He is neatly wrapped in an understated but expensive navy cashmere coat and a russet scarf which emphasises his silver hair. He removes his hat when she turns but she is too surprised to even notice the polite gesture.

"All the buttons look the same," she says. She drops the handset back into her bag.

"You should get your daughter to teach you, Estelle," he smiles.

"Maybe over lunch today," she tells him. He says nothing to this, and she wonders if his silence is meaningful, coupled as it is with the fact that Melissa is nowhere to be seen. She shifts over on the bench, conscious that she is taking up the only available seat, and he sits down, keeping a correct distance, and smiles at her. His eyes are large and dark brown and softened slightly with age – the warm pools of colour look textured, like worn velvet, she thinks.

"It's good to see you again," he tells her. "We didn't really get a chance to talk much the first time." He has an accent when he speaks, a precision of utterance that is well-defined but also musical. There is a heaviness on the letter "L" that she is most aware of when he says her name.

"It was kind of you to let me wait in your office that day," she says.

"Why didn't you come up today? It's cold out here."

"I like the fresh air," she says simply. She does not attempt to explain her ill-defined antipathy to the building – she has only met him once, and he is unlikely to understand her irrational whims, particularly since he owns the building in question.

"Anyway, if the meeting's done…" she says.

"Actually, it's still going on. I played truant, that's all."

She is still wondering how someone can play truant from the sale of his own multi-million dollar company when his telephone rings.

"Perhaps that's them," Alexander says, reassurance in his voice. She looks back up at the tree for something to do while she tries not to listen to the clear voice at the other end. Something about some final queries and wouldn't he like to come back to the meeting?

"Not especially," he says. "Why doesn't everyone break for lunch? I believe Melissa has another appointment…"

There is quiet at the other end, some conferring perhaps, before the metallic voice comes back on the line.

"She says it's nothing important. She'd rather get this thing hammered out and finished."

She can see him press the phone more closely to his ear, trying to block the words from floating out to her across the cool, crisp air.

"Very well, I'll be back in a couple of hours," he says, his tone terse. "Try and have it done by then, will you, Michael?"

He snaps the phone shut, then switches it off. He looks at Estelle, and there is a moment of quiet communication between them. She knows what has happened, and wants to save him the trouble of finding a tactful way to tell her that her daughter will not bother to come.

"I saw the article in *Business World* the other week," she says. "'The King of Catering'."

5

"Those headlines…" he says, with a slight shake of his head.

"I thought it was interesting," she replies. "Especially about your background. Your life in Russia."

He nods slightly, enough to politely acknowledge the comment, but says nothing. Estelle considers asking again, for the few lines about Alexander's early life gleaned from the article suggested a story worth hearing. She decides against probing too much – after all, she knows him only slightly. She pulls a hat from her bag, a preliminary to leaving.

"I'm sorry about lunch with Melissa," he says. He hesitates, and a quick smile moves across his face, which otherwise looks concerned, even nervous. "Would you care to join me instead?"

Estelle pauses, surprised, and while she is thinking, decides against trying to put on her hat blindly and yet elegantly while he is watching. Instead she uses it to keep her hands warm.

"Shouldn't you be going back in?" Estelle asks.

"What for? They all know what to do."

She raises an eyebrow. "I hope so. She may be my daughter, but I don't mind telling you that Melissa has the manners of a piranha when it comes to closing a deal."

He laughs, surprised at her tight appraisal of her own child, and tells her that he doesn't mind, that tough negotiations are a part of most business transactions. There is a short pause between them, a moment when he seems to be debating whether to reveal or explain something. He looks up at the glass building.

"That's where they are. Twenty-sixth floor."

Once again she looks up. It is the type of inaccessible building that she usually associates with her daughter, clean and lean and functional.

"I was sitting there, fifteen minutes ago, sealed inside, looking out of the window like a restless schoolboy who can't concentrate on his math lesson. All I could see was the sky, and beyond that the city and the Back Bay. When I finally came to, someone was asking me something, and I had no idea what it was. Nor did I much care what it was. So, I excused myself and came down here."

"It can't be easy, watching someone else take charge of your business."

"I suppose that must have something to do with it. But I'm not sorry to let it go. It's time."

He rubs his hands together to keep them warm and fixes her with a mischievous look. "So will you come for lunch? Melissa did promise we'd get together the last time. And you can help me play truant."

"It's kind of you, but not at all necessary..."

"Martha, my housekeeper, is at home if you feel happier with a chaperone," he says.

"Trust me, it's been decades since I worried about men being gripped by uncontrollable bouts of passion at the mere sight of me," she tells him. "Don't worry, I'm not scared of you."

"Good. It's settled then?" He stands up, as though it is.

She feels a prickle at this hint of presumption, but her

curiosity about this man has been building. There is nothing she likes more than a good story. And she is cold, and hungry, and does not feel like returning to the desolate reaches of her apartment, or sitting in a restaurant alone.

He takes out his phone again. "Why don't I call Melissa and have her meet us when they're done?"

She nods, grateful for his consideration – that her daughter knows where she is and will join them gives her a measure of security, a final encouragement that she is doing the right thing by having lunch with a man she knows, but does not know. They walk out together, across the squares of sunlight that cover the courtyard. A scatter of auburn leaves floats to the ground before them, and there is something touching to her in the way that Alexander reaches out to feel one as it drops. In the sight of his hand, slightly curved and battered from old age, and Boston winters, and probably from Russian winters too, extending out involuntarily to greet a stray leaf that falls right before his eyes. He watches it settle, feather-like, upon the ground. Then he guides her out to the main doors of the building where the doorman tips his hat and whistles down a cab.

She slides into the red vinyl seats, and Alexander is half-inside too but stops to hand the doorman a tip. His wallet is flipped open – a rich, brown leather casing, which is beginning to show the grainy softness of age. He pulls out a bill and hands it to the man, but Estelle's attention is on a photograph that is exposed inside the open wallet. She sees it for only a second, perhaps two, and it is old and black and white, and perhaps even very slightly out of focus. But the woman in the picture is arresting – she is also young and quite beautiful. Estelle can tell that much despite the fact that the woman is squinting into the camera because the sun is in her eyes. There is something about the photograph, something seductive, something she has no time to think about or define at that moment – but it strikes her as one of those images that contain a whole attitude and atmosphere and that would make anyone stop and take a second look if they could. As Alexander enters the cab, his thumb brushes lightly and very quickly over the picture, and his glance falls on Estelle; then the wallet is closed, and the woman is gone.

He gives the driver his address, and Estelle clears her throat, but hesitates to ask the question on her lips. He looks at her, expectant, a clear gaze with those clear brown eyes, and she can tell nothing at all from them. With a polite smile, she sits back in her seat and looks ahead as the cab moves off.

His house is an old, red-brick building, dating from the days when high ceilings and grand rooms were common. From the days when a growing city could afford to be expansive.

"It's nice to see a place like this that's unconverted."

He nods. "Lots of stairs. Keeps my old bones moving."

"We don't live all that far from each other. We're in a brownstone, it's a lovely building, but we have an apartment. Small, but worth it, to be in the centre of town."

He understands this – he has always lived right in the middle of cities; even in Moscow he had that privilege.

Most people who wanted slightly larger apartments – or any apartment of their own – were forced to move to Khrushchev's new buildings, hastily thrown up, thin-walled and grey, on the outskirts of the city. And many people were happy with that; those blocks gave them space they had never had before. Unless you did well for the Party, or worked in the government itself, rooms at the hub of Moscow were tiny and overfilled.

He holds open his front door for Estelle and she steps into a wood-panelled hallway that instantly brings to her mind an English country house. Instead of portraits of ancestors on the walls, there is a selection of art, some abstract, some figurative, all relatively modern. She half-expects a butler to appear, but the only other sign of life is the understated hum of a vacuum cleaner upstairs. While Alexander hangs their coats and scarves, she looks at the artwork. There are a couple of paintings that she feels immediately pulled into. Strangely, they are abstracts, the kind of non-representative pieces that she usually cannot find any empathy with. But these evoke a certain emotion within her, a feeling of lost love or deep sorrow, and she is unsettled by this, and examines the paintings well, trying to ascertain how the patches of textured colours could create such a sensation. She is about to say something to Alexander when he returns, but cannot find the words to articulate what she is thinking, without sounding pretentious or confused.

"Are you sure about this? I hate to trouble you," she says. "We could just go get a sandwich somewhere."

"Absolutely sure. Cooking is a kind of therapy for me. It will be a simple meal."

Estelle follows him into the living room, a large, light space, with leather armchairs and sofas and a wall full of books and a grand piano. A drawing room from a novel, she thinks. In one corner stands a Christmas tree, a real one, that gives off a fresh smell of pine needles and sap. Windows stretch from the ceiling to the floor, showing a small garden beyond. She looks out at this garden while he fetches a bottle of wine from the kitchen next door. The plants and trees have a feeling of fullness even now, in the late autumn, and she can tell that the slightly overgrown, lush, romantic quality of the garden is carefully nurtured. He returns with the bottle and opens it smoothly and with close attention, and Estelle gives him a glance of query before going over to the piano. She studies the photographs that are ranged over it, and picks up one.

"She's very attractive."

"Lauren, my niece," he says. "She's an artist. A painter. Those are some of her pieces in the hall."

Estelle turns, her interest caught. "Really? I thought they were amazing. But I don't know why. I'm so ignorant about great art, and how it's made and yet…"

"Yes?"

"And yet, if there's anything I would have liked to have been, it's a writer."

And there it is, she has said it out loud, the thing that she keeps so quietly within herself.

He takes a sniff of the wine and concentrates. When he

11

offers Estelle a glass, she takes it, swirls the liquid around as he has done, and inhales deeply. The scent is soft and smoky, a deeply comforting smell, of dried fruit and spice and warm tobacco, and it is a world away from the everyday wine that she is used to.

"Why didn't you?" he asks. "Become a writer?"

She winces, then takes a quick sip. "Don't make it sound so simple."

"Why not?"

She makes no immediate answer. When she does speak, quietly, she feels him leaning in to catch her words.

"Because if it is that simple, I've wasted too much time."

It is a clear, open statement and she is almost embarrassed by it.

"Do you write now?" he asks.

She is dismissive, back in control. "A little. Here and there. Not enough, I guess."

Her eyes escape back to the piano, and it is then that she sees her. The woman she noticed earlier, in the wallet photograph. Estelle picks up the frame.

"This one?" she asks.

"Katya. My late wife," he says. Late. As though she has missed a dinner engagement and might be arriving at any moment. His eyes glance outside, involuntarily, away from the picture and from Estelle's enquiring face; the sky is beginning to cloud over and is giving out a dull, heavy light that reminds him of the past, suddenly. That colourless, oppressive air had been such a memorable feature of the days following Katya's death that even now, he cannot bear to feel it too closely about him. He walks to the door, his tone brisk.

"Could I ask you to accompany me to the kitchen?" he says with an exaggerated bow. "And is there anything you don't eat?"

"Sauerkraut," Estelle says promptly. "If there's one thing I can't stand it's cabbage. Especially when it's all pickled and disguised and wishing it was something else."

"There goes my centrepiece dish," he says.

The kitchen is large, as she had expected it would be for someone in his line of work, and it immediately gives her a slight sense of inadequacy. Painted wooden cupboards give it a homely air, arranged around a vast, gleaming steel stove that takes up much of one wall. Above the stove hangs a wood and steel rack from which shining pots, pans and colanders are suspended. On steel hooks over the stove there are large cooking spoons and a number of other items; tiny frying pans and sieves, mashers and graters – many of which have uses that she cannot even guess at. Here, she notices, there is none of the casual disarray and untidiness that always seems to creep into her own home, no matter how she tries to keep things in their proper place. There is abundance here, but also a feeling of order. With quick movements, he ties on a half-apron.

"I've been longing to be in this kitchen all morning. Thank you for giving me the opportunity."

"You're more than welcome. I wish I had your enthusiasm

for kitchens, but I don't. Which is why I always promised myself I'd marry a man who could cook."

The opportunity he has been looking for. Some part of him has hesitated to ask her outright whether she is married.

"So your husband can cook?" he asks.

"No," she replies with a laugh. "He can't."

He weighs the tomatoes in his hand – they give a little to his touch, the deep red skin showing the slightest beginnings of a wrinkle of over-ripeness. Satisfied, he pours boiling water over them, waiting a moment for the skins to split, before he peels and chops. They are tossed into the pan where smashed garlic and fine-chopped onions are already frying, filling the kitchen with an aroma that makes her feel hungry at once. She watches the chunky freshness of the tomatoes collapsing in the pan, melting into the translucent onions.

"What can I do?" Estelle asks.

"You could grate the parmesan."

He hands her a large block of cheese, rough-edged and pungent. She smells it.

"My god, that's wonderful. And I thought it came from the cow ready grated…"

"Shame on you," he says. "Here." He shaves off a piece with a knife and offers it to her. "Taste this."

Carefully, she takes the cheese and places it in her mouth.

"It's wonderful," she tells him.

He hands her the wine glass. "Now take a sip of that over it."

She is inordinately conscious of his hand touching hers as

he passes the glass over. The cheese is rich and full, with layers of flavour that are completely unlike anything she has tried before. He turns away, as if to give her time and space to enjoy the tasting, and washes basil leaves at the sink. The wine runs smoothly over the lingering taste in her mouth, deepening and rounding it. She resists closing her eyes to concentrate her other senses, and instead, watches him tear the basil into the sauce. He pauses and holds a handful of the leaves under her nose. She smells them and smiles, an acknowledgement of the vibrancy of the herbal scent. She watches as he works, leaning over the pan, and takes another sip of wine, grateful for a moment unobserved to absorb the discoveries she feels she has been making all morning.

They begin the meal with steamed asparagus, dipped into melted butter. They eat with their fingers, cradling the stems, coaxing them into the sauce.

"I don't think I've ever met anyone who loves food as much as you do, Alexander."

"It's just fresh, simple ingredients," he says. "I got used to stale food in Russia, at least some of the time, but here there is no excuse. And I was lucky. My first job here in America was in my brother-in-law's grocery store. I was surrounded by food all day."

"So you really did start with nothing?"

Less than nothing, he thinks. No money and no prospects was the least of it. A heart as dead as a blighted tree was much harder to overcome.

"Yes," he answers.

She looks at him, a pin-sharp gaze, but he will not speak the sorrow in his eyes.

"I remember it so well, even now," he says. "Coming from Russia, I had never seen so much food. So much *fresh* food. So many wonderful breads and cakes, and fruit and meat all in one place. Of course, compared to the delis and supermarkets we have now, it was nothing, but then… I thought we sold everything. Flour and sugar came out of big drums, into paper bags which were weighed."

"I remember," smiles Estelle.

"After a while, I began baking in the shop. Cakes, pies, tarts. We sold them piece by piece."

Slowly, they had added more dishes – brown-crusted meat pies, lentil-rich soups. Shop and office workers began to come in and buy their lunches there, and Alexander would watch them from the kitchen in the back, noting a shop girl's smile as she caught the scent of her soup, or an old man biting gratefully into a pie, unable to wait until he left the shop.

"From there it was a natural progression to catering and canapés," he says, with a slightly ironic smile. He sprinkles the grated cheese into the hot pasta and carries it to the table.

"Who were your clients?" Estelle asks.

"Mostly well-to-do women. Lots of families in Beacon Hill."

"That's where I used to live."

"Really?"

16

She shakes away his interest. "A long, long time ago."

He watches her. Even though she has stopped speaking, he cannot help himself. There is something about her. He searches her face – the high cheekbones are clear, but their defined edges have become a little softened with age. Her eyes are an unlikely shade of bright blue, with an animation behind them that makes them crackle, like neon. He had noticed this the first time they met. He had spent a few minutes settling her in his own office to wait for her daughter, who had remained in his boardroom where they were slowly negotiating the terms of her purchase of his company. He had liked Estelle at once; though their conversation that day did not move much beyond pleasantries, there was a quickness, an ironic undertone to some of her replies which had suggested a vibrant personality, and which found a complement, a ready means of expression in her startling eyes. Melissa's eyes are grey, perhaps after her father. He searches Estelle's face for something of her daughter's cool, veiled look but he can find nothing of it there.

"What is it?"

"I was just trying to figure out if Melissa looks like you."

Estelle shakes her head. "Not much. She has my nose, maybe, but the rest of her is her father."

The pasta, like everything else she has tasted so far, is a revelation. The firm bite of the penne beneath the sweet spiciness of the tomato sauce. Then the balance of the fresh basil and smooth, rich parmesan. She leans back in her chair, feeling slightly indecorous, overwhelmed as she is by a surfeit of pleasure. She takes another, fragrant bite as Alexander asks her if she ever had a career.

"Not until my mid-twenties. I didn't need to work, I suppose. My father was well-to-do, and it just wasn't the thing in those days. One just waited to get married."

"And you did?"

"Not immediately, no." She runs a crust of fresh bread over the sauce that remains on her plate. "All those young Harvard boys that would come visiting." She makes a face at the memory.

"So you began working?"

"Yes, to my father's great consternation. I just couldn't stand sitting around any more, drinking tea, and preparing for dinner parties. So, I got a job, though goodness knows how. I couldn't type, couldn't take dictation....Couldn't do any of the things young women needed for work back then, though I learned pretty quickly. I worked at Boston University. As an assistant to various professors. Mostly in the English Department."

"Why the English Department?" he asks quickly, and she hesitates.

"I always loved books, I guess. The smell of them, the feel of the pages, the idea that whole worlds that I'd never seen or felt before were sandwiched between their covers. Every now and then I'd be typing up a paper or an article, and I'd read something completely unexpected about a book I knew. Or thought I knew. I did a lot of re-reading of classic novels based on those papers."

"When did you stop?"

"After I got married. My husband was the last professor I assisted. In the end, he travelled a lot, and wanted me with him."

"Would you have preferred to continue working?"

"Oh no." She laughs, and feels a slight warmth in her cheeks, which she hopes is not visible. "Not then. I was so in love with him. I couldn't bear the thought of us being apart. Anyway, I still helped with his research, and typing for a while....And then, I had Melissa, and it stopped. Once she grew up, I went back to doing a little reading and typing for him, which I still do. It's been a pretty ordinary life."

"Not really. You could have gotten married out of college, to a suitably well to do young man. But you went to work, which as you say, wasn't the thing to do, and then ended up marrying a professor. I assume marrying for passion rather than comfort. Sounds like you didn't play by the rules at all."

Estelle flushes. She is partly embarrassed that he is interested enough to analyse her existence in this way, and partly pleased. She has never considered her choices in the maverick light that he has cast on them.

"Tell me about your writing?"

"Oh, that," she says, and he senses a shyness in her for the first time. "I'm just an aspiring novelist, I guess. In search of a really interesting character."

"I thought writers are always searching for a good plot. Or theme."

"Oh no," she replies, with certainty this time. "The themes are almost always the same, don't you think? Love, passion, death, betrayal."

She feels a slight pause, which for one moment makes her wonder if she has said something wrong – but then he looks up and smiles his assent.

Back in the living room, sinking deep into soft leather armchairs, with a second glass of wine beside each of them, Estelle considers how to approach the subject of his life in Russia. He has fired gentle questions at her all through lunch, but something about his look or his bearing has made her hesitant to do the same. At last she gestures to the photograph on the piano.

"Your wife was very beautiful," she says.

"Do you think so?"

"Don't you? Such life in those eyes."

"I have never seen anyone or anything to match her in all my life."

He turns, conveniently, she thinks, to the dessert plate, an apricot tart, left over from the day before, warmed through.

"She looks very happy there. In the photo," she comments.

Had she been happy? He thinks, perhaps, some of the time. But with Katya, happiness had never been a deep seated state of being. Rather it had been a fleeting sensation, a series of brief respites from the world as it existed for her.

"She had quite a difficult life," he says blandly. If his guest, the aspiring novelist, is in search of an interesting character, he feels no immediate obligation to provide it. He cuts two generous pieces of the tart.

"I suppose I should be declining politely and thinking of my figure," Estelle says. "But at this stage, what's the point?" She thanks him and sits down again, the plate balanced on her knee.

"You were telling me about your wife?"

"Katya, yes. We grew up during the last part of Stalin's rule, you see. He died in fifty three. And then, by the late fifties, Khrushchev took over." True statements, but vague ones, a ploy to move the focus away from the specific. Estelle moves forward, interested.

"Tell me about Stalin's terrors? Wasn't that when all those thousands were arrested and killed?"

"By the time all the waves of arrests were done, it was millions. Tens of millions, even, when you count all the people who starved to death in the countryside. Unnecessarily, after terrible government policy decisions."

"Why?"

Alexander shakes his head. "That's the terrible thing. For no good reason. Paranoia, perhaps. A wish to keep control and power at any cost. Stalin was a cruel man, and he ruled with fear. You disagreed with him, you died. Very few people will argue in those circumstances."

"But when so many people die, when people are losing their families for no reason…didn't it inspire people to fight against it?"

Alexander considers. His eyes are almost closed with the

21

effort of transporting himself back to that time. He was a child then, during the worst of it. Why didn't people fight it? How much suffering must a population go through before they revolt? Those that did revolt, and many who did not, were imprisoned, tortured, killed. One way or another. He looks away, suddenly.

"Is that what happened…?"

"To Katya? Not directly. We were just children during the worst of it. Anyway, Khrushchev was a change. He still did as he pleased, but there was more accountability. You were allowed to criticise. A little."

He stands up, under pretence of pouring more wine. Suddenly the boredom of the meeting that he has just fled seems comforting, and safe. His movements are measured and careful, designed to gain time. Time to re-balance, to bring himself back to the present, away from a place where Katya's name is suddenly arising naturally, and too often.

"Do you mind me asking when your wife died?"

"1959," he replies.

"Ah. That *is* a long time."

"She was very young. We were very young."

"Do you have any children?"

He shakes his head.

"Do you regret it?"

"No regrets. About anything." He smiles, and she sees that the smile is merely a cover for his lie. He sits down, recalling how he had lain next to his wife at night, coated in a darkness unrelieved by streetlamps outside, and he would imagine her child – their baby – and he had begun to love the idea of it almost as if it had actually existed.

He is concerned that she will ask him what happened. Why Katya died. Even after so many decades he has not found a way, a simplified, subtle way to explain, and yet gloss over what had happened to her. It would be so much easier to be able to put forward an acceptable reason. An illness, a terrible accident. But he has still not learned what one says when it was neither. Estelle is about to ask how he and Katya met, when she notices his quick, nervous movements, his eyes roaming away from hers. She sits back in her chair at once, sorry to have pressed the topic. It is rude of her, a guest in his house, to make him uncomfortable. She is trying to decide how to change the subject when he speaks.

"It's a funny thing," he says. "Even though it has been such a long time, sometimes I can still remember how I felt in those weeks after I first met Katya. The excitement, the dizziness, the agony of meeting the person you had never believed existed. It is a wonderful thing to be truly in love." He looks up. "That is what I remember most about my wife. How very much I adored her."

That much is true, he thinks. All the rest; the betrayals, the nightmares, the waking horror, the guilt; he has packed these away over the course of the years, packed it all tightly into one corner of his mind. No regrets. About anything.

CHAPTER TWO

MOSCOW – MARCH 1956

THE ROOM IS WARM, AND FULL. Most of them are young, about his own age, their chatter filling up the peeling high arches that sweep across the ceiling above them. There are lights, and laughter, and glasses that touch each other musically; an unfamiliar feeling of excess and even decadence that forms a welcome illusion for certain moments during this evening. For certain moments, from certain angles, with his eyes half shut, he can see that the long, narrow room in this apartment belonging to Misha's friends has suddenly regained some of the elegance and life that perhaps filled it so often in another, pre-revolutionary lifetime.

There is a small window at his back, and when he feels a cold draught touch his jacket, he turns, and the preternatural glow of the snow lighting the gloom outside attracts him and makes him look. On the street below he sees a small boy and an old lady. Both are carrying large bundles on their backs.

Both look small and frail under their loads and he watches them for a long minute until they move around the corner of the building and are lost to sight. Probably they are carrying home wood to try and warm their rooms. Or room. He looks at his watch. It is ten o'clock.

It is becoming hot at the party, and Alexander runs a finger along his slender neck, under his collar and tie.

"You look like a government man," Misha had told him, with no small measure of sarcasm, when he picked him up. "Don't you have any casual clothes? This is not one of your state department cocktail parties, you know."

"I came directly from work," had been Alexander's taut reply before he had seen Misha's teasing eyes, and then he had laughed. "Anyway, in the end we are all government men, aren't we?"

A light haze of smoke drifts up high, drawn towards the gleaming, makeshift lights strung up in the corners, and he watches Misha, standing across from him, talking, intent on his own words, then listening to those nearby. There is a buzz of excitement in this room, for the first news of Khrushchev's secret speech has been leaking out into Moscow, creeping through cracks in office windows, gusting into apartments where neighbours have been passing overheard comments up through thin-walled buildings. The speech was made at a closed Congress session but Alexander is pleased that their leader's forthright, shocking denouncement of his predecessor Stalin is becoming known to the people outside. The sense of openness, of freedom that has made some of them light-

26

headed at work over the past weeks will start to infect others too. How can that be bad?

As if he has been listening to his friend's thoughts, Misha turns to him.

"And what do you think about Comrade Khrushchev's brave speech, my friend? That the "cult of the individual" mustn't happen again?"

He pauses and takes a drag on his cigarette. "That old man Stalin was a cantankerous, bloody-minded butcher all along?" Misha smiles thinly, and exhales a long stream of smoke upwards. Alexander does not smoke. He used to, as a teenager, but as a young man, the residual taste of tar, the insidious smell of ash in his clothes, bothers him.

"I think it's about time," Alexander replies. "People will see that things are different now. Really different."

Misha slaps him on the back. "Such an idealist, Sasha." He smiles, but the smile is forced, and when he speaks next, his voice has lowered so that only Alexander can hear him.

"You do remember that our beloved leader Nikita Sergeyevitch was around during all that terror. Doing his part?" The soft tones are a precaution, one that may or may not be necessary here, but Misha, like all of them, cannot get used to any other way when talking about certain subjects.

Alexander shrugs as if to say, you asked me, and Misha laughs. His eyes are smiling now, not just his mouth; he looks happy.

"Don't you feel the change, Misha? In the government, in the people, in the air? There is hope now. Maybe now the

Soviet system will work as it should. As it can. And whatever he may have done in the past – well, at least he is trying to change all that now."

"But can people cope with change? Most of them still worship the old man – even more since he's been dead."

"They saw him as immortal, that's all. Even though he took away husbands and fathers and families, Stalin was a god, to be worshipped and deferred to. He set himself up that way, aloof from the destruction. Khrushchev is different, you can see that. He understands the people. It'll be different now," Alexander adds simply.

"Maybe. Maybe it will be. Maybe I do feel it. Hope. Freedom. Truth. Beauty!" Misha raises his hands over his head and declaims the words and a few drunk people around him applaud before going back to their glasses. He takes a breath and another drink before looking up again.

"Oh, but I've worked hard to build up this cynical surface, Sasha. I'll be sorry to let it go just like that. Don't make me abandon it all in one night."

Alexander smiles at his friend – he cannot remember a time, even when they were boys together at school, when Misha has not had that cynical surface. Carefully cultivated, it had always lent him an aura of sophistication in the eyes of his friends as they were growing up, and even now, in tandem with his startling good looks, it seems to ensure the attraction of any number of women. Alexander turns slightly, for Misha's eyes are wandering over his shoulder. There are two girls standing behind them. He steps aside and allows his friend a free try at them, then scans the room as Misha and the girls talk.

A few couples are dancing in one corner, to the music of three men who sit cramped closely together, brows pulled into ridges of concentration, heads swaying, fingers spinning old remembered melodies from a guitar, a fiddle, a pocket flute. The music has been moving faster, gaining speed slowly as the evening progresses, and now has a rhythm that is well held and infectious. Alexander notices that, in the absence of a drum or tambourine, almost everyone in the room is tapping a foot or a finger in time to the music. He smiles to himself, and as his eyes sweep back towards Misha, his gaze catches on something, and he turns back to look.

She is sitting with two other girls at one of the groups of wooden chairs placed haphazardly around the edges of the room. Alexander watches her intently – he is trying to decide what it is about her that has caught his attention. She is beautiful certainly, but there is something else, something in the proud set of her shoulders and head, that sets her apart from the girls around her. She is talking animatedly, telling a joke or a story, and her friends are laughing, and so is she, but her laughter is controlled – she is smiling, but also watching her audience's reaction. He strains to hear her voice, but he is a little too far away, and the people around him are noisy. He looks about him, with the air of someone who has just woken up, and he realises that he does not know how long he has been staring at her; but now there is a young man who has

29

gone up to her, and who is talking to her, trying his luck, and obscuring Alexander's view.

"Sasha! Where do you wander off to in your head? Come, let's get another drink." Misha gives him a friendly slap on the back, and then looks across the room, to see what sight has turned his friend into a statue.

"The blonde?" he asks, puzzled. He has never known a man less easily pleased with women than his best friend, and this girl looks like so many others that Alexander inevitably turns down.

"No." Alexander moves across a few steps, to see past the young man who is still standing in front of her. He pulls Misha with him, and they both look at the fine-boned, dark-haired girl. Misha's eyebrows go up, and he laughs slightly, hesitantly.

"If you're going to fall, Sasha, don't fall for that one."

"Why not?"

Misha does not answer, and Alexander looks at him.

"You know her?"

"A little. Not so well," replies Misha, with a shrug. "We grew up around each other. My parents knew her parents. They were university professors. They were taken. Years ago. During the war." He hesitates, then makes the final comment, the one he would have held inside were it not for all the alcohol sloshing in his head. "Khrushchev's speech came too late for them."

Alexander's frown deepens.

"For what reason?"

Misha almost snorts with laughter. An excess of vodka is sharpening everything he feels, making him lapse into stating what they all already know.

"For what reason! The same reason as everyone else. They were declared 'enemies of the people'. For no damn reason. Some asshole who worked with them probably wanted their jobs, or their apartment or something, and turned them in."

"Imprisoned?" he asks.

"No. They got their eight grams." It has been a while since Alexander has heard that expression – the slang for the bullet in the head, the reference being to the weight of that bullet. Misha takes a last smoke of the remains of his cigarette and shifts his weight, as though he is suddenly restless.

Alexander is looking back to the chairs where she is sitting. It seems that the young man has been sent away, sauntering with poorly hidden embarrassment back to his laughing friends, and the girl is now listening to the music, watching the guitar player with intent eyes. The musician has fingers that move lightly, flowing like warm water over the rippling strings. Alexander turns back to Misha because a thought has occurred to him.

"Do you…I mean, are you…?"

Misha waves a hand, one that is holding an empty glass.

"No, no, not at all. She's pretty, but a handful. Not for me. You go ahead. If you must." He shakes his head. Alexander nods and pulls his tie back up to his collar and he starts off across the room, stepping through the whirling dancers like a man who has plunged into a stormy lake and is determined to make it to the other side.

"Her name is Katya," Misha calls after him, but there is no acknowledgement from Alexander, who is crossing the room with the solid, blind steps of a sleepwalker.

He is halfway to her when he catches sight of himself in a large, slightly tarnished mirror that was once imposing, and that is mounted on the wall to his side. He does not stop, but is taken aback at the sight of the smart, confident-looking young man who looks back at him. His hair is short and neat, his eyes large, with long lashes. His chin shadowed and strong. The poised, purposeful reflection is unrecognisable to him, because inwardly his heart is pumping so loudly that he can no longer hear much of the music, and he can feel the dry taste of nervousness in his mouth. In a moment, he is standing before her, and she is looking up at him, with the same intent, evaluating stare that she gave to the guitar player a few moments ago. Alexander says nothing, and she waits, somewhat expectantly, for him to speak, but after a short, stiff bow, he offers her only his hand. He is faintly aware that her companions are giggling, made nervous by his intensity, and he begins to feel ridiculous, just standing there, holding out his hand and waiting, especially when he realises that she is not going to take it. The very same moment that he begins to withdraw, however, is the moment that she reaches out. He looks down, watches her slender fingers lying lightly on his palm, and he closes his own fingers over them. The moment feels absurdly romantic to him, but when he glances to her face for recognition of this, her dark eyes only hold an amused, aloof look, and he feels instantly chastened. But he lifts his hand, gently, and she acquiesces and walks with him to the middle of the room where the dancing is, and there they move together, easily. He can hardly feel her against him – she is as light and insubstantial as a shadow, and he looks at her and realizes that this is because she is moving with such unconscious elegance, such unconsidered grace, that he has to prevent himself from stopping to watch. He can feel the heat of her against his palm, and he tries to partner her well, to keep up, although he is not quite sure how, since he can hardly hear the music through the pounding of his heart in his ears.

When the music dies away, it is she that pulls him gently aside. They have remained together there for some moments after the music has finished, and she waits for him to lead her away from the dancers, but the silent, solemn young man seems unaware that the song has ended. She bites her lower lip, uncertain of what to do next. He has said not one word to her yet, which strikes her as odd; and although something about his boldness and resolution has attracted her this far, now she feels her customary sense of cautiousness returning.

"Thank you," she tells him, politely, with a hint of dismissal in her voice that seems to jolt him finally into speech.

"Have a drink with me?" he says.

She glances back to the group she has just left. She does not feel like returning to their jokes and giggles and gossip – not just yet. She looks at Alexander and nods, then, taking his hand once more, she steers him back towards the long tables at Misha's end of the room that serve as a bar. They pass Misha on the way, and Katya smiles at him in recognition, but does not stop to talk for she is preoccupied and sees him only vaguely, as though he were a familiar painting that she is passing while walking quickly through a gallery. When they reach the table, she asks the girl who is watching over the bottles to pour two drinks.

She hands Alexander one glass and picks up the other.

"You are the strangest person I have ever met. And yet," she hesitates.

"And yet?"

"There is something about you that is almost familiar."

She frowns and raises the glass, as though she has just given a toast, and she drinks down the cool liquid. He offers her his own full glass, but she refuses it, and places her hand over his and tries to make him drink.

"Why am I strange?" he asks.

"Because those are practically the first words you have spoken to me."

"And what is familiar about me?" he asks.

"I don't know."

"My smell, perhaps?"

She looks surprised, and then suspicious. "What do you mean?"

"I mean that smells and scents have strong evocations for people, and usually, when you cannot place what is making you comfortable with someone or some place, it is often the smell of them." It is the longest sentence he has spoken to her, and she likes the sound and timbre of his voice. It is reassuring and gentle.

"Are you trying to get me to smell you?"

"No," he laughs. "Only if you want to."

"No, thank you. Some things should be kept for the future."

She cannot think why she has said that. About the future. Without any thought, it just flew out of her mouth, and now he is smiling, he looks happy, as though he is hoping to see her again. She smiles too, suddenly. After all, something has drawn her to this man; perhaps his eyes, which are open and honest and intelligent.

"How old are you?" she asks.

"Do you want to guess?"

"No," she replies, rolling her eyes. "I just want to know. I can't tell from the look of you, whether you are eighteen or thirty."

"I am twenty five."

"Like me." She smiles, as though this satisfies her in some way, and then she closes her eyes. Etched into the skin between those eyes is a furrow of concentration. Alexander watches her, pausing only to ask the girl to pour two more drinks. When Katya opens her eyes, she sees the young man standing before her with his own eyes tightly shut, and a look of absorption on his face. She laughs.

"What are you doing?"

"I'm trying to see what you were concentrating on so suddenly."

"And? What was it?"

"The music?" he ventures, and she smiles her affirmation. The musicians are playing more quietly now, and are almost drowned out under the rising of voices made freer by alcohol and laughter, but the music is there, behind everything, and it is soft and emotive. An older man has joined them, and with his balalaika is wafting a mournful tune that twines out over the heads of the crowd like a long curl of blue-tinged smoke.

"I love this song," Katya says, so quietly that Alexander can barely hear her.

"So do I. Doesn't it remind you of your childhood?"

"Yes. That's exactly it." She looks away from him. "My grandmother used to sing it. She'd make my father play the piano to accompany her, and she'd sing it to my brother and me before we went to sleep."

"Is she still alive?"

Katya shakes her head, but offers nothing more and Alexander looks around, at the deaf crowd, and then back at the liquid eyes of the girl before him.

"Nobody can hear it except for us, I think."

"Perhaps he is only playing it for us," she suggests.

Alexander smiles at the idea. "Yes," he says, and he quickly asks her to dance again, for she seems to be on the verge of tears, as she stands there, alone, listening. His question wakes her from some faraway reverie, from unbidden, unwanted memories – no, they are not even memories, she thinks, it's just a feeling that has enveloped her without warning; that feeling of being a child and being warm, with everything as it should be, nothing complicated or difficult. The smell of onions and fried potatoes still lingering from dinner, and sitting close between Yuri and her mother, and watching her father and grandmother play and sing, and feeling safe and just happy.

"Would you like to dance?" he asks again.

She shakes herself, and smiles and refuses, politely, for she feels that if she continues to focus on that song, even by dancing to it, she will start crying. I must talk, she thinks, say something funny or witty or intelligent to this kind-faced young man. Ask him what he does, where he lives, what he thinks, feels, knows. That's what I am supposed to be doing. He is not what I expected to meet here tonight.

She opens her mouth to address him, and he leans forward a little, to catch the coming words, but they don't arrive. The perfect bow of her upper lip remains open for a second, but no words come out. I cannot speak, she realises; I cannot say one word without crying. It must be the drinks. What is in them?

Her head turns to the bar table, and she sees the second round of glasses sitting there, brimful, their wet bases leaching colour out of the red paper that covers the table. A hand comes into her line of vision, and she sees long fingers and square nails closing around one glass, and raising it up to offer to her.

"Another? Or have you had enough?"

Misha is smiling grimly. Beside him, Alexander stands, attentive, polite.

"I think you know each other?" he offers.

Misha nods, his eyes, reddened with too much alcohol, still upon Katya.

"She's like my kid sister," he tells Alexander. "Which is why I warn her off men like you."

Alexander laughs. "Am I so bad?"

"You're too good, my friend. Too good by a long way."

Katya takes the glass and downs the drink, while Misha watches her. She is restless, annoyed with Misha for interrupting, for breaking the delicate web of memory and gentleness that she had spun here alone with this young man. Now they will be forced to banter with each other, to laugh at stupid jokes that are funny only when you have drunk enough vodka.

"How do you both know each other?" Katya asks.

"We were in the same class at school," Misha tells her. "I was the handsome, brilliant, popular one, and he wasn't."

"Then why were you friends with him?" Katya's voice sounds bored with her own question, as though she is now merely going through the motions of frivolous conversation.

"I took pity on him."

"Are you sure it wasn't the other way around?" Her voice is clipped, with no hint of laughter, and Misha's eyebrows go up and he smiles to cover his displeasure.

She looks at Alexander. He is smiling at his friend indulgently, but there is also a hint of distance in his eyes that suggests he too is beginning to find this conversation tedious. Misha glances from one to the other, with a wry smile now, and through the clouds of vodka that have gathered in his head, he sees that neither of them are finding him charming or amusing. He takes a deep breath that neither one can see. Never mind, he thinks, I'll deal with this later. Now is not the best time. Without another word, he squeezes Alexander's shoulder, and leans to kiss Katya on the cheek. And then, as suddenly as he joined them, he is gone, and they are left alone again, amongst the crowd.

Alexander hands her another drink, and she takes it, then winces and coughs at the burning of the pure liquid snaking down her throat, and he rubs the top of her back with his hand to ease her discomfort, and she leans in to him, and lays her head on his shoulder. Almost as soon as he has absorbed the fact that she really is leaning against him, that he can feel her whole body beneath his hand on her back, she straightens up, with an abruptness that surprises him.

"What is it?"

She shakes her head. "I hardly know you."

He cannot contradict this fact, so he stays silent.

"I want to go home," she says.

"Don't. Please." He turns to follow her movement away from the bar, and when she looks at him, his eyes are concerned and alert.

"Why not, if I am tired?" She looks much stronger now, less fragile. Misha's interruption has given her time to gather herself together, and he knows that her petulant question is only her way of reasserting herself after the lapse of allowing

SHAMIM SARIF

herself to lean against a strange man. She knows it too. She
does not really want to go home to the faded, cold apartment
that she lives in with her friend Maya and Maya's mother.

"Can I accompany you home?"

She shakes her head. "Thank you, but there's no need. My
roommate is over there. We'll go together." He turns to see
the blonde-haired young woman who had been sitting with
Katya earlier.

"And you won't stay just a few more minutes?"

"I'm tired," she says, but her tone is softer now – she is
physically tired, but also mentally weary of fighting her
attraction to this man, just because it is unexpected and
unsettling.

"If you are tired, you should go," he replies. "I only wanted
you to stay because I would like to talk to you, and to see you."
He swallows and makes himself continue. "But that can wait
for another time, perhaps?"

The waiting; the waiting for her to answer, as the crowd of
drinkers clustered at the bar around them grows louder and
louder. He sees the bulbous eyes and reddened cheeks of the
mass of people around him; he watches them shout to get
the attention of whoever is pouring the vodka, watches them
toast each other and drink, and he frowns and fixes his eyes
on Katya's face, on her mouth, so that if her reply is drowned
in the noise, he will still read it.

"Come to see me," she tells him, raising her voice against
the others around them.

He nods, and waits again.

"At my home. Tomorrow," she says, and tells him the address.

He repeats it after her, grateful for her trust in him, and she smiles and turns, and walks away, darting in amongst drinkers and dancers. He takes a step as if to follow, but then stops, because he senses that his time with her is over for now. He only wishes he could have left her with some memorable, romantic parting words, and not with the desperate, loudly-spoken repetition of her address. He turns back to the bar tables and sees Misha at the other end. Misha has seen him also, has been watching him, Alexander feels, and Misha nods and looks away, wrinkling his nose, as if he has just smelt something slightly unpleasant, and orders three more drinks. He had been planning to take them back to share with the girls he has just left, but by the time they are poured, he somehow thinks better of his plan and he drinks them all down himself.

CHAPTER THREE
BOSTON

A FEW WEEKS AFTER THEIR LUNCH, he receives a postcard from Estelle. It arrives at the office, a picture of a
sun drenched boulevard and palm trees, sitting jauntily and
unexpectedly atop the rest of the more mundane mail of
his desk.

"Lots of sun and lots of facelifts (not mine) here in LA," it
reads. "Having a break in the sun while Frank gives a paper at
a literary theory conference. Thanks so much for lunch. Back
on 22nd, for Xmas. Expect you for tea some time? Estelle."

Today is the twenty-second. He is pleased to have heard
from her, for he had enjoyed their afternoon together, even
though by the end of it he had also been a little disconcerted;
with her smiling eyes and quiet questions, she had begun
to stir at the settled surface of his interior, past life. There
were moments during that lunch, admittedly short, when he
had felt the carefully filtered, clear, still pool of his memories

being shaken, the clarity being slightly sullied by a swirl of dust unexpectedly disturbed.

He props the card against his computer screen, with the written side facing outwards, then he walks out and into the glassed-in conference room. His vice presidents are already there, as is Melissa Johnson's small team. Day after day, her people arrive in full, formal business dress, despite the fact that Alexander and all his employees tend to dress more casually. His company headquarters is a relaxed environment in which to work. People have pictures of their children, or paintings by their children pinned to the walls. There are armchairs and sofas amongst the desks, where informal meetings are frequently held. Outside the row of conference rooms is a large kitchen station that looks like a coffee bar. From there, drinks and snacks and samples of new recipes can be collected throughout the day by any employee. From time to time during longer meetings, an assistant comes in with fresh cakes or muffins.

He is immediately irritated by the fact that everyone present already has their laptops flipped open, humming, expectant. It seems to him to be a false show of eagerness. This deal should have been – could have been – completed in principle several days ago. But he has been finding Melissa intractable on certain key points. As soon as the problems arose, he removed himself from the negotiations for two full weeks, a tactic designed to worry her into compromising – but Melissa appears to have nerves strung like steel wires and has stuck with him every step of the way. In retrospect, he realises that anyone who has gotten so far so young in the business world, as Melissa Johnson has, is likely to be a far stronger negotiator than he. In fact, what he has been seeing with considerable clarity during the past several meetings is that for the last decades, during all the time he has built up his business, he has been largely protected. He has always had the majority stake in his own business, he has always been able to run it as he chooses, and he has always chosen to surround himself with like-minded people. He has never bought or sold a company until now, has never had to join in the ruthless games in which others in his position are so well schooled. These past weeks have made him feel like something of a gentleman amateur who has wandered into a kind of financial Olympics where all the other players are highly trained and motivated in a single-minded way with which he cannot quite sympathise.

He sits down, and pours himself some coffee from the pot that sits on the corner of the table.

"Good morning," he says to the room, and there is a ripple of greeting in reply. "Where's Melissa?"

"She's in the bathroom, Mr Ivanov. She'll just be a second."

He nods, and turns to look out of the window while they wait.

Melissa Johnson leans her head against the cool glass of the long washroom mirror and closes her eyes against the overhead lights. The oppressive ache in the centre of her forehead that has been with her since the early hours of the morning has spread now to the left side of her head, and is building into a deep throbbing sensation. She knows that, left unattended, it will mutate into a migraine within an hour or two. Not now, she thinks, please not now. She can hardly leave everyone waiting while she rushes out for medication. It would be unprofessional, and even worse, they would all know she was feeling rough. They would immediately sense an advantage. Alexander Ivanov, she feels, is just waiting to sight a weakness so he can up the deal. She rolls her shoulders, a poor attempt to loosen clenched muscles, and tries to recall the last time she had a migraine. She remembers suddenly, and in some detail – she was closing the telecom deal; they'd worked the whole night, and she had forgotten to eat dinner or breakfast. Her blood sugar had dropped. But that was at least two years ago. Since then she has stayed off red wine and red meat, and cut out chocolate and most carbohydrates. She works out each morning, and most useful of all, she has a set of relaxation exercises that her trainer taught her, which are unobtrusive enough to use even during business meetings.

She opens her eyes, and leans back again. Splashes some water onto her face, and then stands gripping the sides of the basin. She hates the fact that today, when she is so near to closing this deal with Alexander, she is tense enough, apprehensive enough, to give herself a migraine. It does not speak well of her inner strength, or her confidence, and she is someone that prides herself on possessing both in copious quantities. She stands and takes in a deep breath.

Then lets it out through her nose in a series of short, sharp, noisy bursts.

Behind her a toilet flushes, and she starts. Melissa watches in the mirror as the stall door opens and a young woman emerges. Dark hair and eyes, pretty. Tailored trousers, a soft shirt unbuttoned to show some kind of trendy leather necklace around her throat. No jacket. Around thirty years old, Melissa thinks, a few years younger than she. Top level assistant, possibly very low level management. Probably on about sixty thousand a year.

"Hi," says the woman. "You okay?"

"Fine, thanks."

"Sounded like you were having trouble breathing there."

Melissa clears her throat. "No. That was a cleansing breath. It's a yoga thing."

"Ah." The woman washes her hands, using enough soap to make a lather that drips messily over the side of the basin. Melissa waits for her to leave, but she dries her hands and then takes out a small washbag.

"What are you cleansing?" she asks.

The question focuses Melissa on the pulsing pain in her temples. She puts a hand to her head as unobtrusively as she can.

"I have the mother of all headaches," she says.

"Tension?"

Melissa nods.

"Want me to get you something for it?"

Melissa feels elated with relief. "I'd be grateful," she says.

Leaving her bag on the sink, the young woman disappears. She is back within thirty seconds, and deposits two foil-wrapped tablets into Melissa's hand.

"Thank you," Melissa says. She looks at the tablets. "*Aspirin?*"

"Yes."

Melissa shuts her eyes again. "Thanks." She almost breathes the word, for all her energy is divided between this immediate disappointment on the one hand and the effort of pulling herself together on the other. With nothing more than a quick nod to the woman, she turns and leaves.

"How do you want to proceed, Mr Ivanov?" Melissa asks. The directness is typical of her style of work; in a meeting such as this, pleasantries take too much time in relation to their value.

"Let's just get this done," he replies, matching her tone. "I'm sure everyone here would like to get this finished up before Christmas."

"The holidays have never been a big thing for me," she replies. "I think the main thing is to achieve a win-win deal for both sides. And if that means working through Christmas, we'll do it."

Alexander nods, trying to look tough, when really he just feels tired. This is not where he wanted to be three days before Christmas. What he had wanted was to be browsing in delis and supermarkets, with nothing more to think about than what to cook for the next meal. And Lauren will be arriving soon to spend the holidays with him. The idea of spices and fruit and roasting has been slowly insinuating itself into his mind, imbuing him with a feeling of festivity. But that feeling is melting away all too quickly under the searing focus of Melissa's laser-like gaze.

There is a knock on the glass door, and it opens slightly, hesitantly, to show the young woman from the bathroom. Melissa glances at her hand, half-hoping that she has searched her out in order to supply her with a more useful medication, something to stop and kill her headache; but before she can even finish this thought, she is watching Alexander almost leap up from his chair and throw his arms around the woman, who hugs him back.

"I didn't expect you till tomorrow," he tells her, his face flushed, excited.

"I was able to get away earlier. Sorry to interrupt… Betty said I could put my head in…" She glances around, conscious of the room full of people watching them. "Anyway, I didn't have the house keys, so I stopped here."

"This is Lauren Grinkov, my niece," he explains, more for the visitors' benefit, since most of his own team have met her previously. Melissa computes the name.

"Shareholder," she says. "Forty-nine percent."

Lauren cannot help but stare. Melissa's gaze is direct, her posture in her chair upright and yet also very much at ease, as though the company is somehow already hers. Except for her perfectly highlighted dark blonde hair and clear grey eyes, she seems an entirely different person from the tense but polite individual of five minutes ago. There has been no greeting and not even a nod of acknowledgement. Instead, with four words, Lauren feels she has been stripped of all human traits and reduced to the essence of what she represents here and now, in this boardroom, for the purposes of this meeting. She puts down her handbag and holds out her hand. She will force a modicum of courtesy into this exchange if she has to.

"And you are?"

"Melissa Johnson."

"Ah. The potential purchaser."

"Yes."

"Nice to meet you." The comment is more than a little pointed. She pauses, looks more closely at Melissa. "You okay?"

Melissa looks somewhat less comfortable in her seat now.

"Fine, thank you."

Lauren looks at her uncle. Alexander is giving her a look of query, an invitation to stay for the meeting. She nods to him, takes a place on his right hand side and settles quietly into her chair, accepting with a smile the coffee that he places before her.

"We're stalled right now," says Alexander, "and I was telling Melissa that I'd like for us both to be open to compromising a little, if we can."

"For instance?" Melissa's eyes are intent upon him.

In response to a glance, an assistant hands Alexander a printout, several items of which are typed in red ink. His eyes pass down the list and return to the first item.

"The homeless initiative. This was one of the things agreed by your company at the start of negotiations – that they would continue the facilities we have that get the homeless off the streets."

"We're agreed to keep at least 50% of the current shelters. If we can do more, we will."

"They're not just shelters," says Lauren quickly. She had planned not to say anything during this meeting, mainly because her awareness of her uncle's business has always been taken only as far as is needed to understand him. She has always loved the basis of it, his passion for food, the recipe creation; but the intricacies of management and growth and company structuring have never held much interest for her. This point, however, is not about numbers – she knows something about this side of the company. She also knows that she is needled by Melissa Johnson, and she feels the impulse to prod at her a little, to see what sort of woman lies beneath the crisp, brisk exterior. Melissa turns to her now, waiting. She is composed; there are no signs of headaches or cleansing breaths or anything else that might suggest any vulnerability.

"People can go to those facilities, get cleaned up, get clean clothes and live while they try and get work," Lauren continues. "They get help with the interview process, and when they do get jobs, they can stay till they can afford rent of their own. They're not just places to sleep. They help people into homes of their own. If anything we need more of them."

"With all due respect, I'm looking to run a business, not a charity foundation," replies Melissa.

"So are we," says Lauren, crisply. "Isn't that why you're buying us?"

"These are minor issues," Melissa says to the table in general. She seems to be trying to avoid Lauren, to slide out from beneath her haughty gaze.

"Not to the people being helped."

For the first time, Alexander sees Melissa falter, and he is surprised. Certainly Lauren's earnest argument is the kind she would have shredded to pieces with a few pointed rebuffs if he had given it. He looks at his niece. Her head is up, her dark eyes fierce. Melissa takes a moment before replying – she is experienced enough in boardroom tactics to know that snapping back now will only allow Lauren to retain the upper hand.

"You're right, you have a very good business," Melissa says at last. "And it is entirely your prerogative to give away as much of your profits as you like to charitable causes. But it's equally my prerogative, assuming I buy the company, to give nothing if I choose. I respect your choices, even admire them, but they're your choices. Not mine."

It is a clear, logical response and it forces Lauren to nod in acknowledgement. Alexander clears his throat.

"The philanthropic side of things has always been a very major part of our business, Melissa. It's a huge part of who we are as a company." Alexander says. "More to the point, I believe I made clear from the start that it's very important that they are continued by whoever takes over. What chance is there that you can continue everything as is?"

"Everything?"

"The homeless initiatives, the arts foundation, the micro-financing for immigrant start-up businesses…"

"At a cost of eighteen million dollars a year? It's unlikely."

"But not impossible?" Lauren smiles at her encouragingly, radiantly, and Melissa blinks, tapping her pen. She reminds herself that this woman probably doesn't even know a cashflow from a bank statement.

"I'm afraid it is impossible. Maybe we should move on with the rest of the deal."

Despite the fact that this is clearly part of the ebb and flow of working out a business deal, Lauren cannot help but feel this response as a personal affront. More concerning to her is the fact that she can see her uncle wavering. Surely it cannot be so easy for all that he has worked for and believed in to be lost? She can see that Melissa's headache is back, or is at least on its way. She holds her look for a long moment, then turns to her uncle. Alexander has already outlined in his mind a contingency plan. A situation where one of his subsidiary companies would retain control of the charity initiatives, in exchange for an increased purchase price up front, and perhaps a small percentage of sales ongoing. He is considering whether to suggest this to Melissa now, when he catches his niece's look. What he reads there surprises him, but also reassures him in some way – because he finds that he is in agreement. There is a moment's pause as he looks down and examines his pen thoughtfully. Nobody is moving, no coffee cups touch the table, the shifting of pressed cotton shirts against the leather chairs has stopped. Only the background drone of the computers fills the space. He looks at Melissa and shakes his head.

"I'm sorry. Without the initiatives, there's no deal to be made here."

With considerable dramatic flair, Lauren silently zips up her handbag, finishes the last gulp of her coffee and starts to put on her sweater. Melissa looks from one to the other calmly, giving not the slightest hint of her internal impulse, which is to lay her pounding head against the table and close her eyes in resignation.

"Fine," she says, and before anyone else can speak, she excuses herself and is gone.

There is a lively, light feel to the large house now that Lauren is here. From the kitchen, he can hear a jazz CD playing above him, the upbeat sound of it bouncing down the stairs. He wipes his hands and makes his way upstairs. The bathroom door is open, and the bathroom itself empty, but it is still hung about with moisture and steam and scent. The music is coming from the suite of rooms that he has always kept for Lauren alone; here too, the door is ajar. He walks towards it slowly and quietly, wanting to savour this moment, when his niece is home earlier than he had hoped. And some other, smaller part of him is already lost in dreams as he stands there on the landing, imagining a world where he always comes home to find someone there who lives with him, and waits for him and expects to hear his step in the doorway. It is a pleasurable feeling, one that suffuses his whole being for a few moments, and confuses him, the way the gentle waking from a wonderful dream overwhelms and unbalances.

He stops just before the open door. Through the crack of the hinges, he can see her. While the music jumps and dips all around her, Lauren is lying on the bed, entirely motionless except for the occasional blinking of her eyelashes.

He knocks at the open door, loudly, and she sits up at once.

"You look thoughtful," he says.

She waves away the comment, and swings her legs off the bed.

"It's good to be here. Feels like home."

"Good. This is your house, you know. I wish you'd live here."

"I'd drive you crazy," she smiles.

"You mean, I'd drive *you* crazy," he replies. "Don't say anything. I know. Your 'fastidious uncle'."

"You always throw that back at me, Uncle Alex," she said. "I meant it in a nice way. Anyway, I might stay a while, if it's okay with you."

She is avoiding his look slightly and he at once infers why.

"And Carol? How is she?"

She turns away slightly and takes a long time to fasten her leather-strapped watch onto a fragile-looking wrist.

"I don't know," she says, still looking down. "I haven't seen her in a few weeks."

He waits, but she does not elaborate. "I'm sorry," he says at last.

"Don't be. It hasn't been working out for a while now. It's

for the best. I guess I was just surprised at how much I missed her. When she left."

There is a weight to her voice which lends it an unnaturally low tone and which tells him that she is only a step away from tears.

"So it's definitely over?"

"Yeah, but it's fine." She looks up at him now. "You know me. Easy come, easy go."

She regrets saying this as soon as the words are uttered. It is the kind of blithe, throwaway comment that she might be able to get away with amongst people who don't know her so well, but her uncle's kind eyes see directly through her. He read her meaning in the meeting earlier that day, and he can read her now, though he is, of course, too considerate to say anything.

"Anyway, I thought an extended time away from New York might not be a bad thing."

"I would love it," he tells her, and takes her hand encouragingly. "And if your performance this morning was anything to go by, you can help me complete the sale."

"What sale? I thought I blew it."

Alexander shakes his head. "I think you may have saved it. Let's wait and see."

"I hope so. Last thing I wanted to do was ruin your deal."

"Our deal," he corrects. "And I made the decision."

It is typical of him to try and remove the responsibility from her shoulders, for what could turn out to be a bad mistake. She nods.

"Let's go get something to eat," she says. "I'm starving."

Downstairs, she rummages in her bag and hands him a bottle of wine, which he holds at arm's length in order to read the label without searching for his glasses.

"Lauren!"

It is an excellent wine and an excellent vintage. He knows she must have spent a fortune on it.

"Well, I wanted to bring you something nice. I have another – a Burgundy this time – for Christmas dinner."

"You shouldn't be spending your money like this."

"Stop. I do well with my painting," she shrugs. "I'm getting a lot of private work now. Everybody wants to see themselves up on a wall. Apparently there was an article in *Vanity Fair* or *The New Yorker* or somewhere, recommending it. So now I'm in great demand. I've been spending my time in the houses of some of New York's finest. I could tell you some tales."

"Here, have a glass of wine, and let's talk."

She laughs, a deep, happy sound and takes his hand, the affectionate grasp of a mother telling off an errant child. "I have to respect client confidentiality, you know."

"Really? We'll test that after the wine."

She watches him decant the contents of the bottle, slowly and respectfully. Then he loosens a pâté of foie gras from its tin and slices fresh bread while directing her to wash salad leaves at the sink.

"Dressing?" she asks.

"I have homemade vinaigrette from last night. Or shall I make fresh?"

"That *is* fresh. You'd die if you saw what bottled stuff I throw over my salad."

They transport their meal into the living room, spreading everything over a table that sits between the armchairs, and then they discuss the details of the business sale.

"Uncle Alex, are you sure you're ready to sell?"

He has thought about this point a lot during the last few weeks. He sips the wine appreciatively.

"You know that after Katya, this work, building this company became everything to me. But for the last few years, I haven't really felt driven. Not the way I used to. Maybe I'm just getting old. But at my age, I don't want to spend even another month doing something I'm not excited about. I don't have to."

"So what are you excited about now?"

He shrugs. "For now I'll be happy just cooking, and taking it easy. I'm tired, Lauren. Maybe you can teach me more about art too. How long have we been meaning to go around all the museums and galleries together?"

Lauren nods in acknowledgement. The warmth of the fire and the wine have seeped into her muscles, loosening and soothing them, and her head feels heavy. To shake off the feeling, she stands and walks about the room. Her gaze catches, as always, on the photograph of Katya that sits on the piano. Her aunt. The younger sister of Lauren's father, Yuri. Lauren was a late and completely unexpected arrival for her parents, at a time when they had long assumed that they could not have children. Her mother was thirty-seven, her father already fifty when she was born. As a small girl in a crowded, slowly decaying area of South Boston, her father would tell her stories about his old life in the Soviet Union; and often these stories were built around his memories of, and longings for, his own parents and his sister Katya. In these tales, she came to know her aunt as a lively, spirited young girl who always outwitted her more pedestrian older brother. Through her father's stories, Lauren had found in Katya a vivid character for the imagination, to be cheered on in their childhood escapades, in the quiet side streets of a Moscow suburb. She was an heroic, colourful figure in an exotic setting, made up of those qualities that mattered so much to the young Lauren – daring, defiance, laughter, and sophistication of a sort.

It had been a considerable time later that the deeper, more mature knowledge of her aunt had come from Alexander. She remembered only a little of her aunt's husband from her childhood – he had been a quiet, kind presence, but one without much impact in her life until her parents' deaths. In quick succession, Yuri had suffered a heart attack, and then her mother died of cancer, and when she found herself flailing in the ensuing void, she had found that Alexander was there, holding out a hand and emotional sustenance, and she had gratefully allowed him to step in, and confide in her, trust her and love her.

She had understood that at least some of his initial interest in her teenage self had stemmed from the fact that she was related to Katya, that she was a strong blood link to that great love of his. But it took very little time for him to come to know her on her own terms; their relationship had deepened quickly, and he began to love her as if she were his own child. If the line of her chin, or the colour of her eyes, or the tilt of her head offered him an occasional, fleeting, aching suggestion of his late wife, then that was only to be expected and understood. Lauren has never felt that she bore a great resemblance to her aunt, but her hair and eyes are dark, very dark. These features, combined with the simple fact that Katya died young, at around the age that Lauren is now, probably continues to make the occasional passing similarity more noticeable.

Alexander understood that the mystery and tragic elements of Katya's story could have lent it a kind of glamour in his niece's eyes, for she was distanced enough from the events and emotions of that time for them to seem dramatically unreal. And Katya had lived her brief life with an intense passion and conviction that would be irresistible to any young woman. It was with slow inevitability then that Lauren moved away from her uncle's reticence in excavating the past, and towards a trip to Russia to explore the places where he and Katya had lived and grown up. It had been a momentous journey for her, a revisiting of roots that was accompanied by all the romance and excitement of a new city and a wholly different culture. She had visited the usual museums and galleries and the Kremlin, but what she remembers best, what she still savours inside when she recalls that trip, are the small, quiet moments. She remembers standing on a street corner outside the building where Alexander and Katya had once lived. She had imagined them returning there, both weary after work. She imagined them walking out together along the snow-crusted river. She rode the metro that her aunt might have taken on her way to work. Or to so many other, secret places. She had sought out archives that might shed more light on her death and her life, but found nothing more than a sparse, clinical summary that added nothing more to what they already knew. She had even looked, without much hope, for their old friend Misha. Someone who might give her a more intense taste of their lives then, of why things had turned out as they had. She had asked Alexander to accompany her, but he had made his excuses and declined. Without wishing to fully consider his own reasons for refusing, he had simply attributed her fascination to her artistic, romantic temperament, and left it at that.

"I wish you could have met her," says Alexander softly, as he watches Lauren looking at Katya's photograph.

"I would have liked that."

Alexander runs a hand over his head. He is weary and an air of melancholy, of unfulfilled longing, has taken him over. She returns to the fireside, where they sit in silence for a few minutes, and when she finally glances at him, she sees that he has fallen asleep. Quietly, she removes their plates and when she comes back he has nodded awake again.

"You fell asleep," she says.

"I was just resting my eyes," he tells her, and his smile lets them both know that he is lying. "What shall we do now?"

"I'm going to read a bit," she tells him. "And you're going to bed."

He protests, but she is adamant and knows how to handle his insistence; and with an effort that he tries to hide, he gets up from the chair.

"Are you sure?"

"A good book, a glass of wine and a roaring fire. I'm in heaven," she tells him.

She walks with him to the staircase, the panelled hallway cool after the warmth of the flames, and he leaves her with a kiss. She watches him walk upstairs and then returns to the living room. Halfway back to her chair she stops with an abrupt turn, and moves back to the piano. She sits down on the cracked leather stool and lets her hands move over the keys; the ivory is soft, almost powdery to the touch, and her fingers recall their character at once, remembering that they need only the most delicate pressure to coax out the full tone and nuance of each note. She plays for perhaps twenty minutes, a series of melancholy pieces that leave her somehow indulged and depressed. She sits back and looks at Katya's picture once again. She gives it a close, detailed stare that now contains no emotion, only the cool precision of the artist's eye. She is evaluating angles, shade, light, expression. She remains absorbed in this way for several minutes, until at last she steps back with a nod to herself.

CHAPTER FOUR
MOSCOW – MARCH 1956

THERE IS NOT ENOUGH WATER in the whole of Moscow to slake Misha's thirst the morning after the party. His throat burns as he drinks down another cupful. This insatiable thirst always takes hold of him after he has drunk too much – that, and the sensation that his stomach is hollow, burned clean, as though scoured out with acid. He glances down at his flat abdomen, lean and keenly muscled, like the rest of his tall, lithe body. He looks fit and healthy – he is healthy, for the most part, even though on mornings like this, it can take a little time for his body to remember that fact. But six or seven long draughts of cold water, and some strong tea and black bread go a long way to bringing him back to himself, after which he will bathe, and wash his curly cropped hair in the sink, allowing himself to enjoy the feel of the soap lather around his ears and forehead.

Thirty minutes later, he is dressed. Dark trousers and a black roll neck sweater that fits his slim contours closely. Over these he shrugs on a long thin overcoat. He does not bother with a hat. He spends all day at the Aviation Institute, becoming warmer and warmer under the over-zealous heating, and he likes the grasping rush of the cold evening air that plays over his head when he walks out of there at the end of the working day. Anyway, he is not prone to colds, has never been a sickly man, and if you treat the Russian winter like an enemy who has power over you, you will be caught out by it every time.

She is waiting for him at a bar just a few blocks from her apartment. Misha sees her inside, drinking a glass of tea, and he slows down as he approaches. The inside of the bar is illuminated and has an unreal quality this evening, as though it is a festive stage set, placed down in the middle of the fading, dank, slush-lined streets that surround it. And in the centre of the lights and warmth and smoke sits Katya, alone at a small table. He watches her keenly as he approaches, then smiles when she looks up and catches sight of him. He goes straight to the bar and orders two vodkas before he kisses her on the cheek.

"I don't want a vodka," she says. "I had too much last night."

"I know," he says, easily, with a gentle sarcasm.

She waits for him to explain himself.

"I've never seen you act like that with anyone."

She presumes that he is referring to Alexander, and she is momentarily pricked by his directness, and then irritated. What concern is it of his how she acts at a party? A taut reply rises to her lips, but she holds it back at once; for she realizes now that he must have mentioned Alexander for a reason. Misha wastes no time in explaining.

"He's government," Misha says. "Nice position too. Couldn't you tell?"

A pause. "Ah, yes," she says. "Of course...."

Beneath the even tone of her voice, Katya is shocked. Shocked that the man whom she found so appealing and attractive, so unexpectedly, is working directly for the system she so despises. And she is even more surprised that she did not pick up this fact straight away. Now that she considers it, she realizes that the signs were there – the neat, blue suit; a sense of uniformity, a bland correctness, in his manner, his dress, even the shine on his shoes. All these things should have alerted her. It should not have been difficult to spot. In the end those political pigs are all the same, on the surface and deep down.

"I told you I drank too much," she says, and her ironic tone is a cover for the slight pang of disappointment that she also feels in her stomach. She had really liked him, for a while.

"He's so young," she says.

"I know. Nice, too. A little boring, but nice."

He has already drunk both the vodkas. He stands up and pays the bill and Katya begins putting on her coat. She understands that the rest of this conversation is best held outside.

"Are you using him?" she asks, her voice altered in the vast dampness of the outdoor air.

Misha smiles. "Alexander is not easily used. He is a man of integrity. And he would have suspected me if I'd tried for information. Besides, only now is he in a really useful position."

The pause that follows seems to her to be some kind of test. He is waiting for her reply, for the right reply, and it should not be so hard for her to give it. Perhaps it only seems a little difficult because she had liked Alexander. She swallows down the last taste of disappointment that remains in her mouth, and speaks.

"Seems like a good opportunity," she says.

He turns with a half-smile and examines her face. "It is. Could be. If you can keep your head. If you're not attracted to him."

"You know me, Misha."

"Yes, I do." He stops walking and holds her gaze. "That's why I was surprised. Last night. I've never seen you like that with anyone."

She sighs. "I liked him. For a moment. But if he's government, he's everything I work against. It's not a dilemma for me. It's black and white."

"Good."

"But he's coming tonight. To see me. I told him he could," she adds, with as much nonchalance as she can manage.

"You don't waste any time, do you?"

"I don't think that's something you should be concerned about."

He raises an eyebrow, but lets the comment go and they

walk on side by side in silence. Beneath her ribs, deep inside her empty stomach, Katya feels the teasing itch of fear and the flickering of excitement. This could be a big opportunity for her, a chance to directly make a difference. To tap her own source, not to simply pass out information from others.

"Listen," Misha says, and he is all briskness, all business now. "If you can do it, it would be wonderful. Just imagine. But it's not easy to become involved with someone purely to betray them. You have to be emotionally strong. Clear. Clean. Business is business."

"I know."

"I hope so."

She resists the urge to turn away. Evidently she must reassure him a little more if she is to be trusted with this job.

"Misha, he's sweet. Like a puppy. But now that I know who he is, I *can't* fall for him. It's impossible, it would be a denial of everything I am. If you want me to do it, I will."

He finds himself momentarily irritated at her admission that she felt some attraction, any attraction, to Alexander. When it comes to women, he has within him a certain expectation, borne of arrogance, which means that he is always slightly surprised by their awareness of anyone other than he. But her earnest, decisive tone now pleases him, and she can see that. He is not the type to express himself openly; he prefers to play games with people, to keep his responses neutral and unreadable wherever possible. But still she knows him well enough to read the quickening of his step and the bright animation of his manner as he instructs her:

"Very good. For the next few months, you captivate him. Get to know him, allow him to know a little of you, enough for him to fall in love, and above all, get him to trust you. He's a good man, and he hasn't yet had disappointments in life. He's young, like us," he adds, his voice lower, perhaps even hesitant. "He trusts easily."

They are at the crossroads behind her apartment, and he has stopped.

"I'll leave you here," he says. "Think about it a little. Start seeing him, and think about it. You must be sure."

"I am sure."

He smiles slightly. The pleasurable tension of a new avenue, a new contact; the arousal of a new game beginning. A pulse of energy moves through him. He will go out tonight and celebrate. Drink a little and find a girl with pretty eyes to flirt with and make love to.

"Then good luck," he says. "Let me know how it goes. Keep me updated every step of the way."

She nods, accepts the touch of his cold lips on her cheek, and she turns to cross the road, her mind still reeling with the sudden shift that has occurred. Within the space of a few minutes the focus of her evening, and perhaps even her life's work has changed. The heady excitement of attraction and potential romance has brewed within moments into a more bitter, but more real possibility of stolen government secrets, the possibility of making herself useful first-hand, not just as a go-between. This, after all, is what she has always struggled for. Let the real work begin now, Katya, she thinks. You can do it; let the work begin.

One Month Later

Katya squints into the bright morning. She can hardly see her way to school through the snowfall that flurries down around her. There is no hint of a blizzard in this springtime snow; there is barely any wind, and the snowfall itself is not heavy, but her head is light, and the glare of the whiteness that has already coated the streets is dizzying her further. She walks along in the right direction; after all, she knows the way to her own place of work. But all around her, fat flakes of frosted water land gently on the ground, on her head and on her arms; one or two alight upon her eyelashes. She narrows her eyes to close down her field of vision. The snow dances lightly around; when she tries to watch, and follow the descent of some few, particular flakes, she finds them eddying about her, disconcerting her and teasing her, following a balletic path, spiralling downwards, and whirling back up, pausing to whisper kisses of cold moisture against the exposed tips of her ears.

She thinks briefly of Alexander. It has been three weeks since the night they met and she has seen him a few times. Fewer meetings than he would have liked, which is just how she feels it should be; she is teasing out his eagerness. He came to see her again last night, and she had talked to him. That, she knew, was the way to begin. To reveal something

69

of herself, not to probe him, not just yet. And although she has asked him a little about himself, he has been uninterested in replying at any length – in that respect, he seems unlike most other people that she knows. Instead, he has been full of questions to her – her work, her daily life, her thoughts and hopes and fears. She told him of the first two things. I am a school administrator. I run the school. And I get up at this time, and eat that for lunch, and do this in the afternoon, and sleep at around this time. The rest could come later, or not at all. He will wait for her tonight, this time at his apartment. For dinner. She smiles to herself. Although she told him little of real depth, she felt a liberation of some kind simply by speaking to him. Any kind of self-revelation is so rare for her that the mere fact of spending several hours with one human being who is focused solely on her, interested only in what interests her, has given her an unfamiliar sense of release. Of light-headedness. What will happen if she does not find her way back through this shower of snow? What if these pattering, dancing, floating flakes blind her and unhinge her and mislead her, and whisk her far away into the immutable, unending whiteness of the desert, and what if she never makes it home again? The long, pure vista of snow that she sees stretching out before her will continue for ever and ever, she feels, and her head is almost spinning with the seductive pain of being surrounded completely by whiteness and cold, no humans, no life, no end to it.

At the street corner, she stops, disconcerted, and finds that she is standing next to other people. Coated, hatted, bundled black shapes, blurry against the ice. She is back in the city, she suddenly finds, back on the street that she knows by heart, and has been removed from the vast, snowbound Siberian plain of her imagination. So, she thinks, as she crosses the street with the other shapes; so I will continue to live in this new world of mine, I will see him tonight, and he will see me, and we will carry on this game of getting to know each other a little better.

Five minutes later, she is inside the echoing concrete hallway of the school. Her everyday mind is returning as, bit by bit, the brilliant white of her imagination is being painted over with the various greys of this building. The stairs, the floor, the thick metal doors. The grey cabinets and chairs, and her own metal desk. Her grey metal typewriter. The grey skin of some of the teachers. The grey hair of the head teacher, who asks Katya, every few months, if she would not like to teach instead. If she would not like to be out of the school administration offices, and in front of a class of minds eager for knowledge.

Not for the knowledge I would be forced to teach them, she thinks, as she shakes her head again, politely, and laughs. The children would love you, the head teacher tells her; they already do. Her heavy squat body and square rustic head nod to the young woman in hopeless encouragement. Yes, Katya thinks, but children are innocent and superficial. They like me because I am prettier than most of their teachers, and because I am young. They would have crushes on me, the small girls and the small boys. They don't care about anything else. Do they?

She has seen some of their eyes, the little children who come to that school, and she has seen a thirst and an adoration that shocks her. Such naked emotion in the eyes of those children. Smile at them, and they smile. Shout and they withdraw. Hit them and they cower. Such raw power these greying teachers hold. She wants no part of it, not directly. She does what she has to do behind the scenes. Curricula, timetables, state funds. As good a job as any other to earn a wage and fill her days. But she would rather not face that dependence and devotion, that innocence which has already had its new, sharp edges roughed away by state and parents.

She hates herself when she thinks like this, but she does not often think any other way. She herself has cowered, and longed for love from too many different aunts and uncles and friends with whom she spent her own childhood and adolescence. Much of the time, she was even separated from her only brother. There was no-one who wanted to take in two orphans. Two extra mouths to share the thin soups and occasional meats at the table. Two more pairs of feet to buy decent shoes for. In her loneliness, craving the love of her parents and the companionship of her older brother, she learned to turn into her own mind and heart for the satisfaction that she sought. Hours spent learning how to fully use her imagination, teaching herself to fight through to the farthest reaches of her mind in order to remove herself from the lonely, terrifying world she now inhabited. Nights spent holding herself in, learning to be content with her own company, to push away the longing for others, and to trust only herself. A good training, as it turned out, but not the easiest way to live. Alexander is already trying to find a way into this interior life of hers. She smiles and shakes her head at the idea. She walks into the office, and smiles a hello at Svetlana, who shifts self-consciously in her seat. At her desk Katya begins sorting out the stack of letters and memos which has piled up since yesterday afternoon.

The day is passing swiftly for once, and Katya types away, clattering fingers dancing over the keys.

"I can do those for you," Svetlana says.

"I've given you more than enough for one day," Katya replies. Besides, she likes the feel of the keys, and to watch the words being formed on the paper before her. She works with a soothing rhythm that is beginning to free her unconscious mind, and she is finding that her thoughts are drawn repeatedly to Alexander.

She looks up with a start. At her open door, two round blue eyes are staring at her out of an oval face. The eyes are welling with tears. She looks at the boy. He must be five or six, and his knee is bleeding. She stands and goes to him, and kneels down beside him.

"Did you fall?" she asks.

He nods, and the tears pool out and edge down his cheeks. She touches his head affectionately, then stands and briskly gets out a box of tape and bandages.

"Shall I take him to the nurse?" Svetlana asks, half-rising from her chair.

"I'll manage," Katya replies.

"But all injuries are supposed to be reported to the nurse…"

Svetlana's voice trails away, silenced by Katya's look of disbelief.

"It's not a sin to do things differently now and then, Svetlana," she says, with a laugh in her voice. Svetlana subsides, her full lips pursed hard against the mockery.

Katya cuts a small piece of tape, and applies it to the bandaged knee.

"There you are. Is that better?"

The boy looks down, uncertain.

"You are a brave young man, aren't you?" she says.

He looks at her, suspicious. Her amiable, kind tone is unexpected, and he turns suddenly and runs away. Katya watches him go with a small pain in her heart, and some anger flashing in her eyes. Not at the boy, but at everything that has made him push her away. She is almost sitting down at her desk again when she suddenly stands instead, and the abrupt scraping of her chair, together with the metallic slam of the office door which Katya throws open make Svetlana look up, wide-eyed. But Katya is already gone, her chair having fallen to the floor.

She is running down the hallway. It is silent and deserted, for the children have now started their final lesson. But as she flies down the corridor, and turns a corner, she sees her little boy, the one with the cut knee; he is almost back at his classroom. He stares at the woman bearing down on him, and she stops, and they watch each other for a moment. She considers. Another kind word and he will probably run again.

"Come here," Katya tells him, with authority, despite the fact that she is suddenly unsure quite what she is doing, following this unknown child.

He frowns, and then slowly begins the walk down the corridor towards her. He stands before her, and she looks down at the top of his head, her arms folded.

"Please," she says. "Please don't run from me like that," she says, her voice soft and kind now.

Quickly, she passes her fingers through his hair, caressing it, tidying it, and then she turns and walks back down the corridor. She can hear the echoing of her own footfalls clamouring back at her from the hollow walls, but she can hear nothing else. She turns again, and looks at the boy, standing there, still watching her. His soft eyes are too large, too tentatively adoring, too thrilled. She closes her own eyes against them.

"Go back to your lesson," she says, pushing a tone of command into her voice, and he runs from her, back to the classroom.

"Where did you go to?" Svetlana's timid voice makes Katya want to snap back a reply.

"Bathroom," she says.

"Oh."

She suspects very strongly that her secretary's main purpose in life, or at least here at school, is to watch her. Either she is one of those people whose lives are so dull and mean that she keeps herself from boredom by spying on everyone around her, or she has a definite instruction from someone, somewhere to keep an eye on Katya. This would not be unusual, given that Katya's parents were killed under Stalin, as enemies of the state; and her brother Yuri's subsequent escape to the United States did nothing to help the situation. But then, Katya has always relished a challenge, and began her campaign for acceptance and credibility in the Party long ago as a young Pioneer. In her smart uniform – a red hat and scarf over a white shirt, which were some of the best pieces of clothing she owned – she had stood in an orderly row and sworn solemnly to uphold the ideals of Lenin and Stalin. She still remembers the thundering sound of hundreds of childish voices around her, echoing around the hall in which they stood. Soon after that, she had calmly signed a denouncement of her parents, requested of her at the age of thirteen as her civic duty. That had gotten her some points for "heroism" in the Party records. Even then, at that age, with no idea of how she could ever effect a sort of revenge for her parents' deaths, she was clear in her own mind that she wanted to do so. It was always simply a question of how, not whether or not she should.

She glances once more at Svetlana. Her light brown eyes hold streaks of gold within them, and they are superficially striking, but they are always darting, watching; and her delicate mouse-like ears are always twitching. There is plenty of use for unassuming, steady people like her; the local resident's associations, the work councils, the police –

they all use observations from people like that all the time. Katya glances at the clock on the wall behind her. Five minutes to go.

She begins packing up her things.

"It's only five minutes to," Svetlana points out, helpfully.

"I can read a clock," Katya tells her. "I am going home."

Svetlana watches Katya's swift, easy movements. Her admiration of her beautiful superior, with her tall, slim figure and her ink-black hair and eyes has turned to envy over the past year, and even dislike. Svetlana too is pretty in her own way, and as helpful as she can be, and she has tried to make Katya like her, but she will not.

The school bell rings, and a dulled scraping of chairs in thirty rooms above and around them penetrates the thick, solid blocks of the office walls. Katya looks up at her co-worker, and smiles, more kindly. The girl is pleased, and smiles back, coyly, but not without a desperation behind her light eyes that makes Katya shiver inwardly. But Katya smiles again, anyway, before looking back to her own desk, where she picks up her bag. She waits for a moment and listens. Outside the office door, a hundred pairs of feet hustle through the corridor. There is no stampede for the door; even getting out of this place cannot inspire these children with enthusiasm, Katya thinks.

She pushes back her own metal chair, and reaches for her coat.

"Bye, Svetlana," she says.

"Bye, Katya." There is a pause – enough to mark a change of subject, but not enough to allow Katya to escape.

"Doing anything tonight?" Svetlana asks, and her sugary friendliness makes Katya's skin crawl.

"No." She is seeing Alexander. She will go to his apartment, where he wants to cook dinner for her. But that is something private. Even when it has nothing to do with her clandestine work, Katya has never been one to speak of her internal life, of thoughts and feelings, even to her few friends.

"No," she repeats. "You?" she asks, politely, although she does not really care.

"I am re-reading Comrade Stalin's speeches. A little every evening," Svetlana replies.

That should be a stimulating night, thinks Katya, but her eyes lose nothing of their polite smile. "They are very interesting," she says. "Very good."

"I know, they…"

"I have to go."

"Going home, Katya?" she asks.

"I already said that," is the curt reply.

"Oh." Svetlana looks down at her account books once again. "It's just… you don't always go straight home after work. Do you?"

Katya resists the impulsive response, which is to turn and stare sharply at the girl, to evaluate the meaning of her words. Instead, she keeps her head down where it was, in her bag, looking for her hat, and when she finds it, she pulls it out and looks at her with a sigh and says, "Don't you have anything else to worry about?"

Taking a step or two forward, so that she is standing even

nearer to the girl in the oppressive office that they share, Katya puts on the hat, and dons her coat and gloves, slowly and methodically, pulling each woollen casing over each of her own slender fingers. Her eyes are softer now, dancing, with a hint of smiling flirtation in them, and they are fixed upon the girl's eyes. It is a dirty trick, and Katya knows it, but she holds the look anyway, and watches the girl look away, and then watches her darting eyes become inexorably drawn back. Svetlana is confused; something about Katya makes her heart beat heavily and her stomach feel weak.

"See you tomorrow, Svetlana," she says as she walks out at last.

"See you tomorrow." The voice is whispery, hopeful.

Why do you play such games? Katya asks herself. If she is dangerous she will only become more so if you tease her like that. But she does not stop to think about it any more. When she steps outside, the snow is still falling, and with a feeling of pleasure she steps into the tumbling flakes, thinking briefly of the boy in the corridor, and the evening still to come.

His apartment building is new of course, built high and wide, and it overlooks the river. It is no more than twenty years old, and has been built specifically to house government employees; particularly the privileged ones. His own rooms are bright, and very warm; the heated air feels stolen away from some distant, tropical place. The place is brilliantly illuminated with lamps, candles, wall mounted lights. She walks in from the early evening gloom, and immediately she has entered another, more welcoming, more pleasurable world. She places her coat into his waiting hands, and catches the clean, soapy scent of his hair when he leans to kiss her cheek. While he goes to pour them each a glass of vodka, she looks around. What must it cost for the electricity to light this building? And the gas to heat it? Yet who would not want to live here always?

"What are you thinking about?" he asks, handing her a glass.

"How light it is in here."

"A privilege that I enjoy to the fullest," he tells her. "I hate the dark."

"Like a little boy?" she smiles.

"Well, not the darkness really. I mean, the dreary, grey light of winter. The dusk at any time. That sort of thing."

"Yes," she says. "I know what you mean. It can be oppressive."

In the kitchen she stands watching him. He has a chicken. Whole and uncut, and it is roasting in the black oven with potatoes. She watches him cut up winter vegetables and toss them in a dressing of vinegar and a little oil and salt. She offers to help him, but he refuses.

"I love doing this."

She can see that he does. His fingers move with grace and feeling, weighing the knife, scooping up the strips of carrot and cabbage and beetroot, stirring at simmering pots.

"You look very happy."

He stops stirring to look at her, and his large brown eyes are serious and kind.

"I am happy," he says. "I am happy that we met. And that you are here now."

"Thank you." She is slightly embarrassed by his openness. It is not what she is used to, and she walks away a little, under pretence of looking into the oven. Gently, she pulls open the door, and glances in at the roasting bird.

As they eat, he tells her that he works as a first secretary to a minister, a good, trustworthy position. She nods, seriously, without too much interest. She does not want to think about this now. Her first task is to get to know him, let him feel he knows her, and let him begin to love her. There will be time later for finding out these practical things. For now, she remains wholly absorbed by the contents of her plate. The flesh of the chicken is soft and melting; it possesses a texture and taste she has never before encountered, and that bears no resemblance to the stringy specimens of fowl she has eaten prior to this.

"This is an incredible meal," she says. He nods and thanks her.

"Who do you work for, Alexander?" she asks, and her eyes have a glow in them, as though she is sharing a joke with herself.

"A government minister," he repeats.

"From the quality of this chicken, I think it must be Khrushchev himself," she jokes. He laughs, but shakes his head.

"The chicken was not a privilege. At least, not directly. You know Misha?"

"Yes, of course," she replies. "We were friends growing up. Not that close, but we saw each other occasionally."

"We were best friends, when we were boys. He was a genius with physics and mathematics. All the subjects I hated. He'd help me with my science homework, and I'd help him with history and literature. He's still one of my closest friends. The closest, probably."

She says nothing to this, and he shakes his head slightly, to draw himself away from the dark beauty of her eyes, watching him.

"Anyway, his grandmother is part of a small *kolkhoz*, out in the country. She raises all her own chickens and a few pigs and goats. His father was coming in to the city a few days ago, so I gave him the cash for her best chicken, and he carried it with him on the train. Under his jacket. Flapping away, no doubt. And here it is."

She smiles at the story. "Do you always go to this much trouble for food?"

"This was an exceptional occasion," he tells her. "But yes, I enjoy good food – when one can get it. Life can be full of small pleasures, if you take some time now and then to enjoy them."

"Most people don't," she says, which is the closest she can get to saying anything about herself.

"Why do you say that?" he asks, not because he disagrees, but because he would like to hear her thoughts, to draw her out of her reserve.

She takes a drink and considers. "I think people are too used to thinking about the past or the future. There is no consideration for the present. It is taken for granted."

"Perhaps that is because many people are unhappy with their lot in life. They are hoping for a better future. That is the promise this country has made them."

She is surprised at his sympathy for people less well off than himself, but also irritated at his politician's talk of promises.

"Those promises have been made for many years," she says.

"What do you suggest?"

She has already noted four places where bugs may be in this government apartment, and anyway, her true thoughts do not concern him.

"At least the worst is over," she says.

"Yes. The worst is over. Now, after the long winter, comes *ottepel*." The snow melt. Khrushchev's famous "thaw", after the stiff, frozen years of Stalin's rule. He carves more of the meat, and with a smile of thanks she holds up her plate to accept it.

He does not, that evening, specify which minister he works for, but Misha has already told her. She feels edgy, suddenly – nervous, irritable. She takes a few deep, controlled breaths, breaths that he will not notice, and she tries to think. What is troubling her? She smiles at him, and considers. If she is to be honest with herself, she has found that she likes Alexander, more than she can remember ever liking anyone. In the tiredness of the late evening, she wishes for a moment that the calculation and evaluation and consideration of how to steal his secrets would not have to constantly play inside her head, even though she knows that to put them aside, even for a moment, would leave her exposed. They are walking outside now, a walk after dinner, in the wide snowy streets. She has only been trying to do this for a few weeks, and she is already having trouble with him. He is arousing unexpected, unusual feelings in her. He seems to be inspiring respect, and gentleness in her, perhaps because he demonstrates those qualities himself.

"I like my work," he says, when she asks him.

"Passionately?"

"No. How can you be passionate about something you have not chosen to do?"

"Then why not do something else?" she asks.

"Is that how things work in the Soviet Union?" he says, his voice lower. He offers her his hand as they climb over a snow bank to get closer to the softly iced expanse of the river. His grip is firm, and he does not try to hold on for longer than is necessary. They stop under a streetlight and she looks out over the cool blue-white of the frozen water on one side, and the gracious, expansive street on the other, where the buildings are tinted yellow from the lights and the snow. It is how she imagines a deserted Parisian boulevard must look and feel. He follows her gaze, trying to see what she sees.

"It's beautiful," she tells him.

"Yes."

And a world away from the Moscow I live in, and that most people know, she thinks.

They have walked as far as the square, near the Kremlin. There has been a new, light snowfall since the early evening, that has been largely undisturbed. The purity of the crisp, white carpet gives a magical quality to the square and it decorates like fine sugar the tops of distant, golden Kremlin domes and spires that rise up from the walls that close them in. He takes hold of her hand as they both absorb the beauty before them, and she feels warm suddenly, even out here in the cold. Then she quickly glances up, as she always does, at the building that towers over the street ahead of them. It is a habit of hers, a reminder, and at this moment she suddenly feels she needs that reminder more than ever.

"You like that building?" he asks her, noticing.

She shakes her head. "No. Do you know about it?"

He knows that on either side of the grey monolith of the main structure, the wings of the building are designed in slightly differing styles. It looks unbalanced and confused, despite its air of solidity.

"The architect who designed it submitted two different plans to Stalin," she tells him. "And they were both signed off. Or perhaps neither were. Something like that – I forget the details. Anyway, the man was too terrified to ask which design Comrade Stalin actually wanted. So he built half one way, and the other half the other way."

"Is that true?" he asks her.

She shrugs and smiles, but without pleasure. "I think so. It *could* be true anyway, and that's what is important."

He has nothing to say to her in response, so he stays silent, and they keep walking, footsteps crisp on the frosted pavement.

"Tell me about the school. I want to know more," he says. Of course, she thinks. You cannot say much about your work. Not to someone you don't know and trust. Not yet.

"No," she replies. "*I* want to know. How did you get where you are? You are so young, and so…"

"So what?"

"Nice," she laughs. "Tell me, please."

"All right, I will," he says. "Come back for some tea, and I will tell you."

An image of his father swims into Alexander's head from the far edges of his mind, where it usually sits. An image of him excited, angered, passionate, brimming with ideas and with confidence. He was, still is, a good man, honest, and with compassion. At the time of the revolution, he was very young, the son of a merchant, who had inherited a good business from his own father. When the revolution occurred his inherent idealism was overwhelmed with the possibilities laid out by Lenin and his group. He joined the Party at that time, giving up the comfort and security with which he had been brought up, happily and without pride in his actions. He saw no use in arguing for a better, more equal Russia if he himself was not prepared to take the first step. He

86

worked hard and long, moving up through the ranks of the local Komsommol, before taking the next steps into central government. When he came upon corruption and injustice, he explained it away as being an inevitable part of any human endeavour. It would not last long, could not last long, in the new Soviet Union.

Stalin had been his undoing. Not in any physical sense. He was not fired, or sent into exile, or killed. But towards the end, his mind and heart began to silently doubt what it had believed in for so many years as Stalin's methods of rule became unmistakeable, and unexplainable. The pervasive fear that you could sniff in the air like hanging smoke, the terror, the petty-minded spying on one's own family and friends, became too widespread to be passed over or explained away. It began to be apparent to him that almost everyone he knew, from colleagues to friends, were acting from the wrong motives. They only spoke the words that were expected or required; their work was inspired by fear, not belief. It nearly broke him, Alexander told her. He continued to work, but his passion was dying away, like a marching song that fades as the parade moves out of sight. And then when Stalin died, and the political manoeuvrings of his rivals were over, the ascendance of Khrushchev had given him some slight relief. He had used his remaining contacts, and had started Alexander at once on his career in government service.

"He told me that he had hoped to have made a difference during his own lifetime, but that he now placed his hopes in me."

"And is he pleased with your work?"

Alexander nods. "I think so."

"But you don't have the passion that drove him."

"No. That is a rare thing, and everyone must find it where they can."

Katya opens her mouth to reply, but thinks better of it. Why should I be concerned about this young man and his family? And yet she cannot help herself.

"Tell me," he says, for he is watching her hesitate. "Whatever it is, tell me."

"How will you find *your* passion in life if you are following your father's dream?"

Later, alone in the kitchen while he makes her some strong tea to warm them after their walk, he hears her ask that question again. He could not answer at the time, and if he is to be completely honest with himself he was shocked at her words, at her talk of passions and dreams and following paths. It was so different from anything he had ever considered before, and yet there was a sense of some part of his mind shifting, of something falling into place, though he cannot pin down what exactly. As he thinks over their conversation out there in the glow of the snowy streets, he is caught between embarrassment and elation at her incisive, clear mind, and at the way she got the measure of him in minutes, showing him things he had preferred to hide even from himself. For his part, his questions and encouragement and genuine interest in her life has brought him hardly any closer to knowing her than he had been when they first met.

As she sips at her tea, he mentions her parents, a gentle query, and she shakes her head slightly.

"They are both dead."

He nods and waits, so she will understand that he already knows this, but it seems she does not wish to elaborate. He asks something else, to change the focus.

"Any brothers or sisters?"

"One brother," she says, in barely more than a whisper, nodding. "Yuri. He left here. Four years ago."

Alexander nods, but is inwardly shocked again. It is rare for anyone to be able to get out, to escape, for that is what she means. There is no leaving this country; one can only escape, and that is rarely successful. He is about to ask how and why, but her eyes are dark and he does not want to upset her. Her brother's leaving must have made her life harder – not only that he is now lost to her, but that suspicion would automatically be transferred to her, like a blanket that she must always carry around.

She takes a small taste from the customary saucer of jam that he has placed alongside her tea glass, and holds it on her tongue while she drinks. Only then does she look up at him again.

"You know they were taken?" Her voice is matter-of-fact, but her eyes look sad. But then, they often do, he thinks. "My parents, I mean?"

"Yes. How old were you?"

"Twelve years old."

"Just a little girl," he says quietly, and in her mind she curses him, for she is feeling again that strange wave of emotion that overcame her at the party that night of their first meeting. The feeling that she cannot possibly hold everything together any longer, that she is about to scream or cry, or both. It must be him, she thinks. He is the common factor here. It must be him. With a snap, her eyes focus on his face, and with an effort of will that he cannot detect she speaks, coolly:

"They were anti-Stalinists, and they were quite open about it. They knew the risk they were taking."

He is shocked, and disbelieving.

"But they were your parents. And it is not wrong to have an opinion…"

"It is. It was then. And they knew it. And they still kept their opinions, and made them known."

"Didn't you think the same way as them?"

"No. Not really. I was twelve, when they were taken away. I didn't think much about anything, except playing and school."

"And it didn't turn you against the State? Or its systems? Afterwards?"

Is he testing her? Checking her credentials? Her suspicion splashes over her like a sudden burst of freezing water, and it wakes her out of the warm, relaxed state into which he has lulled her. Lured her. It is easier now that she suspects him a little. Now she knows once more where she stands and who she is.

"No. It didn't turn me against the State. My beliefs came to me as an adult, and I have thought them through, and know them to be rational and true."

"And so you remain a good communist to this day?"

She shrugs. "Of course. The crimes or mistakes that one man may have made does not negate a whole ideology, does it?" And I have striven to be the perfect communist, she thinks, to avoid the taint of my parents' beliefs and my brother's actions. And if they must watch me a little more closely, and if that makes my work harder, it also makes it more satisfying.

"No, but they were your parents! Can you be so rational when your own mother has been taken from you? Katya?"

Why does he say her name that way? She closes her eyes and despite herself, she feels the moist hotness of tears searing the edges of the lids. He watches her for a moment, sorry that he has failed to see through her calm, logical bravado. Then he is on his knees by her side, and he touches her hair and finally puts a sure arm around her shoulders.

"I'm sorry," he whispers to her again and again. "I'm sorry." She puts his arm away, firmly, but kindly.

"It's over," she tells him, and when she looks at him her eyes are clear and calm, and her voice is steady.

"It's over, Sasha." It is the first time that she has addressed him by his informal name. She shrugs, and gives him a smile.

"I hardly think of it any more."

She does not allow him to escort her all the way to her apartment. Instead, at the metro station, she insists that he leaves her, and turns back. He is reluctant – he would like to see her safely home, but is also eager for more time with her, even twenty minutes on a train. But she has been shaken by certain feelings that have bubbled up within her while she has been sitting there in his apartment. There was a moment towards the end of their long evening together when she felt herself relax, when she suddenly, unexpectedly, felt that she would be happy never to leave, that she would be content to just stay there with him, this young man who is still little more than a stranger to her. She had noticed this weakness within herself at once, and within five minutes she had come up with a convincing reason why she needed to leave immediately, and she had pulled on her coat and left, with Alexander almost running beside her, at least as far as the station.

She needs time to think, and as she sits limp and tired in the underground carriage, her body swaying with the rocking of the train, she asks herself what she will do next. He likes her, she would have to be blind not to see it, and this is exactly as she would have wished. The more he likes her, the more he will learn to trust her. It will take time, of course, and subtlety and caution, but she can do it.

The train slows inside the blackness of a tunnel, and she blinks away the sudden darkness. The key is to think of him as a means to an end, not as a person. She nods to herself as the carriage emerges into the light of her station. She stands and waits by the door. Forget his kindness, and his handsome eyes, and his open smile. He is a means towards an end, an important end; he is not a person. She steps off the train and runs quickly up the staircase. At the station exit, the freezing night air is waiting for her; the cold pulls her back to herself, and with a deep breath and a nod, she walks briskly back to her home.

CHAPTER FIVE
BOSTON

O<small>N</small> C<small>HRISTMAS</small> E<small>VE</small>, they walk down to Newbury Street. The morning sky is dim, cloud-filled, with a feeling of late afternoon to it. Alexander is grateful for the lights of the shop windows, the coloured bulbs strung over balconies and railings, the mocha-tinged steam that escapes into the chill air from all the coffee shops. Leaving Lauren at a small gallery, he goes to get his last gifts. When at last they meet in Copley Square for lunch, she is radiant, glowing – there is excitement in her face, and the frost has quickened her blood, so that energy and warmth pulsate through her, even through the sheets of cold that beat down from the steel sky. He watches her walking across the paved stones, pleased that she is with him for the holidays, happy to share her liveliness and delighting in the pleasure that shows in her eyes when she recognizes him standing outside the restaurant, muffled up in a yellow cashmere scarf. In moments they are inside, overtaken by dry warmth, talking over the Christmas music, drinking down a small whiskey each. The alcohol curls through him, reaching thin tendrils of heat through his chest and stomach. With a contented sigh he puts down his glass and smiles.

"How were the galleries?"

"Oh, fine."

He smiles. She is hiding something, suppressing it without much success beneath eyes and a mouth that are conspiring to give her away.

"What are you up to, young lady?"

"Nothing. I'm picking up your present after lunch."

"Oh good," he says. "I'm sure it's huge, I'll help you carry it."

"Uh-uh. You're going home; I'll collect it and we'll meet back at the house."

"Are we opening things tonight or tomorrow?"

She shrugs. "Whatever you want."

"It *is* Christmas Eve."

"Tonight it is, then. After dinner."

Lauren struggles into the house, swaying slightly under the weight of the parcel. Now, suddenly, as she carries it over the threshold of her uncle's house, this beautiful, comforting house, she has her first sense of misgiving. Arms aching, she pauses in the hallway and props the present against a wall. It is large, and wound around with an outsized ribbon and bow. In the gallery she had thought the bow a festive, bright touch, but here in the warm darkness of Alexander's home, and considered in the light of her new uncertainty, the gold ribbon appears garish. She reaches over and tugs at it, but the bow is firm and does not unravel at a touch. She pulls off her gloves and scarf, her lip caught between her teeth as she considers.

"Lauren?"

He is calling, from the kitchen of course. She can hear pots sliding on the stove, and the tap running.

"Coming!"

But he is already in the hall, a blue apron around his waist, and a towel between his hands. She looks round and sees him with her artist's perception, for she is still in that other space in her mind, and his age shocks her for a moment. Not that he looks any older than he did the day before, or even six months before, but now she notices him as an older man – his silvery hair, still holding the pattern of his comb; his veined, slightly crooked hands, the light spots that run under the grey hair of his forearms. She greets him and glances at her own hand as it touches his shoulder, and she notices the planes of the bones and the flicker of muscle and vein. She feels like drawing it, immediately.

"Is that for me?"

"Of course," she says.

"Shall I open it now?" he says, playing the excited child, when in reality she knows his small pleasure in unwrapping it will only be enhanced by a period of anticipation.

"After dinner," she says, and leads him back into the kitchen.

An hour before their meal, she is upstairs, immersed in a hot bath, from which he knows she will not emerge for at least thirty minutes. He thinks with pleasure of the new candles he had thought to scatter around her bathroom, and he knows she will be lying there with every one of them lit. Since there will be only the two of them he has decided to serve beef rather than turkey, and the joint of meat is almost done, its savoury juices melting slowly into the pan where the potatoes are crisping. The wine is decanted, and he has the remaining vegetables browning, bubbling or roasting, according to their needs.

When the telephone rings, he considers leaving it, but the bell is persistent, and finally he scoops up the handset and flicks it on.

"Merry Christmas." He recognises Estelle's voice at once. He puts the pan he is holding back onto the stove and sits down at the kitchen table.

"And to you. How was California? Did you succumb to a facelift?"

"Are you implying I need one?" she returns.

"Of course not. I was thinking of your postcard, that's all."

"I have to say, I think LA has nothing going for it except maybe silicone implants and orange juice. How are you? Melissa told me the deal is probably off."

He notes the word 'probably'. Perhaps there is a chance to complete this sale after all. "Yes it is. But it happens. Perhaps it just wasn't the right fit."

"That's too bad." She sounds unconcerned. "Listen, I

wanted to see if you're free to come over for tea tomorrow. And your niece, if she'd like to."

Alexander accepts, trying not to sound over-eager. He is pleased to hear from her. He had liked her relaxed tone, her forthrightness, the lack of formality, during their lunch – as he gets older, he has little patience for the careful treading that most new friendships require.

"How did you know Lauren was here?"

"Melissa mentioned it. In one of her few moments of conversation."

"She's with you for Christmas?" he asks.

"Yes. Right now she's at one end of the apartment typing away on a laptop as thin as a wafer," Estelle continues, "while at the other end, her father is scratching out literary criticism with a fountain pen that looks like something Dickens might have used…"

He smiles at the image, then risks a more intimate remark.

"Sounds lonely for you."

She hesitates. "I'm used to it."

His perception has unbalanced her, and he feels at once that the easy tone of the conversation has been lost. Without remaining on the line for much longer, she simply confirms the time for their visit and hangs up the phone.

After dinner they sit in the living room, almost stupefied by the food.

"I can't believe I ate that much. I can't move," Lauren tells him.

He offers her a chocolate truffle. "Are you trying to kill me?" she asks.

"Certainly not. I want my present first."

She struggles up with looks of exaggerated anguish, but refuses his offer of assistance. With difficulty she slides her package into the living room. He comes to where she holds it upright, and glances to her for permission to open it. She nods, an edge of anxiety scoring into her, as she watches him pick at the tape.

"Just rip it open, Uncle Alex. It's a portrait," she admits suddenly, unable to wait.

"A portrait of whom?"

She smiles and they continue unwrapping together, leaving curls of gold paper all over the floor. He is about to ask the question again, but now enough strips of paper are removed that what was initially just swathes of textured paint now reveals itself as a white blouse, a neck, a throat… then a chin and a mouth – a familiar mouth. The smile freezes on her face as she sees his watching eyes change from anticipation to shock. Or is it horror?

"Uncle Alex?" she says, taking hold of his hand. She has stopped peeling away the paper, but his free hand reaches up and pulls it loose, an impatient, urgent movement. He must see the rest of it at once. He gasps for air, an alarming sound, for in its shock, his body has forgotten to breathe. Lauren's hand is on his forehead, stroking, panicking.

"I'm fine," he whispers.

"Are you sure?"

He does not reply. He is engrossed in the painting. He now realises that he had forgotten what Katya looked like, how she really was. The shape of her nose, the tilt of her chin, the lines on her forehead. Those details that get blurred in memory after months and years, that you find you can only recall by staring at the two photographs that you came away with, and that only return for sweet, ephemeral moments when the beloved's face comes unsummoned into dreams or recollections. He feels he might cry if he speaks so he says nothing, and Lauren knows him well enough to wait in silence while they both look at the portrait. He forces himself to focus on the work involved, on Lauren's achievement, as a way out of the labyrinth of emotion that has suddenly claimed him. His niece, Katya's niece, has captured her aunt with such vivid clarity and life that he has to remind himself that she has in fact never even met her.

"Was it the wrong thing to do?" she asks finally.

He shakes his head to buy time, though there is a part of himself that is almost resentful of what his niece has done. How she has forced right before his eyes, in unrelenting clarity, the vision of his lost wife. His lost love. She waits, sensing that he is displeased in some way – she watches him biting his lip slightly. Perhaps he is trying to regain some control. Then he speaks, as quietly and calmly as he is able.

"Tell me about it," he says.

Still gripping his hand, she speaks, slowly, carefully, explaining how she worked from the two pictures that he has, and from a couple of Yuri's photographs, taken when Katya was a teenager, the Katya that he knew before he left Russia. Her features and facial structure were the same, of course, and gave her different angles and expressions to work from.

"And the eyes?" He looks at Lauren for the first time.

"Are they good?" she asks gently.

He nods. They are exact; so true. They look directly at him while revealing very little themselves. Katya could always have a hint of haughtiness about her, and Lauren had captured that too, but she had also placed in those eyes a fierce intelligence and an infinite sadness.

"When I was thinking about this piece, and how to do it, I went through everything I knew about her, and I realised that basically, there were two Katyas. One was my father's. You know Yuri's stories," she smiles. "The laughing, clever kid sister who was always leading him a dance and getting him in trouble with their parents. And then I knew your Katya. Or at least your stories of her," she adds, to qualify any presumption he might feel she is making.

He waits for her to go on. Tell me, Lauren, what she was like, let me try and feel it again, even though you cannot possibly understand it all.

"That was the Katya I wanted to capture. The bold, strong, vulnerable, angry woman who chose to…"

A quick movement of his head catches her eye and causes her to stop.

"Anyway, that's what I was trying for," she finishes mildly.

"You're a genius, Lauren. It's almost hard to look at."

"I'm sorry. The last thing I wanted was to hurt you… It's

funny, I was excited all the time I was painting it, varnishing, even framing just today. It was only when I got it home this afternoon that I had my first panic attack. Wondering if I was really doing the right thing. It must make you miss her all over again."

They are quiet together for a minute or two before he speaks.

"It does," he says. "I mean, it only sharpens what I've felt for the last forty years. But that's not necessarily a bad thing."

"As long as you're okay with it. I can always take it away."

"No, no. It was a shock, that's all. I just need some time."

He sounds more like himself and she is immeasurably relieved. The self-control, the rationality is back, and she is no longer fearful that she has made a terrible mistake. She leads him back to his chair and pokes at the fire, which has settled down into small, licking flames that curl around the last, luminous log of wood.

"I'll get some tea," she tells him. "Camomile?"

"If you're having some?"

"Yes."

He watches as she goes out to the kitchen, leaving him with a precious few moments alone. He glances at the fire for comfort, but the logs are too dry and are spitting and hissing, putting out a violent heat that causes him to move his chair back a little. Closing his eyes intensifies his awareness of the canvas looming behind him. With conscious, almost ostentatious calm, he turns in his chair, and looks at it, at her, once more. She is watching him with an expression that is half-smile, half-frown, an expression that perhaps she never even had during life, but which captures her character perfectly. He feels a stab of guilt and swallows, but his mouth is dry. He looks for water, but there is only the remains of their wine. Lauren will come soon with the tea, he reminds himself. In the meantime, Katya is regarding him with that slight smile, without accusation or blame. He has always known that she would never have blamed him for what happened – his own pain and guilt have been punishment enough. But that knowledge has only ever reinforced the sense of exactly how much he lost when she died.

CHAPTER SIX
MOSCOW – MAY 1956

THERE IS A LOW, DISBELIEVING WHISTLE from the man standing beside her. She smiles, and watches the sound escape from his lips, and form a question that hovers in the air before them.

"So it's going exactly as we'd hoped?"

She nods and leans over the bridge and looks out onto the river. If she narrows her gaze, the surface of the water sparkles like a field of diamonds under the late afternoon sunshine.

"And he is in love with you?"

"Who knows?" she replies.

"Well, you should know. You *must* know. Or it's no good."

His eyes stay on her and a last outline of amusement leaves her features. In the face of his expectant silence, she gives a shrug; a conceding gesture, a reluctant acknowledgement.

Misha sighs. "Good work, Katyushka. It must be hard too, but you've done well."

Her eyes are downcast, and she appears in no hurry to answer.

"Thank you," she says at last.

He drops his voice, matching her tone. "It's not easy, is it?"

She looks up. Of course, it must be difficult for him too. Much more so than for her. She hardly knows Alexander, while Misha has been friends with him for fifteen years or more.

"But, in the end, Katya," he continues, "you have to make choices in life. Especially in this life of ours. To sacrifice your personal loyalties for a greater cause. Alexander represents everything I despise, and even though he's my friend, I can't live with myself if I'm not doing everything I can to fight the system I hate. It's a hard choice, but I know where I stand."

She is not as reassured by this argument as she feels she should be, not least because it sounds too carefully concise and rehearsed to her ears. It is not that she disagrees with Misha. They have all come out of years of terror and horror, years of becoming used to those crippling moments when your mouth turns dusty with fear, when you hear that someone else you know has been spirited away, when you are glanced at with a guilty look by someone you work with or live next to, or worse, when you are avoided altogether. Where personal loyalty between friends, colleagues, even family, is forgotten in the name of the greater good. Denounce your cousin if he is an enemy of the people. Turn in your neighbour for crimes against the state. Or for anything at all. They might be thinking thoughts that could threaten the Soviet people. She lost her parents because of this ethos, taken to extremes.

But then, perhaps, this choice he is talking of making is not so relevant to her. She is not betraying her best friend, she is only cultivating a source.

"Katya?"

"Yes?"

"Do you care for him?"

Misha watches her carefully, picking through her expressions and movements for signs, but she looks up and meets his gaze without hesitation, her eyes unreadable.

"We are different, the two of us, aren't we?" he asks.

She waits for him to explain.

"I mean we are friends, too. Even if we don't see each other much."

So I can tell you how I really feel? She thinks. Would it be a relief, a pleasure even, to confide in someone, when she has never confided in a soul through her entire adult life? She pictures the scene. Sitting with Misha over a glass of vodka, or some tea perhaps, the way other people do, trying to explain, faltering, confused and perhaps a little shy, that she has been unexpectedly moved by Alexander? No, not moved, exactly, that is too strong a word, maybe touched. Or simply disconcerted. She smiles at Misha. She cannot conceive of sharing her deepest thoughts with him. Especially thoughts that are in need of clarity, and certainty, and definition. No, Misha. Not even you, who I've known since we were barely teenagers.

He sees the cold steel behind the look that she gives him now, and he starts to say something, but her face contracts into a frown of concentration. Her eyes are no longer with him, but are focused on a building several hundred yards away. His eyes move sideways immediately, and they both watch as a large man carrying a shopping bag emerges from the entrance to that apartment block. The man looks about, up at the blue sky, and walks away briskly.

"It's not him," says Katya.

"No." Misha glances at his watch. "It's not time yet. Good. All we need is another one who doesn't stick to his routine."

They face each other again, two friends strolling and lounging out on the bridge, on a day that holds the promise of summer – a day that has drawn out young couples all over the city, and that will tempt more once the day's work is over. Katya is the one facing the apartment block, and as she talks to Misha, her eyes flicker constantly back and forth, between his face and the building. He finds it distracting to talk to her in this way, when her attention is diverted, but there is no help for it – they are here for a reason. But he smiles to himself as he thinks that, even were their positions reversed, and he were the one watching the building, her eyes would still never rest. It is a habit of hers – a nervous habit probably – and he cannot remember a time when she was not like this, darting, sparkling, always moving.

Misha examines his fingers, thinking. He knows little of Katya's private life, but then it has always appeared to him that she has never really had one. He doubts that many men have come and gone during her young life. Perhaps one or two, nothing serious certainly. She is an introverted girl, the type to hold herself in and probably deny any sort of sexuality or passion. Some women, he thinks, are just not capable. Certainly he has never felt able to make any kind of overture towards her, even before he recruited her and they began working together. He glances at her again. She is a beauty, but an inaccessible one – and he is not a man who finds women intimidating. On the contrary, he has always had as many women as he pleases, and he has enjoyed that, enjoyed the fact that he can attract them with only a slight, pleasant type of exertion – of his looks, his conversation, his personality. But Katya has always been just outside his grasp, even though over the years he has reached for her, in his own way; that is, without seeming to do so, for to give the appearance of trying too hard, or caring too much, would go against everything he has brought himself up to be.

"I think you're falling in love with him," Misha says, quickly, but her face reveals little.

"And you would know best."

"Aren't you?" he demands.

Katya laughs, and raises an eyebrow, but her eyes never leave the building.

"I thought that was how it's supposed to be."

"Not in this situation."

She turns away. "I know who I am and what I believe in, Misha, and no-one can ever change that." She is sincere, and he nods, to calm the passion that has risen up in her.

"He is nice to be with," she offers, as an attempt to reassure Misha that she is not hiding things from him. "Easy. I don't have to fight so hard all the time when I am with him. Do you understand?"

"He is exactly what you are supposed to be fighting."

"I know." He catches the irritation in her voice. She is often dismissive to avoid being emotional. Misha speaks again, and keeps his voice neutral – he is probing, but moving around her words carefully; he is a man handling a live grenade that cannot be shaken or dropped without consequences.

"You really do care about him, don't you?" he says.

"A little. But that makes it easier. Imagine being involved with someone who repulses you. Don't worry, Misha; I know what I'm getting into."

Her eyes are scanning people around them, looking for anyone who may be looking for them.

"Are you sure he won't suspect me?" she says suddenly. It is a deep pool she is about to plunge into with Alexander, and she cannot help but look for reassurance, even if it can only be superficial.

"No, he won't. Not if you're always aware. Always. And not if he cares for you the way he seems to. Not if you wait for the right time. When you have his love, and his trust, completely."

In Misha's eyes she sees the recognition of her dilemma, even though it is one she will not voice. It is simply not what she expected, nor how she would prefer to work.

"Fighting an enemy without a face, using strangers, those things are easy. It's not so easy compromising someone you love," he says. It is a gentle probe, his voice is warm, safe, relaxed, so that she might not even notice what he has just implied with his last three words.

"He's not like anyone I've ever met," she says, "but I don't love him."

She senses that he is reassured in the relaxing of his shoulders. He smiles. She is intelligent and quick. Perhaps she will pull it off after all. There is one sure way to find out, but before he can lead into it, she turns slightly, so that she can watch out more easily, and then Misha catches the scent of her, the cool, clean smell that is always hers. She lacks the sweet, flowery, feline perfume, the heavy dabs of standard Soviet scent worn by many of the women that he knows, but her fragrance is honest and real. He looks at her sideways, at her distant eyes and long lashes, at her exotic black hair and finely drawn lips. Standing there in the sunlight, against the cool stone, she looks like an idealized portrait of a person, with no feature ungainly or imperfect. Sasha, he thinks, you may get what you want, but she will be a handful, my friend. Even without the added complications.

"So he thinks you're a card carrying communist?"

"I am," she smiles.

He just laughs.

"Idiot," she says, and touches his nose, then his curly dark hair.

"I'm not the idiot."

"Yes, you are. Look at you. Your nose is all red, and it's not even winter. What kind of Russian are you?"

"I'm not," he says, facetiously. "I came here from Italy last year. I felt like freezing to death and being grey, and never having anything good to eat. I got tired of all the sun, the sea, the delicious food and the dark-haired women."

"Yes," she says. "The women I can believe. Have you ever had one that wasn't blonde?"

"Only kissed." He smiles.

"Who?" she asks, and he frowns.

"You, of course!"

"Oh, Misha. *That*. A teenager's peck – this is what you count?!"

"There he is." Misha says, with no change of tone or expression. He lounges back against the bridge and smiles at Katya. She takes his hand to glance at his watch. He is intensely aware of the feel of her fingers on his arm – they feel light yet strong against the inside of his wrist.

"Good. Four o'clock again. What do you think?"

"I think he's stayed away for an hour every day this week."

"Shall we wait until tomorrow?" She watches their man, short, grey-haired, plump, walking away from them, down the sun-streaked street, where shadows are just beginning to fall with the lowering sky.

"Up to you."

"Okay," she says.

He looks at her. "Okay what?"

"Okay, I'll go in now."

They linger by the bridge for five more minutes, talking with suppressed excitement. They are both nervous, but now

Katya takes two deep breaths and smiles. Misha straightens the collar of her blouse.

"Where does Alexander think you are now? He must know that school is over by now."

"Yes, but the school administrator sometimes works late, to catch up," she says, and her smile has changed a little; he imagines he sees the bright determination slipping out of her slightly, and so he turns, and focuses her mind once more on the job in hand.

"You'd better start," he says.

"Okay."

They walk together towards the building, and as they near the front steps, he calls goodbye, and leans and kisses her on the cheek, an affectionate parting from her friend or brother or lover – who would be able to tell which? Then he strolls away, down the street, relaxed, unconcerned. She watches him go; Misha, who has always been considered something of a subversive, with his daring views and his *bitniki* clothes, the American-influenced jeans and sweaters that give the suggestion of a disaffected rebel, but in a way that offers no real threat. He often plays the role of the doubting intellectual in public, and amongst friends he is usually free with his criticism of the Soviet system; but his anger is carefully controlled for effect, and is never pushed too far. It gives him an edgy persona; he is the maverick employed in one of the State's most trusted positions. In many ways, it is the best cover he could ever have concocted, the kind of double bluff that is the direct opposite of her own strategy of modelling herself as the perfect, non-questioning communist. There is also a large part of him that enjoys the subterfuge and thrives on the danger of the work that they do. Part of him, she feels, is like a small boy who has been given the toys and tools to play spy games, and consequently is always filled with excitement and self-importance.

She turns and runs up into the building. Immediately, she has good luck. An old man is coming out, and holds open the heavy front door for her. She wishes him "Good afternoon," and starts up the stairs. Above the ringing of the cold cement under her feet, she hears the old man turn and call after her. She stops. A nosy one, probably. One of those who know everyone in the building.

"Who are you here for?" he asks, his voice shaky.

"Sasha," she replies, and is shocked that she has used his name as the first name that comes to her, that she has already dragged him into this part of her life. Usually she replies any male first name – something different each time, of course. Using the diminutive makes them think she is on intimate terms with whomever she's visiting, and with luck, makes them hesitate as to whom she means. She smiles at the old man, and continues up the stairs, showing no hesitation. She is relieved when she hears the acknowledgement and the slam of the door.

It does not take her long to open the inner door. She has knocked first, of course, just in case, but she can sense that the apartment is empty. Immediately, she walks down the short hallway and into the bedroom. There is a chest of drawers and on the mattress, the sheet is caught up in one corner, as though the bed has been lifted. Sure enough, in an improvised pocket beneath the springs, she finds the code sheets. Some cable transcripts too, which look old and pointless. They may be hidden as a decoy. She takes them to the small table, and lays the pad down, avoiding moist rings of tea spills. From her inside pocket she extracts a camera, and leans down to fit the whole page into the viewfinder. She snaps, winds, and lifts the top sheet, then snaps the one below. She gets into a rhythm at once: click, wind, lift, click, wind, lift. Kneeling down, she stuffs them back into the mattress pocket.

She stands quietly in the middle of the room and frowns. It has been almost too easy, and she still has plenty of time. She runs a finger over the shelf of books above the bed. Nothing stands out. Then she goes through the drawers, and the desk, and his books. Then the bathroom. The floor and basin are dirty and marked, and tiny chest hairs are curled into every corner, but the mirror is surprisingly clean. Vanity? she wonders, and she stops there herself and looks at her face. It appears gaunt and closed off, and distrustful. She is startled, as though she has caught an unknown woman standing right behind her, and then unsettled, for this is not how she sees herself in her own mind. She wonders if this is the face that Alexander sees. As she thinks of him, her face softens, and this change in her features is so clear on the unrelenting surface of the mirror that she quickly turns away.

She has what she came for, and so she removes the film and tucks it inside her shirt, places the camera into her handbag. Quietly she moves across the floor, and closes the front door behind her. By the time she emerges onto the street, the sunlight has begun to recede, and it feels cooler than before.

She walks slowly down the street, and around the corner. She cannot see Misha anywhere. She slows down slightly, but does not look behind, not at first; but then she can sense him walking up behind her, and without thinking she turns to look. He is not there. As she looks ahead again she bumps into him.

"Katya!" he says, for there are many people around now, leaving work. "How are you? What a surprise."

"Yes, isn't it?"

He laughs. "What the hell do you think you were doing?"

She swallows, then sighs. "Sorry. I thought I felt you behind me."

"Even worse. Don't ever look for me, and don't ever wait for me. If they get one of us, they mustn't get the other."

"I know."

"Don't ever wait for me, Katya."

"I know. I'm sorry."

Her step becomes a little faster, as though she is trying to pull away from the conversation. Misha keeps up.

"Did you get everything?" he asks.

"Immediately. All under the bed."

"Again?"

She nods. "Will these people never learn?" she asks dryly.

"They would," he says, walking her in the direction of her

apartment, "but they never think it'll happen to them. More paranoia – that's what they need."

"You don't think they have enough? They rule with it."

"Maybe they need to bring some into their own homes. They're making your job too easy."

She pushes her hands deeper into the pockets of her long cardigan.

"Don't worry, it will never be too easy."

They walk quietly for a few minutes before he broaches the thing he has been considering all afternoon.

"It's time you took something from Alexander."

She seems startled. "Already?"

He nods. "Just once. Just a test run. See how it works."

He wants to see how *she* works, to test her, she is sure of it. He is concerned that she has lost control of her emotions, that she will begin to like Sasha so much that she will no longer want to betray him.

"It's not the right time. He'll suspect. I don't want to ruin it before we've even started."

"I think it's time," Misha repeats. His tone now is authoritative. He has slipped into his role as the senior one in this partnership. She is his recruit, his responsibility, his agent. In the end, she must follow orders.

"Fine," she replies. "What do you want me to do?"

"You see him in the evenings, don't you? Does he bring work home?"

"Sometimes."

"Anything interesting?"

"I don't know, I haven't looked yet. I was trying to be careful."

"Take whatever he brings next time," Misha says, and his tone is the same, firm, leaving no room for argument. "Photograph it, copy it, remember it if you have to – you decide."

She nods. "Give me a week or two."

"Sure."

They have reached the corner of the street that she lives on. The light summer green of the trees casts little pools of shade onto the uneven paving stones, and in the fading sunlight, the yellowing concrete of the apartment blocks looks warm and burnished. Misha stops here, and kisses her goodbye, and as he grasps her hand fondly she slips the camera film into his palm. From here he will turn back onto the main street and walk down to the metro. No other words are exchanged between them, and she is glad of it, for he has ended the day in a way that she had not anticipated and she is feeling more than a little perturbed. He is already walking away, and she watches him disappear around the corner. She stands, lonely on the quiet street, and waits until she can no longer hear his footsteps.

CHAPTER SEVEN
BOSTON

"So tell me about this person we're having tea with."

"Her name is Estelle." Alexander watches Lauren butter her fourth piece of toast. "How do you have the appetite for breakfast after last night?" he asks.

She bites into it with relish. "Want some?"

He shakes his head. Perhaps when he was younger, and his digestion a little better than it is now, he would have been able to eat like that; though in fact he has always been satiated by a little food of excellent quality, rather than quantity for its own sake. It is a fastidious tendency that has served him well through all the years building a business based around food.

"And she's the mother of the awful Melissa?" Lauren asks. "How did you meet?"

She continues eating while he tells her; she is listening intently, but is giving the impression that she is more caught up in her breakfast than in the details of her uncle's story. She has sensed something interesting here, an attraction on his part, but she wants him to speak freely, without noticing that she is probing deeper feelings.

"Anyway, Melissa wouldn't leave the meeting to have lunch with her, so I brought her home. I liked her."

"How come?"

She dusts toast crumbs from her hands as he talks; he mentions Estelle's wit, her quick mind, her unnaturally blue eyes. The romantic slant of this last observation is not lost on Lauren.

"So are you going to ask her out?"

"Of course not. She's married."

"Happily?"

He stands up to pour more tea. "What's that supposed to mean?"

"I don't know. I guess, if she's unhappily married, would that be less of an obstacle for you? In pursuing her?"

He is taken aback. Not because the wish that Estelle was single has not crossed his mind, but because he is disconcerted that his innermost thoughts, which strike him as ignoble, have been guessed at by his niece.

"You know me," he tells her, tersely. "I wouldn't even think like that."

"I know. But passion has been known to drive people to madness."

"It's hardly passion. We just met. It's a friendship, barely. A possible friendship."

The city is as quiet as Lauren has ever known it, the heavy, grey light adding to the sense of isolation, and desolation. They walk together without speaking, glancing in at the window displays of the closed shops. Then, deliberately, they turn off the main road and stroll through silent back streets. Cooking smells slip into the air around them as they walk past the brownstones that loom up on one side. Across the broad, deserted street, through the stark winter trees, the vast river lies cloudy and still.

A few windows have coloured lights or candles in them, but the decorations here in this street of academics and students are largely subdued or absent. Few residents remain here during university holidays, and it shows. Only one house on the corner sports a garish display on its small front patio. A large plastic Santa Claus, streaked with soil and snow melt, stands forlornly in a flower bed; behind him a plastic reindeer lies on its side in the earth, staring up at the sky.

"That's a nice look," Lauren comments. "Take a tip for next year."

They walk back up the street, purposefully now, scanning the door numbers until they find Estelle's entrance. There are lights in the second floor windows and Estelle's voice floats over the intercom, altered and indecipherable; the door clicks open and they walk in and up the stairs.

She is waiting on the landing, and Alexander stands aside for his niece to precede him. It is innate courtesy on his part, but he is also grateful for the buffer, for someone to shield the unlooked for nervousness that he now feels. Before they reach the top of the stairs he hands the bouquet of roses that he carries to Lauren. Estelle receives them from her with a smile, but is slightly awkward, he feels, and fusses for a while over the flowers as she leads them into a long, narrow hallway, lit with lamps that cast a delicate light onto pure white walls. Before they manage more than a few steps, a voice thunders out from a darkened hallway to their left.

"Christmas Day. It must be Santa Claus."

In the dimness of the unlit passageway stands a tall man whom Alexander assumes must be the husband, the professor. The balance of his large body looks strangely precarious, as though a slight breeze, or a gentle push, might cause him to list to one side. He is holding in one large hand an even larger cup from which steam rises.

"Not even the tooth fairy, I'm afraid," Alexander replies.

Estelle smiles. "This is Lauren, Frank. She's an artist. And Mr Ivanov, her uncle. It's his company that Melissa was trying to buy."

"Ah. Ivanov, you say?"

Alexander nods. The professor raises eyebrows that are unkempt but expressive.

"Are you of Russian extraction?" he asks.

"Yes, I am."

"You know, you share your name with a play written by your compatriot, Chekov?"

"Ivanov. Yes, that's right."

"Do you know it?"

"A little." Alexander smiles, and so does the professor.

"A rather dull play, is it not?"

"It has never been one of my favourites."

"And tell me, is your Christian name also Mikhail, like the character?"

For a brief moment he feels like a schoolboy, standing there, being given a sneaky test by the teacher. Perhaps Professor Johnson knows no other way of communicating.

"My name is Alexander," he replies. "Not Nikolai, as I believe the other Ivanov was called."

There is a barking noise from the hall, which Alexander takes to be a laugh, because Estelle smiles also. Perhaps he is imagining it, but he sees a trace of pleasure in her eyes – perhaps she is pleased that he has kept up with her difficult husband. In the meantime, the professor turns around and continues walking away from them. Lauren's eyebrows are slightly raised; she is beginning to understand from where Melissa must have learned, or inherited, her somewhat deficient communication skills. She glances at her uncle, her lips curved into a half-smile.

"You will excuse me if I take my tea in my study, Mr Ivanov," Professor Johnson calls over his shoulder.

"Of course."

A door clicks shut, and he is gone. Estelle sighs slightly.

She doesn't remember the last time she was able to enjoy this banter of his, this brand of humour, even though she is the type who enjoys laughing. She has always been an easy-going counterfoil to the foibles and moods of her husband, the more serious professor. An out-going character to balance his deep introversion. She has a wise-cracking, dry, quick sense of humour that he had liked when they first met, which was so long ago that on the odd occasions when she recalls those memories to her mind, it seems to her that they play themselves out in black and white. He too was ironic at times – is still ironic, but in a less pleasant way than he used to be. His intellectual strength has made him impatient, or even contemptuous sometimes, of people who try to engage him. She does not remember him being like this before, though she is willing to admit to herself that this may be nothing more than a trick of nostalgia; the inevitable filtering out of the hard pieces of grit through the fine mesh of memory. What she remembers is watching sly-eyed through his study door at the university, as she typed in the reception area outside. He would leave his door ajar during the summer months, when the sweltering Boston heat rose moistly up the red brick building and overflowed in through the windows.

She remembers watching him teach his students. A tall, imposing presence he seemed to her, lowered into a wooden captain's chair, listening intently while different young boys and girls, by turns nervous and bold, read aloud their essay for the week. He listened well, and without self-consciousness, so that she felt sure that he was not aware that she half-observed him. Later, when they were together, he would laugh, a gruff sound that seemed to her to match perfectly the rough-hewn contours of his features, and he would tell her that he had always known that she was watching him. She would listen to him, intrigued, absorbing into her own mind the lush overflow of words, of poetry and prose and criticism that issued from that room. The inside of his room always looked summery in her mind – she could not remember it dark or cold, although it must have been so for many months at a time. But whenever she put her mind to it, she could still summon up the smell of old books and dust that pervaded it, no matter how bright the light that washed the walls. It was the smell of scholarship and absent-mindedness, and it brought to her mind the sensation that she was stepping into one of those Victorian novels that she loved so well. She would often put her head into the empty room before she left at the end of the workday, just to get a last lungful of that air, a sense of understanding and kinship with the professor, and with the contents of those age-speckled books, something to take home with her; an unusual need that she could never explain to anyone.

"Come on in. He doesn't mean to be sarcastic," she says, leading her guests into a kitchen that blazes with light and seems the direct antithesis of the dark hallway outside. "It's just his way. I think too many years shut up with only his books have left him not knowing how to speak to people. Even to say hello."

The kitchen is large, for an apartment, and about half of it is taken up with a well-used wooden table and chairs. The table is already set with cream coloured china, the perfect delicacy of the plates and cups at odds with the lived-in, almost faded feel of the rest of the kitchen furnishings. There are only three settings, Alexander notes. Evidently she has not expected her husband to join them, nor her daughter.

She talks mainly to Lauren at first, asking her about their Christmas, and Alexander watches them, his eyes drawn particularly to Estelle, for his morning conversation with Lauren is still playing on his mind. He tries to be casual in his examination of her, but when Estelle looks to him, politely, during the course of the conversation, she is instantly disconcerted. He transfers his attention at once to the slices of cake that sit on the table before them. Lauren has already tasted a piece.

"This is amazing…"

Alexander tries it and asks at once for the recipe but Estelle appears hesitant.

"It's kind of an old family secret."

Alexander shakes his head. "Everyone has a price, Estelle. And when it comes to food, I can usually find it."

"Really? Now I see the no-nonsense businessman." She frowns and pours cups of aromatic tea. He can see her considering whether or not to tell.

"Well, since you are a man who loves his food so much… It's an autumn cake. You have to wait till fall – preferably late fall."

He sits a little forward in his chair, intrigued.

"You need to dress up warmly," she continues, nodding at Lauren. "And then… do you know Fisher's Pond? Where all the berries grow?"

Alexander nods.

"You walk over there. When you get to the northeast corner, where most of the fruit bushes are, turn left down the pathway."

"And then?" he asks.

"And then when you get to Marion's Bakery Stall, you go in and buy as many as you want from the counter. She makes them fresh every day except Monday." The women look at each other and laugh.

"Come on, Uncle Alex, didn't you see that coming?"

"I had you going, didn't I?" Estelle adds, with satisfaction.

"You have a naughty streak, Estelle."

"Sorry I couldn't oblige you with a new dessert recipe. What will you do now?"

He tastes his tea. "Maybe I'll suggest that whoever eventually buys our company contact Marion as a potential new supplier."

"Of course." Estelle shakes her head. "And before you know it, Marion will be a conglomerate, and her cakes will taste like plastic."

The strong tone of her words leaves a slight pause hanging between them for a moment, before Alexander puts down his cup.

"Firstly, have you considered the fact that Marion, whoever she is, might not want to go on baking only ten cakes a day for the rest of her life? And secondly, not all big business means poor quality."

"Maybe, but you have to agree that companies like yours

are the exception rather than the rule. And," she adds with a note of triumph, "even you are on the point of selling out. You know things won't stay the same. That home-made touch that you're so famous for will probably disappear."

"I'm 'selling out' because I'm getting old and I want to do other things with my life."

"I know. I'm not accusing you of taking the money and running. But no matter what your reasons, the outcome will be the same."

Her eyes dance; she seems impassioned by this exchange. Lauren is noting the change in her electric blue eyes and the sudden colour in her cheeks.

"And Melissa?" Alexander asks. "Do you include her as part of those impersonal business machines that you seem to hate so much?"

He stops short, realizing that his niece is giving him a warning look. But Estelle does not seem insulted as much as eager to explain.

"Melissa and I don't see eye to eye on many things. And definitely not big business."

"Well," Alexander tells her. "I'd like another piece of the cake that's causing all the trouble. And I don't want you to throw it at me, so I'm retiring from the debate."

He holds her glance a moment longer than is necessary, a way of making amends for the altercation. She understands and is grateful that he has been generous enough to shift the focus of the conversation. For her part, she turns to Lauren.

"I can't tell you how much I loved your work. The two

abstracts in your uncle's house. They left me with such a feeling... I don't know why, or rather how they had such an effect."

Lauren is flattered. She had almost forgotten those paintings, but Estelle's remarks bring back a momentary sense of what she had felt when she produced them, several years ago.

"Thanks. They're pretty old pieces, though. I do portraits mainly now."

"I'd love to see them. Whose?"

"Oh, some socialites. Some old money, some new. A lot of your favourite corporate types. More and more. They're mostly the same. They like to see themselves in suits, tailored but relaxed. The arms are usually folded, and the expression – that has to be strong yet benevolent, tough with just a hint of condescension."

"Sounds like you have it down to a formula," smiles Estelle, but Lauren does not smile in return. Just for a moment, she finds she cannot. Her own flippant description of her work is still ringing in her head, and Estelle's remark has distilled it, has given it the unforgiving effect of a fluorescent light being snapped on in a pitch dark room. Lauren has, for that instant, perfect clarity about her work – and she is horrified at what she sees. A formula.

Estelle clears her throat during the ensuing silence – she is unsure of anything right at this moment except that she seems to be upsetting one or other of her guests every time she opens her mouth.

"I have to tell you, my Christmas present is anything but formulaic." Alexander is smiling, intent, desperate to alleviate the distress he can read in his niece's face. With alacrity, Estelle grasps the line that has been thrown.

"Really? What was it? Your present?"

There is the slightest hesitation from Alexander as he realises that his quiet gallantry has led him to a point where he will have to mention things that he had no wish to talk about.

"A portrait," he says. "Of Katya."

Estelle appears immediately intrigued. "I'd love to see it," she suggests, and Lauren nods.

"You must."

She is too considerate and polished to allow this unexpected realisation about her work to keep everyone off-balance and floundering. She will simply store it up in the back of her mind to think over later, if she dares.

"What about tomorrow?" Alexander suggests. He is almost surprised to hear himself say it. Although he would like very much to see Estelle again, the focus on Katya and Russia does not come easily to him. But the offer has already been made by Lauren, and it would be rude to ignore it.

"I'd love to," Estelle says. "I'd like to look at your other work again too."

She feels recovered now from the previous, edgy exchanges, and eager to ask him something about himself, and about Russia in particular, but she feels a little apprehensive of those soft brown eyes of his watching her unwaveringly, as though daring her to probe the secrets that they guard so politely. She decides against skirting around the subject since he seems so adept at side-stepping.

"Tell me about Russia, when you were there. Or the Soviet Union, rather? It's fascinating to someone like me, born and brought up here."

He regards her kindly but without openness. "What do you want to know?"

"Everything. How was it back then? Did you have to fight for a loaf of bread? How did you get from Russia to America? When did you leave? *Why* did you leave?"

There is a pause. Lauren drinks down her last sip of tea, even though it is cold.

"Gathering material for your novel?" Alexander says, and he is instantly sorry. The comment seemed to just slip out of him, unconsidered, and he had meant it as a light comment, to divert away from those questions of hers, questions that he has courted, but which have already thrown him off balance; but instead he feels he has been unkind, and accusatory.

"No." She offers no further explanation or justification – her denial is vehement enough without them, and he apologises at once.

"I'm sorry. You must think I have the worst manners…"

"You met my husband," she replies, with a slight smile. He shakes his head as if to assure her that he will not be made to feel better so easily.

"I left there just before Katya died," he says. "1959. I was twenty-eight."

"How old was she?"

"The same age as me."

Estelle winces. In the expectant silence that follows, he senses more questions about Katya's death, and so he quickly moves on.

"It was hard back then," he tells her. "I can hardly remember it sometimes, and at other times I can think of nothing else. My wife has always remained the most real thing about Russia for me. But we didn't struggle the way many people did. My father did well in the civil service…"

"A good communist?"

"Yes. He came from a well-to-do family. At least they had money before the revolution. But he believed in the fight for equality. For a better life for everyone. It was a real belief for him, and he gave up everything he had to follow Lenin. Then, he began to rise in the party ranks, during the early years of Stalin's government, and he got back some of the privileges he had had before – a better home, better food."

"But surely that wasn't the communist ideal…"

"Exactly. But it is hard to keep completely aware of ideals when you are hungry and cold and have a wife and baby."

"And did you follow the same path?"

"There was no other path to follow in the Soviet Union. If you were given the opportunities I was given, you didn't turn them down. But I began to see many things that did not make sense. People were brainwashed." He pauses, considering.

"Perhaps that's not quite right. We were simply brought up not to think for ourselves. Because thinking might cause you to question things, and if you questioned the Communist Party, then you were a threat, a loose cannon. They wanted everyone to conform – to think and work the same way, for the common good, supposedly. Katya made me see these things more clearly. She always thought for herself, and believe me, that was incredibly unusual in Soviet Russia, especially during Stalin's time and just after. It seems normal to us now, in the west. But it was so different then. It was like suggesting the world was square. But I carried on with my work because there was nothing else to do. Maybe I thought I could make a change from within the government. I don't know. And I was always reassured by the beliefs of my father, because he was a good man. I was too much reassured."

Estelle waits, hoping for more. She is interested and intrigued; but the effort of revealing this much seems to have been enough for Alexander.

"You worked for the government?"

"Yes."

"Interesting."

"Not especially. I had a decent apartment and a good enough life with Katya."

"And she changed your way of thinking?"

"She enlarged it and shaped it and refined it. She was a long, long way ahead of me on that score. She even found ways to challenge things…" he breaks off and takes a sip of tea.

"How?" Estelle asks. He can feel her watching him carefully. Lauren shifts slightly in her seat. He is suddenly defensive, tired of speaking after his unaccustomed openness; and then, with a timing he could not have wished for, the kitchen door opens, and he is spared. Melissa Johnson stands just inside the doorway, where she concentrates on pulling off her charcoal grey gloves.

"Hello, my darling. I didn't realize you'd be back so early," Estelle says.

Melissa blinks. "I'm not back – I just forgot some papers. Where's dad?"

"You really have to ask?"

Melissa turns and only then realizes, with considerable surprise, that it is Alexander Ivanov who is sitting in her mother's kitchen. Even more discomfiting, his niece is with him, watching her with an amused look in her black eyes. Alexander stands, and hesitates between a handshake and a kiss, but Melissa leans forward for the latter.

"We were just talking about you, earlier," Alexander tells her.

"Really?" Melissa leans over to shake Lauren's hand, and gives her mother a wry look. "All good things, I'm sure."

Estelle smiles. "We were discussing big business."

"And I suppose I was cast as the big bad wolf?"

"Of course."

Just visibly, Melissa takes a breath, although she keeps the sound of it packed down inside herself. Her eyes look tired, Lauren notices, and she chooses not to take up this line of conversation, but Estelle has already moved on.

"I was also spending your money for you. Lauren is a

portrait painter and I told her you might commission a portrait one of these days."

"Of myself? I don't think so."

Melissa lays her gloves on the counter but keeps her coat on. She takes the empty seat beside Lauren.

"Do you do other things than portraits?" she asks.

"Sure." At least, I used to, she thinks. "But I don't like my potential clients to be beaten into commissioning anything by their mothers."

"Don't worry about that," Melissa says. "I won't do anything I don't want to. I'd love to see your work though."

Lauren opens her mouth to speak, then glances at Alexander, a glance of query.

"Why don't you both come over to my place tomorrow?" he tells her. "Your husband too, if he'd like to. We can see some of Lauren's pieces, and then Melissa, you and I can talk business. Or not, if you prefer." It is an elegant way to re-open the negotiation, and Melissa takes advantage of it with good grace.

"Sounds good. There are a few suggestions I have that I'd like to go over with you, anyway. I tried you at the office yesterday and today, but you weren't around."

A sigh from Estelle.

"It's Christmas," Lauren says quickly, easily, a smile in her eyes.

Melissa looks at her, and her grey eyes seem less austere for a moment. "And you all think I'm the grinch."

"Never too late to change," Lauren says.

Melissa holds her look. "I can try, I guess. What time do you want us tomorrow?"

"About eleven."

"So time to stop in at the office first."

"Or to just stay in bed," suggests Lauren.

Melissa looks at her. "Possibly," she says, and smiles.

Alexander coughs slightly. He is somewhat surprised to see his feisty niece charming the woman she so recently dismissed as 'awful'. Melissa's eyes take in the table, lingering with feigned disinterest on the cake .

"Would you like a piece of this?" Lauren asks, offering her the plate.

"Is it carb-free?"

"No, but then it's not taste-free either."

Melissa shakes her head. "Please, don't try and break all my rules in one day. It may be Christmas, but my goodwill to all men only extends so far."

She stands up, reaches for her gloves, and is ready to leave almost as abruptly as she arrived. Lauren watches her, bemused.

"I have to get going," she says. "I guess I'll see you all tomorrow."

CHAPTER EIGHT
MOSCOW – JULY 1956

THE METRO IS CLEAN AND CLEAR just after school finishes. If she is able to leave by four o'clock, the ride is easier, quicker than the bus. But today she has had work after her school administration job is over; she has had to carry a message and some documents and she has had to lie. She has helped to set in motion a train of events that will undermine, delay and irritate the people and the system she hates. The usual necessary work, but it is occasionally distasteful nonetheless. And now it is late, seven o'clock, and she steps off the train with a hundred other people. She lands lightly on the platform. Before her feet lies an expanse of polished marble blocks. She watches the shoes of her fellow passengers tap and scrape across them. The walls rise high with the smooth, veined marble too, except where they end in pale grey stonework, carved firmly into imposing images of Stalin, Lenin and other heroes of the Party. Above her head hang glass chandeliers, wide bowls of glittering glass that blaze light into the subterranean cavern. The height, the space, the dramatic beauty – these have become an everyday phenomenon to the commuters who use the metro, to people who only know homes where the ceilings hang low and the walls are thin enough for a forceful fist to punch through. Katya pauses and blinks – she is standing suddenly in a ballroom, in another, pre-revolutionary world, where at any moment a flock of white-necked women will be escorted to dance by tall men in ties and long jackets and waxed whiskers. Something she has read of in Tolstoy perhaps. Someone bumps into her shoulder and she spins round. An old woman disappears across the station without any word of apology. Katya rubs her shoulder, and follows the rest of them out and upwards, away from the subway station, away from this "people's palace" built by Stalin.

What use is a station that looks like a ballroom when people are still struggling for meat and milk?

Out on the street, the air is fresher, and she turns and walks quickly into her apartment block, for Sasha will be coming soon, and she wants to bathe and change out of these clothes that she feels are soiled from the places they have just been. It is a strange idea of hers, but she cannot rid herself of it. Whenever she finishes such work, her real work, she changes all her clothes from her sweater to her underwear and washes them all, no matter how clean. She thinks it is her way of separating the strands of her life, or maybe, she laughs to herself, she believes the ideas of the people she deals with will rub off on her like a germ.

She is ready twenty minutes early, and she waits as the minutes drip by, glancing to the open window for any sign of him. She hears a firm footfall on the road below, and immediately there is a feeling of hollowness in her chest, a pleasant emptiness that she knows is a strange type of anticipation. She stands casually, with her face up against the grimy window pane and peers down, but it is not him. She breathes in to slow the sprinting of her heartbeat. This is all new to her, and all wrong, she thinks; very, very wrong. She should not be waiting like this, like a hopeful puppy, looking from windows. She has to try and be more rational about the whole situation. It is just one more step on the path you want to take through life, Katya.

Of course, it would be much easier if he was petulant, or unkind, or hungry for power, or even just ugly or inconsiderate. But there is time for her to uncover these things about him. No-one is without their bad points; she just needs to look harder to find them. And then she can work to subdue these unlooked for feelings, these slow droplets of escaped emotion that are slowly filling up inside her. It will be easier when she finds out what a bastard he really is.

She knows he will probably come slightly before the appointed hour, for he too has trouble keeping away from her, and sure enough, he is fifteen minutes early. He has taken the metro to her area, and has tried without much success to use up the extra time by walking slowly for much of the way. Now that he is before her building, though, within a hundred paces of her, it is easier to slow down, to savour the anticipation of seeing her within a very few moments. Her block is uniform, indistinguishable from the others around it except for the numbers on the front. He sighs slightly. The apartments are depressing. Pre-fabricated, hastily thrown up by Khrushchev to help solve the housing problems of the city – there are a million more people living in Moscow now than there were only ten years ago. They have served their purpose well, these apartment blocks, but the people who live in them call them *khrushchoby*, a joke that combines their leader's name with the word *trushchoby* – slum. They are better than slums, certainly, but are not comparable to the stone and brick buildings in which Alexander has grown up. He moves quickly through the dank, gloomy stairwell. She lives on the top floor, the fifth. These blocks are rarely higher, for they dispense with the luxury of elevators also. Her door is thrown open before he reaches the top, and she is looking out for him.

"Katya," is all he says, as he reaches her and lifts her up into a hug and spins her around and kisses her. His briefcase and two parcels are dropped onto the floor. She pushes the door shut behind him, and he glances around.

"Where's Maya?"

"Gone out. She's eating with her workmates. And her mother's staying with her sister in the country for a week."

He smiles, kisses her again.

140

"Will we always be this excited to see each other, Sasha?"

"Always, my love."

"Even when we are ancient?" She has asked the question from her heart, without thinking, but as soon as the words are spoken she feels a weight in her stomach, a weight that makes her feel slightly sick. This suggestion of hers that they will be together until they die, when she knows that she is only with him, supposed to be with him, for one reason. It is difficult to remember sometimes. To stay aware, in the way Misha said she should always be aware. But if she tries to be aloof with him, or distant, or if she holds herself back in any way he will feel it. The relationship will not progress, and the game will be over. She has to let herself go, to immerse herself in the role of a woman in love, even when the acting begins to come too easily, and she no longer has to think so hard about her lines.

"Especially when we're ancient." He pulls back from her and looks at her eyes and mouth and face. "You will never be old in my eyes, Katyushka," he says, gallantly, and with complete honesty.

"Are you sure?"

"Completely. Are you hungry?"

She nods. She has not eaten since her lunchtime meal of bread and soup from the school canteen.

"I brought bread and some fish," he tells her. He holds up his prized packages with a flourish. She cannot help but notice that his briefcase, perhaps full of papers from work, is still lying on the floor, behind him. Perhaps he sees her glance at it, for he smiles and reaches to pick it up. Should she offer to take it, to put it in the bedroom with his jacket or will that be too obvious? In fact she is saved from the decision, because he himself passes her the food parcels and turns and strides into her bedroom, depositing the rest of his things there.

"Where did you get fish, Sasha?" she asks as he walks past her again, into the tiny area of the living room that passes for her kitchen.

He smiles. "Never mind."

She feels a quick burn of anger in her stomach. He will not say, but she knows he has ready access to special shops, to the types of food that most people could never have access to or afford. He senses her feelings, and regrets that he dismissed her question.

"I know I have privileges," he tells her. "But I just wanted you to have it. The fish, I mean. I wanted you to enjoy it."

He is caught between repentance and the wish to give her everything in the world, and she sees his uncertainty, this dilemma.

"Is there any dessert?" he asks.

She pushes away the remnants of her anger, and stops at the entrance to the kitchen. She holds out her arms, offering herself. Her eyes are teasing, but her movement is slightly awkward, for she does not quite know how to be so relaxed and affectionate with another person; she is still learning to open out her natural insularity. He smiles and puts his arms around her, pulling her close to him, willing her uncertainty to crumble away. Then he kisses her hair, loosens his tie, and rolls up his shirt sleeves, for he has no intention of letting her cook for him.

First, he reaches into the kitchen drawer, feeling for a match, which he applies with caution to the back of the oven. She feels the slow heat rising at once, and can sense just a tiny bit of escaped gas.

He tosses the parcel of fish up behind his back and it drops onto the small plywood counter in front of him. Katya is laughing suddenly – at the fish, at his playfulness, at the fact of him being here. She gives him a knife and watches him slit open the layers of paper.

She shrieks.

"What?" he asks.

"It looks alive!"

"I promise you it's not," he replies.

He slams the handle of the knife smartly down on the chipped counter-top and stamps his foot. A flourish to start the cutting of the fish. He picks up the blade, and holds it up to his face, so that he is looking down its silvery length at Katya's expectant eyes.

"Ready?" he asks, voice solemn.

She nods. "Ready."

"And so." He grabs it by the tail and turns it over with a slap, merely for effect, and then, in a flash of strokes with the blade, he has decapitated it, and removed its tail. These parts are deftly and swiftly wrapped up in the old, oily paper, and pushed to one side.

"Better?" he asks her and she nods.

"What's next?"

"Gutting," he says.

"Let me watch, then."

He begins work with the knife, and she moves closer, near to his moving arm. He is concentrating now, enjoying the attention to detail required of him, and she sees the tip of the knife caressing the soft belly of the fish, watches the gentle strokes with which he cleans away the scales. He handles the knife with respect, as though it were an ally of his, working with him to subdue and prepare this clear-eyed creature.

Again, his wrists and fingers move so quickly once the fish is cut, that she barely sees a glimpse of the soft, red, spilling insides before they are also gone.

He turns his head to look sideways at her, and she enquiringly meets his glance. "Does the smell trouble you?" he wants to know.

"No. It is a fresh fish."

"Yes, but still."

She is mesmerised by his hands. The long bones of the fingers, visibly lined with gentle muscles. Their lithe, light touches, the patient, repetitive movement, the firm strokes of his fingertips, the careful caress of his palms. In a matter of moments, in too short a time, he is finished with his task and wiping his hands, and she sighs slightly that it is over.

"What is it, my Katyushka?" he says, turning to her. His mouth is near to hers, his warm breath on her nose. She stands very still, not yet able to lift her lips to his, but not wanting the sensations of this moment to end – there are times when his easy intimacy seems wondrous to her.

"I could watch you cook all day," she tells him finally, and he laughs, his mouth still close to hers, but not touching. He does not know why, but he feels he must leap across a chasm that lies hidden within her to reach their next kiss.

"Is that what you want me for? To cook for you all day?"

"Yes," she tells him. "That is exactly it."

"How was your work today?" he asks.

"It went well. Are you going to bake this thing?"

Their flavourings are few; some salt, dried herbs and some vinegar. He wraps the fish and puts it in the oven.

"What did you do?"

"At work?" she asks.

"Yes. Why did you have to work late?"

"It's time for the school reports – again," she adds wryly. "So much typing. It gets boring." She shakes her head at the memory of her afternoon's overtime work, trapped in the office of the school administrator, a fictional two hours which is completely real in her mind at that moment. In fact, with Svetlana's help, she had finished typing the reports by lunchtime.

"I can imagine. Aren't you tempted to rewrite the bad reports as you go along?" Alexander laughs, but she is serious as she replies.

"Sometimes. Sometimes I have… re-phrased them. So they are less harsh. They are so uncaring, Sasha. They call the children stupid and dull and useless."

He looks at her. "I am glad that you re-write them then."

"I don't change them completely, just…"

"I know. But I'm glad."

"And yours, how was your work today?" she asks. They walk together to the small sofa and sit down. She likes the warmth of his leg touching hers, feels a stir of desire, but will not, or cannot show it.

"I don't know." His eyes are troubled. "It's not the same since…"

"Since what?"

"You make me look at things in a different way, Katya."

"But I'm proud of you. And your work. Why am I ruining it for you? Because I told you it was your father's path?"

He looks at her for a long time, thinking about the answer. His eyes are still considering when he leans over gently and kisses her throat. She closes her eyes slightly against the pleasurable touch of his lips on her skin, and looking up at her, he catches that moment of release.

"No. Not just that," he continues. "I don't know how to explain. Everything looks new since I met you. It's as though I was sleep-walking through the world up until now. You have sharpened all the blurred pictures that I had in my mind, and now I feel that I see things – or begin to see things – more clearly. I'm not really helping people, Katya. All I can do…"

"All they *let* you do," she says, fiercely, and he shrugs.

"All I can do is push paper from one side of my desk to the other, and try and argue a small point or two in meetings, or watch and wait and hope that things will improve. I begin to see it in a different way. A very different way." His voice is low, and she moves even closer to him, allowing his arm to press her to him, so that when they speak they can whisper. Just in case.

"How did you see it before?"

"You know. I like Khrushchev."

"You know he followed Stalin around like a little puppy," she says, with an ironic smile. "His little *liubimchik*."

"Look. Everyone believed in Stalin unless they figured out what he really was about. And if you figured that out, you were trapped anyway. Khrushchev did what he needed to in order to survive. I think some of these new ideas of his are good. Not all of them will work, but he has begun sweeping away that hero-worship that people had for Stalin, and that fear, that terrible, terrible fear. I think he's really trying to help now. It's just... there are no controls. He overrides Bulganin, Malenkov, all of them. And they're all watching their own backs, trying to keep their positions. Sometimes at the expense of doing good work. But it is changing," he says, almost to himself. "At least now they're trying to control people by giving them something, not by threatening them."

"But they are still trying to control people?"

"I don't know. I think so. Possibly." He gives a wry, desperate smile. "You see, with one question you open up a new way of looking at things for me. I begin to see things differently now. And once you do that, you cannot go back to the old way of thinking can you? Can you, Katya?"

His last question is softly spoken, almost a plea. She hears it, but her eyes are focused on some faraway point, somewhere that he cannot see.

"No," she tells him. "You can never go back."

He looks at her a moment, and swallows a sigh. "Come on," he says, pointing at the stove. "It must be ready. Let's eat."

While he is filleting the fish and slicing bread, she has excused herself and disappeared into her bedroom. She quickly applies a little lipstick, for that is what she has ostensibly come here to do. In the mirror she eyes the briefcase. There is no time to consider, she must simply do it. She walks over to the bed in her bare feet, as silently as she can, and flips open the catch. It makes a sound and she glances at the door to see if he may have heard, but he is busy outside, and the background throb of the cooling oven is probably all he can hear. Inside is a notebook, full of clean paper, and one folder containing five sheets of paper. She scans them. They seems to be minutes of a meeting, something to do with defence research. They are in his handwriting; probably he was appointed to take the minutes. She reads two of the pages within a minute, memorising what she thinks are the key names and points. She will write them down later, when he is gone.

"Katya," he calls.

She slips the folder back into his bag – she can hear him coming to find her. Quickly she twists the catch closed again, and she is up and at the door of the bedroom, kissing him as he crosses the threshold. She stays in the kiss for a long time, to his surprise and pleasure, for she needs a few moments to recover herself, to slow the adrenalin that is coursing through her and making her hands tingle. Unexpectedly, she is also wracked by guilt, immediately. She is completely consumed by it, without any warning, without her even having to think through what she has just done. She leans her head against Alexander's shoulder, positioning herself so that her face is hidden from his gaze. You've done what you were told to do, she reminds herself, as he holds her. You've done what you've always wanted to do, and it will be all right when you get used to it.

Later, she lies back on her bed with one arm crossed protectively over her stomach and chest. Often these days she misses him when he leaves, but tonight she is grateful to be alone. With her other hand she rubs her temples, as though soothing a headache. There is no pain there, but there is confusion, and she does not like it. She has been unhappy since the moment she opened his briefcase. It is the kind of thing she has had to do many times before, but today's assignment, with Alexander, was the most difficult to execute. Partly because he knows her so well and is sensitive enough to read her every look and expression; and partly because for the first time in her experience, she simply did not want to do what had been asked of her. She knows this move was made too early, and that Misha only wanted to put her to the test, but she knows also that there is something more at play here. She is worried that stealing secrets from Alexander and abusing his trust and love will not become any easier as time goes by.

All her life has been a struggle against confusion, a wish to keep things clear. Ambivalence and uncertainty are of no help to someone who has chosen the path she has taken. You must believe in what you do and why you do it, even more so than any communist leader who sentences millions of *kulaks* to death with the stroke of a pen must be certain that he is acting for the greater good, or at least for his own good.

"I do believe in it," she says, in a whisper. That is not the problem. She will fight the system that made her an orphan, that killed her parents and everyone else's with such brutality, until she dies. But now she is falling in love – she can barely allow herself to even think the phrase in her head, much less admit it aloud – with a man who represents that system and is deeply involved in it. What does that make her? A traitor to everything she has lived for, probably. A traitor to the cause of making amends for what happened to her parents. A traitor to the anti-communists, to the Americans whom she indirectly works for.

She thinks about Alexander, running through her conversations with him in her mind. She is sure that he is a good man, and this makes her think of the others that she works against, steals secrets from, lies to. Are they good and just working in a system that she considers bad? She rarely knows these adversaries well enough to judge, but it is possible, probable even, that the majority are good, but unthinking. Unquestioning. And in a state where questioning and thinking can cost you your life, or your freedom, can they be blamed?

But Alexander has told her that she has made him think. Or start to think. His boss is not Stalin, it is Khrushchev. Would his questioning cost him his life now? Perhaps not, but his career certainly. He would be left with nothing if anyone found out the thoughts that are winding their way into his head. Or that he was falling in love with Katya. No, that would not cost him anything, not yet, because nobody knows what she really is. What she really does. But they might find out – she lives with that awareness at all times. And then what would happen to him?

She laughs slightly, a laugh of sarcasm at her own thoughts running in that direction, imagining this life with Alexander, and the potential consequences for him. As if his future should be of any concern to her. She should only want to know him to access his information. Khrushchev may not be the same breed of monster as Stalin, but the system is the same, and it still stinks. His crazy agricultural 'reforms' are still leaving people starving. And Misha has just told her the latest disaster for his father and grandmother out in the country. Their co-operative farm, their small *kolkhoz*, is being forced to buy all their old tractors and equipment from the government outright and at inflated prices, leaving them with huge debts that they can never hope to pay off. And here in the city, who you are and whom you know are still the only certain way to progress. Alexander himself is where he is today because of his father. These, Katya, are the kinds of things you must keep in your mind.

But for the first time, she is discovering that the head and the heart can have two different wishes, different motives, different objectives. Her heart is a frightening organ, to Katya. She neither trusts nor understands it. When she was twelve, and she watched her mother and father being hustled out of their apartment with guns pressed to their heads, leaving half-finished plates of food behind them, her heart broke. Where it had been, there remained only a hollow, into which she swallowed her tears of terror at what they might do to her parents, and the desperate fear that she could not speak, the crude fear of a child being left all alone. Those roughly hurt emotions left raw, open wounds that no-one but she could slowly try and soothe. And since then, her heart has been sitting quietly within her, untroubled by much more than the effort of pumping her blood through her veins. There is nothing more that she wants of it, for she knows that it is a fearsome, ruthless animal that can rise up and rip out the rest of her organs in a second.

"Katya? You awake?"

She jumps. She has been so absorbed in her thoughts that she has not even heard Maya return.

"Yes. How was your dinner?"

"Good." Maya stumbles to her bed, a few feet across from Katya's and Katya can smell the slightly acrid, smoky smell of a bar on her friend. "I drank too much, of course. I'll have a hell of a headache in the morning. How was your date?"

Katya gives a half-smile in the dark. My date. "Fine. He's nice."

"About time you showed some interest in someone. Men are not all pigs you know." Maya is unbuttoning her clothes, pulling on a nightdress. She wanders slowly to the dressing table they both share, where brushes, towels and soap are all kept so that they will not be taken from the bathroom out in the hallway that they share with the two daughters from the apartment upstairs.

"I didn't think they were," replies Katya. "I'm just…"

"Picky," finishes Maya.

Katya laughs. "Perhaps."

Maya disappears to the bathroom, and Katya lies looking at the pattern that the moonlight makes on the corner of the ceiling as it plays through the small, high window of their room. When she returns, Katya whispers to her.

"I like him, Maya."

But the drink, or exhaustion, or both have made Maya deaf to her roommate's half-whisper. Katya listens as the girl clambers into her bed, giving a slight moan of relief or pleasure at lying down between cool sheets after a warm, tiring evening.

"Goodnight," Katya calls.

But Maya is already asleep.

CHAPTER NINE

BOSTON

A LEXANDER CANNOT WALK HOME FAST ENOUGH, and Lauren is having to work hard to keep up with him, to enclose him fully beneath the capacious umbrella that she carries.

Courteously, he tries to slow down, and smiles at her briefly, but his face reflects a series of indefinite, discomfiting emotions – irritation, nervousness, depression. His thoughts are black-edged with melancholy. Around them the settling evening darkness is being made weightier by the relentless drizzle, and they are both grateful for the lights of home that come into sight when they turn into their own street at last. The two hours at Estelle's apartment have unsettled him fully, have left him unmoored and feeling exposed. He tries to pin down which aspects of the afternoon have led to his present mood, but he senses that there is something insidious at work here, something that has crept into his mind and now lies curled up and threatening inside his head. He glances sideways at his niece. He had seen pained surprise and yet such clarity of vision in her face earlier, when Estelle's comment about her portraits had stung her. The idea of such unexpected awareness, such sudden and complete illumination is strangely attractive to him. If he could have felt that clear about certain things in his life – in his younger life especially – would he have taken a different path?

"So what do you think?" Lauren asks as he unlocks the front door.

He is embarrassed to realize that he hasn't heard anything she has been saying. With a look of apology he shrugs off his coat, and then takes hers.

"I've been miles away. Sorry."

She follows him into the living room, where he paces about, switching on lamps, lighting the fire and putting on some music. He keeps moving, diligently, but it does not seem to help – wherever he goes he feels that he is being followed by the eyes of Katya's portrait. Finally he looks at it, a hungry, desolate look, until he becomes aware that Lauren is watching him, and he smiles at the picture, as though taking pleasure in it, as he would with any present.

"I just thought that it might be a good project," Lauren continues. "Sketching, and then painting the two of you."

He looks at her, not understanding.

"You and Estelle."

"Are you serious?"

"Absolutely." She remains standing, even after he sinks

into his armchair. "I've been thinking about a series. Sort of based around the Seven Ages of Man."

Her choice of title makes him smile. "I don't suppose I would be number six, would I?"

"What?"

"Of the seven ages of man."

"I haven't decided yet. Maybe not."

"You know how to hit an old man where it hurts."

"But Uncle Alex, you have such character in your face, such romance in your eyes…"

"Please. You should be ashamed of yourself, trying to charm a man my age."

Despite his banter, he is distracted, she can see that, so she decides to leave aside her idea for a while, even though she is keen to discuss it with her uncle. She has deliberately chosen a theme, an underlying idea that she can think about and work on, in order to try and bring some emotional and intellectual depth to the next portraits that she does. She wants to discuss with him what Estelle had said earlier about her work sounding formulaic. She had felt a cool prickling of fear at the realisation, so sudden and yet so clear, that Estelle was right – what she has been doing for the past few years has lost any edge, any philosophy. Her work is now steady and comfortable and plentiful and if she is to be brutally honest with herself, meaningless. She is living the kind of easy, uninspired existence that is precisely what she has always despised in others and dreaded for herself. She has always assumed that being an artist of any kind somehow implied a sense of integrity in your work – the kind of integrity not so easily found in other fields. Like business, for instance. But then she sees the fervour with which her uncle has built his company, from the seeds of his passion. And now it occurs to her to wonder whether Melissa Johnson's devotion to her work might represent a passion also. Perhaps it is harder for Lauren to recognise because it is rooted in the day to day work of deal-making and consulting, rather than in a desire to make a life's work out of an art or a single love like Alexander's love of food and cooking. She glances at her uncle once more, hoping to talk through some of this; she is astute and sensitive enough, however, to tell that he is in one of those rare moods when he has no wish for company. Leaving him with a kiss on the cheek, she tells him she wants to have a bath, and he nods. A sigh escapes him – it has risen from deep within, on the tide of memories and feelings that have been stirred up by Estelle and her questions. He smothers the sigh under a smile, and just before his niece leaves the room, he calls her back.

"And Estelle? Where does she fit into the Ages of Man?"

"I guess she'd be number six. Of the seven. She has a great face – such life and movement in her eyes. What do you think?"

Whether she means to ask his opinion for her being the sixth, or of her eyes, he is unsure, but he nods mildly, and gives away nothing of his pleasure that Lauren's new idea might throw Estelle and himself together more frequently.

He sits, prodding at the fire, a pointless gesture since the logs are burning well. He is missing Katya. Not in the vague, intermittent way that he has fallen into over the years, but in a deep, urgent, aching way that he fears will give him no respite. He puts down the poker and buries his face in his hands, trying to stop himself turning to look at the portrait that leans against the wall behind him. He does not feel his age, despite the dampness affecting his knee, and the silver of the hairs on his arms. He feels young, very young, and as though he has just lost her. The memory of the intense, pure pain that her death inflicted on him is easily summoned up at this moment. He remembers that at first he had been shocked and disbelieving, desperate for answers. He had focused on trying to get those answers, to find a way to see her, to look at her poor dead body for himself, to see that it was really true that she could have been removed from the world so quickly and brutally. He had not been able to do so, of course, and then he could no longer resist the feeling that he was slipping, that his hands were grasping to a sharp ledge of life, and that below him there was the comfort of an abyss, an infinite drop into oblivion. The taste of that drop, the sensation of falling was so sweet that there were many times he had nearly let go. It was so simple, it was the work of one moment to lift a hand away and plunge downwards. To continue to cling to the brutal roughness of life seemed the harder course but he followed it doggedly; a young, grief-torn attempt to make himself suffer just a little of what she had suffered.

"I'm so sorry, Katyushka," he whispers to the portrait. He wants to touch her, to hold her close, to bury his face in her soft, black hair, to be able to feel comforted by a pair of arms around him, without having to speak, or ask, or explain.

He also knows that when he left Estelle's apartment no more than an hour ago, he had wanted to touch her as well. It is a hard truth for him to admit to himself – that he wanted to feel some human warmth; and in particular, *her* warmth. The touch of her hand on his own. But Estelle is married. To a man he wishes to believe is uncaring and cold, but who may be a very different person when he shuts his books at night. And Katya is dead. Long dead and disappeared, and all that remains of her are a few tiny grains of memory, many of which he suspects are more and more embellished in his own mind as time passes, and those few grains will themselves dance away into thin air, as though blown away by a breeze, as soon as his own life is over, leaving nothing more of her, anywhere, ever. Except for a portrait, an arresting, accurate portrait, which will be of a woman of whom no-one knows anything.

His rational instinct is to try and break out of this mood, and his thoughts move almost automatically to his kitchen and to what he might cook. But he has no appetite after the tea and cake they have just had, and besides, his fingers feel stiff from the cold. He stands and glances through the bookshelves on his left. The familiar titles jump out at him, in a familiar order, and he pulls down an old novel and begins to read for a while. His eyes trace the lines in a purposeful, direct manner, for he is eager to be pulled into some other world, and is prepared to work hard to manage it. But it seems to him that the book is not helping him at all. He tries again, selecting poetry this time, but this does little except indulge his mood. He is almost relieved to look up and find that the fire has burned down. Going upstairs, he takes a hot shower, calls goodnight to Lauren, and goes to bed.

He sleeps until nine the next morning, which is unusually late for him, and which throws off his sense of the day to come. But the early part of the night was seared with dreams of Katya, and one in particular had hung about his memory for several wakeful hours in the night. It had seemed unrelentingly long, and he was relieved when he awoke, but also disturbed. In the dream, he had gotten out of bed and gone to the window, except that it did not look like his bedroom window, but was divided into several smaller, wooden framed panes of glass. He had the sense that he was inside a dacha somewhere outside Moscow – there was a grand entrance hall, and wicker chairs on a wooden verandah, and a feeling of sunlight in the house, that reminded him of a dacha for government officials that he and Katya had once stayed in during a summer holiday. And in the dream it was summer; he could somehow sense that it was windy but warm outside, but he had gotten out of bed because he had heard a woman's voice, laughing. Wiping at the dusty glass, he saw Katya outside the window. He felt that she must be a ghost, because she was moving in strange ways.

At one moment she seemed to be at a great distance, and he could see her bare feet and the swirling hem of her summer dress. There were moments too, when she seemed to be right next to him, when he could feel her touch on his arm, could breathe the scent of her neck. These moments lifted him into a kind of tormented ecstasy – for somewhere in the back of his mind he understood that she was not real. He was grateful to wake up after falling into a final, fitful sleep in the early hours, and pleased to remember that Estelle and Melissa would be visiting in a couple of hours.

Estelle's desk, in contrast to her husband's, sits under a window in their living room, where the sunlight floods it in the late afternoon. She cannot bear the artificial light that he labours under in his study, but he tells her that he prefers it – that way his books and papers are lit the same way at midnight and at midday, and there is nothing to distract him from his thoughts. She sits down, with a trace of self-consciousness, despite the fact that she is alone in the room. For she feels a definite sense of purpose today, something different from the usual vague possibilities that lead her to her desk at other times. She pushes back the leather pen-holder, the box of white letter paper and envelopes, and the untidy stack of bills that usually claims her attention when she sits here. She wants space today, a feeling of clarity and openness, and when she has cleared a good empty area around her computer, she begins. A new document, a blank page. She begins writing.

The snow has blurred the outline of the woman standing outside; to Alexander, she appears as something ghostly.

Of course, names will have to change, particularly since most of this will be fiction anyway. She types in a little more, then highlights the whole piece and taps the delete button. Her fingers are ill at ease on the keyboard today. Letters are flying up to her touch in the wrong order, and the keys are conspiring against her. She opens a drawer, and pulls out a handwritten paper of her husband's. The sort of thing she usually types up in minutes, with no problems. She attempts to copy it onto the computer.

Undoubtedly, the extreme deference with which the writer approaches his subject provides a sense of ..

She has no trouble typing this. With impatience, and a sudden decisiveness, she thrusts the paper back into the drawer, and pushes the computer screen farther back on the desk. Now she checks her fountain pen, and looks around for a pad of paper. She will write this thing in longhand if she has to. One lies beneath the sheaf of bills, and she reaches for it, noticing as she does so that the electricity payment was due last week. Twenty minutes later, she is still writing cheques when Melissa knocks at the open door.

"Does genius burn?" she asks. It is a quiet reference, to *Little Women*. It is what Jo March's family asks her when she is writing. Estelle looks at her over the top of half-moon glasses.

"I'd forgotten about that," she says. "How long is it since we read that book?"

It is not a question, but a recognition of a time long past, of the shared history of mother and daughter; but Melissa has an answer:

"I was twelve," she said. "I remember because you read it to me every night the week before I went to summer camp."

Estelle nods, recognising Melissa's deeply held emotion simply by the precision and detail of her recollection. "I liked reading to you," she tells her.

"I liked listening."

"Come here."

Melissa goes and stands before her mother's chair. Estelle's arms are up, outstretched, and Melissa leans down to accept the embrace with something like relief.

"I miss you," she says quietly.

Melissa wonders at how such a short, hackneyed phrase can suddenly have such a reassuring effect. Perhaps it is the feel of her mother's arms around her, after too long an absence.

"Thanks," she says. "Listen. We have to go in a little while."

Estelle puts away the untouched pad of paper. "I'll go get ready."

"Good," Melissa replies. "I don't want to be late."

On her way to answer the doorbell, Lauren glances at the paintings that hang on the walls of the entrance hall. They are the two abstracts that Estelle had mentioned, old pieces that she worked on perhaps six or seven years ago, and that catch her attention for a second, because they are good. She has an immediate, vague recollection, little more than the kind of transportation of mind that a certain scent or taste can effect; she has, suddenly, a hint of the ideas she was working out when she painted them. That hyper-awareness, that sensation that a moment of grace was close to being grasped. The doorbell rings again, a long, insistent ring this time and she hurries forward and throws it open. Estelle and Melissa stand on the doorstep.

"You know, patience is a great virtue," she says to Melissa.

"So they say, if you're sure that what you're waiting for is going to show up."

"I was on my way to the door." She stands aside to let them in.

"But I didn't know that for sure. It's a big house. You might not have heard the bell. We could have been waiting here forever."

Lauren rubs her forehead.

"Am I giving you a headache?" Melissa smiles.

"Yes. And don't try and alleviate your guilt with a lousy aspirin either. I'll expect a shoulder massage."

"If that's what you want."

Estelle takes in this exchange with some surprise. Melissa's reply, the directness of it has seemed to cause Lauren to flush. She walks briskly ahead of them, showing them into the living room, and immediately, Estelle sees the portrait of Katya. She stands close before it.

"She is quite stunning. The painting is stunning. It must have been hard for Alexander."

"I can't decide whether it was the best present I've ever given him, or the worst."

"Has it brought it all back?"

"I think so. Though he's trying to put a brave face on it."

Estelle turns back to the portrait. She is finding herself increasingly intrigued by this woman and her story – whatever it might be. She seems enclosed in mystery, and that mystery reeks of danger, of undiscovered secrets and hidden passions, Katya's portrait looks back at her, with unknowable dark eyes and Estelle feels momentarily effaced, lost under the gaze of this young, immortalised woman.

Alexander pushes the door open with his foot because he is carrying in a large platter covered with canapés. He wishes them all good morning, and holds the door for a middle-aged woman in a white apron, whom he introduces as his housekeeper. She carries a bottle of champagne and a tray of gleaming glasses. It occurs to Estelle that if she spends more than a little time with this man, she will end up as big as a house.

"Your husband wasn't able to come?" Alexander asks.

"He's with another woman right now," Estelle says. "I asked him to join us, but he won't leave her."

There is a stifled sound of exasperation from Melissa.

"Dad's an English professor. The 'other woman' is George Eliot."

"For now," adds Estelle. "But next week, it'll be someone else."

Alexander smiles, but Estelle feels her daughter watching

her keenly, almost clinically. This kind of ultimately inconsequential talk is so alien to Melissa that Estelle does her best
to repress it when they are together, but occasionally it will
declare itself. While Alexander pours drinks, Lauren is drawn
back to talking about the portrait.

"I just wanted to try and capture a woman that you could
believe one would feel deeply about," she explains.

"You've done a great job," Estelle replies. "It makes you
want to know more about the person portrayed, and yet...
and yet, you feel you already know her, or at least part of her
character, just from the expression, and the eyes. Actually, you
resemble her quite a bit, don't you think?"

"Maybe just the colouring. Eyes and hair."

"I think there's something more," suggests Melissa.

They all consider the painting once again.

"I love the way she's standing, with her arms folded," says
Estelle. "There's something relaxed and almost haughty about
her, but also, the hands grip the elbows just a little too tightly,
and doesn't that suggest a little defensiveness?" Estelle steps
back from her analysis and imagining, and looks uncertainly
at Lauren. "Or am I way off base?"

But Lauren is elated.

"That's exactly it," she says. "Those are the kinds of
complexities that made my aunt such an irresistible subject
for me. It's hard to put a portrait into words, but that's a great
description."

"Estelle writes," Alexander says, partly to interrupt Lauren.

"It shows," says Lauren. "What do you write?"

Estelle ponders, as if trying to choose between her many styles and forms is a great burden.

"Nothing, really. Sum total of my output to date? Five short stories, and half a novel which is so bad it makes me cringe, but which cost such an effort that I can't actually bear to throw it away."

"One of my art teachers told me once that those old canvases which have taken the longest time but are going nowhere – they're the ones to paint over first."

"You mean a brand new novel?"

"Sure. Any ideas?"

Alexander is watching her, Estelle knows, and she turns to meet his look for a second.

"A few."

"Care to share them?" Alexander asks, handing her a glass.

"Not just yet," says Estelle. "Genius can't be rushed, you know."

CHAPTER TEN
MOSCOW – AUGUST 1956

THE RESTAURANT HAS BEEN LOUD and smoky and filled with talk, laughter and dancing. It is a Georgian restaurant, on the ground floor of an apartment block near her own. The food is rich with tomatoes, nuts and spices, the atmosphere carefree; somehow reflective of that southern heritage. They finish their meal – a chicken *satsivi* and some fried aubergine, and they watch two soldiers dancing with three women in the centre of the room. They are stamping their feet and swinging around – the people at the tables closest to them are having to be careful of their drinks. But everyone is smiling – their enthusiasm and excitement are contagious. Alexander watches Katya watching the dancers.

It is the end of the week, and both of them have had a busy time at work. Alexander is happy to be here with her, but he can't help but feel tired and subdued, eroded by a poor week of meetings and discussions that he feels have led only backwards. She is smiling as she watches the dancing, but her eyes are not part of the smile. She has been lively this evening, and he has hardly been able to take his eyes from her, but at the same time, something is making him uneasy. She seems to be behaving with him as she sometimes does with other people whom she does not know so well – not falsely, but not altogether relaxed. There is an air of effort about her convivial conversation and about her laughter, and he wonders inwardly if something might be bothering her.

He drinks down his last mouthful of sweet Georgian wine, and fills her glass with what remains in the bottle. She looks at him.

"You look so young with your haircut," she says, reaching across to ruffle his hair. He puts a defensive hand to his head, and laughs.

"Do I look like a boy?" he asks.

She smiles and shakes her head. Then she leans across the table and kisses him, a light brush of the lips that lingers over his mouth, becoming slowly deeper, until he can taste her tongue running lightly over his own, can feel her mouth pulling at his. After a minute, she moves away, leaving him dizzy. Then she turns back to watch the dancing as though there is nothing else of interest to her just now. The shadows that play about her face tonight are textured and thick, accentuated by the array of lamps and candles that light the restaurant.

He passes her another piece of the *khachapuri* bread that

she likes, rich with cheese and eggs, and she breaks off a bite and washes it down with the last of her wine.

They walk back to her apartment, holding hands, not speaking. The late-night air is cool, even here, where the narrow streets are bound by high, grey buildings, and he is happy. Even his fatigue is pleasurable when it is relieved by her company. When they reach her apartment, he walks behind her up the stairs. The concrete walls and tiny stairwells are oppressive, and he is relieved to get away from them, even into her small, dark living space. Maya, as usual, is still out. Maya's mother is asleep in her tiny cupboard of a room, the door tightly shut. They go into the bedroom and Alexander sits on the foot of her bed, draws her to him, and kisses her.

"Happy anniversary," he says.

It is not a particularly significant day, but while they have been strolling home, he has been calculating in his mind, and has come to the conclusion that today they have been together for five months exactly. Katya looks up with a jerk, almost as though he has reached over and slapped her. She stares at him coolly.

"What is it?" he asks, feeling a mild panic grip him.

"What *are* you talking about?" she replies. Her tone is harsh.

"I was just thinking... I was just thinking that we have been together exactly five months. Today. An anniversary."

"Oh." She stands up abruptly, upset still, and embarrassed. As she knew would happen, he is on his feet in a moment, and has moved to hold her, but it is hard for him to do so for she has the palms of her hands pressed over her eyes. He holds her from behind, cradling her in his arms, and kissing her neck.

"What is it, Katyushka? What is it, my love?" he asks, and despite herself, she feels the tears begin to fall. He holds her more tightly.

"Is it so bad to be with me?"

She laughs, slightly, as she weeps, and shakes her head. He kisses her hair. He can smell the metallic, inky smell of the school in it.

"Tell me. What are you thinking about?" He pauses. "What anniversary?"

Almost at once, the sobbing stops, and her body has stiffened beneath his hands.

"Come here," he says, and he takes her hand and pulls her down onto the thin mattress, and lies next to her, precariously close to the edge of the narrow bed, shifting closer so that her head is against his shoulder, and his arms are around her. She has stopped crying, and he waits, rubbing the top of her back gently, as if soothing a child, and he listens to the breath entering and leaving her, rhythmic and slowing.

"Tell me," he says, and for the first time, she does.

"Fourteen years ago today," she says, as though beginning a bedtime story, "I was sitting at the table in my parents' house. Having dinner." She stops to take a deep, ragged breath, and then she smiles.

"I loved that table. It was a big wooden thing that my

grandfather brought on the back of a cart from his *dacha* years ago. We all had our own places at that table, and our parents let each of us carve our names into the underside of it, at the places where we each sat. It was easy, the wood was soft." She stops and looks at Alexander. He is thinking whether to ask her where the table is now, but decides against it.

"They were quite strict, my parents. They never let us do anything like that usually. But anyway, they let us put our names in the table. We were all there, both of them, my brother and myself. They were laughing a lot over dinner, my mother and father. There had been some joke at the university, some piece of research that had crossed over into both of their fields – I forget exactly what – and they were explaining it to us, and they were excited and happy that the unthinkable had happened, and they would have to work together for a while."

"Go on," says Alexander, softly and with trepidation, for he knows how the story must end, even if he has waited this long to hear from her how it started.

"We were sitting there, having dinner. I was twelve, Yuri quite a bit older. I was the afterthought, the baby they didn't expect. They were so shocked when they found my mother was pregnant," she adds, with a quick laugh. She is telling him things now that he already knows, putting off the moment when she must put into words the thing she has never spoken of before. He puts his lips to her forehead and waits, and after a moment, she speaks again.

"We had finished the meal, almost, and we were about

to have dessert – I remember, because we rarely had any, not during the war anyway, and I was looking forward to it – when there was a knock at the door. That knock that for the last ten years people always waited for, but never really believed would happen to them. People are so stupid sometimes. We were stupid. Maybe to survive. Better to blind yourself to the danger than have a heart attack every time someone knocks at the door. Anyway, nobody was nervous. No-one thought twice about opening that door, although I suppose it would have made no difference if we had tried not to. We all knew that Stalin was arresting people, all over again. Jumpy from the war. Looking for collaborators, more enemies of the people, as though any could have been left after the thirties. But that knock was supposed to come at three in the morning, not nine at night. That gave us a false sense of security, I suppose, even though we all already knew someone who had been interrogated, or who had been imprisoned, or killed. Especially my parents. They knew lots of so-called intelligentsia. That was what they were, after all. And non-conformist intelligentsia at that. The worst sort of people."

He is stroking her hair, but she seems oblivious now, her voice brittle and still carrying the residual sound of tears. She is staring up at the ceiling, watching the whole scene again.

"So we opened the door – Yuri did, I remember, because my parents were still at the table, still talking, one eye and ear on the door, waiting to see who had come to visit. And then they were inside, pushing Yuri to one side – poor Yuri, he used to blame himself after that for opening the door, as if that would have changed anything. And they showed some papers – some kind of stupid identification – and they grabbed my father by both arms, shouting that they were arresting him for crimes against the State, and then my mother, too; they pulled her up, and her chair fell over, and my father was shouting at them not to hurt her, and we were watching, just shocked, I think. There seemed to be so many of them, but you know, there were only three men. They just seemed so powerful. They *were* so powerful. They had my parents out of our apartment in a matter of seconds. Seconds. They did not even have time to turn their heads and look back at us, or say anything to us. By the time I ran forwards, crying for my mother, she was gone. There was no trace of her, or my father. We never saw them again."

Her eyes are bright, but she is not crying, and he holds her, his own tears dropping unnoticed into her thick, black hair.

"I felt so helpless," she is saying. "So helpless, and lost. I miss them so much, Sasha. I miss my mother so much."

In his short life, Alexander has rarely encountered situations when he does not know how to respond, or what action to try. He has simply never been faced with such raw emotional trauma in someone he loves, the kind of primeval pain that no-one outside can heal. He watches the narrow shadows thrown about the room by the streetlight outside. Her back and shoulders start to shake with sobs that she cannot control, and he tries to hold her even more closely. Then, after a few minutes, she sits up on the bed, and glances at him, her face tear-streaked and red, and she pushes back her hair and stands up. He reaches out to hold onto her still, but she is back to herself now, and she touches his face gratefully and releases herself from his hands.

"Yuri looked everywhere for them. The Lubyanka, the Butyrka prison, the police stations. It was as though they had vanished into thin air. How did he get away with that for so long?" she whispers.

"Fear," Alexander says. "He ruled with fear. We were all relieved when it was over." Then he regrets what he has said, for while his dislike of Stalin is mainly intellectual, hers comes from an emotional pain he can barely imagine.

"Not all. Not even most, Sasha. Everyone was distraught when he died. Even your father."

"Not in the same way."

She lets it go, but he knows what she means. His father, who was so disenchanted by Stalin, was still devastated by his death. Millions of Soviets, most people, were. The emotional reliance on their leader had been so deeply rooted, the respect that grew from fear was so ingrained, his insidious charm so great, that it was difficult for people to imagine how the country would cope without him. Or how it would even exist without him.

But since Stalin's death, Alexander thinks, his father has allowed himself to think about things in a more balanced manner, less emotionally perhaps. He has allowed himself to deconstruct the source of his disillusionment and disgust. Khrushchev's early, far-reaching movement towards de-

Stalinization helped to shock him and others like him into reconsidering the years that had gone before – to face the fact that the torturous methods of terror were a direct result of Stalin's orders and way of governing. And even now when Khrushchev panics that he is losing control of his reforms, and makes sudden reversals into stiff, harsh governance, such reversals only throw into relief the inconsistencies and injustice of the system that they became used to. His father, Alexander thinks, has become a man who sees that his life is not built on a series of solid, upright bricks, as he had once thought, but on a set of rubber, shifting blocks that are beginning to show holes.

"When did you find out what had happened to them?"

Katya can do no more than whisper now. "Maybe six months later. We were lucky to ever find out I suppose. Apparently they were taken straight to a state farm owned by the NKVD. At Kommunarka, just outside the city. No-one knew that it was one of the secret places they sent people to be killed. They refused to sign confessions that they were enemies of the people. But then there was a report that Yuri saw – he bribed an official – it said that my father had stated for the record that he had been wrongly arrested – that is was Stalin who was the enemy of the people." A twisted smile passes briefly over her face. "I'm sure it was true. That he said it. My father always had a good sense of irony."

"And so they shot them. My father was a historian, a good one, and therefore an intellectual terrorist and my mother…

well, my mother's mistake was to be his wife. To support him. Those six months, waiting to find out if they were dead or alive were the worst. I had such dreams. That someone was holding my father over a balcony. I would watch, wait, on a knife-edge, praying they would pull him back. But always, with the gentlest, lightest movement, the hand would let go of him, and he would fall to his death. I would wake up crying, I was so sick with sadness." She clears her throat. "Don't make me think about it any more."

She walks out, away, into the hallway and then into the tiny, damp bathroom, and looks at herself in the mirror. "Sasha?"

"Yes?"

As she suspected, he has followed her and is waiting outside, in the dank hallway. Above him, in the corners of the low ceiling, he can see patches of dampness and the white bloom of mildew beginning to take hold.

"What are you doing with me? Misha told me once that he tried to warn you away from me the first time we met. At the dance."

"I didn't even hear him," Alexander replies. "I was a man possessed."

He sees the shaking of her head amongst the shadows in the bathroom, as she watches herself in the mirror.

"Ah, but possessed of what, now?" she asks, without humour, and she leans down to splash icy water on her face. She feels sorry for him for a moment, for even though he is the same age as she, she can feel his childlike helplessness in the face of her grief and anger. She runs a hand over her burning eyes, and thinks to herself that she will go in and lie down next to him and let him hold her, and let his warmth and love enclose her in so that she does not have to see or hear anything else ever again. That will help her, and it will help him also. But for now she remains standing there, fiddling with her hair, for she is thinking. She looks at her eyes in the mirror, and knows they are the same as her mother's, and from this starting point she tries to reconstruct her mother's face as she recalls it – the rough, dark hair, the high, broad forehead and long nose, uneven from some childhood mishap. The face appears to her – a face, any face really, not truly as it was. She is trying too hard to see it, and it has been too long, and Katya herself was too young. All these circumstances conspire against the retaining of the perfect memory, and she sighs. She comes out to the hallway and together they walk back to her room.

"I can't even remember what my mother looks like," she tells him, and he nods and walks her back to the bed. His body is warm compared to the cold air of the apartment, and she closes her eyes, places her mouth and nose almost flat against his chest and breathes his smell and listens to the blood pulsing around his body. Now she will begin once more the process of forgetting it, that terrible thing that once happened, so many years ago. And what a hard process it is, every time she recalls it, to then tame it and push all of it back into the farthest, unlit recesses of her memory where it will never stay willingly, but lies waiting like a sly, hungry animal; waiting for her guard to drop, for her shell to crack open and let it back in.

She feels safer with Alexander's arms around her, and his sensitive, kind eyes watching over her, but she also feels brittle and cold inside. She had made notes on the information she had gleaned from his papers that night, several weeks ago, and she passed them to Misha the next day. He had been satisfied in some way, and since then, she has not had to do anything similar. But since that evening she has begun to dislike herself, and the feeling of self-disgust is especially strong at times like this, when Alexander is watching over her with more care and adoration than she has ever received in her life. She sighs. Perhaps she will not think so hard about it for a while. Just for a few weeks. She is too confused to consider anything properly now. Perhaps she will just relax a little, and enjoy her time with him, and then, when Misha wants her to begin work, she can decide what to do. She feels tears prick at her eyes again, and tries biting her lip to hold them back, but they will not be held. They are tears of anger at what happened to her parents, tears of self-pity for the lost child she remembers being, and tears of frustration at the dilemma she now feels, because she is not at all sure that there is any decision to be made by her, about Alexander; she is almost sure that there is no way out.

CHAPTER ELEVEN
BOSTON

ESTELLE OPENS HER FRONT DOOR. She is dressed entirely in black – trousers, a turtle neck and a scarf that swathes softly over her shoulders. The effect is elegant, effortless. A faint smile of approval passes over Lauren's lips as Estelle shows her in, guiding her to a drawing room which Lauren takes in with a precise glance. The original floorboards are exposed, sanded and varnished to a warm brown colour which matches the outside of the fireplace. On top of the mantel is a photograph of Melissa as a child, sitting on her father's shoulders. There is an element of the dashing, the Byronesque, about Professor Johnson in the photograph. His face shows a casual pride as he holds onto his child. Melissa is smiling, the kind of fully released expression that is so much more common in children than adults. Lauren looks away, to a couple of old rugs placed beneath leather sofas. The soft grain and folds of the leather might make an interesting background, she thinks, and she suggests that Estelle take a seat there. Tinged with self-consciousness, Estelle takes a few moments to find a comfortable position, but Lauren is busy unfolding her easel and setting out her pencils.

"Just give me a bowl of fruit," Estelle says. "I can pose as a still life."

"I see you as anything but a still life," says Lauren. "Just relax. The point of sketching someone at home is to have them be comfortable."

"In their native habitat," comments Estelle.

"Exactly."

Lauren refuses the offer of a drink or breakfast; she has a nervous tension in her stomach and in her hands which, if harnessed correctly, can be helpful to her work. She begins drawing, talking to Estelle as she does so, inconsequential chatter, the kind that she can manage easily in order to keep her subject relaxed and interested. They talk about her husband's work, and then her daughter's.

"Melissa can be a little short sometimes," Estelle says suddenly. "She doesn't even realise she's being less than gracious. Her mind is always moving at a hundred miles an hour, always thinking about the next thing, and words or communicating just take up precious time."

"Is that how your husband is?" Lauren asks.

Estelle smiles. "Yes. But he means well, mostly."

"And if it's too much bother for either of them to communicate, who does that leave for you to talk to?"

"I don't know," says Estelle wryly. "Maybe I should get a therapist."

Lauren smiles. "Well, how about talking to me? Tell me about your story ideas."

"For my great novel, you mean?"

"Uh-huh."

"Don't laugh," Estelle instructs.

"I won't."

"Alexander and Katya."

Lauren laughs.

"I'm serious," says Estelle. "Your uncle is an intriguing person, and Katya – well, there's just a ton of drama and mystery that seems to hang around her."

"It's not that mysterious," Lauren replies. "He just doesn't like to talk about it much."

"Why not? Can the wounds be that raw after so many years?"

Lauren stops drawing. "I don't think it's that. He feels somehow responsible, and therefore guilty, for what happened to her. He had to make some hard choices before he left Russia. And she was the love of his life. I guess in the end, he's not a heart-on-his-sleeve kind of guy. He'd rather keep it all in."

"Which doesn't make my job any easier. Anyway, I just want to use them as a starting point. For a fictional piece. Unless he authorises me to write the official version."

"I'd love to see that," Lauren says, and Estelle looks at her, unsure if she detects a note of sarcasm, but Lauren gives her a glance of confirmation.

"No, I really would. You see, for a long time now, I've thought there was a lot more to the story than even Uncle Alex knows. He was out of the loop of what was happening. And there are loose ends that just don't tie up. I don't think he was as responsible as he thinks."

"You're forgetting – I still don't know what happened. Only that your aunt died. Care to fill me in?"

Lauren rubs at her eyes with her hand. "I'd love to. But I think we should clear it with your lead character first, don't you?"

"I suppose."

Lauren looks at her closely.

"You have the eyes of a naughty child, Estelle. I need to find a way to capture that."

Estelle gives a half-smile, but does not reply. She is involved in the idea of this story. Of Katya. A different era, an intensity of life so far removed from her own. Aware that she has fallen silent, she looks at Lauren, but she too is absorbed, her attention moving more fully to the paper before her, to the lines of charcoal darting over the page. Estelle sits watching the young woman working, and she can feel that she is rapt, excited, interested. Everything that Estelle is afraid to allow in herself when she sits at her desk. She is suddenly overtaken by desire, and wishes she was there now, with the glow from the setting sun on the wall behind her, and her pen flowing across the lined sheets. When Lauren leaves, she decides, she will write. Anything. She will describe the portrait of Katya. Then she will describe Katya herself, or rather the character she wants to begin sketching.

"So you wouldn't mind me using your story as a starting point?"

Alexander has only been in Estelle's apartment for ten minutes, but he is already ambivalent about having come. At first he had been secretly disappointed that Lauren preferred to sketch Estelle in her own home rather than having her come to their house. He would have liked to have constant proximity to his new friend without having to contrive reasons for it. But he has resolved to simply acknowledge the fact that he would like to see Estelle more, and so has offered to come and walk his niece back home when she has completed her morning's work. For Estelle, Alexander's arrival seems the perfect opportunity to ask the question that has been in her mind all morning.

"You're planning a whole novel?" Alexander asks, and she nods.

He is pleased that she is excited about writing, though disturbed about her choice of subject. Her eagerness and enthusiasm are clear to him, and she seems different, more vibrant, when she talks about working. After years assisting her husband, probably with little thanks, and no outlet of her own, she has something that is driving her.

"I've already started researching. Books and the internet. The big impression I've found so far is that Khrushchev made a huge difference. Just in attitude, and atmosphere, after the dictatorship of Stalin. There was less suspicion, more openness."

Alexander nods. "Yes, it was like that, mostly. Khrushchev was not infallible – he made many mistakes, often because he was rushing through changes to avoid opposition, but he was a big step forward. They called it the "thaw", that period. That's when I was working in the government."

"It must have been an exciting time."

Alexander studies his hands, thinking. It has been so long since he has thought of that time and place as anything other than threatening, and choking. Had he thought it exciting once, when he first started? Probably. But that was before Katya. Before the very institutions that he had been reared to respect and serve began to threaten what he loved most. He blinks away the thoughts.

"You seem happy," is all he says to Estelle, and the directness of his comment makes her look away for a second.

"I guess I am," she says. "But I know these things are hard for you to talk about, and contrary to the impression I may have given up till now, I hate to be a pushy broad."

"I can't pretend that I relish going over things that I haven't considered for many, many years," he says.

"Maybe it's time you considered them again," Lauren says.

He is suddenly irritated. "I've kept them at arm's length all this time for a reason. They are painful subjects for me."

"I know, but the more I've looked into my aunt's life, the more discrepancies there seem to be."

Alexander rubs his chin. "Can anything be changed by all of this?" he asks.

"Maybe," Lauren says. Her face shows determination and life – the same qualities he recognises in himself, though perhaps not as frequently any more.

"Katya is dead," he says. He is getting tired of saying it, and of thinking it. "Nothing is going to resurrect her. Estelle, I want you to write, more than anything. I think it's wonderful, and if I can help by providing your starting point, or even with telling you what I know about Katya's life and death, I guess I'll do so. But I won't have a whole investigation re-opened. Nothing can be served by all this re-hashing and probing."

His hand hits the table for emphasis, and although he has meant the gesture merely to emphasise his point, to his embarrassment, the teacups shake slightly.

"That's not in the spirit of study and enlightenment, Mr Ivanov."

He turns to see a looming outline in the doorway.

"Professor Johnson." Alexander stands and shakes his hand.

"Enlightenment can never be achieved in this case. It is always a good thing to know when to leave something be."

"Stop, stop," the professor replies, a note of delight in his low voice. "You're opening up too many wonderful debates all at once. The nature of enlightenment, the nature of achievement itself... Ah, we could talk for hours."

Alexander sits back down. "With respect, I don't want to open up debates. I want to close them."

Professor Johnson does not comment further, only nods, and then makes his way to the fridge. Estelle is up already, bringing him a glass, into which he pours the contents of a can of tonic water. He drinks a sip and looks at the company at the table.

"Excellent protection against malaria," he informs them, taking another drink.

Lauren laughs, and his eyes fix on her. They are fierce, and bird-like, giving the impression of continual movement and extreme concentration at the same time.

"You remind me somewhat of my wife," he tells her. "Though not superficially you understand. Something in the eyes. 'All the wild summer was in her gaze…'"

Estelle smiles, but busies herself with scooping tea leaves into a pot.

"Thank you," says Lauren.

"William Butler Yeats," continues the professor. "The quotation, just now."

He is a big man, broad in the chest and shoulders, and yet somehow he contrives to look lanky. He walks slowly back to the door of the kitchen, placing his legs gingerly, as though they have not been tested away from the confines of his desk for some time. He shakes his head when Lauren asks him if he will join them.

"I don't take afternoon tea," he tells her. "I have to save something to look forward to in my old age."

Alexander can see Lauren examining his face and frame, placing him against an empty canvas even as she smiles at his joke. And then something happens, something which Alexander would give much to be able to undo. He reaches for his teacup, but Estelle is still pouring milk into it, and their hands brush, and without thinking, he reaches out to hold hers to steady it. The touch is brief, intimate, and he feels it in every fibre of his body, and a second after the nervous, pleasurable tension has faded, he is appalled that the professor might also have seen and sensed what has happened. Estelle glances up at her husband as she pours Lauren's cup, but he is not looking at either of them. Alexander cannot help but feel, however, that the professor does not miss a trick.

Estelle's voice is bright when she breaks the pause. "I'm stealing Lauren's research on Russia for my own purposes."

There is a slight snort from her husband, a residual response to what he has just seen perhaps. "Not another book attempt, my dear?" he says.

Estelle is silent, compact, pulled in suddenly. Like an animal on alert. Professor Johnson smiles at once.

"You know, you mustn't feel badly about appropriating Lauren's research. After all, much of academia rests on the study of stolen books and papers."

Perhaps he feels badly for having denigrated her attempted work, or perhaps, Alexander thinks, he just feels badly that he did so in front of their guests. But Estelle's glance at her husband is kind, if cautious.

"Never mind, Frank," she says, and he seems to take this as

an absolution of a sort, and with a cough, he turns and walks back down the hallway.

It takes almost two hours for them to go over the history of Alexander's life with Katya as he remembers it. His discoveries, her decisions, and then her death; the central issue, as overpowering as a poisonous gas to the rest of the conversation. It is here that he has always been at a disadvantage when faced with Lauren's probing and questions – for what he knows is hearsay. He was not there before, during or afterwards, and he cannot therefore know precisely what happened and when. That is Lauren's point, one that seems to make sense to Estelle also. It is now, for the first time, that Alexander recognises something of Melissa in her mother's clear eyes, a reflection of the careful sifting going on in her mind.

"I think there's a lot more that we could try and find out. Especially now," Lauren tells him.

"Why now?" asks Alexander.

"Because I found out that Misha is alive," she says gently. "Their best friend in Russia," she adds, for Estelle's benefit.

Why this should hit him as a physical shock, he has no idea. It is not as though he had known or believed that Misha was dead. But for all the years since he has left Russia, his thoughts of Misha have been like those of Katya – rooted in the past. In some ways, it was as though they had died together. He had rarely thought of the possibility that he still existed, and he had always told himself that this was because it would have been too difficult and too dangerous for them to have kept in touch for the first decades. This was true enough, but if he is to be honest with himself, that close friendship with Misha was also the strongest remaining reminder of Katya, and Alexander had found in the immediate aftermath of her death that he wanted a clean break, a pure, deep cut that would sever him from their country, and from everyone and everything in it.

The women watch him expectantly, but he is at a loss. He has been feeling his grip on the afternoon, on the whole situation, loosening for some time, and now his head feels light and as though it is filled with cotton wool or the meringues that he is so fond of. Everything is soft, there is nothing solid to grasp hold of, and he hates the feeling. It is how he has imagined the onset of senility might one day feel, and the very idea makes him want to shiver.

"How long have you been keeping all this from me?"

"I wasn't hiding it. I didn't know if we'd find him, and I didn't want to bother you with it unless we did. It started when I went to Moscow last year. I couldn't find him then, so I hired a private agency – a detective, really – to look for him."

Alexander nods. "And?"

"They've found him. A couple of weeks ago. Still living in Moscow. I've been trying to find a good time to tell you."

Alexander feels the last thread unravel in his mind. He can no longer think or feel. He touches his forehead, and Estelle hands him a glass of water.

"He was in Moscow, when Katya died. He was her best friend, and yours. He must have tried to learn something about her death. And since you were never able to speak to him, you don't know what he might have found out."

"You want to see him?"

"I think so. Don't you?" Lauren's hand is on his shoulder. Estelle is sitting forward in her chair.

"I think we should." Lauren continues. "I think a trip out there would help a lot. I could help you figure out the full story, and Estelle says she'd love to join us – it would be a great chance for her to do some research. I think it would be good for all of us. Maybe it would help you, Uncle Alex."

He does not reply. His throat is still dry, despite the sips of water.

"Uncle Alex? All I'm trying to say is that there are all these missing pieces, and maybe it won't change anything, but don't you want to know the whole story, once and for all? You might even find out that you weren't as responsible as you feel. That's what I'm hoping," she adds, her voice dropping.

He is listening, she knows, but he makes no sign, he is just leaning forward, eyes staring at the floor. When she looks up at Estelle, the blue eyes are thoughtful. With a glance at Lauren, Estelle shakes her head slightly, and Lauren nods, knowing she has taken things as far as she can for the moment.

Lauren has an image of her own mind as a canvas, spattered with wildly coloured paints, colours that are random, without any coherence, colours that are bleeding into each other, forming a coagulated mass that is confusion and uncertainty. This bewilderment has been with her since she began having doubts about her work. But now, the re-visiting of Katya's story is also seeping into the mess. She has not previously had any doubts about looking for Misha and going to meet him – she has been more and more convinced that the loose ends, the unknown parts, of Katya's story should be found. How can partial information be a good thing, when the full story is potentially available? How can ignorance be better than knowledge? But the distress she is causing her uncle is causing her to reconsider.

She is reading a memoir about Africa when the telephone rings. She is still surrounded by dunes and desert as she answers, so it takes her a moment to realise that it is Melissa, but when she does recognise the voice, the book drops and she sits up. After the standard pleasantries, she offers to call Alexander to the phone, but Melissa refuses.

"I'm calling for you, actually."

"Really?"

"I've just been given two front-row seats to the ballet. For tonight. And I wondered if you'd be interested to join me. It's *The Nutcracker*."

"I'd love to." Lauren feels the confusion in her mind spreading again, although now the feeling is a pleasant, heady one. As soon as she has accepted it occurs to her that perhaps she should be checking with her uncle first regarding the etiquette of the impending business deal. They arrange to meet at the theatre, and only when she hangs up the phone does it occur to Lauren that perhaps this invitation is part of closing that deal as far as Melissa is concerned.

The theatre is warm and dark, the lights of the stage reflected softly back onto the entranced faces of the audience. Without moving her head, Melissa takes a sidelong glance at Lauren. She seems fully engrossed by the dancing, her eyes following the light movement of the leads, her mouth slightly upturned, happy. Melissa looks back at the stage. The music is dramatic and moving, but she does not know enough about ballet to be able to tell whether the dancers are superlative or merely good. She will ask Lauren later what she thinks. In the meantime, she is a little restless. There is still another hour to go, and Melissa can think of a number of things she could do in that precious amount of time – she could be working, or working out; she could be catching up with the news on TV, or even taking a long soak in the bath, a luxury she rarely has time for. But she is here, with a guest, and she makes an effort to relax about the wasted time. When did life become so frantic that to sit still, listening to music that she cannot even imagine having the brilliance to write, become something she has to remind herself she enjoys? Clearly, Lauren does not see it that way, nor do most of the people sitting here around her. With cool analysis, Melissa wonders if she is slowly losing whatever capacity she once had for pure pleasure, for learning, for art, for spending her time outside work in a way that might not be the most efficient, but that could be the most enlightening. She resolves to relax and enjoy the rest of the performance. Then, later, she will make an effort to schedule in some down time, perhaps an art gallery. Something she can ask Lauren to show her.

Later, over dinner, Lauren questions her about her parents. Melissa's conversation is terse and to the point, but with an undercurrent of dry humour that Lauren finds particularly amusing when she talks about her father's lack of awareness of anything outside his books. After a few moments, though, Melissa's tone changes, becoming more subdued.

"You know, the last two times I had dinner with them, my mother's been talking non-stop about Russia. And my dad answers all her questions, but it never once occurs to him to ask why she's interested. He has a kind of purity in his thought process which I admire, but I guess it can blind you when you're in a close relationship."

From Melissa's slight shifting, and the movement away of her eyes, Lauren senses that this is her hesitant way of explaining something of herself, but she decides not to pursue the point at this moment.

"Why is Estelle so into Russia?"

"Because of your uncle. And Katya. I think she's developing quite a fascination." She smiles. "Everyone seems taken with this woman, whom none of us have ever met."

"I guess when I was younger, Katya seemed like a comic book heroine to me. Exotic and exciting, leading a double life. Spying, the cold war, all that stuff."

"But you still admire her, don't you?"

"Sure. I mean, she lost both her parents very young, in the most horrible way, and yet found a way to be so strong, so sure of herself and what she believed in. Even when believing it meant defying everyone and everything around her. She lived with passion and I aspire to that."

Melissa smiles. "She sounds a little like you. Losing your parents, living with passion. I mean, you don't become an artist to get a regular income. You do it because you love it, right?"

Lauren has not considered herself in the same light as her aunt since she was a teenager, and is even less inclined to do so now.

"I think I have a long way to go before I'm anything like Katya," Lauren replies. "She really knew what she wanted in life. She had a purpose."

"And you don't?"

Lauren hesitates. "I love painting. I'm just tired of portraits. I've been playing it safe for too long. Taking commissions that don't stretch me intellectually or physically. I'm not learning anything new."

"That's a problem," says Melissa. "You don't ever stay still in life. If you're not stepping forward, you're falling behind."

"Did you get that from a desk calendar?"

Melissa sighs. "You love thinking of me as a corporate robot, don't you? I might not be able to express myself poetically, or through art or whatever, but I know what I believe. Sorry if it sounds trite."

Not for the first time, Lauren finds herself cursing her own quick tongue. She has also continually overlooked the fact that here in front of her is a woman who is also passionate about what she does.

"No, I'm sorry," she says. "I really am. I've been giving you my artist's superiority complex from day one, and you don't deserve it."

Melissa smiles and re-fills their wine glasses. "You have been pretty feisty. But nothing I can't handle."

"Oh really?"

"Yes, really."

There is a pause, and Lauren looks at the dessert menu noting that Melissa has pushed hers to one side.

"I don't suppose you'll split a chocolate cheesecake with me?"

"Too many carbs. And the fat grams...."

"If you do, I'll take you around the Museum of Fine Arts, and show you a few things. If you want to."

Melissa frowns. "So let me get this right. I have to eat a dessert I don't want in order to win a trip around a museum that I haven't asked for?"

Lauren nods.

"You're a hell of a negotiator. For an artist."

"Do we have a deal?"

Melissa smiles. "I love cheesecake. And I'm pretty sure I can learn to love art. I'm going home to New York for a few days. But maybe when I get back?"

Lauren sits back in her seat and smiles. "I'll hold you to it."

CHAPTER TWELVE
MOSCOW – OCTOBER 1956

O N HIS BED, SHE LIES NAKED, and trembling. He cannot see her shaking in the cool darkness, but his hand can feel the tiny tremors in her muscles as it passes gently over the skin of her stomach. He has pulled back from her kisses, the kisses that she sometimes uses to shield her face from his eyes, because she knows that when he is so close to her he cannot watch her. The desire that had overwhelmed him a few moments ago has cooled slightly, a conscious, monumental effort on his part, because he wants to see her now, and know what it is that is passing through her mind or heart, and that is leaving a shivering imprint on every fibre of her body.

He sits alongside, and when she tries to pull him down towards her, he carefully takes possession of the hand that grasps his shoulder and brings it to his mouth. With his eyes closed, he kisses her fingers, every joint of every one, slowly, slowly. Then her palm, warm and salty. He holds it pressed against his face for a few moments, and with his other hand touches her chest, between her breasts. Her breath comes shallow and fast, and the trembling is there still.

"Sasha," she whispers, and he brings her palm down to his own chest, holding it against his heart, and looks at her, tenderly, quietly, willing her to tell him anything she wants to tell him.

"What is it, Katyushka?" he asks, his voice low.

She shakes her head very slightly and turns it away from him, towards the window, and in the thin moonlight or streetlight that penetrates the curtain, he sees tears gleaming on her cheeks and eyelashes. Without taking even a moment to undress, he lies down alongside her. Although he cannot see her turned-away face, he can hold her, and his arms encircle her whole body, his hands caress and stroke her wherever they rest – her waist, her hip, her thigh. Her shaking seems to become stronger. He can feel her ribs against him, the soft down of her back against his arm, her thin shoulders, all shivering.

"What is it, my love?"

A shift of her head, towards him. She brings up a hand to try and wipe her face, but he is holding her so tightly that she cannot reach. He guides her towards him, and willingly now she turns over, so that her head is against his neck, and he can feel the wetness of her eyes and nose on his skin.

"What's wrong?"

But she shakes her head, and a sound comes from her that is like a laugh, but it rises from so deep within, and is laden with such raw emotion, that he cannot be sure what it is, or what it means.

"I'm so happy with you, Sasha."

It is the first time she has ever told him anything like that. Even during their most intimate, tender love-making, she has been unable to bring herself to respond to his quiet speaking of his own love.

He feels dizzy with pleasure, with a deep, uncontrolled joy, and he closes his eyes and kisses her forehead and eyes and holds her as closely as he can. He never wants to move from here, or let her go, or get up from this bed, ever again. In a little while, it occurs to him to ask her again what he had asked her a few days ago. "Katyushka, will you marry me please?" She had not answered, had been withdrawn and confused beneath her insistence that she needed time to make a decision. He had felt sick with despair, for how could anyone need time to answer this question, unless the answer was really no? But here, now, he knows that she loves him. But he does not ask. The moment is too precious to break, and besides, she will answer when she is ready.

The trembling of her limbs has ceased. She lies quiet and peaceful against him, her breathing even and deeper. He lies still, wondering if she has fallen asleep. But there is a slight tension in her legs, which she is deliberately holding fast against his own that tells him that she is awake.

"Sasha," she whispers. "I will marry you." And then in a tiny, quiet voice: "I love you."

He kisses her head as a reply. Nothing will induce him to

release his hold of her right now – and she does not try and look up or kiss him. They lie there, complete, silent, and in a few moments he feels her arms relax and her hand fall away from his leg. She is sleeping.

She can somehow tell in those moments of falling into sleep that she is about to have the dream again. The knowledge comes to her subconscious like a sixth sense, and she always struggles to pull back to wakefulness, but it is a useless attempt, like trying to sprint out of quicksand. It is terrible and inevitable, but she is fully trapped now in the swirling current of her slumber, and there is no way for her to rise to the surface, to pull away from the dream and burst up into the fresh air. He feels her limbs twitch against him, and he smiles that she has slept so quickly and easily. Another sound comes from her throat, a moan, and he kisses her and rubs her back.

She sees her mother in a cell, windowless, airless. The smell of faeces and urine soaked into the walls. Her father is there somewhere, too, in another part of the jail, but she never sees him in this dream. Only her mother. And her face is so clear, so well-remembered, it gives her a pin-prick of pleasure in the midst of her anguish, for when she is awake, she can never fully recall her mother's face. Her mother is sitting in a corner of the cell, which is garishly lit to prevent her from sleeping; and she seems strangely calm, but the calmness comes from resignation or despair, something that hurts Katya more than seeing her mother's panic or anger would. She knows her mother has refused to sign a piece of paper, her fabricated confession to her crimes against the state, and from somewhere outside the cell, Katya can hear herself begging her mother to just sign it, don't let them hurt you, just sign it.

"But then they will shoot me anyway, Katyushka, if I confess," her mother says. Just like that, coolly, without recognising her daughter's fear and anguish. She knows it is an effect of the dream that makes her mother so distant and unaware, but it pains her anyway. Doesn't she care that she will never see Katya again, or hold her or kiss her?

Then she is beaten. This is a terrible part of the dream for Katya, but she knows that this is only the start. She feels a primal yell rising in her throat, as two of the guards go in on her mother, jabbing with rifle butts, swinging with black boots. They are heavy men; she sees one of them is short, with a thick neck and shoulders, and the sound of his gun thudding against the prone body on the ground is sickening. There is a wetness, a squelching to the sound, when they have been hitting for long enough. Then she can hear her mother gurgling, blood filling her mouth and throat and eyes. Then comes the worst part of the dream. Another man unbuttons his trousers, he is a guard, she thinks, and the heavy man is still there, laughing now, and her mother is being pulled out of her corner, being uncurled, her limbs pushed apart, and now she hears her mother sobbing. The guard drops down on top of her with quick brutality. There is a savage, relentless grunting from his slack, open mouth as he rapes her, an obscene groan of pleasure as he thrashes

203

about on top of her, his hands groping her dress, grasping at her breasts.

"Just sign it," Katya begs. "Just sign it."

She signs it. In the end. And then she is taken out of the cell, and Katya watches her being walked outside, and her mother's knees are buckling and her face is unrecognisable now, a bloody pulp, and her dress is badly stained and streaked, and she has a cigarette burn on her neck. And when they get her outside, they will put her against a wall, with a few others, and shoot her. But she never sees that part. Which is why the rape is always the worst.

He has been shaking her very gently for a few minutes now, since the screams began, tiny, strangled, primeval sounds, as though she is trying to shout and gasp for air at the same time. He is hesitant to wake her suddenly from such a deep sleep. But then her breathing slows and the noises stop. There is a tear escaping from one eye, and her mouth is contorted in pain or sadness. He rubs her back and strokes her head, whispering to her that she is fine, nothing can hurt her. And her face slowly relaxes, and within a few minutes she is awake.

"You were having a bad dream," he tells her.

She wipes a hand over her eyes and face; she is panting for breath. She turns over, and looks away from him, up at the ceiling. Suddenly, she does not want to feel his hands on her. She shifts again, so that the warmth of his body is held slightly away from her. Now the coolness of the air can reach her hot limbs and she is grateful for it.

"Katya? Do you remember what it was?"

"What?" she asks, her voice hoarse.

"Your dream. You were so unhappy. Do you remember it?"

Her breathing is heavy, barely controlled. All that she can do is shake her head.

"Are you sure?" he wants to know. "Are you okay?"

She takes some deep breaths and then she can turn to look at him, clear-eyed. "No, I don't remember any of it," she says. "Nothing at all."

She closes her eyes and pretends to sleep. She is still holding herself a little away from him, and he can sense that, and she knows he is hurt by it, but he shifts away from her anyway to give her the space she is now craving. Then she hears him get up, quietly, and go into the bathroom. The sound of the water running in a thin stream into the bath. He will be a while. She opens her eyes and takes an audible gulp of air. The dream is fading from her mind, much more quickly than usual, because on waking she has remembered that she has just agreed to marry him. She blinks hard and wipes away a light sheen of sweat from her cheeks and nose. She has been in a state of suppressed panic for days, since he first asked her, considering whether she should marry him for his information, or whether she should refuse him because she would only be using him. She wonders what she was thinking just now, when she said yes; and then she realises she was not thinking at all, was not being rational, controlled, sensible. She agreed to marry him just now because she loves him, and at that moment that was all she could feel and think and know. She turns over onto her back and looks at the ceiling. What on earth is she going to tell Misha? How on earth will he ever understand?

CHAPTER THIRTEEN
BOSTON

THE EVENING SHADOWS ARE stretching fingers of dusk into the kitchen. Lauren stands before the stove and notices the reflection of the weak, late winter sunshine slipping down the walls of the room. It is a warm colour that slides away, and it leaves a solemn darkness in its place. It is the kind of twilight that she loves, that has an atmosphere of early spring about it, and she glances quickly at Alexander. He is busy whisking together eggs and milk, and has not yet noticed the fading light. She is glad of it. In this house she can rarely indulge her appetite for the quiet dusk, or the velvet cover of nighttime. A surfeit of lights and lamps and candles chase these tones away whenever Alexander is near.

"When do you plan to leave?" he asks her, grinding salt and pepper into his eggs.

"I was hoping *we* would leave next week."

With a deliberately cavalier gesture, Alexander cuts a large knob of butter and puts it into a saucepan.

"I wanted scrambled eggs, not a heart attack," Lauren comments.

"You wanted to learn to make *my* scrambled eggs," he says. "And I'm not running a health farm. Wait till the butter is just foaming."

Obediently, she watches it melt.

"I'm not going on this trip," Alexander says suddenly. "I told you that from the start, and nothing has changed. If you really think you can find something, then fine. Come back and let me know what it is."

Lauren tips the eggs into the pan.

"Keep stirring," Alexander instructs.

"So you do want to know more?"

"No!"

She is startled by the harsh decisiveness of the reply, but she will not look up from the stove. She moves her wooden spoon back and forth amongst the gently setting eggs. Watches them intently, giving herself time to harness her instinct to yell back at him, and giving him time to gather himself. She can feel that he has taken a step back and is standing awkwardly beside her. He takes out his handkerchief and wipes at his face. A long minute or two passes this way, during which he dare not guide her about the eggs, even though he is longing to take over. Instinctively, she lets go of the spoon and turns the handle of the pan so that it is within his reach. Then she looks up.

"Well, maybe you should start wanting to know, Uncle Alex. Or stop pretending that you don't. No," she cuts him off before he can utter even a sound in defence. "And don't think of trying that terse tone again with me. It might work in business meetings, but I'm your family."

"Keep stirring, Lauren," is all he says.

She takes up the spoon again. "Looks like they're nearly done."

He sets two places at the kitchen table, and puts slices of bread into the toaster. Within a few moments, she brings the saucepan over to him and he checks the eggs and nods approval. She divides the contents between their plates and waits for him to sit down.

"Now, listen to me, Uncle Alex. The reason I've been pursuing this thing is because I think you've been wrong all these years. Wrong about blaming yourself for what happened to Katya, and wrong not to have checked it out before now. I think someone else was involved."

"That much is obvious. But what does it matter? I started the ball rolling. I started the investigation."

"But someone else finished it. Brutally. No arrest, no trial. That wasn't Khrushchev's new way of working, was it?"

"It could have been," he says. "We've been through this before. Things don't change overnight in any government. Khrushchev made big strides towards transparency and accountability, but old ways die hard. And the KGB dies the hardest. To them, what Katya and I did was treason."

"And what about Misha?" she asks quietly.

The telephone rings, and gratefully, he reaches over and picks it up. There is a gruff, unfamiliar voice at the other end.

"Is this Mr Ivanov?"

"Yes, it is."

"President of the Chekhov Appreciation Society?" A brief bark of a laugh follows. The professor. Alexander begins to feel a faint throb of headache invade his temples.

"Is everything all right, Professor Johnson?"

"Ah, that's the thing, you see. I'm not quite sure."

Alexander is not in the mood for games, and he waits, silently, for an explanation.

"I would love to meet you, if you've time," Frank Johnson offers at last. "There are some things I would like to discuss with you."

"Such as?"

"I would like us to meet face to face."

"Very well."

"Good," he says. "Can you come tomorrow?"

"Where?"

"To my office. At the university. English Department, in the Grayston Building on…"

"I know it."

"Ten o'clock." It is a statement, not a question.

"Noon would be better for me," Alexander replies as politely as he can. In truth, the time is of no great relevance, but he feels an impulse to bridle against the professor's presumption. He hears some pages turn, and above the noise of paper, a sigh of irritation.

"I have a tutorial at twelve. How about eleven?"

"Sounds fine. I'll see you tomorrow."

Lauren is watching him, confused.

"What's going on?"

Alexander takes a small bite of his eggs, then pushes the plate away and rubs at his aching head. "The professor wants a duel," he says.

The following day dawns with the kind of pure, hard sunlight that suggests coldness, and Alexander is up early, sitting at his study desk, high on the top floor of his house, under the sloping eaves, watching the blue of the sky turn from a deep azure to a pale, icy sheen. Padding into the kitchen in his robe and slippers, he prepares bacon and pancakes for breakfast, leaving the door wide open in the hope that the scent will drift up the stairs and wake Lauren.

Within a few minutes, she appears, hair wet from the shower, and sits down at the table with her head leaning tiredly on her hand.

"You smell lovely," he says. "Very clean."

"I am very clean. What smells so good?"

He fills a plate and deposits it in front of her.

"My God. I'm going to weigh three hundred pounds by the time I leave here."

"Do you want me to take it away?" he asks, and her arms move protectively around the plate. He watches her for a moment, pleased that something has healed between them.

"What is it?"

"I've been thinking about what you said yesterday." He sits down and in the next few minutes, tries to explain to her about Misha. How they had been in the same class at school since the age of eight, how the ties of friendship that had bound them were far too strong to be pulled apart even by slightly differing ideologies or political loyalties.

"But you did differ?"

"Not much. At university, we both questioned the government a lot – quietly though. We talked for hours about the changes we wanted to see, how we would make a difference from within. You see, he was in the system, like I was – he had a good research job in an exciting field – aviation and space exploration. Remember, the Soviets launched the world's first satellite in fifty-seven. It was a great time for him, but he couldn't discuss it much; so much was new and secret. I remember, we had such a celebration when he got the job. My first serious hangover." Alexander smiles at the recollection.

"I was so proud of him, and yet I was anxious too – eager to find my place in life, to start working as he had. He graduated from the Institute of Aviation; he'd always wanted to fly. He was as disillusioned as Katya and myself after the years of Stalin. But, though he hated to admit it, I think he felt there were possibilities for change under Khrushchev."

"Why did he hate to admit it?"

Alexander shrugs. "That was Misha. He had this cynical, devil-may-care attitude, and that meant not appearing to give much respect to anything or anyone."

"He sounds like a character," she tells him. Then, more softly, she adds. "And I look forward to meeting him."

Alexander stands up from his chair as though she has thrown her hot tea in his lap. Then he pauses, trying to cover the sharpness of the movement.

"I'd better get ready," he says, and goes upstairs.

Under the soothing pulse of a very hot, very long shower, he tries to argue down his internal resistance to Lauren's and Estelle's planned trip to Russia. Either they will find something, or they won't. If they do not, which is the likely outcome, nothing will have changed. If they do, would he not want to know any other detail, any other small crumb of information about Katya that they could bring back to him? Only when he starts dressing does he remember the professor, and he consciously takes a little extra time in choosing what to wear. It is strange that after the turmoil of the past few weeks, and despite the anger and headaches, there is a part of him that feels more alive and invigorated than he has for months. Perhaps because there are challenges to face once more. A part of him is longing for the pain of Katya's loss to be fully understood and then buried forever. Another part wants Estelle to help with that process. And yet perhaps all that has happened is that he has begun to acknowledge something he has pushed aside for too many years – that he has dealt badly with the aftermath of his wife's death; that he has taken the easier route away from it, a route of disassociation, not involvement. He used his grief and horror as a good enough excuse not to return to that worst of times, but forty years later, it is becoming apparent to him that he has been naïve to think that he has ever had a choice in the matter. Perhaps all that he has managed to do over the course of his life is to delay the same moment of confrontation he has been trying so quietly to erase.

Lauren is still in the kitchen when he comes back downstairs. She has a fresh pot of tea and a newspaper before her, and has waited here to try and win him back, to once again smooth over the roughness that keeps edging between them. Her eyes look him up and down over the edge of the broadsheet.

"It doesn't matter how spiffy you look, he's going to hate you. Probably more so."

Alexander laughs. "Should I wear my oldest clothes and forget to brush my teeth?"

She wrinkles her nose. "Maybe not. Whatever you do, you'll never compete with his rumpled, professor look. Better to stick with what you know." She stands and kisses him on the cheek.

"You look very handsome," she says. "Good luck."

With the aid of various signposts, he makes his way to the English Department. Inside, the brick building is dark and poky, though impressively panelled in wood, and in the gloomy lobby he sees the back of a woman typing and speaking on the telephone. After a few moments' wait, he looks in at her door.

"Professor Johnson?" he whispers.

She places a hand over the receiver. "Up the stairs – third door on the left."

"Thank you."

His name is written in rolling script on a small card insecurely attached to his door. There is an air of impermanence about the sign, which adds to the gloom of the place. Alexander removes his hat and knocks firmly. There is a rustling of papers, and a gruff "Come," and he enters.

Frank Johnson's thick iron-coloured hair is swept back over a craggy forehead and disjointed nose, but several locks have escaped and hang limply over his brow. He is closely shaven, but has cut himself recently, low on the chin. He stands to shake Alexander's hand, and he seems even taller somehow, perhaps more so in the confines of this small room – perhaps four or five inches over six foot.

"Good of you to come. Sit down, sit down." He points vaguely behind Alexander. There is an old, wooden chair which holds a tall pile of books, including a complete works of Shakespeare. Professor Johnson reaches over and tries ineffectually to push the books away, but his action seems surprisingly frail. Alexander turns to help, and together they clear the books onto the floor, and he sits down.

"Something to drink?" the professor asks.

"No, thank you."

"I'll open a window. It can get stuffy in here, and I tend not to notice, you know."

Alexander acquiesces gratefully – the room is more

than a little oppressive. While he waits, he looks at the bookshelves that surround them. As he would somehow expect in an English professor's room, they are stacked to overflowing, with books placed horizontally wherever there is the slightest bit of space. Further tall stacks lie on the tops of the bookcases themselves. As he glances at titles and authors, he can see that the books had once been laid out in some kind of chronological and regional order, but that the thread has been lost somewhere along the way. Directly in front of him is a case devoted entirely, it seems, to Irish works.

The professor is watching him when Alexander turns back.

"I like books."

"I noticed. Irish literature?"

"A fondness of mine, if not truly a speciality. The Irish have a certain…" He sighs, and places his enormous hands behind his head while he selects the right words. "A certain… wildness, a certain desperate enjoyment of life which often overlays a certain darkness and blackness of soul. Which reminds me not a little," he says, with a sideways glance at his guest, "of the Russian temperament."

Alexander is at a loss. The comment sounds innocuously general, but is clearly aimed at him.

"You don't agree?" Professor Johnson asks.

"On the contrary, I think there is a lot of truth in what you say. But I also think one has to be wary of speaking in generalisations."

"Indeed. Let's choose some specifics, then."

"Very well."

"I wish to know a little more about you, Mr Ivanov."

"Please, call me Alexander."

"Thank you. I wish to know more about you, Alexander."

"May I ask why?"

"You may. How can I put this?" His fingers tap along the papers on his desk and he glances about, as though searching for a book that will perhaps help to explain his meaning.

"I'm a man of routine. I am at home almost all of the time, and then two days in the week, I come here, to this esteemed institution of learning, in order to tease out some semblance of a coherent thought process from the young minds entrusted to me."

"You don't work full time?"

"I work all the time. But not here. At home."

"I see."

"Wherever I'm working, I am home every evening, and I have dinner there with my wife."

Alexander catches the first gleam of suggestion in the professor's eye. He nods in a non-committal way, and waits for him to continue.

"Every evening we talk a little. About various things. Our daughter. My work, even, now and then, though I blame myself for not being as open and articulate as I would like on that subject. We talk about music sometimes. Sometimes," he says, staring off at a point somewhere behind Alexander, "we don't speak much at all. Anyway, what I'm trying to say is, we don't speak about Russia."

Alexander wonders if the professor rambles this much in his tutorials.

"You don't discuss Russia?" he repeats.

"Ah," the professor says, lifting a triumphant finger, as though Alexander has somehow proved a point for him. "We never *used* to. We never *used* to. And then, out of the blue one day, we were eating dinner, and Estelle begins talking to me about Russia, and Stalin, and Khrushchev. Asking me questions, you know."

Alexander shifts slightly in the chair, which is uncomfortable.

"I thought nothing of it at the time," Professor Johnson continues, "and I answered her questions as best I could, which is to say, I answered them rather poorly. Russian history is not my best subject."

"I'm sure you know a lot…"

He raises a hand. "Anyway, I discussed various things with her, and then she mentioned you, and how you had met, and so on, and that was the end of that. Or so I thought."

"And then," he says, "we met, you and I, over tea, a couple of times. And now it's beginning to happen again." He sits back with some satisfaction, as though his explanation is now complete.

"What's happening again?" Alexander asks, puzzled.

"The Russia questions. Again and again. And again. And do you know something? Every last one of those conversations somehow ends up being about you."

"Oh."

"I am not a brilliant man when it comes to emotional or psychological affairs," he says. "But it would take a dunce not to make the obvious conclusion."

Alexander's stomach drops. "I see," he says quickly, hoping that the aforementioned conclusion is so obvious that there will be no further need to articulate it.

"My wife has found something in you." He makes it sound distasteful, as though it might be a ringworm or a virus.

"What do you mean?" Alexander asks.

"*Something*," Professor Johnson replies, as if unsure. He pauses, and looks out of the window. "Something that attracts her. Something she does not find in me. Attention, perhaps, excitement, understanding; I have no definite idea."

Alexander sits forward in his seat, and assures Frank Johnson that he is a man of some integrity at least, and that he is certain that his conduct has not been inappropriate.

The professor laughs, heartily, but the pressure of sound cannot quite cover the tone of concern beneath.

"*Inappropriate*," he repeats. "I'm sure it hasn't. I am not, after all, accusing you of a sordid affair, or of any type of affair whatsoever."

Alexander holds his look. "What *are* you accusing me of?"

The answer takes such a long time to come that Alexander begins to think that the question has been forgotten. Professor Johnson swings around in his chair, and looks out from the window, and all that can be heard in the tiny room is his laboured breathing, and Alexander's own quiet shiftings on the chair. When, ever so slowly, that chair of his begins to creak back around again, Alexander feels his limbs stiffen in anticipation.

"I accuse you," the professor says, rubbing at his huge forehead, "of endearing yourself to my wife. Of conversing with her in a way that pleases her much more than my way. Of giving her something to look forward to each day. Of making her happier in a way, but also somehow more dissatisfied. In short, I accuse you of coming between us."

"We are friends, nothing more."

"Please…" he says, raising a hand. "You are taking her to Moscow."

Alexander stands up. "It seems to me that this is something you should be discussing with your wife, Professor Johnson. I don't make her decisions for her."

"That's the easier way of looking at it. You have certainly influenced her."

"What would you have me do? Stop seeing her?" Alexander wants to know what his view of the situation is. He does not, as yet, feel compelled to let the professor know that Estelle will be travelling to Russia without him. There is a principle at stake here.

"There's the thing," Frank Johnson says. A slow smile spreads over his granite face. His teeth are a little crooked, Alexander notices. "Logically I cannot see a reason why you should. As you say, you are friends, nothing more."

"But?"

There is no further comment.

"Then what is your reservation?" Alexander asks.

He looks down, with a sigh, and waves a hand as if to close off this particular line of conversation. When he glances up again, his dark, heavy eyes look infinitely tired.

"You confuse me, Alexander."

"Imagine how I feel."

A brief smile at this. "You see, I can't decide what your inner response has been to our discussion," the professor says. "It seems to me there are two general possibilities. That as a man of integrity, as you call yourself, you feel your conduct has been, and will continue to be, nothing less than honourable, and therefore there is no need to stop... socialising with my wife. Or secondly," he continues, "that your intentions toward her are in some way inappropriate – be they romantic or otherwise, and that, as a man of integrity, you think that perhaps you should stop seeing her."

Alexander sits silently for a moment, for he feels he is being pushed to agree to the latter suggestion.

"At least in both scenarios I am a man of integrity," is all he says. "You know, Professor, feelings rarely conform to the 'general possibilities' that you speak of." He is buying himself time.

"True, but that is very rare," comes the reply. "I believe, Alexander, that feelings are not quite as complex as people like to give them credit for. Usually, there is one main force driving you in any given situation – jealousy, anger, compassion, even honesty – and these will condition your responses. Time and again, the same responses occur to the same situations. All part of that human condition, that people are so fond of invoking." He turns again to the window. "You see it in history, in science; and, of course, in literature. Very little changes in novels over the years," he says with a sigh. "Style, primarily, and the method of writing, but the rest of it, well…" He raises his hand and waves it dismissively at the window and then turns so that he is facing Alexander once more.

"What sort of man are you?" he asks, suddenly.

"Modest," Alexander replies.

"Ha!" he barks. "Amusing, but you don't get away that easily."

"Why are you concerned with my character?"

"I may not take a minute interest in the day-to-day details of my wife's life," he says. "But I am interested in what makes you interesting to her."

"I am honest, and direct, and reasonably kind. I love learning, and I love life – I find it exhilarating most of the time."

"Good qualities, all. What else?"

"I can cook."

A shout of laughter. "I know. Ever since I can remember my wife has been telling me that she always wanted a man that could cook. And now she has the 'King of Catering'."

The silence that follows is awkward, unwieldy; and Alexander does not know how to grasp and subdue it. The professor will not look up, but watches his own large fingers, as he laces them in and out of each other. In his mind, Alexander curses *Business Week* for that circus-like headline.

"Perhaps you're making too many assumptions about what

she wants," he offers at last. "If it's any consolation to you, I can tell you that it seems to me that your wife already has what she wants. And whom." He tries to stop there, graciously, but finds he cannot. The professor's potential discomfort is of no concern to him at this moment.

"Except perhaps for a little encouragement regarding other things she is interested in – like writing, or travelling. Whether she is able to write brilliantly is irrelevant. And subjective. The point is she wants to try. And the encouragement to do so may be all she lacks."

"Perhaps," Frank Johnson replies abruptly, frowning. "But from what I have read of her work, which I admit, is not that much, she is not a great writer. She may improve, but the chances are that, at the end of the day, she will contribute nothing to the world by typing prose into a computer. Even I don't attempt it. Because it's difficult for me to encourage mediocrity. It goes against everything I stand for. I know it's harsh in one respect, but there it is. Can you understand that?"

Alexander nods. "Yes. It's a view I try to uphold too. But I don't think you're giving her a fair chance. She's hardly begun. And when she does begin, who sets the standard that decides whether her writing is worthwhile or not?"

The professor frowns slightly, but does not reply. Then he reaches a big hand across his desk to the shelves of Irish literature, like a child reaching for a worn, loved blanket, and he extracts a small paperback book, whose title Alexander cannot read.

"Joyce," he says, raising the book. "'The Dead.' A fine short story. Do you know it?"

"I've read it. But it has been a good while. I don't remember much."

"Good. May I?"

Alexander nods, and watches as he leafs quickly through the pages. They fall open easily at certain places, those which he particularly likes, he presumes. Why the professor has decided to read to him, he cannot say. Perhaps he feels, as Alexander himself does, that they have exhausted whatever they have to say to each other. It takes him only seconds to find the place he is looking for, but as he lifts the book to read, there is a knock at the door.

"Two minutes," he shouts, and there is a muffled noise in reply. "My twelve o'clock tutorial," he says. "A good boy, but a feverish imagination. Now, where was I..." He looks back down at the book, and after a short pause to indicate the end of conversation and the beginning of the reading, he begins:

"The air of the room chilled his shoulders. He stretched himself cautiously along under the sheets and lay down beside his wife. One by one, they were all becoming shades. Better pass boldly into that other world, in the full glory of some passion, than fade and wither dismally with age. He thought of how she who lay beside him had locked in her heart for so many years that image of her lover's eyes when he had told her that he did not wish to live."

He looks up. "Have you ever loved a woman so much that you felt unable to live without her? I haven't."

Alexander is deeply saddened by this admission. He would have been better pleased if Estelle was married to someone utterly devoted.

"Yes," he replies. "My wife, Katya."

"But you *have* managed to live without her."

"I have had little choice."

Professor Johnson shrugs, a gesture of dismissiveness, and Alexander feels he could easily hit him then, with his ironic tone and his air of superiority.

"My life with and without my wife is something you will never know anything about." He stands up to leave.

The professor stands, also, quickly. "Wait a minute. You're right. I push things too far sometimes to no real purpose. It was bad of me. I apologise. Please don't go."

Alexander is burning, with anger, with sorrow, with confusion again, but he remains there. He forces himself to read the titles of a row of books behind the professor's head. Then he takes a breath.

"Your tutorial is waiting," he says.

"He will wait."

"I'm sure, but I must go."

"Do you like it?" he asks quickly, pointing at the book.

A pause. "Very much."

"Good. I had a feeling that you might. Please," he says. "Please."

The pleading tone sends a shiver down Alexander's core,

and he feels both contemptuous and pitiful. He does not sit down, but neither does he make a move to leave, and at once the professor continues:

"I like this piece, that's all. I think it is a fine, melancholy piece of writing. And I'm trying – in some sense – to learn what it means." His large voice softens at this last sentence. He looks up. "May I continue a little?"

Alexander nods.

"Generous tears filled Gabriel's eyes. He had never felt like that himself towards any woman, but he knew that such a feeling must be love. The tears gathered more thickly in his eyes and in the partial darkness he imagined he saw the form of a young man standing under a dripping tree. Other forms were near. His soul had approached that region where dwell the vast hosts of the dead."

"He was conscious of, but could not apprehend, their wayward and flickering existence. His own identity was fading out into a grey, impalpable world: the solid world itself, which these dead had one time reared and lived in, was dissolving and dwindling."

The book closes with a snap.

Alexander cannot speak. He would like to – he would like to tell Frank Johnson that he reads beautifully, for his anger has left, to be replaced by something deeper and sadder, but his throat is dry, a sensation that is becoming too familiar these days.

"I wanted to know if you would see in it what I do," Professor Johnson says. "Purely selfish motives. One is always looking for understanding."

As he speaks, he makes his way to the door, and opens it. Outside, a blond-haired young man scrambles to his feet from the floor where he has been sitting, and at a signal from the professor, comes inside the room as Alexander leaves. The windowless hallway is dark and cold, and Alexander turns briefly to look back at that tiny room where only a desk lamp makes an impression on the shadows of the winter's afternoon.

"I thank you for coming," Professor Johnson says.

Alexander nods briefly. Placing his hat back on his head, he turns and walks quickly away.

CHAPTER FOURTEEN
MOSCOW – NOVEMBER 1956

MISHA TOLD HIM THAT HE WAS naïve to think that his wedding day would be the happiest day of his life.

"The most *nervous* day, my friend," he had said. "Or the most frightening. But happy? You won't have *time* to feel happy."

Alexander buttons his newly pressed shirt, and carefully tucks it into his trousers. He feels his chin and cheeks, shaved just two hours ago at the barber shop that is in the courtyard of his building. They are smooth, but in his current fastidious mood he fancies that there is a slight stubble there already, and he goes back into the bathroom to shave once more. He leans well forward over the basin, his feet too far back because he does not want to splash any water or soap onto his clean shirt. He loves clean clothes, and so does Katya. Some evenings, when they meet at her apartment, he has noticed her walk in and throw down everything that she is wearing in a pile to be washed.

He rinses his razor in the bowl, and dries it, aware that there is barely any difference in the state of his chin, the shadow being either imagined, or too slight to be gripped by the blade. It matters little, however – half the pleasure for him is in the preparation, and in quiet anticipation. He pats his face dry, and goes back out to the slightly tarnished mirror that stands on the dressing table. The table that he will now clear of his things, ready for Katya to use. He looks at his face. It is a handsome face, so he has been told, all the years of growing up as the only child of his parents. It is also a serious face in the mouth and the eyes, although those eyes have a latent sparkle, and show a personality that appreciates irony. He wonders how his face would look diluted into the features of a little baby, and then he shakes his head, because what he really wants is a baby that looks like Katya. He imagines a tiny body held close to his chest, imagines breathing in that baby fragrance of sweetened milk. He buttons his starched collar, and smiles at himself in the mirror. Misha was wrong, he thinks. This really is the happiest day of my life. The only cloud on his horizon is the fact that he must face another two hours without Katya, two hours that they must spend apart, each of them getting dressed up and ready so that they can finally spend the rest of their lives together.

He is at the registry office, with Misha, nearly an hour early. They both stop together at the entrance, which is imposing in its monolithic austerity.

"My grandparents were married in a church," Alexander says, and Misha nods.

"Mine too. Even my parents were."

It has been many years now since the majority of churches were converted for other uses, or vandalised, or simply destroyed. The clergy and those faithful who had tried to continue the practice of their faith, were sent away to the camps. Or just shot. So many were found dead in those early days that after a little while people became slowly numbed, immune to the shock. Alexander does not remember the incident himself, but he remembers his mother telling him, one evening, in a voice choked with urgency and tears, that their own local priest had been arrested and taken away. They had never heard of him again.

Misha walks into the grey-stoned entrance slightly ahead of Alexander. The latter follows, his eyes passing over the clean, scrubbed floor, which gives off a faintly antiseptic smell. The windows are high up and the cold, grey pillars induce in him the feeling of a prison. He sniffs. A church would be more atmospheric perhaps, but impossible for someone in his position. He imagines a smell of incense, a glow of stained glass, a cross over an altar. It is a romanticised vision, and anyway, he has no real belief in God, and certainly no belief in religion as such. Both he and Misha were taught that religion was nothing more than a means of controlling the minds of the population; something that Alexander, after much argument and consideration, still believes to be true. It is beyond his comprehension how anyone can simply subscribe to an entire school of thought, based on a book or a self-enclosed set of teachings, from an ancient era. To have faith in such things, blind faith, appears to him to be a convenient way of excusing such people from any thought or reasoning. But then he remembers how he and Misha laughed ironically that instead of icons of the Virgin, they were all now given overblown pictures and statues of Stalin to worship. One cult had simply replaced another. But while he senses from Misha no existential questioning, no philosophical uncertainty, Alexander remains quietly unsure, and unsettled. He has a sense sometimes, deep in the night, of revelation, a sudden realisation of his own infinite smallness, and he feels the world itself getting smaller and smaller, subsumed into some vastness that creeps in on him from the shifting edges of consciousness. He cannot say what it means, and this fact alone is what troubles him.

They speak to the girl at the counter, and explain that they are here for a wedding, and with a smile she winks at Misha and sends them up two flights of stairs.

"Why do women always react that way to you?" Alexander asks him.

Misha is almost forced to shout over the ringing sound of their footsteps, climbing the concrete stairs in unison.

"They can't help it, my friend," he says. "They just can't help it."

Katya's uncle has arrived even before them. One of her few relatives, and perhaps the only one she has any contact with,

he is old and infirm now, but he hurries to stand up when he
sees the two young men approaching down the hallway. He
was once a priest, back in the twenties, but now he works
at the railway station, selling tickets. Misha and Alexander
quicken their pace, and Misha puts a gentle hand on the old
man's shoulder to guide him back into his seat. He is smiling,
and mumbles some words, which they have to strain to catch.
He has spent seven years in the camps and his face was beaten
so much that now his speech is barely recognisable as such.

"Thank you for coming, Dimitri Petroyavich," says
Alexander.

He nods and catches Alexander's hand in his own, in a
handshake that he holds for a long moment. The vein-ridged
hand has a permanent tremble now, but it seems in that one
grasp to convey congratulations, gratitude and blessing all in
one, and it brings a feeling of tears to Alexander's throat.

"I need the bathroom," Dimitri says, suddenly. The two
men stand again and Alexander walks him down the corridor
to the toilet, and then returns back to Misha.

"They have wrecked him," he says.

"They wreck everybody. Sometimes it is better just to be
killed quickly than to go through what they go through."

Misha's slow, ironic voice is harsh and hard, and Alexander
touches his friend on the shoulder, disturbed by the depth of
anger he sees in his eyes. Misha reaches for his cigarettes.

"They wiped out the clergy," he continues, striking a match
with vehemence, "wiped them out, Sasha!"

"I know."

"And then, our great Comrade changes his mind – he thinks bringing back the church will help to bring the country back together, after he ripped it apart himself during the stinking war, and so he says, okay, tortured priests, come back. Come on back to your churches that I spat on. Practise again the things I killed you for yesterday." Misha keeps the anger in his voice very low, a habit they have all assimilated from their anxious parents since they could talk, and now he shakes his head in disgust.

"If I were that priest, if I had endured what he had and seen what he'd seen, I'd have the shakes too." He pauses. "And then, the rules of the game only change all over again."

Misha restlessly begins to walk about, smoking his cigarette. Alexander stands too, and starts to explore the cavernous hallway from the other side. His stomach is clutched by a sick feeling, one that passes over him often, when he thinks of this world about him, and the many changes that still must be made. From the corner of his eye he watches his friend, sees the deep inhaling and exhaling, sees him calming down a little. Alexander reads a few general notices taped onto a board, and then glances at his watch. When will she be here? he thinks. Misha is at his shoulder suddenly. Alexander turns.

"My best man," he tells Misha. "The best man."

Misha shakes his head. "*You* are the best man, my friend," Misha says. "As far as Katya is concerned. You are the best man."

"Really?" His tone is earnest and the question too quick. Misha looks at him.

"Really. She adores you, Sasha. Even she can't cover that up."

Alexander nods, and thinks of her – she must be almost ready, preparing to leave. Attending her this morning are her flatmate Maya, and Maya's sister-in-law. Uncle Dimitri will take the place of Katya's own father and brother. She is missing Yuri today, he knows; she misses him often, but will rarely admit it, as if to do so would be to somehow dishonour his decision to escape. It has made life hard for her, especially now that she is marrying a government official. She has perhaps been under some surveillance from the KGB, and so has he, her background checked and re-checked. It is probably only because her record for the Party is exemplary that they have been able to come this far undisturbed.

The two young men wait together, marking off the minutes silently. Alexander is just thinking to check on Dimitri, when the old man emerges. He moves slowly down the hallway, and continues on past the bench where they sit, motioning to Alexander to follow him. He does so, walking with him until they reach the other end of the corridor.

"My son, how are you today?" Now that Alexander's own dark head is bent right down to Dimitri's white one, he can better understand what he says.

"I am fine, Uncle. Very happy," he adds, honestly, but not without a trace of self-consciousness. He glances up, waiting for the old man to speak, and he sees a swollen mouth, the skin and lips bruised and twisted into a shape that is unnatural and harsh. The eyes that meet his own are dark and dulled with age. Alexander watches the old man weighing his words. His brown suit smells musty and slightly damp, as though it has been hanging unused in an old closet for years.

"You are sure you wish to marry?"

"Yes, Uncle."

"Katya. You will look after her?"

"Yes, Uncle. I love her."

Dimitri's face is stern, his mouth set into a downturn, and Alexander feels a sense of foreboding. The old man seems displeased, unconvinced about something.

"What's wrong, Uncle?" he asks.

The grainy eyes turn to him, surprised. "Nothing. I am very happy she found you. That you found each other."

Alexander nods, and swallows. Nothing else in the old man's face has changed, and he realises now that he has been smiling all this time. But the attempted grin has been foiled by the palsied, frozen mass of skin around his mouth. For a moment, Alexander cannot take his eyes from the lower part of Dimitri's face; in his mind he visualises the kind of brutal beating and cutting that might have led to such a gruesome countenance.

"Her parents were very dear to me. Atheists, you know – intellectuals often are." Dimitri gives a chuckle that ends in a wheeze that comes up from the bottom of his chest. Alexander smiles. "But they were good people. They helped me to hide, for a while. When the trouble came. And then, they themselves…" he does not finish the sentence, for the wheeze has turned into an unhealthy cough, and Alexander nods to indicate that he understands, and at the same time tries to pull back slightly from the hacking breath that is invading his own.

"Good luck to you, my son," he sputters, finally, dabbing at his eyes with the handkerchief that Alexander has given him from his own top pocket. He raises his trembling hand and pats Alexander on the back. Alexander thanks him, and straightens up, and together they walk back to the bench that sits before the registry office door, where Misha stands waiting.

People are coming inside. Only one or two, here and there, but then, there will not be so many people at the wedding anyway. More will come afterwards, to his parents' apartment for the celebration lunch. Now, suddenly, after a slow beginning, things seem to be happening. Misha has found an official to open up the door to the small room where the wedding will be held and Alexander's parents have arrived, calling to him from the top of the stairs and he turns and comes to meet them, watching his mother quieting his father, who is apt to talk too loudly when he gets excited.

"My son," says his father, embracing him heartily. His mother's greeting is more delicate, more hesitant. She is conscious of her makeup and her clothes, concerned that they should not become creased. They ask if Alexander is well, and he tells them that he is, and then he leads them in and looks for where to seat them, for he has no idea of the formalities and protocol of a wedding, and behind him Misha comes up, moving languidly as always, and without an effort he takes over the parents, and guides them to their places. Alexander watches them as they sit down and arrange themselves, watches his mother trying to reclaim parts of her own seat that his father has somehow spread himself over, watches her fidgeting, and his expansiveness, and he smiles. It is not how he sees himself with Katya in thirty years time; but his parents' movements are familiar to him, and they are reassuring on this day, in this unfamiliar place, where suddenly he feels very much alone.

He turns and looks about. There are people nodding and smiling at him. Several young men of his own age – his work colleagues and a few friends – come up to shake his hand and he accepts their congratulations, happily and without speaking much. His mind is filled with her now, with the thrilling fact of his impending marriage; he is finding it hard to articulate anything else, and so he just nods and smiles. He looks at his watch, and is surprised to see that she should be here within five minutes, and when he looks up, with the astonishment still upon his face, he sees Misha, and Misha laughs slightly and shakes his head.

"What happened to your handkerchief, my fastidious friend?"

Alexander smiles. "Dimitri Petroyavich needed it more than I did."

"Here," Misha says, tucking his own handkerchief into Alexander's top pocket.

"Thank you, Misha."

"You are welcome, my friend."

Twenty minutes have passed, and Alexander has felt them like twenty lashes on his back. He stands facing the registrar, and alongside him he can feel Dimitri, with his trembling hand and beaten mouth, while his own naked back, wearing its wedding suit, lies exposed to the eyes of the people now sitting in two orderly, murmuring rows behind him. She has not come. He feels Misha tug at his arm, a firm pull, and he turns, relieved to have some diversion, to have someone to look at, someone who can tell him what to do. He has never been good at acting, at pushing his own raw emotions down so that they do not crack the façade of his expression. Misha can do it, many men he knows can   but he has never learned the trick.

"What is it?" he asks.

"Come and sit down with me," says Misha. "Let's sit down till she comes."

Alexander obeys placidly. His heart is so heavy that he can feel it resting like a leaden mass in the base of his stomach... She has not come. He looks at Misha, who shakes his head.

"No way, my friend. She's coming. Trust me."

Misha is not at all sure that she is coming. He is beginning to worry that she has had a change of heart. That at the last moment, after all the encouragement he has given her, she has been unable to reconcile this marriage, which he knows has become a love marriage, with her work. Misha is momentarily annoyed. He has invested a lot of time recently in making her see that this is the best way she has to make a difference, to help kill the system that killed her parents. And

SHAMIM SARIF

it has not been easy because she is emotionally aware of all his psychological tricks, and because she is intelligent and worst of all, has a stubborn integrity that she is now focusing on the wrong things.

Misha sighs and puffs his cheeks. Perhaps, he thinks, this way would be better for them both in the long run. It will certainly save Alexander possible heartbreak. But the opportunities we will miss, Katya... Misha shakes himself inwardly and tries to remember that today he is the best man. He looks at Alexander with concern, and sees that his friend is looking down, his eyes fixed on the floor beneath his feet. Alexander is deeply wrapped up in the misery of betrayal, in a cold mist of sorrow that envelops him like a shroud. Then, to his right, he feels a movement, and a sideways glance reveals that Misha is standing up. He pats Alexander on the back and leans down to whisper in his ear.

"I'm going to find her. Give me a few minutes. I'll be back."

A tiny tremor of anticipation ripples through the assembled company as Misha turns and walks easily down the centre of the room and outside, leaving the metallic door to slam behind him.

Running down the front steps of the building, Misha looks around. He has no idea where Katya might be; she may be at home, having changed her mind, for all he knows. He turns left onto the street, and he almost knocks over Maya, who is coming along the pavement from the opposite direction. He stops and watches her, and she stares back, her breath short from her hurried walk, pooling into the cold air in clouds. He waits silently, for even though she is Katya's roommate, her name has somehow escaped him at this critical moment.

"She wants to see Sasha," she offers, finally.

"Where is she?"

"Down there, by the metro."

Misha nods, and moves aside for the girl to pass him, before he walks very quickly down the street and around the corner. He can see Katya standing outside the metro station entrance, her eyes already looking for Alexander. When Katya sees him she gives a rueful smile, but also takes a small, unconscious step back. She has not expected to see me out here, Misha thinks, and she would probably prefer not to. He shakes his head and gives an easy laugh when he reaches her.

"They don't perform weddings at metro stations," he says. She makes a good attempt at a smile. Her dark hair is pulled back from her clear-skinned face and her haughty cheekbones. Her eyes look almost liquid, and they are slightly red around the edges, but he cannot tell whether this is from crying or sleeplessness or the cold. She glances at his watch, and rubs at her temples. Misha watches her, trying to maintain a semblance of sympathy in his expression, when in truth he is already beginning to lose patience. He will not speak and help her. Let her think, and then say what is bothering her.

"I don't think I can do it," she says, finally.

"Your fiancé is not going to be happy," he observes, but she shakes her head, and he frowns, a sense of misgiving hitting him in the gut. She is looking down at her feet when she speaks again.

"No, not the wedding, Misha. The rest of it." Now she looks up at him, unflinching. "The work. I don't want to do it any more."

He puts a hand over his eyes – he feels tired suddenly, and this is not at all what he was expecting to deal with. Never in all the time he has known her did he seriously suspect that she would want to stop working against the government. Not completely. Not for some man. It has always been too deeply a part of who she is. It has been all that she is.

"You're not thinking straight," he tells her. "You're emotional and confused."

She shakes her head, and gives a short laugh. "Yes, I am, but it's more than that, Misha. Please try and understand. I can't explain it to anyone else. I love him. And I can't lie to him. It doesn't feel like the right thing to do anymore."

With a considerable effort, Misha manages to bite back a sarcastic response, but it hardly matters, because she knows him well enough to guess what he is thinking. He takes her by the shoulders and looks at her face, pinning her down with a firm gaze.

"I thought this was your life's work?"

"It is."

"You mean, it *was*."

Her eyes look pained, as though he has forced a realisation upon her. He waits, certain that he has pulled her back. But she nods, and frowns.

"Yes. I mean, it *was*."

"My God, what has happened to you?" He sighs, unsure of what tack to try next. Then he has an idea. Perhaps honesty will work. For a moment, he tries to focus hard on what he is really feeling.

"You know, Katya, I'm surprised. For me, this work has always been important, always meaningful, but I do it for reasons that are intellectual. Well thought out reasons. To be simplistic about it, I have political convictions and passing whatever secrets I learn at work out to the other side is the best way I know, the most efficient way, to fight for those convictions."

She nods, listening.

"But you. You have a drive that even I don't have. For you, it's personal. They took a gun and shot your mother and your father through the head, for nothing. Never mind that they had young children crying for them back home. Never mind that they were honest, decent people. Never mind that they were probably sick and crying with fear. They shot them anyway. And left you with no-one. Now that's a basis for conviction." He shrugs, shakes his head, paces a little. "I'm surprised at you, that's all."

He has touched nerves with his brutal, obvious depiction, he is sure of that, because she will not meet his eye for a few moments.

"Misha," she says finally. "I'm just not sure it's the right thing to do. Not this way. Not like this. You see, I always thought I would end up with someone like myself. Or like you, who is on our side, against the government. Not someone inside the government, who I can't say anything to, and who can't help me, or understand. It's ironic, I know. Believe me, nobody has laughed and cried more about this than I have. But in the end, I love him. There is something very good and decent about him. He represents this terrible system, but he is not an evil man. I have a feeling there is another way to fight this battle…"

"Really?" he says with exaggerated interest. "And tell me, what is that way?"

"I don't know yet."

"Ah. Well, then."

She looks at him angrily. "I don't want to hurt him, Misha. I won't hurt him."

"Of course you won't. He'll never know…"

She shakes off his wheedling, and he stops short. Then tries again.

"Don't lie to him, Katya. I've told you already, you have nothing to do for two years. Two years. I don't want you to do anything except run your school. Nothing else."

"We only agreed that to avoid suspicion. So he doesn't find me out at once."

Misha shrugs. "Yes, whatever. But you have two years, and in that time, you don't have to lie to him. Then, when the two years are up, we'll talk. See how you feel then."

"I know how I'll feel then. I won't want to do it, and you'll try and make me…"

Misha smiles, his look almost indulgent. Oh no, Katya, you

don't know how you'll feel. You imagine you will feel just as you do now. But in two years, Katyushka, the delicate bloom will be off your new love. You will be used to each other, and beginning to be irritated with his fastidious ways, and tired of having someone with you all the time. You, who are so jealous of your privacy, of your solitude, have chosen a man who is passionate and probably obsessive. He will drive you mad. Yes, in two years, it will be so different. He will probably have moved up in the world, and his information will be all the more valuable, and you will be tired of him Katya, you will be ready to remember who and what you are. My recruit, my agent, my source.

"Fine," he says, his tone entirely reasonable. "Just marry him. You love him, he loves you, it's all beautiful. Marry him now, and we'll talk again in a couple of years, and we'll decide then. If you don't want to, you don't want to. Okay?"

Alexander tries to slow down as he approaches the metro station, to give himself a few moments to think, but he sees her standing there, with Misha, the two of them looking at each other, neither speaking, and he finds himself by her side in a second. Around them people hurry up and down the metro stairs, or walk purposefully along the street. He sees all these moving bodies around him dimly, as scattered blurs, and as Katya takes his hand and looks at him, their stillness amid the bustle gives him the feeling that their private world has stopped and that time has halted with it. From outside his consciousness, Misha puts a hand on his shoulder and squeezes reassuringly.

"I'll leave you two for a moment. See you inside," he says, and he is gone, absorbed into a body of people that have just spilled out from the exit.

Alexander takes her hand and waits.

"I'm sorry, Sasha," she says. "I knew you must be waiting for me, but it didn't seem real. It felt so peaceful and isolated out here. I almost couldn't move."

She hears her own words and laughs quickly. "I mean, the street is not peaceful, and there are people all around, but…"

"It doesn't matter," he tells her. "You don't have to explain."

But she owes him something, they both know, for being late, for making him come to see her on the street when by now they should already have been married.

"I just had to see you," is all she can say, and her fingers tighten around his, a desperate grasp, like that of a scared child.

"You would have seen me in there. I was waiting for you." He has only wanted to be understanding and kind, and he is disappointed at the petulance he hears in his own voice. She looks down, ashamed.

"I know. I wanted to see you alone, though, not in front of all those people."

"You've changed your mind?"

But she shakes her head. He is momentarily grateful, but forces himself to focus on the fact that she has still not explained herself.

"You don't seem certain about this," he says. "It is better to call it off if you..."

He trails off, inviting her to fill in the rest, for he cannot fathom what it is that troubles her. But she says nothing, just stands watching him blankly. In her mind is a series of sentences, phrases and unconnected words that are telling him things about herself that she has never spoken before. She takes a breath, lets her lips part slightly. If she exhales, gently, without thinking, will any of those words or explanations begin to emerge from her mouth so that he can hear them? She waits. Nothing comes. He is looking at her and his eyes are probing, trying to read thoughts that he cannot guess at. She presses her lips together and then smiles at him, slightly. It will be all right. She has told Misha her view of it, and he knows she is serious. The confusion in her mind about her work, her life, her parents – there will be time to consider all of this. After they are married. She takes his hand and puts it to her face then turns her mouth into his palm to kiss it. The love she feels for him is wondrous, amazing to her. She cannot believe that leaving it behind would be better than embracing it. Embracing him. "What is it?" he whispers.

"Can we go and get married?" she says.

He watches her still. It is not enough for him.

"I am so sure of you," she tells him, her face serious, earnest. "I love you so much."

"Then why are you out here?"

"I was worried. There is so much you don't know about me. So much I haven't let you know."

She can hardly believe that she has spoken the words. That she has brought herself this close to the point where she will have to reveal her secrets. The idea elates her, and then drops her again. For he will never marry her if she tells him.

"I want to know everything about you, Katya. And there will be time for that. Our whole lives are for that."

He has not pressed the point, probably because he does not understand it; so instead, he is giving her a way out, and hastily, she takes it.

"Yes, you're right. I think I'm just feeling too emotional. No-one has ever come as close to me as you have, Sasha, not in my whole life. It's wonderful, but there are times when I'm afraid."

"Of what?"

"That you're not real. That what we have found together is too good to be real."

He lifts her hand, and raises it to his lips, and holds it there. His eyelashes close, and brush against the warm skin, and he holds his eyes shut against the noise about him, and concentrates on the scent of her and the taste of her. She reaches out to stroke his head, but he does not look up, or move at all. In the pause that follows she can hear the low rumble of a train arriving under the ground beneath them. A gust of wind whirls up and into the street. His head is warm against the skin of her hand, and inside the recesses of her mind, she hears again that childhood tune, played by the balalaika that they heard at the dance on the first night that they met.

After a few moments, she tugs at his hand and as he looks up, she starts walking, back towards the registry office, pulling him with her.

"Wait, Katya. Are you sure you will be happy with me?" he says.

She stops, turns, and looks at him. He has not asked if she is sure she wants to get married. Rather, he is concerned whether she will be happy. It is typical of him to do this, to look a step beyond, to what really matters.

"If you want the truth, I was once sure that I could never love anyone enough to want to be married." Her eyes are clear and open as she looks at him. "But I want to marry you, now. Because yes, I'm sure I will be happy with you, and you with me. Despite everything, I am sure."

She begins walking again, and the question is in his mouth, so close to being uttered – 'Despite what, Katya, despite what?' – but she is ahead of him now, and he hesitates to keep pressing, to break the fragile beauty of this moment; and so he follows after her, catching her hand in his own, and consciously pushing his worry out of his mind. He smiles when she turns to kiss him as they go.

CHAPTER FIFTEEN
BOSTON

MELISSA HAS THOUGHT A LOT ABOUT Alexander Ivanov on the flight from New York. He remains something of a cipher to her. A brilliant businessman who behaves like an old-school gentleman. A philanthropist who donates large portions of his wealth to others – probably to alleviate the remains of his old communist guilt. A man devoted to his work, but not at the expense of those around him. There is much to admire in him, and perhaps something to learn – and his company is not in bad shape either, so that she is pleased that he has called her and given her another try at the deal. His telephone call two days ago had been brief and he had focused only on arranging a time for her to come back and discuss the sale – he had made no mention of the terms he might be looking for but she has schooled herself well enough in the strategy and psychology of deal-making to know when to hold back questions, and she simply agreed to fly in. She can look for all the answers she wants when they are face to face.

He shows her into his own office. There are two walls of books, mostly related to food and wine, and a slim laptop sits on his wide desk. His paperwork is stacked neatly on assorted trays; only the centre of the desk, right before his chair, is a confusion of paper, pens and correspondence.

"Good to see you again," he tells her.

"You too," she says. "I hope we can work this out."

When he had first met Melissa he had thought her cold. The impression had been a function of the brusque tone of her words, and their concise content, but he had changed his mind before that first meeting was over. Even though she has often stretched his patience, and made this sale impossible so far, at times he has enjoyed working alongside her, and he feels that sense of satisfaction again now, as they begin to talk about the details of the business. She is wholly focused when she works, always absorbing and learning from him everything she can. He notes that her mind seizes instantly on whatever he says and refines it, looking at an issue from every side to see how it can be improved, or streamlined, or both. He is learning a lot from her, about cleanness and precision of thought. He is precise also, even fastidious, in many ways, but often his business mind is clouded by his creative process, the part of him that produces new recipes and ideas. Hers is not, and that seems to provide her with a permanent clarity of vision.

"We can discuss details all day," he says, "but I have to ask you if your position has changed on the charitable initiatives?"

"How much are you willing to negotiate?"

"Not at all. I want to sell but I don't need to. And I have interest from other buyers."

She sits back in her seat and closes her notebook.

"Can I ask you something Alexander?"

"Sure."

"When you lived in Russia, did you believe in communism?"

He would never have predicted such a question from Melissa, who so rarely crosses the personal with the professional... He wonders if there is a ploy here, a trap to lure him into some counter-argument.

"Yes, I did," he says. "There was nothing else to believe in. Why do you ask?"

"I'm interested. You're the model of capitalism and free enterprise now. How do you move from one extreme mind set to another so easily?"

"It wasn't easy. And yet it wasn't hard either. The first belief – in communism – had been drummed into me from childhood. I knew nothing else, and was convinced, for a while anyway, that such a state was the fairest way for everyone to have something. But I began to change my mind even before I left Russia. I still thought that everyone should have opportunities, but I was less convinced that this was the way to achieve it. I knew the system was flawed, but I began to wonder if the base ideas were flawed too...There was too much cost to individual expression, individual thought, and no mercy for those who rebelled..."

He stops short, and she is quite sure that this last sentence has reminded him of his wife. There is a look of utter desolation in his eyes. Then he blinks, hard, noticeably, and he is back with her. He smiles.

"Then I lived here, worked hard. Rose on my merits, as they say. But it still troubles me that most people in the world are born without any opportunity to start a business, to feed themselves, to take advantage of the positive things that capitalism and democracy can bring. And I believe very strongly – and so does Lauren – that we have a responsibility to use the wealth that we have well."

"Does everybody have the same responsibility?"

"I think so, but I can only control what I own. Which is why I am refusing to sell if you, or anyone else, compromises the philanthropy."

Melissa says nothing, and he glances at his watch. He has a six o'clock conference call which is due to begin in five minutes. He excuses himself, and closes the meeting without suggesting a further one. She will contact him, if she wants to, once she has considered what they have discussed.

The apartment is too dark and too quiet. She can tell at once that her mother is not at home. She puts down her suitcase and looks down the side hallway at her father's closed door. The carpet leading towards it is old and worn out in a line slightly to the left of the middle which is her father's accustomed route out of his study. It is his habit to touch the wall as he walks along, and so the pile of the centre strip of carpet looks clean and thick by comparison. She wonders if her mother walks down there – has reason to walk down there – more than once or twice a month.

"Dad?" she says, in a voice that is too small for him to hear.

She turns and goes into the kitchen and switches on lights. Scans the fridge for food. There is parmesan cheese, a platter of raw meat, the sight of which turns her stomach, and some fruit and yoghurt. Then she turns again and walks determinedly down the unwelcoming hallway and stops outside her father's study door. She knocks and opens it.

"Hey," she says.

With a single push of his foot, he allows the swivel action of his chair to bring him slowly around to face her. "Hey," he replies. "When did you get back?"

"This afternoon."

"Business?"

She nods. He blinks, trying to disengage from the literary world of the nineteenth century that has absorbed his brain without release for the past few hours.

"Where's mom?" she asks. A simple question to help ease him back to the world of the apartment, the world of his family.

"In the kitchen, I think."

"She's not home," she tells him, a reminder. He frowns, remembers.

"She's at the movies. She'll be back by eight, she said."

"Did you ask her what she's seeing?" She gives him a half-smile, a way to soften the accusation that underlies her question. She knows that usually he would not think to ask.

255

"*Doctor Zhivago*," he says, and his voice is a curious mixture of triumph and regret. "She's in a Russian phase, you know. She's set on going over there next week. Lauren asked her."

"My mother's scoring better than me."

He grins. He loves the utter dryness of her wit, the complete unexpectedness with which it darts from her serious face. He indicates the chair beside him. On its seat are open books, and its back carries various outer garments which Frank Johnson alternately wears and discards throughout the day, according to his mood and temperature. It is a chair that has not been sat upon for some considerable time.

"Why don't you go to Russia?" he asks. "Very interesting place, you know."

"I know."

A pause. "You like this girl?"

Melissa gives a short laugh. "What makes you ask?"

"Oh, I pick things up. Your mother and I discuss you quite a bit, you know." He waits, giving her time to reply, but she says nothing. He watches her with a frown, then turns back to his papers, reads the last sentence he wrote, scratches out a word and replaces it with another. Then he turns back to her. She looks at him, a little amused but mostly irritated.

"What?" she asks.

"Try," he says, turning back around in his chair. "Try, and see what happens."

"Maybe," Melissa says. "Maybe I'll ask them. I need a vacation." Her father's back is to her now, and his pen is working up and down on the paper once more. She stands up and puts the books and cardigans and scarves back on the chair.

"Just get another ticket," he says suddenly, just as she reaches the door. "Or better yet, persuade your mother to stay here with me."

Melissa waits silently, hoping that he will turn around and that she will be able to read in his eyes the full meaning of these last words. But he does not look up from his work. She closes the door behind her, gently, and goes back to the kitchen. From there she will call Lauren and see if she will come out with her for dinner.

Estelle is trying to locate within herself what she imagines Alexander must feel when he cooks. She moves about her kitchen purposefully, trying to shake off the heady languor of the cinema, that sense of loss that she felt as the vivid screen darkened, taking with it that other world of Russia, revolution, passion and snow. She is preparing steaks and pasta, and she tries to look at and handle each ingredient as Alexander might. Initially, this only makes her conscious that her pasta is not Italian-made, and often turns out a little soggy. And that she has forgotten to buy fresh basil to tear into her tomato sauce. She opens the fridge and pulls out her new purchase of fresh parmesan. A whole piece of real cheese, not the ready grated imitation strands she usually scatters. She serves the pasta while the steaks lie warm in the pan, and she grates the cheese over the hot sauce. It smells wonderful, but still she cannot build up quite the enthusiasm or the delicacy of handling that Alexander shows. The steaks land in their allotted positions on the plates with a slap, and she wipes her hands and walks out to the hallway.

"Frank!" she calls. "Dinner!"

She has said those two words in exactly the same way for as long as she can remember. Sometimes she has an impulse to vary the phrase. Occasionally she does so. She will shout, "Dinner's ready," or "Shall we eat?" But usually, it's the same. Why this should bother her now, she does not know. Except that most things about her usual routine have been feeling restrictive over the last few days. She listens for a grunt of recognition, which is generally the signal that he will take another five minutes or so to emerge from his study; but instead the door is flung open immediately, and he is walking down the hall towards her.

"Smells good," he says.

She turns and precedes him into the kitchen.

"Fresh parmesan."

They sit down in their accustomed places, and with one of their worn, blunt knives, Frank Johnson saws at the meat on his plate.

"Parmigiano Reggiano," he says, in an exaggerated Italian accent. "The king of cheeses." He leaves a slight pause, and then: "Tell me, do we owe our initiation into the king of cheeses to the 'King of Catering'?"

Estelle feels a jolt at her husband's acuity – occasionally, she mistakes his absorption in his work, and his lack of attention to any detail outside the walls of his study, for a lack of perception. And then she is invariably caught out.

"Why, do you prefer ready-grated?" she asks.

He gives a grin at her side-stepping, and lets her know he has recognised it by not bothering to answer. They continue to eat in silence for a few minutes. He is conscious of the high, metallic scratch of her fork on her plate; she is trying not to listen to the liquid sound of his chewing.

"What's that?" he asks finally. With his knife he points to a book that lies on the counter behind her. She glances around, playing for time, even though she knows what he is gesturing at.

"It's a book," she says.

"Ah, so it's going to be one of those evenings, is it? If you want me to stay quiet, just say so."

She looks up at him, repentant suddenly. She did not mean to be dismissive, but is not sure she has the courage to carry through the conversation that will result from a proper reply.

"Sorry."

"It's all right."

"It's a book about the Cold War." She takes a breath, steeling herself just a little. "I'm reading it as research for my novel."

He makes no comment for a moment, while he chews another piece of meat. He always eats the contents of his plate one item at a time – he will first eat all the steak, then the pasta.

"For pity's sake, Estelle," he says when he has finished. "Not the whole writing lark again."

Now it is her turn to concentrate on her food, although the last thing she feels she can do is swallow it. But she attends to the strands of spaghetti winding around her fork as though there is nothing else of interest to her at this moment, for she cannot bear to look up and let him guess how much he has hurt her. When the fork is loaded with pasta, she finds she cannot raise it to her mouth, and so she lays it gently down next to the remains of her steak.

"Yes, the 'writing lark' again." She picks up her plate and takes it to the sink, feeling the anger rising through her body. "Is it so terrible, that I have something that I enjoy doing, and want to do?"

"No," he replies, evenly. "But it must be done well."

"By whose standards?" She turns on him, and comes straight back to the table, standing with her arms crossed. But he does not reply. He looks down at his plate where the parmesan-coated pasta lies untouched.

"Are you the divine authority on all literary matters, Frank?"

"I have trained and read a lot. Literary criticism is my life's work."

"Believe me, I know that! If anyone knows it, I do." She picks up the volume on Soviet Russia and moves away as if to leave the room, but something holds her back. If she walks out now, there will be an end to it, there will be an impasse between them, the same impasse that has never yet been crossed. She wants him to understand her, for once. If he can. If she can explain. She sits back down at the table, holding the book against her chest like a heavy talisman.

"Listen, Frank. We always argue about the same thing, and in the end it's beside the point."

"I don't agree," he begins, but she cuts him off.

"Just listen to me for a minute, can you? It doesn't matter if I write like Shakespeare, or if I turn out the worst sort of badly-written romantic trash. Because I'm happy doing it. And I am your wife."

"So our relationship should excuse poor writing?"

"No. Our relationship means you should support me, and be happy that I'm happy in whatever I'm doing. And then, if you feel I need help, then help me to improve. Not by being sarcastic and dismissive, but by showing me how to change, helping me with what to read, how to phrase things. You do it with your students for goodness' sake. Be kind, Frank. That's all I'm asking."

"Be blind, you mean."

"Goddamn it!"

He cannot resist the impulse to be facetious, but there are moments when she feels he must try. She gets up, wanting to bring the book down on the table with a crash, to vent her frustration, to jolt him from his sanctimonious attitude. She is at the door when he almost shouts, which is unnecessary, since she is no more than two feet away from him.

"Estelle, wait!" He reaches for her hand, but it is clutching the book, and she will not give it up to him.

"I'm sorry. That was a stupid thing to say." A pause. "Don't go away to Russia."

"I want to."

261

"To be with him?"

She is taken aback, had not considered the fact that he would probably assume Alexander would be going too.

"To research," she replies. And then, although she does not feel he deserves the comfort, she adds, "He's not even going."

He looks up at her, his hair dishevelled and his eyes pouchy with exhaustion. "Then why didn't he say that yesterday?"

Estelle takes a step back into the room.

"What do you mean?"

Her husband pushes his plate away. "He came to see me yesterday. At the university. I asked him to come."

"Why?"

"I'm not sure."

"Why didn't you tell me?"

He waves a hand. "I didn't want to make a song and dance about nothing."

"Well, you are."

As if he has not heard her, he continues. "It's strange. I really liked him. He kept me at a distance – very proper and correct and reserved. But I liked him, even as I tried to dislike him because he is attractive to you."

Is his slight pause hanging there, waiting, hoping for her denial? She says nothing, and he speaks again:

"Under that polished veneer, in his eyes, I could see that he has a gentleness to him, and also great passion about many things. A passionate man. Attentive, kind."

"He is."

"And I am not, of course."

For a man of such advanced age and intelligence, he reminds her of a wheedling child too frequently.

"You're a good man, Frank," she says quietly. "But attentive? Kind? Passionate, except maybe about your books? No."

They are the harshest words she has ever spoken to him, and she feels badly, but relieved, as though something shameful has finally been revealed. He is watching her, unflinching.

"You knew who I was when you married me. And you have known for the last thirty years. Why are you only complaining now?"

She looks down. "Maybe I've changed. People can, you know. Sometimes it's a desirable thing, to progress as a person. Maybe the ideal thing would have been for us to change together."

"Spare me the popular psychology."

But she hardly hears him. "Is there a statute of limitations on complaining? If you've put up with something for thirty years, is it too late to put in a request for a change?"

"Now you're being facetious."

She pauses and takes a breath which manifests itself as a long sigh. When she speaks again, her tone is calmer and less harsh.

"The truth is, what I just said hurt you, and maybe that's why it's taken me so long. It's not an easy thing to say."

She puts the book down, and touches his shoulder. There is no response and so she walks back around the table and sits down opposite him.

"Frank," she begins, but she can get no further before he

stands up and walks out of the kitchen, back down the dark hallway. She looks at the doorway where she seems to still see the large outline of his frame and, stunned, listens to the thud of his study door and the turn of the key in the lock.

CHAPTER SIXTEEN

MOSCOW – JANUARY 1959 – TWO YEARS LATER

Katya hurries into the apartment, throwing off her coat and walking straight into the kitchen.

"I have to hurry," she says, kissing Alexander on the back of the neck. "I have to leave again in half-an-hour."

He looks round at her; he is retrieving some butter from their new refrigerator. He taps the solid block unhappily, then looks again at the temperature dial.

"This refrigerator won't just cool things," he complains. "It insists on freezing them."

He leans in towards her, butter in hand, waiting for her to kiss him again, on the mouth. She does so, smiling.

"At least it works," she tells him. "What did Irina leave?" She lifts the lid on a pot of food that sits waiting on the stove. He looks across.

"Stew," he replies. "She says we are keeping the place too

clean, and that she didn't have to work the full four hours so she left back some money."

Katya is taking down two plates and gathering cutlery. "The last honest woman in Russia," she says.

"I gave it to her anyway," says Alexander.

"And the last philanthropist," she comments, hoisting the pot to the centre of the table.

He comes over to her, carrying several slices of dark brown bread, and two opened bottles of equally dark beer. They sit, and begin spooning out the stew, bowls full of steaming, scented sauce and small pieces of meat.

"Where are you going to, in such a hurry?" Alexander asks. He loosens his tie, and watches his slim, ravenous wife dipping her bread into her bowl.

"The school play, remember?"

"Ah, yes. And tell me, what does the school administrator have to do with the schoolchildren's play?"

She sighs. She knows this light, bantering tone of his, but cannot enjoy it tonight, does not want to cope with the request for attention that underlies it.

"The school administrator has everything to do with it," she says. "All the staff has to be there. To meet the parents, and cheer the children. You know how it is." She looks up.

"How was your day at work?"

"Bad."

"The same problem still?" Katya asks, concerned.

"We are losing a lot of valuable information. They have

been watching all of us for weeks now, but I know it's someone from outside."

"Are you sure? Who else but an insider would have been able to get so much information to Washington for so long?"

He shakes his head. "I don't know. It doesn't make sense. But they must be found. The atmosphere is becoming more and more paranoid. None of us trusts each other any more."

"So you've told Oleg?"

"I've told everyone. At every level. They're worried."

"Ah," says Katya, nodding.

"What is it, my love?"

"So the man who came to check the wiring in the building this morning – he was putting in more listening devices?"

Alexander shrugs. "Probably."

"When they find whoever it is, they'll kill them, you know."

"Perhaps," he says, without satisfaction. "Can I come with you?" he asks.

She rolls her eyes. "I'd love it, but I couldn't let you sit through yet another version of *Peter and the Wolf*."

He says nothing, and she continues. "They're primary school kids. You'll be bored. Won't you?"

"Yes."

They eat, and she feels badly that she has been so unequivocal in her refusal. After a few moments, he looks up at her and smiles, so that she should know that he is not upset about it.

"Do you really want to come?" she asks, gently.

He shakes his head. "I really don't," he tells her. "But I will miss you, that's all."

"I know. So will I." She touches his hand across the table. "It won't be long. I should be back by nine, at the latest."

"Okay."

When they finish, they both rise with their plates, but Alexander takes Katya's from her. "Go and get ready," he says. "You have to leave."

Five minutes later she is back in the doorway to the kitchen, watching him wash up the dishes.

"Why don't you leave them for Irina?"

"I don't like the mess. And I don't mind doing it."

"Thank you," she says.

"For what?"

"For doing that. And for being here."

"Where else would I be?" He goes over to her, drying his hands, and kisses her. "Go on. You'll be late."

She nods and turns in the hallway, and tells him goodbye.

He frowns. "Are you going to be on the stage?" he asks, and she laughs, her head back and her delicate throat exposed.

"No way. I'm not an actress."

She opens the door. He is turning to go back to the kitchen when something makes him stop and look again. She is still standing in the doorway, framed there, smiling at him, and when he turns to look, she makes a sweeping, faux-actress curtsey and blows him a kiss. He laughs, and she is gone.

He is lying on the bed, reading through the reports he has brought home with him, when the telephone rings. It is his mother. They want his help with a young man who works at the bank. The young man, it seems, is too talented to be working as a mere clerk, and they have asked Alexander to see if he can find a place for him somewhere as an assistant.

"He's here now," says his mother. "If you are not busy, come over with Katya and speak to him. Tell us what you think."

He is pleased to have something to occupy his time, for this evening has already dragged without her there, and so he tells his mother that he will come, and that he will bring Katya, if he can pick her up when he goes past the school.

He puts down the solid black receiver, and then picks it up again. He dials the number of the school where his wife works. There is no reply.

"Of course," he tells himself. "They are all watching the play."

He cuts off the call and while he considers what to do, he tries the number again. This time, a man's voice answers.

"Is this the school?" Alexander asks, frowning.

"Yes."

"Who are you?"

"I'm the caretaker. Who are you?"

"I am Alexander Ivanov. I am looking for my wife, Katya. The administrator?"

There is a grunt that, from its tone, Alexander assumes to be a grunt of recognition.

"Is she there?" he repeats.

"No, she's not here. Nobody is here. It is nearly eight thirty at night, comrade. Nobody is here."

The man sounds genuine. "What about the play?" asks Alexander, his stomach dropping slightly.

"What play?"

"The school play. *Peter and the Wolf.*"

"They did that last month."

Alexander pauses. "Are they doing it somewhere else, perhaps?"

He can almost see the man shrug. "Where else would they do it?" he asks, reasonably.

Alexander does not even remember thanking the caretaker, or saying goodbye, or any of the formalities that he knows he must have completed before putting down the receiver. His heart is filled with a mixture of misgiving, fear and anger. If she is not at the school, where is she? Is she safe? Why did she lie to him? The question that recurs most often in his head. "Why did she lie?"

There is something about what has just happened that, deep down, does not shock him quite as it should. Something in his wife's personality or nature that has made him almost expect something like this. There has always been a tiny kernel, a hidden part of her that he feels he has never seen. The certainty of this feeling has, however, been worn away over the months and years of their marriage by Katya herself. She has told him time and again that he is not logical, that he is insecure for no reason, and when she asks him what she has done to make him feel the way he does, he cannot point to any one thing. And he, knowing that she does love him, and knowing also that she would not hurt him, has slowly come to disbelieve his own gut feelings.

But now he sits forward in his chair, and then gets up and goes and lies, fully clothed, on his side of the bed. He is feeling sick with anger now. She must be with somebody. In his mind he thinks back to all the times he has felt uncertain about her, and those feelings are gradually refined and magnified until they are all that he is aware of. By the time the hallway clock chimes half past nine, he is so sad and angry that he is again sitting up. He pulls out the new *Literaturnaya Moskva* magazine –– he likes to look through the poetry and commentary, now that censorship has eased a little – but at this moment he cannot begin to make sense of the firm lines of print through the blood pounding in his temples. The telephone rings, and he snatches it up. He hears his father's voice, and dispirited, Alexander tells him that he has a bad headache, and cannot come over. His sentences are terse and tense, and the conversation is over in seconds, after which he walks helplessly around the apartment, looking out from every window, waiting, waiting for her to come back.

It is ten o'clock now, and he has checked his watch more than ten times. Still, there is no sign of her. She is never late. He goes to the window and looks out at the street, but there is only the night guard. No Katya walking back up the road, no muffled sound of the outside door closing, no footsteps flying lightly up the stairs. For the first time, he begins to be afraid. The anger at her settles down within him so that the burning in his stomach is now like faintly glowing coals and not the licking flames of the last hour. He paces up and down, hoping she is all right, and wanting her to come in so that she can tell him the reason for the lie, for there must, he realises now, be a reason; a simple, logical reason.

At almost eleven o'clock, he is slumped in the armchair, listless, and for a few minutes he has ceased waiting on a knife edge, so that when the muffled slam of the downstairs door finally comes, he is surprised, and sits up, wondering whether he has heard it correctly. He has, for there are footsteps on the stairs, and they are hers. Before she can even place her key in the lock, he has opened the door. His manner is cool and distant, but is belied by his appearance – reddened eyes, unkempt hair, creases in his shirt where he has turned back and forth on the sofa, trying not to worry about her. She takes him in while she stands there on the threshold. She says nothing for the moment, but neither does she walk in. Something momentous has occurred or is taking place. A turning point, and she must read it and assimilate it and understand how to deal with it before she even thinks about opening her mouth to speak.

"Where were you?" he asks.

She steps inside and kisses him on his cheek, and she can feel that he has resisted the impulse to turn away from that kiss, and that he suspects something.

"I'm so sorry, Sasha," she tells him, her voice normal, neutral. She is speaking more to the listening devices that she is sure are in their apartment, than to him directly. "The play finished at nine, and then Elena was ill. Svetlana and I stayed with her until her husband came. He took her straight to a friend of theirs who is working at the hospital. He's a doctor. The friend."

"I called the school." His voice sounds sad, the harshness falling away despite his intentions. She is so plausible, so believable, she loves him, she would surely not lie – not with such detail.

"My school?"

He nods. Of course.

She smiles. "It wasn't there. It was at the 6th district school. A joint production. We did it last month for Christmas. They did it now for New Year. Here," and she is holding out a yellow leaflet, printed with the school names, and a picture of Peter trapping the wolf, and the date and the time and the place. He takes it and scans the information. He feels suddenly ridiculous, standing before her with his wild eyes and accusing manner.

"I should have explained properly. I was in such a hurry, I'm sorry."

"What was wrong with her?"

"Who? Elena?"

"Yes."

"I'm not sure. Seemed like food poisoning to me. She ate some meat at dinner that was a few days old. She got it with rations, but it was the last piece, someone brought it out from the back for her. They probably had it in the shop for a week. It happens."

He runs his hands over his head, brushing down his hair with his fingers, and then re-tucks his shirt. She has not yet taken off her coat or gloves. She holds her hat in one hand.

"Are you tired?" she asks him.

"No."

"Shall we go for a walk? It'll relax you."

He feels angry again, let down in some way. Irritated that she wants him to relax, when it is her late return that has so troubled him. But before he can say anything, she pulls off a glove and places a hand over his lips. The fingers stay there, and when she knows he will not speak, they trace the line of his mouth, and her own lips go up to meet his.

"Come on," she says, and he gets his coat and hat.

Outside, there is snow falling, very lightly, a few, delicate, downy flakes, flakes that are barely felt when they touch the skin. When she looks up at the deep grey of the night sky, she sees the white flecks tumbling down, the light weight of them making their descent seem too slow, a pace that seems out of tune with the laws of gravity, and she feels dizzy for a moment, and nauseous.

Why is she out here with him, when they should be in the warmth of their home, getting ready to sleep? What does she *want* to tell him? When she had first walked into the apartment, under the weight of his suspicion and anger, she had been concerned, perhaps even hopeful, that she would need to tell him things, to admit certain truths. But now she has told him the surface facts, about the play, and about Elena

274

falling sick, and she can perhaps still wriggle away from his deeper uncertainties without too much effort. So why has she brought him outside? What does she *want* to tell him?

"I thought you had lied to me, about the play," he says. "What could I think? Especially when you were so late."

She has not lied about the play. She needs a good, true alibi for whatever she does. A lie about a play or about a woman going to a hospital, would be too easily found out and exposed. No, she has been at the play, she has sat through *Peter and the Wolf* again, and she did sit with a comforting hand on the deputy head teacher's back watching her vomit into the stark white toilet of the school cloakroom. She tells him this again, and he nods.

"Why did you doubt me, Sasha?" she asks. She is so much in love with him that she can hardly keep her rational mind working. Her impulse is to throw her arms about his neck and beg him to forgive her for feeding his doubts, for she has been lying to him, for the last three months she has been lying. Or, at least, not telling him everything – about where she has been, what she does, whom she meets. For three months, after the two year break that Misha insisted was necessary to avoid suspicion, she has started working again, her real work, stealing his thoughts and papers and transposing them, and passing them on to the people who will use them to fight his government. His employer. His life. Even now, on the way home from the school play, she has dropped off a camera film containing snapshots of documents. Her husband's documents, private papers from his workplace.

She has felt every minute of these past three months creeping slowly by, because she has hated every second of them. She had known that once the two year grace period was over, Misha would try to play on her doubts, on the fact that she had once sworn to dedicate her whole life to fighting the communist system. As she had expected, he had teased, and pushed and wheedled and manipulated, but still she had held firm, and even though in her mind she found some of his arguments persuasive, she would not betray her husband – she had come to believe that she must live with integrity in her own house before attempting to do so out in the world. But then Misha had played his trump card.

"Remember, Katyushka," he had said, with a cool smile. "You already betrayed him once. Before you were married. Imagine how devastated your husband would be if he found out the love of his life married him only for his information."

She had hated Misha at that moment. She had seen at once, at last, that he had made her steal from Alexander that first time, not as a test of her resolve, but to have something to hold over her if the plan went wrong, if she fell in love. She knows that it is that kind of foresight and ruthlessness that makes him such a good agent, but she never expected that he would use such tactics to blackmail her. She had felt trapped, confused, desperate; and so she had agreed to start spying on Alexander – anything to avoid him learning that she had betrayed him already. But instead, with each passing day, with each completed theft of his information, she has become increasingly tangled in the net, increasingly unable to find a way out of her dilemma. Until the weight of guilt has built up to such a level that part of her is now willing her husband, her victim, to find her out, so that she can confess at last, and put an end to this waking nightmare, however terrible the consequences may be.

Alexander is no longer angry, but neither does he seem embarrassed, or sorry for having accused her. Something still troubles him, she can tell, and she now realises that it is this new awareness of his that has made her bring him out onto the wide, silent, snowy street, away from ears and eyes that should not observe them.

"Why did I doubt you, Katya? I don't know."

"You know I love you?"

He stops and looks at her, then nods. "Yes. But when I phoned the school, and the caretaker said there was no play, I felt terrible, and yet, a small part of me was…" he touches the snow that sits on a black railing behind them with the tip of his gloved finger. "I was not surprised. And I can't think why that should be."

His eyes are searching hers for an answer. He has not used the diminutive of her name since she has returned, and there is a coolness to him which is new to her, and that she hates. She is the one who keeps certain aspects of herself aloof, not him. And now, a few short months later, she cannot even manage that. What has she become? she wonders. Something better, or something worse?

"I have something to tell you," she says, quickly. Although she is far from decided about what she wants to say, she must

277

put out a sentence that will make it more difficult for her to stop. He waits for her to continue, and he looks small against the broad background of the snow. She gestures to a bench, and together they walk to it and brush off the crisp ice that has settled upon it, and they sit down to talk.

With innate politeness, he waits for her to sit first. He is filled with misgiving. She has something to tell him. It cannot be something good, that much he knows. Is she having an affair? Is she in love with someone else? He examines his gloves and waits for her to speak. She touches the back of his neck with such affection that he cannot imagine that she does not love him any more. Then she speaks.

"I have been lying to you, Sasha," is her first sentence. "Or, at least, I have not been honest with you. Since we met. Since before we were married."

He cannot say a word. His large brown eyes meet her's, mute with dread.

"Sasha, you know how the murder of my parents has affected me?"

Perhaps it is cowardly of her to approach it in this way, roundabout, giving the justifications first, but she cannot just come out with it. He nods. It is the first time she has spoken of it as murder, rather than "loss" or "death" and he senses that there is a reason for the new directness.

"Well, I became a Pioneer after that, just like you, a good young Party member, and no-one could fault me. I denounced my parents in writing, just like they asked me to, and I followed the road that one takes in order to get along. And then, when Yuri escaped to America, suspicion was thrown on me again, and I worked even harder to prove myself a model communist, and I succeeded quite well."

She takes her hand from his neck and presses her stiff fingers between her knees. Snowflakes settle on her coat for a moment, then melt into the woollen fibres where they will sit, slowly making her wetter and colder.

"I did all that for a reason. And the reason was not a love of communism, or the government. Quite the opposite. You know I look at things differently from most people, but I have never told you how differently. I hated Stalin. I hated his government. I hated his paranoia that infected the whole country, so that it became everyone's paranoia. To not be suspicious, to not be sneaky, to not be fearful – would have meant to not be alive. To survive, your neighbour had to reveal five names of traitors, whether he even knew them or not. So that you never knew who was watching you, or was being beaten at that moment into giving your name as an enemy of the state, just because they had to give someone's name. I hated the so-called communist ideal that could allow people like Beria to rape as many young girls as he wanted, and that let Khrushchev and Molotov and all the rest of them live in huge houses and eat well while the working people starved. I hate the fact that, even now, we have a 'proletarian aristocracy'. I know, because I married into it." She cannot help but laugh, bitterly.

"Is that what communism is supposed to be about? That,

with you, I can live in a beautiful apartment overlooking the river, while with Maya I have to live in a cold cell of a room while her mother sleeps in a cupboard?"

He doesn't reply, but his eyes are fixed on her with surprise and sympathy.

"You're right," he says. "But things can be changed, slowly…"

"No. I don't hate the communist system because it has been abused, Sasha, I hate it because it cannot work, even when there isn't a dictator in charge. It stifles people, it kills freedom of thought and expression, everyone and everything must be the same, uniform. Well, people are not the same. There is no room here for artists, writers, poets. Look what they just did to Pasternak. The whole world is praising his book, he won this prize, the Nobel prize. And here, in his homeland, he is driven to despair. Treated like a criminal. It is unforgivable, Sasha. And it's not just writers. If anyone, a farmer, or a clerk, a train driver, wants to work extra hard and try and make something of himself, or if he wants to invent something, or try to do something he enjoys or loves, is that so wrong? Or if someone has a good business idea – why should that person not be able to do as he pleases, and even make money and live in the big house that now only a politician can live in? At least he would be there on merit. That's how it is in America."

Alexander cannot speak; he is caught between shock and amazement at her words. He is trying to take it all in, trying to absorb her passionate defence of the enemy, of capitalism, and he is absorbing it, easily, because her words are seductive, because they are rational. And behind it all, he is waiting, still waiting for her to explain how she has been dishonest to him, for he cannot yet see what point she is moving towards.

"Anyway," she continues, a little more calmly now, "from the age of thirteen, I knew what I wanted to do with my life. Most people don't, ever. Especially here, where there is no room for wanting. We just do what we're told, don't we?"

His head is light, reeling from her words. *I knew what I wanted to do with my life.* It seems so simple and clear, but so alien. How did she learn even to think in such a way? He is full of admiration, suddenly, for her swift mind, for her unconventional thinking, even as he is apprehensive of what it has led to. She is talking again, and he looks at her closely, to listen better, to allow not a word or nuance to escape him.

"I wanted to fight the system that had caused my parents, two kind, intelligent, *innocent* people to be brutally killed. I wanted to revenge the pain they put me through. Taking my own mother away from me. And from Yuri. And millions of other children. Shame on them, Sasha." Her voice breaks, the tears bubbling under the cracked surface of her sentences. "Shame on them. How did we let them get away with it for so long? Why are we still?"

He puts a hand on her shoulder, which is shaking from weeping now, and waits as long as he can before asking:

"How did you fight it, Katya? Tell me…"

She takes a sudden, gulping breath and looks up. Her gloves wipe the edges of her eyes.

SHAMIM SARIF

"I'm an agent," she says, simply, in a whisper. "I work for the Americans. I have done for years now."

"*What?*"

She knows he has heard, so she shrugs and says nothing else. Takes more breaths of the moist, cold air. A flake of snow dances into her mouth, burning away instantly on the heat of her tongue.

What she has just revealed seems meaningless to him, almost beyond comprehension, and yet it makes perfect sense.

"You had no idea?" she asks. He shakes his head. And then a thought begins to form that he can hardly articulate. But he must try. He looks at her, jaw slack, eyes anguished, and tries to form the words. Nothing comes out, but she hears them as clearly as if she has just been inside his mind.

"No, no, no," she says, and she grasps his gloved hand, and pulls it to her breast, her heart. "That is not why I married you, Sasha. It's why I almost didn't. It's why I said I had to think about it when you first asked me, when every part of me was crying yes." She pauses, and touches his head. "Do you remember on our wedding day, when you came to meet me at the metro? Well, I nearly told you then. But I was too weak," she says, with a trace of bitterness. "I told myself I was just being careful, but really, I was weak. And, anyway, I had agreed not to work for two years, to avoid suspicion, and I was sure I would never start again. But I did. A few months ago. It has been killing me, Sasha, and I can't do it anymore. I wanted you to know."

282

She is crying again, but there is no sobbing, no change in her voice, only tears which simply slide down her cheekbones, which are gaunt and starkly shadowed in the half-darkness. He cannot move. He just stares at her, shocked.

"How could you have lied to me, Katya? All this time? And *spied* on me?"

She shakes her head, unable to speak. He feels anger tingling in his throat and hands. The sheer purity of the emotion is making his voice constrict, and his head reel. He looks away.

"How could you betray me?"

"I couldn't. Since marrying you, I haven't worked for them actively. And now, I've started again, they asked me too, they blackmailed me into it. They said if I didn't do it, they would tell you anyway. And I was scared to lose you. But I can't lie about it any more, Sasha, I can't..."

She finds that she is calling after him, because he is walking away from her now, almost stumbling through the snow, in an effort to distance himself from her quickly, as quickly as he can. He cannot look at her, or hear her pleading voice, not now, not when he does not know if he can ever again trust a single word that comes from her mouth.

He does not return home for five hours. It is very early in the morning, the small hours, the hours that feel diminished to her, in the way that her whole life feels suddenly diminished and meaningless now that he hates her. In those five lost hours, she has passed through fear, and sorrow, and self-loathing, and dread, and now she sits at the kitchen table, in the dark, drained of feeling and of thought.

He has walked for five hours, with numb feet and a cold heart, and during the last hour of anguish, as he walked past the restaurant they went to on their first wedding anniversary, and past the bridge that they have so often crossed together on their way to visit his parents, he has begun to remember something of their old life, the one they had before tonight, and he has also begun to attribute some meaning to the fact that it is Katya herself who has confessed her betrayal.

He walks into the house, and switches on all the lights and comes into the kitchen. There she sits, squinting in the sudden glare like a newborn animal. She has been crying a lot, he can see that, and despite himself, his heart goes out to her. He takes his frozen hands from his coat pockets, and picks up the coat that she has left draped across the table. He hands it to her, and almost automatically, she rises and puts it on, and follows him out of the front door, down the stairs and into the silent street. He turns and looks at her, eyes stern.

"I can't lie to you any more," she whispers, simply. "Even if it means it's over between us. I love you."

He believes it, and he is tired of anger, and of pushing her away, and he cannot bring himself to ignore her pain at this moment. His fury and his hurt are beginning to be subsumed now by his heart. Uncertain of what to do, he puts his arms around her, and although the action is mechanical, it stimulates something within him, his love, his care, and he finds himself feeling relieved that she has said what she wanted to say, even if he has no idea what to do with her words just yet. After a moment, he kisses her forehead, inhales her, the cold skin where it meets the warmer scalp, and holds her to him.

"You don't hate me?"

"No... but I wish you could have told me before."

"I know. I said nothing because I was so afraid of losing you, and instead, I just made it all worse."

He glances around. Suddenly, even the quiet glow of the snow seems threatening to him.

"What are we going to do, Katyushka?" he whispers. "I'm so scared."

He has spent the last several weeks alerting his department to the fact that there is a mole, or a leak of some kind, never suspecting for a moment that the leak was himself. Through Katya. The realisation that she may be caught at any moment, that she may be wrested from him and into prison, ignites a fear within him that for the time being subsumes his sense of betrayal.

"What have I done?" he asks. "Because of me, they're looking for you. What have I done?"

"You did your job. You did the right thing." Her voice is muffled against his damp collar, but it is as though he does not hear her at all.

"What are we going to do? We can't stay here. They'll find you." He cannot think properly, he needs time, and he needs his rationality back. Then, in the midst of his confusion, an idea comes to him.

"I'll cancel America," he says.

SHAMIM SARIF

He means the diplomatic delegation that he is going on the following week. It is an honour to be chosen for the trip, part of the group accompanying Deputy Premier Mikoyan to Washington, New York, Chicago, even Los Angeles – part of the new diplomatic openness between the two countries. It will be Alexander's first time out of the Soviet Union and he has been proud and excited about it, eager to go and see and explore this other culture, this other world, for himself. But now it seems faintly ridiculous to him, this schoolboy enthusiasm, when all this time his wife has been connected so deeply with the United States, has been involved with organisations that make a mockery of the surface diplomacy that he represents. And on a practical level, this trip is also something that will keep him away from her for a week, just when he must be with her. He must find a way to understand everything that is happening, and make a plan, and protect her – and himself. But how?

"You can't cancel it. Nothing could be more suspicious…" Even as she speaks, she has raised her head and is now staring at him, with eyes that are wild, almost prophetic, filled with revelation.

"No. You must go. You must. Don't you see? Then you will be out of here, at least. We will be out. I'll join you, they'll help me get out. If I offer them your information… Sasha, we could do it. We could leave here."

"Leave?" He is still stupefied. "How can we leave?"

"You have a ticket already. I will follow you."

"Katya, this is insane. Stop talking this way."

286

"Think about it. What choice do we have? Jail, or worse."

"It will never work…"

"Can we stay?" she asks. "Can we stay?"

He stares at her for a few minutes while he thinks about her question. He is trying to consider all the options, looking at remote possibilities, suggestions, ideas. The hurdles they face are hard, perhaps insurmountable, but dealing with them is infinitely soothing to him for it involves thinking, deciding, practicality. Her lying, her betrayal, her pain, her reasons – all these things are too overwhelming for him to think of at this moment, and the focus on immediate, practical issues is strangely calming.

"Let's go," she pleads. "I'm so tired of it here. We can't even talk to each other in private except in the street. Let's go. Please. Maybe there we could really make a difference. We could tell people how things are here. The terrible things that have happened."

His mind is staggering under the weight of her idea. Let's go. As if they can just stroll out of this country with no difficulty and no consequences. Let's go. As if they have no life, no responsibilities, no ties here. They are of this place, born here, raised here. And she especially, has been scarred here. And, he realises, they are not welcome here any more. They are not accepted, or acceptable. She is a traitor to the government, and he is too, because he loves her and because he trusts her so much that he is willing to listen to what she believes in and to try and understand it if he can. In the end, she is all that is important to him. So they are both traitors.

And they live in a place where there is no real dissension without terrible consequences.

"Sasha," she says again. "Can we really stay here any longer?"

He thinks for a few moments, and then just shakes his head, for he is beginning to admit to himself that, despite everything, he does not see how they can.

CHAPTER SEVENTEEN
BOSTON

They lose each other in the confusion of the airport for a few minutes, until Lauren finds Melissa looking in the window of an electronics store.

"I was just looking for you," she says. Her laptop case is slung over her shoulder, and she holds a cappuccino in one hand.

"Oh really?" Lauren asks. "And did I come with a DVD and a one year warranty?"

Melissa smiles. "I just glanced in there as I was going past..."

"Sure."

"Got this for you." She holds up the coffee.

Lauren smiles her thanks, and takes the cup. As they walk to the first-class lounge to wait for their flight, she asks Melissa about Estelle. "I can't believe your mother dropped out of this," Lauren says "It's not like her."

"As far as you know," Melissa replies. Lauren has found that the easiest way to entice Melissa to talk more is to meet her short comments with an expectant silence. She checks them into the lounge while she waits, watching Melissa's darting eyes take in the people around them.

"My mother has this feisty, fun thing going on," Melissa offers at last. "But when it comes to the crunch – well, she's always taken the easy route out."

"Meaning?"

"Meaning, she doesn't have the guts to follow anything through. My father only has to have a moment of drama, and she drops everything. I mean, look at him. He's had the passion and drive to follow his love of literature all his life – even when it's been at our expense. I've always wanted a career in business, and I've built one. But she's never really followed through on anything. Sometimes I wonder how much she really wants to be a writer. If you can't get started by this age, when will you?"

Lauren stands to get some water from the complimentary bar. The collecting of bottles and glasses gives her time to collect herself, so that she will not have to embark on a week's trip by losing her temper.

"Don't you think that's a little harsh?" she asks when she returns to their table.

"No, but you do." The grey eyes smile.

"Yes, I do. Maybe it would help her if your father and even you were encouraging about her writing. No drama, no sarcasm, just some positive feedback."

290

"Maybe. But at the end of the day, she shouldn't need it. Either she really wants to write, or she doesn't."

"Oh, to live in your world, where everything is so black and white. Must be great. No trouble figuring out work, family, relationships…"

"I didn't say it was easy," Melissa returns. "I've found a way to get through the mess of everyday life, that's all. At least with work and family."

Lauren considers whether to ask the next question.

"And relationships?" she says.

"Haven't had one for a while," Melissa says simply. "When you've had your heart broken, you don't necessarily feel like jumping back into the fray right away." She shifts in her chair and pours more water for them both.

"Anyway," she says briskly. "Explain it to me. About my mother."

"I just think that she might not have the confidence to write. Especially if your father is busy judging her all the time. And also, it's understandable that she might not want to upset him. Or her marriage of however many years. Seems to me like she gets the burden of keeping things together in your family."

Melissa waits.

"Think about it. You and your father are busy doing exactly as you like, no matter what the cost to your relationships. So who keeps you all together?"

Melissa checks a monitor that hangs above them.

"Well, maybe you have a point. About my mother. I'm

not sure, but I'm going to think about it." She points at the screen. "They're calling our flight. Now you've made me feel guilty, maybe we can call my mom and check in on her before we leave."

Estelle hangs up the telephone, sits at her desk, and starts crying. For the duration of the call from Melissa and Lauren, she has managed to convey brightness and excitement for them and their trip. But as soon as the receiver is back in its cradle, she cannot hold the tears from edging out. There is nowhere else she wanted to be on this day than boarding that flight to Moscow with them. She has pictured it all in her mind ever since Lauren suggested it, has hoarded the anticipation that she felt to herself in the dark hours of the night when she would wake up, bubbling over with excitement. After a couple of minutes, she stops crying, wipes at her eyes and nose. Leaning back in her chair, she looks out at the hallway. She can see one half of her husband's door at the far end of it, closed to the world and to her. But behind that door, he is happy, or comfortable at least, pleased to know that she is there in the apartment with him.

"You old fool," she says, to herself. The desk before her is clear and clean, and the computer is switched on. There are no emails, and no bills waiting to be paid, and no reason for her not to sit here and try to type out a chapter, or a few pages at least. Except that she has decided, at last, that she will not bother any more. She opens a fresh document, and watches the cursor blink. With a sudden, decisive movement, she picks up the telephone and dials Alexander's number.

"Alexander Ivanov."

She hangs up and is immediately mortified by her own behaviour. She dials again.

"Alexander Ivanov."

"Alexander? It's me."

"Estelle! I was worried about you. Lauren told me you weren't going to Moscow, and I called you, but you never called me back."

"I'm sorry about that. It's been a crazy few days."

"Are you well?"

She feels like crying again. She realises that she is rarely asked that question, and the realisation strengthens her brand new resolve.

"Yes, I'm fine, thanks. Listen, Alexander, I was wondering. *My Fair Lady* is playing at the Colonial Theatre. Frank doesn't want to see it, so I wondered if you'd be interested?"

"I'd love to. When were you thinking of?"

"How about tomorrow? There's a matinee at three."

"Sounds good. I'll pick you up at twelve."

"That's early," she says.

"Well, maybe we can make a day of it?"

"Okay," she says. "But don't pick me up. How about if I come to you?"

"If you prefer," he says. "I'll see you tomorrow."

293

When he opens his front door to her the following day, he greets her with a shake of the hand, a formality that seems incongruous now that they know each other so well, but one that he almost cannot help. Since his meeting with Frank Johnson, he has been on edge, questioning his own motives in pursuing a friendship with Estelle. She looks at his hand for a moment and then takes it.

"Enchanté," she says, with a half-curtsey. When they look up, her eyes hold a familiar half-laugh. Alexander smiles, and leans to kiss her on the cheek.

"Is that better?"

"Yes indeed," she replies.

"Shall we?"

"Sure," she says. "Do you mind if we walk? Or take the T? I feel like seeing the city a little."

They stroll to the nearest station, to catch a T to Beacon Hill. Across from them, as they walk down to the platform from the busy Saturday afternoon street, they can see the overland station. She looks over at it, remembering. She recalls waiting at different Boston stations for her husband to come home. He would travel all around the country on lecture tours, and once they had Melissa, Estelle rarely joined him. He loved to take the train. He always hated the individual concentration on the mechanical, and the reliance on the ability and good will of others that came with driving. Trains, he liked to say, were much more civilised. Someone else worrying about steering and braking. A night on a train could leave you with a new novel read and absorbed into the mind, a good dinner, eaten and digested, and time for a sleep. A night in a car got you to a destination with nothing else accomplished.

She smiles to herself. She sees herself down there on the platforms, waiting, waiting for his train, walking down with it, watching for the doors to open. After the first couple of times, she knew that he would never be among the few eager young men hanging out of the windows. He was always busy inside, in the shaded carriage, putting away books and papers, shrugging on a jacket, waiting by the door. He was not a hanger out of windows. She never stopped looking up at those train windows though, for she liked to see the joyous faces of those boys, the breeze shifting through their hair, their tanned arms waving. Her husband was not boyish. She had met him when he was thirty-six, but even in the few photographs that he possessed of himself as a teenager, he had a dark, heavy look that precluded any real sense of youth. He had loved her, but there was never any trace of puppy-dog adoration or young, eager passion about his love. It was mature and reasonable, with a depth that showed itself now and again when he found himself caught off guard.

Alexander walks on beside her in silence, for a glance at her face has revealed that she is far away. When at last she looks back at him, with a sudden movement of her head, he smiles and gives her a querying look.

"I was thinking about my husband," she says.

"I see."

A few minutes later they are walking through Beacon Hill. The tall, imposing houses of rich red brick, the ornate streetlights, the quaintly cobbled streets – all of these form the backdrop for distant memories for both of them. Estelle walks a half-pace ahead of him, her eyes clouding with recollection. Without speaking, he follows her through the narrow streets, and into a broad, cobblestone road; the type of street that he remembers well from his early days in Boston, delivering food in those first months and years, building his catering business from his brother-in-law's kitchen.

"It's here," she says, and she turns to him with a smile of delight.

"Your house?" he asks, looking around.

"My father's," she nods. "They'd moved here by the time I finished college, and I lived with them for two years. It was a fun couple of years, let me tell you. My parents loved people. They were always entertaining. The parties! And dinners."

"Sounds like a lot of cooking."

She does not answer. Her eyes frown and she shakes her head vaguely, then continues walking up the street towards her old home.

"What is it?"

"Nothing. We had a full time cook," she says, turning to him. She stares at Alexander for a moment, with a look of concentration on her face, and then she shakes her head, as though throwing off a wild idea, and as she stands before her old front door, she begins to tell him stories of her father and mother.

She is remembering those Beacon Hill dinner parties. The light, the abundance, the enjoyment. She realises now how much she misses the bustle of guests, the casual, lively inflow of people into the house for tea or drinks or dinner. Her mother did not cook. Few people did, when entertaining. They had a cook, or a housekeeper at least. And then, from time to time, her mother would engage a caterer. Someone she had found whose food was incredible, or so she told them. Estelle does not remember who it was, or even when it was, but a moment steals into her mind as Alexander asks her those questions. A moment of memory that she feels may not be real after all, may perhaps be an imaginative extension of what she has learned about Alexander's early work here. She sees in her mind the quiet excitement of the early evening, just before one particular party. She sees herself in a pale blue satin dress (can her memory be that good?) walking into the kitchen where Perpetua stands at the stove, stirring, and arranging. Picking up a canapé. She remembers that, and complimenting Perpetua on it.

"Not me, Miss Estelle," she can hear the cook saying. "That gentlemen there."

She had looked at the back door, which hung open to the night, a block of black in the white, light wall of the kitchen, and she had seen the smudged, soft silhouette of a young man. That was all. She had not looked into his eyes, or seen his face, or spoken to him, and he nodded and was gone in a moment, leaving her with a polite smile on her face, before she turned to go back to their arriving guests.

It crosses his mind, briefly, that he may even once have catered a party at her parents' house; until she tells him that they had had a cook. In truth, he cannot remember a single doorway or alley that he walked through all those years ago. Many of the houses look familiar in some respects, but many are also similar to each other, and the details have long been lost to him.

"We should go, Alexander. We'll be late for the show."

He offers her his arm, and she takes it, as he points upwards. From the heavy, late afternoon sky, soft curls of snow are just beginning to tumble down. She blinks her eyes against the sudden fall of flakes, but the change in weather gives her a sudden sense of satisfaction. The snow adds a new sensation of quiet, dulling their footfalls and the sounds of traffic below, and gives a feeling of intimacy, as if the two of them are the only people left in the world. Together they walk down the street, where the thin lamps are spreading fingers of diffuse yellow light above their heads, catching the soft swirl of snow in their beams, until they find a taxi. He holds open the door for her, listens to her voice giving the driver the theatre name. As he walks around to the other side of the car, something makes him stop and look back for a moment, up the winding street at the tall brick houses, but still, no clear memory comes back to him.

They have to wait a few minutes for a table for supper after the show, and while they wait, Estelle pulls out her mobile phone and calls home, as Alexander tries valiantly not to listen.

"No, we're just having some supper, Frank. Won't be long. There are cold cuts in the fridge, and there's fresh bread on the counter." A pause. "On the counter. No, the other one. By the stove."

She smiles thinly at Alexander.

"Okay. See you later."

They are shown to their table, and as he waits for her to sit down, Alexander asks the question that has been in his mind for the whole day.

"Does he know you're with me?"

She nods.

"And he doesn't mind?"

"Oh, I'm sure he does." She smiles at him. "You look confused."

"Do you blame me?"

His eyes are clear and warm as they watch her; the soft lights thrown by candles and wall-lamps suit their deep brown colour and the firm contours of his face.

"Let me ask you something. Why didn't you go to Moscow?"

She sighs. "Don't get all logical on me. I don't know what I'm doing any more, or why. If you really want to know, all I can tell you is that a few days ago, we had a blow-up, Frank and I. No broken plates or anything…" She pauses, conscious that she is rambling slightly. This depth of revelation about her marriage does not come easily to her.

"Anyway, he was upset about my writing ambitions, and about the trip to Russia, even though I told him you weren't going. And most of all, he was upset about you."

He waits for her to continue.

"So, ever the understanding wife, I told him I wasn't sure I really cared about writing the damned novel. Not enough to fight with him all the time. Or have him carping and criticising over my shoulder. And that if he really begrudged me the trip to Moscow, I'd rather cancel it. And I told him that you had never been planning to go with us anyway."

"And how much of all that is true?"

She laughs, but without humour. "Just the last bit. That you were never part of the trip. And here's the funny thing. I think that's the only part he didn't believe. Because you didn't mention it to him when you met, and he sees you as an honest man."

Alexander nods. "Ah yes. We met at his office last week."

"Yes, thanks for getting around to telling me. He only mentioned it in passing, almost by mistake. Quite a secretive couple, the two of you. Anyway, the irony of the thing was that he liked you. A lot. Meaning, I think, that he could see why I like you. He thinks you're a passionate man. He's just concerned that you're becoming passionate about me."

She can hardly believe she has said it, but those last words hang in the warm air between them like echoes. He looks to her, and she sees him swallow, follows the constriction of his throat as he decides what to say. A waiter has approached them, has introduced himself, and is waiting for a response that does not come, for Alexander cannot look away from her. She glances up at the waiter and says something, she is not sure what, and he goes away. And then Alexander's hand is reaching across the table for hers, and she sees it as though watching the whole scene happening in a movie. Perhaps a script that she has written, or would wish to write. His fingers are reassuring and tentative at the same time, and she holds them back, for just a few moments. And then she pulls her hand away. He takes his hand back, too, and picks up his menu.

"So, if you agreed to stop writing, and cancel Moscow, why are you sitting here with me?" His tone is slightly curt. "Surely cutting off our friendship was part of the deal too?"

"It was, in an unspoken kind of way. But then, having made all those concessions…"

"Sacrifices."

She raises an eyebrow in acknowledgement, and continues.

"Anyway, as soon as I'd said all that, in fact, even while I was saying, I realised it was all complete lies. I still wanted to write. I sure as hell wanted to go to Moscow. And I didn't want to lose you. As a friend."

He feels tossed about, rocked emotionally, like a man struggling to control a small boat on a rough sea. A moment of bliss is followed by a fall from grace, and the pattern is repeated. They have talked about other things for a while now – the play, the theatre in general; it is his way of trying to get back on an even keel, but it seems that nothing can restore his equanimity tonight. He is not happy with the food either. The scallops are overcooked, and over-seasoning has killed their inherent sweetness. He toys with them, as she finishes her meal.

"Will Lauren call you from Russia?" she asks.

He is not sure about this. Usually she would keep in touch, but she knows of his antipathy to the whole trip, and she may take that as a signal to lie low for a week.

"You know, she really just wants to help you. To maybe help you see that you were not the cause of Katya's death."

"Lauren is a very kind person. She loves me, and hates to think of me suffering, and I think that has clouded her thinking up to now. The facts are that I defected, and left Katya there, in mortal danger."

"Did you have a choice?"

"I could have stayed with her."

"But I thought they would have caught you both?"

He nods. "Probably. But it was such a long shot, to try and get out the way we did. I was swept along, I never had time to think things through. She was so excited, and so desperate to leave, and I couldn't see another way. Neither of us could."

He finishes his wine, and re-fills both their glasses.

"I do remember well feeling so confused during that whole time. I was struggling – not only with the dangers we were facing, but with the fact that she had been betraying me, that the woman I trusted and loved had concealed a double life from me."

"Were you angry?"

"Yes, of course I was. But you know, I never felt uncertain that she loved me. She went through a huge change to marry me. She had to find a way to balance her beliefs and her love for me. She was a brilliant, fearless woman. She questioned everything."

"In what way?"

"In every way. She questioned the way things were run, the way people thought – and in the Soviet Union, anyone who questioned anything was a potential traitor. Because they were thinking outside the usual parameters. And those parameters were hard to escape. We were so cut off from the outside world. From different countries, different cultures and beliefs. It's hard to imagine such insularity now. But, Katya thought for herself. That's why she was always evolving, even at her young age. And that ability to think, to ask, to consider, is one of the great gifts that she gave me."

He takes a drink of water. "And in return, I left her there to perish." He knows this is harsh, and not true, but he is melancholy and angry, and in the mood to be brutally flippant.

"That could hardly have been the case," Estelle says.

"It's not far off," he replies.

"What I did was unforgivable. A high-profile, total embarrassment for the government. And they wanted to punish me in the worst way, but I had asylum, and they had no way of touching me. Except for one."

His eyes look older now, watery, and profoundly sad. Estelle does not know anything she can say to relieve him.

"They ruined your life," she says, softly.

"They did for a long while. It was hard to let go of."

"Have you managed yet?"

He looks up at her, uncertain of her meaning.

"To let go? Of Katya? Have you managed yet?"

"Does it matter?"

"Maybe. Maybe not. It may have stopped you moving on. It may still be stopping you," she adds.

Once again, the lurch of sudden emotion in his stomach. Is she trying to tell him something?

"What do you mean, Estelle?"

"I mean that it may be stopping you from moving on with your life."

He hears her, and hesitates, then decides that he must ask the question, that he must know her meaning, or her desire, once and for all.

"You mean…" he says gently. "With you?"

"With me?" she replies, and the negative tone of her voice is an icy shock to him. She shakes her head, trying to seem definite, and succeeding, for he is not in control enough to read her well. In truth, his reminiscences of Katya, her brilliance, her dedication, her youth, her daring, have left Estelle feeling more than a little deficient and completely inadequate. She feels that she herself has none of those qualities, and in a life that is passing by faster with each day, she feels little hope of cultivating them.

"No. I don't think so," she says, with a firmness that is overcompensating for the uncertainty that she feels inside. "What is happening between us must find a different ending. But," she adds, in a voice whose brightness and banality she immediately despises, "there are plenty of fish in the sea."

He leaves her at the table a few moments afterwards and makes his way to the bathroom. He feels unsteady, but forces himself to walk purposefully. At the mirror that is fixed over the row of frosted glass basins, he stops and examines himself. Why had he been so thrilled when Estelle had suggested that they go out together? Ostensibly, because he had felt like an afternoon of theatre and he had been pleased for a friend to share it with. There were other reasons, however, reasons he has taken care not to articulate even to himself. The fact that he feels his pulse race whenever he sees her; that the intense look of her startling, intelligent eyes watching him can make him lose his train of thought; that he wants to know more of the thoughts that live behind those eyes; that he has longed to spend more than just an hour or two in her company.

"Soap, sir?"

He looks across. Reflected beside him in the mirror is a young man, of about Alexander's own height and weight. For an odd, head-spinning moment, he feels that he is looking at his younger self. He turns, hastily, to look behind, and the young man is there, in the flesh; no more an apparition than Alexander himself is. He shakes his head slightly.

"Excuse me?"

"Soap?" The young man indicates the basin next to him, which he has filled with warm water. He holds up the soap dispenser with an encouraging smile.

"Thank you," Alexander says automatically, and holds out his hand. Methodically, he washes up, rinses his hands and takes the small towel that the attendant now offers.

"Cologne, sir?" the young man asks.

Alexander looks at him blankly.

"A splash of cologne, sir. For the ladies," and he smiles.

"Ah." Alexander looks down to see before him an array of colognes and fragrances lined up on a silver tray. The attendant waits a decent interval, then says kindly:

"My wife loves this one. Says it makes me irresistible." He holds it up, poised to spray.

"Your wife?"

"Yes, sir," he says, and under Alexander's keen gaze, a little colour comes up to his cheeks and his dark eyes smile.

Instinctively, Alexander turns away, and leans back down to the basin where he splashes his face with cold water. Quickly, correctly, the young man puts down his cologne, and hands him another towel. Alexander rubs it over his face, holding it over his eyes for a moment, because just then he does not want to look at that boy and his flushed face and glowing looks. He can feel him waiting behind him, sensitive and aware, holding his breath, not wishing to disturb the troubled old man. Alexander removes the towel, and places it back into the attendant's outstretched hand. He straightens his tie, and clears his throat. Quick as a flash, he picks up the scent again. Probably, Alexander thinks, he feels I can use as much help as I can get.

But Alexander simply holds up a hand and does his best to smile. "No, thank you. I just think… I think it's best to just leave everything as it is."

"Good choice. You look perfectly fine as you are, sir."

"Thank you," Alexander says. He hands the young man a five dollar bill, and walks out.

Estelle wishes that, just once, she could arrive home to a welcoming apartment. One where the hall light is turned on, where perhaps some music is playing in one of the rooms, where there is a welcoming smell of hot toast or even flowers. A home where there is a sign of some life other than her own. Throwing down her handbag, she flicks on the lights, deliberately walking from room to room, illuminating the whole place, except of course for her husband's study. In the kitchen, she puts on a pot of coffee, and switches on the radio. She is irritable, and restless, and feeling badly for Alexander, and sorry for herself. She knows she is unlikely to see him again, and she feels deeply and surprisingly bereft, stripped of something vital.

She sits at the table without moving and waits for the coffee to brew. When she has poured herself a cup, and is flicking, unseeing, through the *Atlantic Monthly*, she hears the slow click of the door down the hall. Something within her stiffens, and she moves her head from side to side, easing a tension in her neck that she has suddenly become aware of. His steps come shuffling down the hall – for some years now, he has ceased to pick up his feet properly when walking – and then he is in the kitchen.

"Smells good," he says. "What is it? I'm hungry."

"It's coffee," she replies.

He sits down expectantly. In one hand he holds a sheaf of

papers, which he does not offer her yet. She can read on his face a look of triumph and relief; it is the look that follows the satisfactory conclusion of a piece of criticism or writing that he has been struggling with. Very soon, he will offer her the papers he is holding to read.

"It's nine thirty, Frank. Why didn't you eat?"

"I didn't know what to eat."

"I told you. On the phone. Cold cuts."

A flicker of recognition. "Ah, yes. I forgot. Just carried on working after we spoke."

Stifling a sigh, she stands and goes to the fridge, where she takes out pickles, and meat and bread, and she makes him up a plate, and pours him coffee. While she does this, he tells her what he has been doing – how he has broken through on the Joyce paper he has been working on, and how he is ready to have her read the first draft. He pushes the papers across to where she sits. She sees this from the corner of her eye, but does not look up. She is trying to swallow the irritation and bitterness she feels. She does not want to pick up the paper, does not want to congratulate him, certainly does not want to struggle to read his abstruse prose right at this moment. She almost smiles at the irony – she, who unwillingly spends eighty per cent of her time alone even when he is in the house with her, just wants to be left in peace right now. She places the plate before him but does not yet sit down.

"Don't you want to read it?" he asks, biting off a piece of bread.

"Maybe tomorrow." She rubs a hand over her eyes. "I'm tired. It's been a long day."

This is where he could ask, if he wanted to, if it even occurred to him – what did you do, what did you eat for dinner, why are you tired? But there is nothing of course; he is simply not used to asking, and so he just nods, manfully trying to cover his disappointment.

"I'm going to bed, I think, Frank."

He nods, crunching into a pickle. "I'll be in soon. I just want to tidy up the loose ends." He slides the paper back around to his side of the table and within seconds is absorbed in it again. She wishes him goodnight and goes out.

In the privacy of their room, she sinks down onto the bed for a few moments. Then she stands, and reaching up above the wardrobe, pulls out a worn, voluminous leather bag. Opening drawers and cupboards, she puts into it her favourite casual clothes, and some spare toiletries. Then she snaps it shut and pushes it under the bed. Without undressing, she lies down on the bed again, and closes her eyes to think over the day that has just ended. Within a few minutes, she has fallen asleep.

CHAPTER EIGHTEEN
MOSCOW – JANUARY 1959

K ATYA HAS FELT INDESCRIBABLY DIFFERENT during the last few days. A feeling of radiance, of sheer weightlessness, has taken her over. It is as though her heavy, blood-filled organs and the solid hard muscle of her heart have been pulled out of her body, and in their place is a suffusion of light. It is an entirely new feeling for her, something she has never before experienced, and she knows it is happening because she has fully revealed herself to him, because at last there is no longer any part of her that is cut off, sealed or contained.

In her tired grey office, she types letters for the headmistress, her fingers playing over the keys, their clatter soothing the swirl of her thoughts, and tying her to the ground, to her everyday life, albeit with the slightest of threads. It is a pleasurable feeling, to be tugged back down to earth now and then, for it throws into relief the freedom she feels in her heart. Svetlana is stealing more frequent glances than usual at her co-worker, for there is something irresistible about her face today, in the glowing smile that lurks within her dark eyes, and in the quick grace of her movements. When the bell rings, Katya smiles, and offers Svetlana a piece of chocolate, a treat to savour on the way home.

"Thank you."

The girl is thrilled to receive such a gift from Katya. Since she has been married to Alexander, since she has become the wife of such a well-placed young politician, Svetlana has only admired her more. In her eyes, Katya has ascended to the highest level that any young Soviet girl can aspire to. Svetlana takes the chocolate and places it in her mouth, reverently, holding it with her tongue against the roof of her mouth, very lightly, so that it will melt as slowly as possible.

Alexander's last hour at his desk drags, but he stays there, in his distraction, not wanting to draw attention to himself, even by something as innocuous as leaving early with a headache. He massages his temples, his fingers pausing, then pulling lightly on his hair. What is he to do? With a strange irony, he has never felt more sure of Katya, and their relationship than he has in this past week, for he has felt at last every crevice of her heart is wholly open to him. But he is sure of nothing else, although there is not a waking moment when he is not turning over in his mind the arguments and ideas that she has been sharing with him.

He too has disliked Stalin's regime, and the people who

took part in it, although his willingness to face up to the harsh facts has certainly increased since he has met Katya. The burden of awareness has always been the problem; the sheer weight of acknowledgment – of mass starvation in the countryside, directly linked to insane collectivisation policies, of a rule of fear and terror in the cities, and of war and destruction everywhere – has often been too much for people to consider and digest. Easier to keep moving, keep working, keep concentrated on earning the next meal, than to think too carefully about such nightmares and what lies behind them. But the problem for Alexander is that now there is a change; everyone can feel it. He remembers the first, soft breath of it sweeping through the room at that party where he and Katya first met. The results of Khrushchev's carefully leaked speech to the closed congress. He considers for a moment. He trusts Nikita Sergeyevitch, even where he has been misguided or hurried, and even though there have been mistakes, terrible mistakes. There was the brutal, bloody Soviet response to the revolt in Hungary – a result of panic and confusion, not reasoning. And now, the mass planting of corn in an attempt to emulate the cornfields of America; they all have the sense that Khrushchev's primary motivation is bravado, not necessity. Now they are beginning to struggle for bread, the people on the street, and they call him the *kukuriznik* – the maize freak. But even so, his leader is working with a good will, even where his foresight may be lacking. Alexander feels that to be true. Books and magazines are being published now, American books, and more importantly, Russian ones. There are rumours that more are to come, books that tell of the hardships of the *gulag* and the war.

But then, he has begun to question the whole communist ethos. The seeds of that questioning had been within him, had been germinating through meetings and work which had been frustrating and often hopeless. But now he wonders if even a good leader and a good government can make something worthwhile of such a system. Oh, Katya, how you have taught me to start thinking. And if every man starts to think for himself, and believe different things, then how can such a system survive?

And yet, the goals and ideas he has grown up with linger on. He always wanted to work for his country, to make a difference from within the existing framework of government. He had hoped that there would be more revolutions for the Soviet Union, but quiet ones. And things are progressing; there is more accountability, a little more respect for the individual.

"But they listen to us in our own apartment, Sasha."

He does not recall when Katya actually said those words to him, but he hears them now as clearly as if she is standing in the room with him. He glances up at the imposing leather-covered double doors of his office, his head still resting on his hands, but of course there is no-one there. He sighs and looks down again. Maybe she is right. Maybe it is time to make a difference from without. Perhaps it is the only way. Today, at work, he has found something out, some news that he has been dreading. She is in immediate danger. He rubs his head again. There is no way out of this place. And yet, if they stay, they will both end up in prison, or worse.

There is a knock on his door. It is Sergei, the departmental driver.

"Working late tonight, comrade?"

Alexander shakes his head, and gets up. "I have a headache," he says.

Sergei smiles, a brown-toothed smile, and puts his cap on his head.

"Then come, I'll take you home."

From the soft cradle of the back seat, he sits quietly, mind blank, watching the mustard buildings of the central city blur past the window. The movement accentuates the throbbing in his temples, and so he faces forwards, and watches the back of the driver's head. The head is small, and fits Sergei's thin, small frame. The fragile bones and unformed muscles of a boy who grew up during the war, hungry. Starved of even the most basic nutrients. There are so many like that, of a slightly unnatural height and shape. Sergei is from Leningrad, and suffered more than most in surviving the brutal German siege. He has told Alexander how his grandfather, who was already weak from old age, died within weeks of the food supplies being cut, and how his mother then boiled the old man's shoes over and over again to make a soup from whatever goodness and flavour she could wring from the soaked leather. No one had much back then, but thanks to Alexander's father's position, he got through it incomparably better than many other boys his age. When Germany attacked the Soviet Union in 1941, he and his family were evacuated with other government-related families to Kuibyshev. By the edge of the flowing Volga, Alexander lived with his parents and aunt in two small rooms. It was a strange, short interlude in his life, but they were kept safe, distanced from the worst traumas of the war. He puts away the recollections and sighs silently. He is tired, but the weariness is not a physical sensation.

There are long moments when he finds himself removed from the problems and issues that they are facing now, in these last days before his trip to America. At these moments, his mind returns to the fact of Katya's betrayal, her lying. He finds himself thinking back to dinners they have had, evenings when he has waited for her to get back from the school, times when she has given him such detail about her day's work. At which of those times was she lying? Or omitting to tell him the things that really mattered to her? Which of his papers did she pick up from the hall table where he would leave them as he walked in some evenings? He pictures himself in the bath, and Katya outside, silently sliding documents from his bag, photographing them, or copying them, her eyes darting up now and then to the closed bathroom door. Her open smile when he emerges, clean and shaved. He is so regular in his routine that she must have been able to calculate to the minute the time she had for reading. For stealing.

He is staring out of the window at his own building, his eyes focused far away from it, when he realises that the car is stationary. He sits up abruptly, catching Sergei's amused look in the mirror, and taking up his neat pile of papers, he gets out. He leans down to the driver's window, which is slightly open to the frosty evening.

"Thank you, Sergei," he says.

The chauffeur smiles an acknowledgement and presses down on the accelerator, his taillights disappearing into the thick, dark evening. The main door is vast and old, and sometimes, in this cold, requires a push of the shoulder to open. Alexander slips in while it is just ajar, and continues quickly up the stairs. He has lived in this block for nearly four years, and he has never before noticed the dark length of grain that snakes like a fine vein of feathers down the gritty, dirt-darkened wood of the banister. His hand slips along it as he walks. The whole day has been like this – he has been seeing very clearly, noticing that which he had not caught sight of before.

They will go to the Bolshoi that night. He has had an invitation from his superiors, and they will dress up now, after work, he in a dark blue suit and tie, she in a simple, fitted black dress. She does not wear the fur throws and overstated jewellery, or the overpowering scent that many of the other wives do, and by comparison she sometimes appears to the others to be under-dressed or unfashionable, but to Alexander she always looks coolly elegant. After the

SHAMIM SARIF

ballet, which they will watch from the front stalls, or perhaps even from the box reserved for the party leaders, they will have a glass of champagne with his boss and his colleagues under the brazen chandeliers of the Metropole Hotel; a drink that it would be impolite and impolitic to refuse. And so another evening will pass, another few of the precious last hours that they have together before his trip will be gone, wasted on people they do not want to see, in places where they do not wish to be.

The following night they go to visit his parents. They eat there, a robust meal which Alexander helps his mother to complete. There are many dishes prepared this evening – borscht and meat and sausages and cheese – because this is a meal to celebrate Alexander's trip to America. He is leaving the following day, and his father is swelling with pride and pleasure that his son will accompany the Deputy Premier of the Soviet Union, will be part of such a prestigious delegation. Alexander does not know how he manages to do so, but he smiles, and even laughs once or twice, and tries not to let the aching fear in his belly overcome him when his father hugs him and wishes him a safe journey there and home. *And home.*

"Well done, my son. This is everything I wished for you." He grasps the back of Alexander's neck. "It's everything I wished for myself too, but I am happier that it has worked out for you. Well done, Sasha, well done."

Alexander hugs him back, feeling that he is betraying his

318

father with every breath. If only you knew, Papa, if only you knew what I am planning to do. To walk away from all these opportunities that we are celebrating here tonight, to walk away from my work here in this government, the work that is making you so proud. He breathes in deeply, in an effort to take control of himself, and he takes in the smell of his father's shirt and skin. They are scents that were once familiar, but that now remind him only distantly of his boyhood. He wants to stare at his parents, to take in every last detail of their faces, their speech, their eyes – to commit them to a memory that will never fade, for after tomorrow, that is all that will remain to him of these two people whom he has known longer than anyone else. His eyes begin to fill, and he busies himself slicing more cheese and handing it around. When he reaches Katya's plate, he looks up at her, and she pauses in her chatter and smiles at him, encouragingly. The sight of her makes him feel worse, though, for he realises that spending this final night with his mother and father, attempting to hoard away the details of their faces and characters for his future remembrance, is a luxury that she never had with her own parents. He sighs inwardly and sits down.

"Cheer up, Sasha. America will be more fun than you can imagine." Misha pats him on the back and Alexander smiles.

"Wish you were going, Misha?"

"Absolutely. I hear the women are...."

Katya hits his shoulder playfully, and they all laugh. Alexander is pleased that Misha has been able to join them.

He has removed the burden of conversation from Alexander's shoulders and has made this a lively two hours, full of jokes and laughter. Katya is also in good spirits, has been so since the night of their talk, and Misha's laconic humour has been a good foil for her. Between them, they have entertained the Ivanovs, and kept at bay the spectres hovering before Alexander's troubled eyes.

Now it is late, and Alexander and Katya walk home alone, spurning the two stops on the metro in order to have some peace and privacy amongst the few people who are out on the cold streets.

"You were quiet tonight," she says, her eyes upon him, concerned. "How is your headache?"

"Fine. Not very bad." They walk a little further. "Katya?"

"Yes, Sasha?"

"I'm afraid."

"So am I. But everything will be fine, my love."

His steps slow down and he waits for her to meet his eyes, and then, when he can see his own misgiving reflected in her anxious gaze, he speaks again.

"You don't understand. There was news at work yesterday. I haven't had time to tell you." He pauses. "They've caught someone."

She takes a moment to digest this.

"Who?"

Alexander shrugs. "No-one's even supposed to know. The rumour is it's someone high up, working for the Americans."

A slight laugh. "It all seems so strange. Our lives. This catching of spies. It's like one of those stories – 'Red Leaves'. It doesn't seem real." He is referring to the series of articles about the outwitting and capture of American spies in the popular magazine *Ogoniek*.

"Everyone seems relieved now, but I'm worried," he continues, with panic in his voice. "That person will talk. Do you know anything about it, Katya?"

Misha was just at dinner with them. That is all she knows, and she breathes in the ice-laden air gratefully. There might be others who might know her identity and her role – she cannot be sure – but at least it isn't Misha that they've caught.

Katya shakes her head. "I don't know what's happening."

"It means they're getting closer." He doesn't add "to us."

They hold hands, and both of them are quiet, thinking now of the practicalities of leaving. How do you plan to do the impossible? His part is undoubtedly the easiest. He will leave the next day for Washington. It will be a long journey, one plane solely for the whole delegation. Once they arrive, he will behave well and carefully, for they will be assiduously chaperoned, and on the following evening there will be a banquet for all the diplomats and attendees. It is then that he must target someone, and quietly make known his wish to defect. He must do it then, must cross over, that night, before any more time passes, for every day may bring his superiors closer to finding out who has been leaking information. In the meantime, Katya will wait until the night of the banquet, and then make arrangements with her contacts here to leave at once. And he will wait, with the Americans, for Katya to join him. And this is where his imagination goes blank. He knows she will bargain her way out by offering his information to her contacts here. But she has been able to tell him very little else, and the timing is so important. He needs detail to feel secure, and now, in this most nerve-wracking of times and hardest of decisions, he has none. Whom will she speak to, how will she escape, and when and where will they ever meet again?

"I don't think we can plan to move any more quickly than we have already," she says, and there is a tone of query in her voice.

"No, I've just been thinking about it. I can't see how."

"Good; then we'll just think about the plan and wait and it'll be over with soon. So soon, Sasha. Within a few days. Less than that." She is whispering to him now, and he nods and tries to feel something of her optimism, or strength of purpose, but his fear is so intense at the thought of all that can go wrong, that he feels himself shivering as they walk. Her hand snakes into his pocket and grasps his, through their gloves, and he squeezes it, but does not look at her. How can he leave her when he does not know what will happen to her?

Outside their building she steps onto a snow bank piled by the road. The surface is icy and brittle and her boots do not sink into it. Standing above him, her face is pink with cold, and her black eyes contain a glitter that seems to reflect the sparkling surface of the ice, refracted by yellow streetlamps. She looks different just now, like a stranger, and he feels a crisp chill clasp his heart, remembers again how deeply she has lied to him. But in America they can begin again. A life together, without threats or lies or pain.

"Will it be this cold in Washington?" she asks him.

"I don't know. Maybe not."

"Take your galoshes and your gloves, just in case."

"Yes."

Inside the apartment, they shed coats and hats and gloves and she holds him immediately, for a long few minutes, in the warm darkness of the kitchen. Then she goes to the bathroom. He hears the water running, her muttered words, perhaps complaining at the temperature, and the familiar sounds of her footsteps, and her undressing. He follows her in, having taken off his tie and belt and opened the top buttons of his shirt.

"You're bathing now?"

She nods, and steps out of her underwear. She dips a foot into the water.

"It's late," he says.

"I know. But I don't think I can sleep. Not right now. I feel so strange."

She slides her body into the water and shuts her eyes. The bath is a little too small, and so her knees are bent, emerging pale and bony from the warmth. He sits on the side of the bath, leans over and kisses an exposed knee.

"Why do you feel strange?" he asks.

Her eyes stay closed, but a single tear escapes out onto her cheek. He leans forward to her.

"This is our last night together, for a while," she whispers.

He is grateful for the last three words, clings onto them as though they are a life belt around his neck. He holds a hand over his eyes. He feels as though he is sinking.

"I can't bear it," he whispers. "I can't bear to leave without you."

Her hand emerges, dripping, and takes his. His shirt cuffs get wet, and she pulls back, but he does not care about that now, and he grabs the hand back and will not let it go. Her fingers entwine with his and she sits up slightly, so that she can grasp him properly. His head leans forward to hers and he breathes the words into her ear.

"I don't want to go. How will you manage? Can't I go with you?"

She shakes her head, a definitive movement, but her eyes hold understanding and a sympathy for his anxiety. She whispers into his ear.

"You must go. It is our only hope. I'll arrange everything as soon as you've gone. Immediately." She kisses his ear, with her cool, moist lips, and sits back in the bath.

He stands up and goes to the basin to wash. She is right, of course; they have been through it all already. She cannot arrange anything for herself until he is safely out, or he will be jeopardised. And then, the details of her trip are uncertain, even for Katya – she does not know as yet what route she will take, where she will be hidden, how she will travel, until she has advice from those who will help her. But will they advise her well? He watches her in the small mirror, her eyes closed as she lies there in the water. Please keep safe, my Katyushka, he thinks. Please keep safe, and come to me soon.

CHAPTER NINETEEN
MOSCOW

Sheremetyevo Airport in Moscow has a dinginess to it that always seems to Lauren to be somehow fitting. At the passport control, she turns to Melissa to say something, and the woman in the booth snaps at her to face forwards. Above them, a fluorescent tube casts an unforgiving light. Even this gives Lauren a slight thrill. She knows it is one of the last vestiges of bureaucratic authority or state control that she will feel here in this city.

The National Hotel is one of the finest. The marble reception area and plush carpets lead up to bedrooms which lean towards opulence. Maroon velvet curtains and a view towards Red Square. Lauren looks out – electronic billboards dominate the paved square before them. Tourists mill out of the metro station below, or sit outside, drinking coffee. And beyond are the proud statues and towering onion domes and spires of St Basil's cathedral, the shapes and views that speak of the older city, the one she has always imagined and conjured from books.

When she turns back to the room, Melissa is sitting on the edge of the bed. A double bed.

"Do you want me to see if they can switch us to a twin?" Lauren asks.

"Not on my account." Melissa shakes her head, holding Lauren's intent look for only a moment before she abruptly begins to unpack.

They eat their first dinner at the Pushkin restaurant, and the following lunch at the Central House of Writers, because Lauren has read about it in a novel and they visit the Kremlin museums, where Lauren talks Melissa through some of the art works. She speaks shyly at first, giving only small, brief bits of information, until Melissa keeps asking more questions, subtly drawing her into longer explanations. Melissa finds that the golden, gilded churches, and the heavily exotic art are becoming much more fascinating to her than she would have imagined, because of Lauren's ability to illuminate them, to mix snippets of political history and social background with art history. She is also able to point out the different paints or textures or techniques used, and to tell Melissa why they were popular at the time, or what effect they were used to achieve. It is a new world that she is slowly unlocking, a world of patient craft and devotion and inspiration, and Melissa takes it all in, her eyes intent on Lauren's face as she listens. She is experiencing a specific excitement, the kind of exhilaration she has always felt when learning something entirely new; from sensing a new aspect of life opening to her. It is a pleasurable sensation, and one that she has not known for some time.

The following day, they meet the investigator who has taken on Lauren's brief. He feels like a throwback to another time – he has the rumpled, sleepy but sharp-eyed look of a fictional American private eye as he talks them through the hours he has worked and at last, gives them the address he has found for Misha.

"Good luck," says the detective. "What do you want to learn from him?"

"We have questions about the old days. A long time ago."

The man shrugs. "I hope his memory is okay." He makes a drinking motion with his hand. "The guy looks shaky, you know?"

There is no telephone number, so they simply arrange for a guide who can also act as interpreter to come with them the following morning, and a stocky young man presents himself in the hotel lobby a little after ten o'clock, introducing himself as Boris.

Misha's apartment block is about half an hour from the hotel. They take the metro, Melissa marvelling at the stunning stations, carved from marble and stone, glowing with ornate chandeliers, inlaid with stained glass the colours of wine and jewels. Boris outlines the history of the stations for them.

"I thought people were starving in the thirties," she says.

"How did the government have money to burn on this kind of thing?"

"They didn't," Lauren replies. "But they wanted to make a statement to the world. What amazing things socialism could achieve – the most spectacular underground system ever. Oh, and the tunnels could always come in handy as bomb shelters."

"Dual purpose. I guess that justifies it," says Melissa, with heavy irony.

But Lauren does not reply; she is thinking now about what she wants to ask Misha, and how she will approach the subject of Katya. She does not want to shock Misha, but will try and lead in gently, once the greetings and catching up are over with. She is hardly aware that they have stopped before a building of sandy yellow brick. It is surrounded by others that are much the same, but on the ground level of this one is a restaurant. The windows of the kitchen and dining room are thrown open to the spring air, but a slight haze of stale smoke hangs around the ceiling. At this time of the morning, the place looks deserted.

The guide hands Melissa back the piece of paper with Misha's address on it, and starts up the stairwell.

"It should be here somewhere," he assures them. They follow him through a dim, grey walkway that has a residual smell of old rubbish about it, and he finds the door. Lauren takes an audible breath, and Boris smiles, pausing with his hand poised to knock.

"Ready?"

She nods, and Melissa touches her back as if to reassure her. Boris taps politely, and they wait. There is nothing. He knocks again; then finally pounds the wood with his fist, and now they hear someone grumbling, a shuffling on the other side of the door. It is flung open, and an old man peers at Boris. The guide asks the man his name.

"Mikhail Ardonov," is the reply. "Misha, to my friends," he adds. "And to the ladies." He speaks in Russian, and gives Melissa and Lauren a quick, appreciative glance before dissolving into a racking cough. His breath is eye-wateringly acidic, and Melissa turns away her head as discreetly as possible.

Boris has been given his instructions beforehand, and he explains that the two women are researching and wish to speak with him, and after a couple of moments conferring, they are led inside. The apartment is dark and damp-smelling, but over the staleness of the air, the smell of vodka persists, pervasive, almost antiseptic.

There are only three chairs in the living room, so somewhat gingerly, Boris sits on the floor. There is a greasiness to the carpet which has come from years of dirt and unmopped spillages, and there is one armchair that clearly belongs to Misha. It is covered in worn green velour, and is caved in on the seat. The coffee table beside it holds cigarettes, two used, finger-smudged vodka glasses, a newspaper and a remote control for the television.

The old man's chair faces Melissa, and it is to her that he directs his initial comments, in Russian.

"Would you ask him if he speaks any English?" Melissa says to Boris. The question is relayed and Misha shakes his head.

"*Niet*. No. Good morning," he adds, in a hearty bellow. "Goodbye."

"Very good," comments Melissa.

"That's all he can say, in English," says Boris. "Don't worry, that's why I'm here."

Misha attempts to smooth back his hair, which is unruly, and mostly black, though heavily and dramatically streaked with silver, and he asks if the women are from England.

"No," says Lauren. "From America."

Misha hums the opening bars of "The Star-Spangled Banner." Melissa sighs slightly.

"Where are you staying? One of the nice hotels, hey? The Metropole?" Lauren catches the trace of sarcasm in his tone.

"The National."

Misha shrugs as if she is splitting hairs.

"It's been a long time since two such pretty women knocked at my door. What are you researching?"

Lauren clears her throat. "I'm researching my aunt's life."

"Your aunt? Why did you choose me to talk to?"

He looks at her, and as he does so, the end of his last sentence falters slightly, so that Boris waits to see if there is anything else. But Misha has fallen silent, and is staring now, peering at the woman sitting to his right. He leans across and pushes the curtains further open, so that the room is suddenly brightened by the slanted sunlight. Lauren shifts a little in her chair, and watches him back, taking in his yellowed skin, and gaunt cheeks. Now Misha's hand is reaching for his glass, and bringing it to his lips, but it is empty. Boris says something to him, offering water perhaps, and Misha just holds out the glass. The guide takes it and disappears into the kitchen. When Misha opens his mouth, only a wheeze emerges.

"Are you okay, Mr Ardonov?"

Misha ignores Lauren and puts his fingers over his eyes. He seems reluctant to take them away but does so at last, for Boris is pushing a glass of water into his hand. Misha takes a sip, and speaks to the interpreter.

"She reminds me of someone. Someone I knew long ago." When Boris tells them this, Lauren can barely keep still.

"Who?" she asks.

Misha shakes his head. "Who are you?"

"I am Lauren Grinkov."

There is a long silence. Misha sips at his water, then stands up, throws the remainder of the liquid into a dying pot plant, and extracts a bottle of vodka from the bureau behind him.

"What do you want?"

"I want to talk about Katya. My aunt. I am her brother Yuri's daughter."

"I don't remember anything from those days. It was a long time ago."

Lauren glances to Melissa – this is not how she has expected the meeting to progress. Melissa turns back to Misha and speaks.

"Mr Ardonov, we've come a long way. If you could help us out, just a little."

"You see," adds Lauren. "I'm very close to my uncle, Alexander. And it is he that I am concerned about." They wait for Boris to translate.

"Sasha is alive?" Misha says in almost a whisper.

"Yes, he is. He lives in Boston now. He was thinking about coming with us, but… anyway, I have a letter for you. From him."

She listens to the overlapping of Boris's translation, and waits expectantly, but there is no response.

"He's happy and well," Lauren continues, "but I feel he has never ever really recovered from Katya's death. And a lot of that is because he does not really know what happened to her. In fact, he blames himself for leaving her here, in danger. Not that he had much choice. From what we understand."

Misha laughs mirthlessly. "Everyone has choices in life. He ran off as quickly as he could."

"So you do remember?" Melissa says. Immediately, she asks Boris not to translate that remark, but Misha casts her a hostile glance – her tone is plain in any language.

Lauren speaks again, her voice even, her manner persuasive.

"The fact is that my uncle was gone, and you were her best friend here. Is there anything you can tell me about the time leading up to her death? Did you see her, or talk to her?"

"I told you, I don't remember. This all happened thirty or forty years ago. And I have spent those forty years drinking too much vodka. And now the doctors tell me I don't have much time left. A few months, maybe. It kills the liver and then the brain, you know, vodka. And sometimes, if one has good luck, it kills the memory first."

He stares off into the middle distance while Boris relays this to the women.

"I don't buy it," says Melissa, quietly. "He's sharp as a tack."

"Then why would he be so difficult about talking to us?"

"Beats me. But he hasn't even looked at you since he noticed who you look like."

Lauren nods to Boris to let him know that she is ready for him to translate again. But before she says anything, she stands up and walks the two paces to Misha's chair. She squats down before the old man, so that he has nowhere to look except at her face. She speaks directly to Misha, and her voice is soft, so that Boris has to concentrate hard to hear her.

"I know this must be difficult for you. But my aunt Katya is important to me too. I really need to know what happened to her."

His eyes dart away, and fix down on his knees. There is a slight shake to his hand, which Lauren has not noticed earlier.

"What difference does it make now?" he says.

Lauren sighs. "You sound just like my uncle. It could make all the difference in the world. Mr Ardonov – imagine being him. Imagine losing the love of your life, and then spending every day of your life blaming yourself for her death."

He is looking straight at her now, with sharp, hollow eyes like caverns, almost devouring her features. The expression on his face shows the difficulty of the task he has set himself. Then, suddenly, a veined hand reaches up and pushes at Lauren's shoulder, almost putting her off-balance. She stands and takes a step back, shocked.

"You must leave now. I have nothing more to tell you." His shaking hand goes to his glass again and he takes a drink. When he looks up, something in his face has hardened.

"Goodbye," he adds, harshly, in English.

Boris shrugs at Melissa and gets up, but Melissa waits for Lauren to make a move before she too stands up. They pick up their bags, and after a moment's consideration, Lauren takes out a package and hands it to Misha.

"Here, Mr. Ardonov. To say thank you for seeing us."

He does not reach for it, or even look at her, so she leaves it balanced on the edge of the table beside him. On top of the package, she leaves the letter that Alexander has given her, and a card from their hotel.

"We're here for four more days. At the National. We leave on Saturday. If you decide you can remember anything."

There is no response, so Boris thanks him and they leave.

For some time after they have gone, Misha sits motionless in his chair, watching dots of dust spiralling down through the same shaft of sunlight that revealed Katya's niece's face to him. Finally, he takes another drink, and rips open the envelope. The note is short, but he leaves it on his lap where it falls for a moment, before flicking it open to read it.

"Misha –

It has been too long that we have not been in contact, and I am sorry for it. You will have met Lauren by now, and will know that she is Katya's niece. Perhaps you will have seen it in her face before she even explained. She is like a daughter to me – the daughter I wish I could have had with Katya. I know you will treat her well, but I ask you, in memory of our old, long friendship, to look after her and help her if you can in her quest to find out what happened to our Katyushka. There is not a day when I don't miss her, Misha. I know you must too. I also know you must have done all you could to help her, and I have never thanked you for that. I thank you now, my friend."

There are a couple more lines to the letter, but Misha does not read them. He crumples the note in his hand and puts it on the table beside him, and puts a hand to his eyes, where tears are beginning to pool. He cannot believe this. He can count on the fingers of one hand the times he has cried during his entire life. As if to divert his own attention, he roughly pulls open the brown paper on the package and leaves the hotel card where it falls, on the floor. The wrapping holds a frame, and when he turns it around, he finds a small brush and ink portrait of Katya, signed by Lauren. A tiny, animalistic sound is forced from him, almost involuntarily, for the likeness is incredible. He lets the picture drop onto his lap and covers his eyes again. His shoulders give an involuntary shake. Then, with a sudden force of emotion and energy, he picks up the frame and hurls it across the room. It bounces and lands face down on the dirty carpet, but does not break. Leaving it there, he staggers into the kitchen for vodka.

The night-time darkness in the room is thick, unalleviated by any glow or shadow from outside, for the crimson velvet drapes are heavy and full. Lauren lies in bed, thankful for the blackness blanketing her. Her disappointment at the meeting with Misha is deep and the searing touch of it is only now beginning to recede. She turns from side to side, wondering what it is about Katya that is so hard for the people who knew her to speak of. Beside her, Melissa shifts a little, and Lauren turns towards her. Her shape has become discernible now, as her eyes have adjusted to the darkness. Her back is to her, and she can see the slight rise and fall of her arm, moving with her gentle breathing.

Slowly, giving herself time to pull back if she wishes, Lauren reaches out her arm beneath the covers so that her hand lays almost flat on Melissa's back. She can feel a calm stillness in the body she is touching, so that she knows that Melissa is awake and aware of her touch. Gently she lets her fingers move down her back, caressing the bare skin, feeling along the length of the spine to the hollow of her lower back. There is a slight shiver beneath her fingers, and she lets them rest here for a few long seconds. Then she traces a line back upwards again, until she is stroking the base of Melissa's neck. Without another thought, Lauren shifts closer to her, and her lips follow the line her hand has just taken.

"Are you sure about this?" Melissa says quietly.

"Yes."

Melissa says nothing more, and Lauren cannot trace her feelings.

"Do you want me to stop?" she asks.

Gently, lightly, so that she will not disturb the subtle spell of this moment, Melissa turns around so that her hands can reach up to enclose Lauren's face.

"No," she says. "Don't stop."

For Melissa, the days have passed in a strange combination of heightened awareness, and blurred confusion. Her laptop has been left untouched for the week, and her impressions of Moscow remain caught up with the sight and touch and scent of Lauren. She dislikes the feeling that she is slipping out of control, but there is also a new pleasure to even everyday sensations now that she does not want to give up. She takes a soothing gulp of black coffee and through the doors of the restaurant watches the occasional activity in the lobby. It is before seven o'clock in the morning, and too early for breakfast to be served, but she has found someone to bring her a pot of coffee. She is an early riser, has always been, and today she has been too restless to stay in bed alongside the slumbering Lauren. Their packing is almost complete, and they have several hours before their flight. She has a taste for solitude sometimes, for time alone to think things through, a trait she has inherited from her father.

The sound of talking attracts her attention. There are two men in the lobby now, and she looks up as she savours the warmth of the cup in her hands. An old man is making his way past the doorman. He has been stopped because he is not well-dressed; or rather, his clothes look old and unwashed. But he is inside now, and making his way to the desk clerk. With a jolt, Melissa recognises Misha. Putting down her cup, she goes out to the lobby, where she watches from a discreet distance. Misha is carrying a small, battered brown suitcase. He puts this down on the counter before the disconcerted concierge, and the two men have a voluble discussion. The concierge appears reluctant to take the case, and makes Misha open it. He does so, finally, and she can make out nothing more than a small pile of clothes and an envelope. The case is examined and snapped shut again. She hears Lauren's surname being mentioned, and the concierge scribbles a note. Before he has even finished writing, Misha is turning and walking back out through the lobby.

He has a slight limp from his hip that makes him walk slowly, and Melissa watches him, computing, deciding. It takes only a second for her to hurry across the room and cut him off before he reaches the front entrance. He stares at her, then rolls his eyes as though he cannot believe his bad luck and tries to sidestep her. She is asking him to wait, saying that she must speak with him, and the doorman steps in to halt the old man. Misha stops with a frustrated gesture, and looks furiously at Melissa, then barks something at her. She looks at the doorman.

"He wants to know what you want with him?" the doorman obliges.

"I just want to talk to him. Will you ask him if he will have a cup of coffee with me?"

The request is forwarded, and Misha shakes his head vigorously.

"He says he must go. He is tired and old. You must please leave him alone."

"I can't. Tell him I will follow him until he agrees to speak with me."

Misha lets out a stream of bad-tempered invective that the doorman does not care to translate, and he takes a further step away from them, but Melissa has already slipped a fifty dollar bill into the doorman's hand. With a quick, belligerent movement, he blocks off the door and all but pushes Misha back inside. Melissa reaches for Misha's arm. It is thin and frail under his grimy, grey jacket.

"Please," she says. "Just a few minutes."

Misha pulls his arm away, and sizes up the fit, young doorman.

"How much did she give you, bastard?" he asks him. The doorman smiles and moves his large frame more squarely in front of the door.

With an irritated sigh, he turns suddenly and walks towards the restaurant, and Melissa follows, stopping to ask the concierge if he will translate for them. The man seems reluctant, but comes out from behind his desk.

"Oh, and bring that suitcase with you," Melissa says, pointing to the brown case that waits on the counter.

"It is for Miss Grinkov," says the concierge, by way of asserting himself.

Melissa picks up the hotel phone and dials their room.

"I need you down in the restaurant. Quickly," she says, and she hangs up, anxious to ensure that Misha does not get away. But he is sitting sullenly at the first table, just inside the restaurant doors. She sits down beside him, with the concierge across from them. The suitcase has been left behind, she notes, but there will be time to deal with that later.

"Would you like coffee?" Melissa asks.

Misha glances at his watch, as though hoping he might be able to request a real drink. He waves a hand impatiently, and shakes his head.

"What do you want?" the concierge asks Melissa on his behalf.

"I want to know why you came here. What did you leave for Lauren?"

"It's there. Go and see if you want to."

"Why didn't you ask to see Lauren?"

Misha's anger seems to seep away slightly, and his eyes hold a suggestion of sorrow, even fear.

"I just wanted to leave the case for her. That's all. I am a dying man, I have one last thing to do, and now I have done it. Okay?"

His aggression has no effect whatsoever on Melissa's composure.

"Why didn't you ask to see Lauren?" she says again.

Misha looks at her, irritated, but his voice when he replies is lower this time.

"I don't want to see her face again."

"Because she looks like Katya?"

Misha does not bother to reply. The concierge repeats the question, and he looks away.

"Why does that upset you so much? Why do you feel so badly when you remember Katya?"

Still, Misha looks away, at the floor, but now the fierceness of his gaze is replaced with something deeper – again that mixture of sadness and fear, Melissa feels. Behind the old man, Lauren has come into the restaurant. She has washed up, and the hair around her face is damp, but her eyes still hold a haze of sleepiness. She looks at Misha in surprise.

"Mr Ardonov?"

Misha jumps in his chair. Lauren's hand goes to his back, soothing, reassuring, but her touch and her anxious gaze only seem to upset him more.

"Look at her," Melissa says. She nods at the concierge, who is watching in confusion, and has forgotten to translate.

Misha disregards the request. "Tell him again," instructs Melissa. "Look at her. Look!"

He looks up. Lauren's face is just above his, her hand still on his shoulder, and he looks into her eyes, takes in her nose and mouth and chin. His hand comes up and clutches at her arm. The pain and horror in his own face appals the women as they watch.

"What is it?" Lauren asks, quietly. "What is it?"

Melissa is looking from Lauren to Misha, gauging. They are near a breakthrough of some kind, that much she can sense, but how not to let it slip away?

"You know something about her death, don't you?"

The concierge looks shocked, but she repeats the question and instructs him to translate it. Misha hears it and at last his eyes pull away from Lauren. His eyes are watery; though whether these are tears, or the familiar rheumy moistness of age and alcohol, Melissa cannot tell.

"You know something."

"Melissa…?"

"Trust me on this one," Melissa says brusquely, and her eyes never leave Misha. "She's Alexander's niece. Your best friend's niece. Don't you owe him and Katya that much?" She pauses. In the quiet of the vast room, they can hear only the clinking of plates being laid out.

"You're dying," Melissa says softly and he looks at her, a wounded glance, as if she has taken too low a shot at him. But she remains unfazed. "You're dying," she repeats, her voice clear. "If you clear your conscience, what do you have to lose?"

Misha clears his throat, and lets go of Lauren's arm. He mutters something to the concierge.

"He says he will have some coffee now."

Melissa nods, and orders it from the waitress who is

setting up tables at the other end of the room. Misha is speaking again.

"And he says that you should sit down." The concierge indicates a chair for Lauren. "Because what he has to tell you may take a while, and now he is ready to talk."

CHAPTER TWENTY

MOSCOW – JANUARY 1959

KATYA HAS BEEN LIVING ON HER NERVES for the past two days, and she is feeling light-headed and a little fearful, now that Alexander has left, and his own anxiety is not there to balance her optimism. The café, at least, is warm and smoky and crowded, and the steam that collects on the windows to her right somehow gives her a feeling of reassurance, and safety, as though the vapour is wrapping her up and enclosing her.

He will have arrived in Washington. In her mind, she has followed him through each possible hour of his day. Right now, he should be at the opening banquet. It will be ending, or may already have ended, and this is when he will have made his move. A flicker of worry passes over her face, then she nods to herself. He will have already crossed over by now. He is safe and well, and waiting, that is all she must believe and remember. And so now it is up to her. Across the table, Misha watches her, clear-eyed, as though reading her thoughts, and he smiles, a grin of encouragement, when she glances back at him.

She pours him more tea, and he helps himself to another spoonful of jam. Then he takes another, with a wink at her, and she laughs and pushes the saucer nearer to him. He leans forward again.

"So. Do you miss him?"

"Yes."

"Already?" Misha laughs.

"I know, but I can't help it."

The smile leaves his eyes and they look at each other, serious now. He is thinking about what she has told him, just now, here in this café, full of after-work drinkers. He had not seen any of it coming. That Sasha, of all people, has defected. Or is about to. That she is planning to join him, and needs help. And that this has been decided because someone has been caught, and does he know who it is? It has taken him some minutes to recover himself after the surprise of all this information, and to get his thoughts in order. He does not know quite what to do. He will have to take instructions, he will be forced to. She wants to leave now, needs to in fact, but he has explained to her that it is difficult to arrange things that quickly. And she has nodded, absently, almost without hearing him. She has that look of removal in her eyes now, as she watches him drink his tea. It is as though she has already gone, escaped. He can tell that there can be no pulling her back now – she is too far gone to be brought back by any means. There is a lightness to her, an excitement, that he has never seen previously, and that makes her look more beautiful than he has ever noticed before. He puts his glass down, gently, onto the tiny saucer, and reaches for her hand. It is an affectionate gesture, a touch between friends, and she will think nothing of it. He looks at the fingers lying in his palm, and he caresses them slightly with his thumb. If he holds on any longer, she will begin to be uneasy about his touch, will feel at first simply that it is not quite appropriate, and then she will begin to understand the depth of repressed emotion that lies behind it. And then she will pull away, embarrassed, confused, perhaps even repulsed by him. He lets go abruptly, and takes up his glass again, draining the dark amber liquid. He looks at her again, and now his gaze is cooler and more distant, which is good. For a moment, he is proud of himself. He has always been able to find the way to let go when he has needed to.

"I need to get things organised," he says. "Give me a couple of hours."

This alarms her. "No. The moment they know he's gone, they'll come and get me."

"One hour, then. Meet me back here in an hour. You must prepare. You don't know how long and hard this journey is going to be."

From beneath the table, she slides out a small brown suitcase. "I am prepared. Here. This is everything I'm taking. I'll wait here. I feel better waiting here. If I go home, anything could happen."

He watches her for a few moments, considering possibilities, thinking through the best strategy.

"You're right. Wait here then. I'll be as quick as I can."

She stands up with him, and kisses him on the cheek.

"You should do what I'm doing, Misha You should come with me."

He laughs. "Don't worry about me. I'll be fine."

"But you must be in danger too…"

"I know how to handle myself, don't worry."

She nods, sighs at his bravado. "An hour then?" she says.

He nods, and she waves as he leaves. She tries to look after him as he walks away, watching him through the window, but two men have left just after him and are blocking him off from view. Anyway, the steam has risen so high on the glass that she cannot see properly. After a moment, she rubs at the window with a finger, and leans down to peer through it, but he is long gone now, and besides, it is snowing again. The flakes are banging up against the window like demented moths, and even though she is inside she turns up her collar and shivers.

He is back in an hour, just as he promised. She stands up at once, in the smoky dankness of the café, and he offers her a drink, which she refuses, and so he holds open the door for her. Walking out onto the street, he takes her suitcase from her. Her eyes are flickering, nervous as she walks alongside him, watching him for a sign of where they are going.

"A safe house," he mutters. "It will do for now."

"And then?"

"Then, I'll get you travel papers, and you can start off."

She nods. She has a hundred other questions. Whose house is it? Which route will she take? When can she hope to make it out? But there will be time later for these questions to be asked. It is probable that Misha still needs time to find the answers anyway.

Their pace is brisk, fast even, and it is hard work for her to match his speed at first, especially through the damped down, slushy grey snow on the edges of the street. She aims her feet towards the centre of the pavements, where the snow is worn away entirely. He gives her a sideways glance of encouragement, then veers off down a side road. She hurries to follow him.

"What do you have in here?" he asks, hefting the suitcase from one hand to another.

"Hardly anything. Clothes, the photograph of my parents, you know the one. And Misha, I have to give you this."

She pulls at his coat, forcing him to slow down. He is reluctant to do so, but her gesture is urgent – she wants to give him this while they are still alone, before they reach the safe house. She glances around, but the street is a quiet one, on a gentle downhill slope, and there seems to be nobody about.

"What is it?" he asks.

She reaches inside her coat pocket and brings out a slim white envelope, which she holds out to him as he walks on. Alongside him, she sounds slightly breathless.

"Here, take this, Misha."

He takes his other hand out of his pocket and reaches for the envelope.

"What is it?"

"A letter. For Sasha."

Misha smiles and puts his hand away again. "Give it to him yourself."

"In case I don't make it. In case anything goes wrong."

For a moment, she thinks he has not heard her. He is striding onwards, his eyes intent and focused ahead, and now he turns into a smaller street. Buildings of light stone loom around them in the gloom. They both stop, and glance around and up at the sky. Misha watches his breath puff out above him.

"It will all be fine," he says at last.

"You never know what might happen," she insists.

He looks over his shoulder, then quickly takes the letter, and tucks it inside his shirt, then starts walking again.

"I don't know when I would ever see him again."

She shrugs. "You would get it to him, eventually."

"Would I throw up if I read it?" he asks, with a grin.

"Probably. It's just a love letter, Misha."

He nods. They are walking more slowly now, in a thick evening darkness. She looks up. They have turned again, and the alleyway where they are now has no streetlights, leaving only the glow of the snow to illuminate the atmosphere around them. Flakes are falling, slowly, languidly, and one catches on her eyelash. She blinks it away.

"Misha? You will be careful, won't you?"

He pauses to look at her, taking in her open, concerned face.

"You're the one that needs to be careful now, Katyushka."

He seems nervous for her, Katya thinks. He probably knows even better than me how hard it will be to get out of here.

"You know what I mean," she tells him. "You're putting yourself at risk, helping me."

He looks down, shakes his head. "Don't worry about me."

"I do. You're a good friend Misha." Her hand is on his face, and her lips come up to kiss his cheek. There are no houses here, only a lonely patch of waste ground to one side. For a moment, she thinks she can smell the tiny wild flowers that grow there, the scent of them sweetening the evening air, before she remembers that it is snowing, and that nothing can have grown in that cold, solid earth for months.

"Just be careful, Misha. I will be out of here, but you won't. And if they've caught someone already, they'll torture and threaten him until they make him talk."

"I know."

"I worry that that person will end up betraying you."

She is restless, and stamps her boots to keep warm. Then she takes a step further, as though encouraging him to start walking again, to get going. But he is not moving. He walks to the side of the alley, near a brick wall, and places her suitcase down on the ground. She follows him there.

"Are we waiting here?" she asks.

He nods slightly, and takes her hand, drawing her closer to

him. She can feel the warmth of him beneath his coat. She frowns; his heart is beating very quickly.

"Katya," he says, in a hoarse whisper. "I have to tell you something."

His head is above hers, his face pressed down into her hair. He takes a breath, inhales the scent of her, and she tries not to pull away, but she is peturbed.

"What is it, Misha?"

He bends his head and whispers in her ear. "You should be careful that that person will not end up betraying you."

She does not understand his words, but for the moment, it is as though words, and everyday signals and clear human contact are irrelevant. Something more primeval has taken her over. There is a strange sensation within her, an awareness of something terrible coming that cannot be averted, an almost preternatural sense of pre-warning. She stands there, cold and yet warm, against Misha, and she can hardly believe the realisation that is coursing into her body. The downy hair at the nape of her neck is raised. His hand comes up, caressing her hair, and it is then that she feels the cold metallic muzzle against the side of her head. It slides against her ear, and down to her chin.

"Misha?" she breathes.

He is whispering into her ear. "I know, it's almost too ironic to be true. It was me that they got, you see, Katya? It was *me*. And now I have to help them."

She is dizzy with shock and disbelief. This cannot be happening, not now, not today, not when she is so close to freedom, not from him. Without warning she finds herself choking on a sob.

"You *have* to, Misha?"

"Yes."

"No, you don't. You don't."

He moves her shoulders slightly, so that she knows to turn and look behind her. Some small distance away, a distance magnified by the snow and the darkness, she can see the smudged outlines of two men, watching them.

"They're KGB," he says. "My new permanent escorts."

"How did they… how can you do this? You're not really going to, are you, Misha? Misha?"

There is a sound on the street that intersects the alleyway a hundred yards away. She waits, breathless, but they are young men down there, laughing and full of vodka, and they walk past. Even if anyone were to bother glancing into the alleyway, the air is too dark and the snow is falling too thickly for them to be seen. And even if they were seen… Misha's arm is around her waist. Her body is held close to his, and anyone would think they were lovers, nothing more.

"Is Sasha out? Did they stop him?"

"He's out," he says, with almost a sigh, and she feels a moment of relief, for his tone and voice are so familiar. "And I wish you could have gotten out too. Maybe you could have, if you hadn't chosen me to confide in just now."

She is still in confusion. "Who else could I…? You're the only one I know, Misha, the only one I trust. Trusted." She makes a noise, a sound of bitterness.

"Well, they want to teach your husband a lesson. And you. They're angry, Katya. Very angry."

She feels tears at the rims of her eyes, and they are painful. It is as though they are turning to ice before they can even fall, mocking her sorrow.

"So it's me or you, isn't it?" she says. "That's the choice they gave you."

"I tried to keep you out of it… *You came to me*, remember?"

"Fucking bastard," she says.

"Shut up."

"No!" She sobs, suddenly. "I only want to get out of here and live, Misha. I don't care about the rest of it any more. About all this."

She can hear the tears in her own voice, and her eyes are blurred with the salty water.

"Please, Misha. How can you let them win?After everything we've lived for, and believed in?"

But he is pretending not to listen, she feels. Her breathing comes harder, for she is fearful that he will do it at any moment.

"Please don't kill me, Misha, please don't." She pulls away slightly. "I don't want to smell your coat and your… smell, as you kill me," she says.

This makes him stop, and she feels a sense of respite. A moment to think. A second to imagine Sasha. In the back of her mind, she realises that today was one of the few days when she did not say to herself, "Katya, you might die today. You might be killed today." She has always been fully aware of death, and more so in recent times because of the nature of her work. Usually this thought comes to her before too much of the day has passed, and she always makes sure to focus on it, sometimes imagining possible deaths, and sometimes thinking of her misery at leaving Sasha. She hoards these thoughts consciously and regards them as talismans against the thing that has been thought of actually happening. But she does not remember having thought about her death today. She has been lax about it for many days now, swept away by her excitement and her hopes of the life they have to come. She has been so wrapped up in her visions of Sasha and herself, away from here, away from the lies and deception, just the two of them together, in love and happy and working, that she has completely forgotten to imagine the worst. And now look what has happened. Perhaps, she thinks, there is something to be said for superstition after all. Perhaps the fates do not like to be taken for granted. She wipes her eyes and nose on the sleeve of her coat.

"Misha, how can you betray me...? And what we've been fighting for?"

"Shut up. Stop talking."

"Why, am I making you feel guilty?" With a swing of her fist, she hits him in the jaw, and tries to break free of him, but it is impossible. The men watching begin to move forward but then Misha hits her hard, on the side of her head. She staggers for a second, and then straightens her thin shoulders and faces him. Her ears are ringing from the blow. He shoves her backwards, turning her so that she is facing the wall and he is standing close behind her. So that he doesn't have to see her face, she thinks. She fights a whimper that rises in her throat, because now she feels truly terrified for she knows that it must happen now. She tries not to panic, tries to keep an image of Alexander in her mind. He hits the top of her head, and at the same time she feels a foot kick the back of her knees, making her drop hard to the ground, kneeling.

"You fucking bastard. How can you, Misha? It's *me*. Please, Misha, just let me go. Please, I don't want to die like this." This pitiful pleading will not move him, she knows, but she cannot think well at this moment; she cannot stop herself from crying.

There is no reply, but there is an inhuman sound from his mouth. Is it anguish or anger? He puts a foot on the back of her neck, and presses, with surprising control and gentleness, so that her head is pushed forward so far that beneath the wet snow she can smell the dirty tar of the alley, and the trails of old urine that have trickled down it for years.

"Let's just get this done, Katya." It is anguish she hears in him.

"I have one thing to say," she says, through her weeping. "I'm pregnant, Misha."

Why she has said it she does not know. He would never let her go because she is pregnant, but it has been in her mind all day. She has been waiting to say it to Sasha when they meet again; all afternoon she has been imagining the joy and excitement in his face when he hears it, and so the words have been rolling around in the front of her mouth, waiting to be spoken aloud. And now she has spoken them.

"I thought you never wanted children." Now his voice is harsh. He has switched off, and is pretending that it is not Katya under his boot and gun here in the filthy alley.

He is right. She had gotten pregnant despite her precautions, and she had always taken these for she had previously had no desire to bring a child into this world of theirs, a world in which she could see little hope. And then there was the burning mark of the loss of her parents. She has always known the risks associated with her work, the risks of capture and death, and she has never wanted to leave her own child motherless, to put her own child through what she herself suffered.

When she had realised the reason for her nausea and her bloated stomach she had wished silently, in the late night darkness of their bedroom, for a miscarriage. But that was before the hope of escape. Before the vision of a life with Sasha in another place, where it would be just them, and their baby – no bugs, no cameras, nobody watching them, nobody for her to spy on. A place where she could fight communism openly. She can hardly believe what is happening. She hates herself for ever wishing the baby dead, and now she is angry with herself, for she feels that she has brought this fate upon herself. It is irrational, but she feels it. Here, in this soiled, cold alley, she has been given the means for her tiny baby to die, and she has to die with it. She turns her head to the side and whispers.

"Misha, please, don't do it. You can help me. I don't want the baby to die. Come away with me. Let's make a run for it, right now, you and I. We'll go away together. You don't want to stay here working for the KGB for the rest of your life. Come with me. We'll live happily together. We can do it."

She pauses, and he is still behind her. She can feel him wavering, she is sure of it. Something has touched a nerve. Perhaps, like her, he feels that, even if the odds are against them, he has nothing to lose by trying. Perhaps one more round of persuasion will clinch it.

"You and me?" he says, softly, and she hesitates. Something strikes her as being wrong here, but before she can think about what it is, she speaks again, desperate to secure the advantage.

"Yes. You and me and Sasha, together. Think of it."

He kicks her hard. This one is between her shoulder blades and now she cannot breathe. She knows at once where she has made her mistake… 'and Sasha'. Now she sees with such clarity, as though a spotlight has suddenly been trained on her. He is in love with her. She sees it now, understands finally the desperate need she has sensed, but dismissed, in certain of his looks and touches. And by reminding him that she is going to Alexander, that she loves his best friend, that she is pregnant by him, she understands at once that she has just lost her last chance of evading death.

She rocks forward on her knees so that her forehead touches the dirty ground, and she waits for the spasm to pass. The kick has thoroughly winded her. Perhaps it is better if I pass out now, she thinks, before he shoots me, but her lungs instinctively fight for breath. She sobs slightly. She wants to go home. She is scared of dying like this, like her parents, with a bullet that will explode through her brain, erasing her and her baby from the earth, leaving Sasha alone with the horror of it. It seems too hard that this black destiny should descend on her now, when they have come so very close to the happiness they imagined together.

"Sasha," she whispers. She pictures him in her head, which is pounding with fear. "I love you, Sasha."

Misha closes his finger around the trigger of the gun. This is taking too long. He is tempted, briefly, to pull her up and kiss her, to know at last how it would feel to have her lips on his, to taste her warm mouth and tongue with his own, to savour what Alexander has enjoyed for all this time without even thinking about it. But that will only make it harder than it is already. He closes his eyes and concentrates on the blackness that is revealed to him. He is blocking out sight, blocking thought, blocking all sense; but from somewhere, he can hear a buzzing. His right ear is buzzing – from where Katya has hit him, probably. Misha keeps his eyes tightly shut a little longer, and pretends that the buzzing he hears is the distant sound of an aeroplane. He pictures it flying a straight course across an imaginary horizon. How he loved aeroplanes when he was a little boy. Little Misha. Keeping old newspaper cuttings of the first, heroic, Soviet pilots. Pictures of them in their beautiful planes, pictures of them meeting Comrade

Stalin. With his classmates, he had watched them flying over Red Square on national holidays, had watched them being saluted by their leader, amid cheers. That was all he had ever wanted to do when he was young. Get into a cockpit, cheered by admiring crowds and fly up into the grey sky, away from the city, and up high above the clouds where, his father had assured him, the sky was always blue.

He opens his eyes and glances down at the top of her head. His gaze is steady now, and cool, and he knows he has crossed the line in his mind, so that now she will give him no more trouble. Without another moment's thought, he pulls the trigger, twice, and stands back, dispassionate, as she slumps forward.

CHAPTER TWENTY ONE

BOSTON

NEITHER OF THEM SPEAKS MUCH during the drive home from the airport. During the long flight back they have been depressed and agitated by turns. They have talked about Misha's confession, examined his words from every angle, pieced together not only the facts of the case, but the emotions of it too. Now, during the final leg of the journey home, it is as though all of that artificial, nervous energy has drained from them. Lauren in particular is tense, deeply upset. Each mile along the highway is only bringing her closer to Alexander, and she does not quite know how to tell him what they have learned.

"I feel like we've been away for months," Melissa says.

"Missing the office?" Lauren asks, smiling.

"Sure, but that's not what I meant. I kind of got used to Moscow. Felt immersed in it, and in Katya. I think I'm still in shock."

Lauren nods. "I know."

They turn off the highway and into the warren of back streets that leads directly to their neighbourhood.

"Do you want to have some dinner with us? I can pretty much guarantee that Uncle Alex will have an amazing meal waiting."

"I'm sure he will. But I think you'd better do this alone, don't you? This is going to be incredibly hard for him."

"I know."

Melissa swings the car into Alexander's street, and slows before the house. She gets out and helps Lauren up the front steps with her bags. As she hands her the last one, their hands touch. Melissa entwines her fingers with Lauren's and squeezes. Then kisses her on the cheek.

"Good luck," she says. "Call me later and let me know how it went."

Before she has even driven away, Alexander has opened the door, and is embracing his niece. He waves to Melissa, and then helps Lauren into the house.

"So good to have you back. I have dinner all ready."

"Smells great."

She follows him into the kitchen, where he is all movement and energy. When he looks at her, she is watching him with compassion, or is it pity? Something about her look causes a vague sensation of coldness to invade his chest, and when she asks him if she can have a quick shower before dinner, he is almost grateful for the idea of a few extra minutes to collect himself now that the excitement of her return is beginning to give way to a nervous tension – curiosity about what she might have found out.

"Go ahead," he tells her. "I need a few minutes to finish dinner anyway. And then, I want to know about Moscow."

She smiles, sensing the effort that he is making to take a distanced interest in her trip. He wipes his hands on a cloth and looks at her.

"Go on. Then you can come back and tell me everything."

"Moscow's looking more and more like downtown in any big US city," Lauren says as they eat. "The ads, the coffee places, you know. At least, part of it seems that way."

"And the rest?"

"The rest of it still looks like the place of my imagination. The place I always visualised you living. Dramatic buildings, the churches you walk past where suddenly a group of people are chanting prayers, the old babushkas on the street corners, those solid grey Soviet buildings. The spires of the Kremlin. It's a strange combination."

"You romanticise it too much."

"Maybe. I can't help it."

Alexander pushes away his plate. He has eaten less than half of the food on it, she notices.

"How are you, Uncle Alex?"

"Fine."

"How's Estelle?"

Now his eyes avoid hers, and he stands up to load more salad into her bowl.

"I don't know. I saw her the day after you left. A week ago, nearly. We saw *My Fair Lady*. You should see it by the way."

"Tell me. Something happened."

He sits down, pinned there by her insight.

"Nothing, really. Without actually talking about it as such, she made it clear that she wasn't interested in pursuing any relationship with me. Not one that might trouble her husband."

"Were you surprised?"

"No…" He pauses, hoping he will be excused from saying more, but she only waits. "I guess I was somehow hoping for more from her. So, I thought it best that we stop seeing each other altogether."

"How does she feel about that?"

"I don't know. I got a note about a week ago. She said she was going out of town on her own for a few weeks. To get her bearings, think about things."

"What things?"

"I have no idea. She wants to write, you know," he adds suddenly, with warmth. "But she seems somehow afraid of that man and his opinions."

"The professor?"

Alexander nods. "I don't think she even likes him. Maybe she loves him, from habit, or duty, but there's no passion there."

"Isn't passion a lot to expect after thirty years?"

Alexander fixes her with a look that holds in it a weight of anger and sadness. "I don't think so."

She is silent, sorry for his distress, unsure of what to say.

366

"Without passion, what is the point of living?" he tells her, his tone still bristling with emotion. She nods, wanting to placate, wanting to understand.

"And Misha," he says, suddenly. "Tell me, did you find him?"

"Yes," she says, looking down. "We did."

Lauren begins to recount the details of her journey over a dessert of chocolate cake, beginning with how the detective found Misha, and then moving onto their first visit to Misha's apartment. She does not hurry her words, for she wants time to carry her uncle slowly along with her, before the real story is thrust on him. She has no trouble managing this – despite all Alexander's previous protestations that he does not care about Russia and the details of what happened, he is in fact hungry for facts, and descriptions, and sights and every one of her impressions is of interest to him. He wants to know what Misha looks like, how he behaves, does he have the same sense of humour, what is his apartment like? All these Lauren answers, obliging her uncle with her painter's eye for detail and nuance.

"So you learned nothing from him?"

Lauren catches an undertone of disappointment in his voice, and she feels slightly sick. Of course, deep down, he was really hoping that we would find something out; of course he has always secretly wanted every fragment of Katya that he can grasp hold of. The fact that Lauren now has plenty to tell him does not make her feel any better. In all of her imagined outcomes, she never dreamed that the story she discovered would be so very difficult to recount.

"We learned nothing from him at first. He was very hostile to us, actually. Melissa noticed it more than me – she knew instinctively that he was hiding something under all that anger. I mean, I waltzed in there expecting to be received like a long-lost princess. His good friend's niece and all that. But instead, he cut us dead. Threw us out of his apartment, practically."

"How strange," Alexander comments. Lauren nods but moves quickly on, relating how she left Misha the letter and a brush and ink portrait of Katya – one that she had used as a study for the main portrait. Alexander stands up at this.

"Come, let's continue this in the living room. I have something to show you."

She follows his neat, padding steps out of the kitchen – he has not bothered to begin clearing their plates, an unusual oversight.

In the living room the curtains are still open to the blackness of the night beyond. And Katya's portrait is hanging there, on the large wall to their left. Although the size of the canvas is perfect for the space, she dominates the room, thinks Lauren. Not the picture, but Katya herself.

"What do you think?"

She smiles. "It's a good place to put it. But it isn't too much for you?"

He shakes his head. He had worried about that at first – that was why it has taken him so many weeks to hang it.

"She was the most important person in my life for such a long time," he says. "I didn't want to be afraid of that any more."

His simple sentence brings the threat of tears to Lauren's eyes and quickly she goes and closes the curtains, a task that gives her a few seconds to compose herself. She has a lot more to get through tonight.

They sit together before the empty fireplace, and she watches her uncle bend down to light the neatly built pile of kindling and logs. He is lean and economical in all his movements.

"So you went back to see him?" Alexander asks her over his shoulder.

"No. I wasn't expecting to see him again. And then, on the day we left – this morning in fact – a funny thing happened."

Was it only this morning, she wonders? Her fatigue from a long day's travelling has been subsumed by the emotion and shock at the outcome of the morning's meeting with Misha. Alexander is watching her, patient, calm. He feels carried along in this whole current of events, but the feeling is not unpleasant. Not if he can keep balanced and sanguine, the way he feels now. Perhaps his relaxed air is only superficial, or perhaps it indicates a deeper peace with what Lauren has chosen to do – in any event, he is calm as he waits for her to continue. She smiles slightly and puts her hand over his. Then she leans back and begins to tell how Melissa had caught Misha leaving something at the hotel for her, and how she had kept him there.

"What did he bring you?" Alexander asks.

369

"I'll get to that," Lauren says.

She talks on, paying particular attention to Misha's reaction to her own resemblance to Katya. Melissa had told her that he had not wanted to see Lauren again, that he could not bear it, and that her arrival in the restaurant had been the beginning of his confession.

"Confession?" Alexander sits up slightly, and now his surface calm has fragmented; without putting up the slightest fight, it has shattered like a barely frozen crust of ice on a puddle.

"He told us that he knew all along that Katya was working for the Americans. Because he worked with her."

There is a pause while Alexander digests this. He is clearly stunned.

"Misha worked for the Americans?"

She nods. "He was Katya's main contact for years. He recruited her in fact. They worked closely together. For the most part, he used her to smuggle out research he was involved in at the Aviation Institute."

"I can't believe this. It can't be true."

"It is. They recruited him out of college, apparently."

She waits, allowing time for this to settle in Alexander's mind. Her uncle is frowning, thinking, shaping ideas.

"So did he know her plans to escape? Did he try and help her?"

Lauren becomes aware that her lips are pursed, as though she is trying to avoid having to let out the next words that she has to say.

"She told him. After you had left. In fact, she timed it as well as she could in the circumstances, just minutes after you had defected."

"She knew I'd got out?"

"Not for sure. She hoped. Anyway, she didn't breathe a word to anyone until then, he says. Even him. She wanted to be as sure as she could that you were safe. But then she needed his help. And she told him that the government, or the KGB, had caught someone, and that she was worried that that person would talk and compromise Misha and herself."

Alexander nods. "That's why I left so quickly. The opportunity was there, and we had to take it. Otherwise they would have found her."

"Yes, they would have. They would have found out both of you, Uncle Alex. You do know that, don't you?"

Her concern to reassure him, and reinforce the point acts as an instant alert to his senses. His stomach sinks slightly with misgiving at what she might be about to say. But try as he might, he cannot weave a path through his thoughts and conjectures to prepare himself by imagining possible outcomes. He sits slightly forwards in his chair, cradling his wine glass, waiting anxiously.

"Uncle Alex, it was him."

"What?"

"It was Misha that they'd caught."

Now distant possibilities begin, vaguely, to jostle for position in his mind, but he cannot make sense of them.

He has a sense of dread, like a small patch of acridity in his throat, but he cannot reason out why.

"But Misha was with us the night before I left. We had dinner with my parents, I'm sure of that. How could they have caught him?"

"They let him go."

"Why?"

"Don't you see, Uncle Alex? He switched sides. To protect himself. He became a double agent."

He says nothing, but his mouth is slightly open as he thinks over this revelation. "Of course," he says, softly. "Of course."

She nods. She goes over to his chair and perches on the arm of it. Takes his wine out of his hand and places it alongside hers on the table. Her hand is on his back, and with bitterness she recalls touching Misha's bony shoulders, reassuring him, in much the same way not so long ago.

Alexander can hardly speak, but he must articulate what he is thinking.

"Misha betrayed Katya?" is all he can get out, in a hoarse whisper.

She holds her uncle close, and pulls his head to her shoulder, as though trying to cocoon him, insulate him from her next words.

"Uncle Alex, he pulled the trigger."

He is unresponsive – it is as though she has spoken in Chinese, and he cannot fathom her meaning. He looks at her, his eyes wide, trusting, as if willing her to explain again, to explain that what he just heard is a mistake.

Lauren is crying, she cannot help herself. "Uncle Alex, he shot her himself."

"No…" is all he can say, and then there is a moment of complete stillness in the room. All life, and breath, and sound and movement has ceased. And then the shoulders beneath her hands are shaking.

"Oh God, Uncle Alex, I am so sorry. I thought you ought to know. I thought I had to tell you."

She is holding him hard against her as he cries. She is helpless in the face of his grief, and has no idea what else to do. To her relief his shoulders stop moving after a few minutes, and he just sits quietly, beneath her hands, composing himself. She releases her hold on him when he shifts. He is reaching into his pocket for a handkerchief. She stands and pokes the fire, and waits for him to finish wiping his face and blowing his nose behind her.

"Are you sure it's true? He told you this himself?"

She nods. "I'm so sorry, Uncle Alex."

"How could he?"

"I don't know," she says. "I don't know."

He is sitting very still again. It is as though all life is draining from him.

"I'm sorry," she repeats. "Sorry to tell you this." She wants to find something to do to help him, any small thing, even though he is so far beyond relief, and so she offers to fetch him some water. He nods, and she hesitates for a moment, because his breath is short now, his chest moving too quickly. He nods again, and quickly, she turns and hurries out.

In the cool darkness of the kitchen, the light of the open refrigerator door illuminates her face. Just as she reaches in for a cold bottle of water, she hears something. She stops, head up, listening. The noise comes again. A crash, something falling. Then another. Without stopping she runs back, the bottle clutched in her hand, listening to the continuing noise, and she throws open the living room door.

He is standing up, almost panting now, and in his raised hand is a small vase. It appears that this vase is the only breakable thing in the room that is still in one piece. She throws the bottle onto the sofa and goes straight to him taking the vase from his hand, and putting her arm around him. He sits down, covering his eyes.

"How could he? We were his best friends in the world. How could he?"

"I'm sorry, Uncle Alex." There are shards of broken glass beneath her feet. She is a little fearful now, for she has never in her life seen him do anything remotely violent, and she does not know how to reach this part of him that is so wounded it cannot speak, only act.

"Don't be. I don't want to have another secret, or unanswered question in my life ever again." He is shouting now. "Do you understand? However hard it is, it's better than lies."

She makes reassuring noises, but he cannot hear them. His eyes are everywhere, moving wildly.

"I have to kill him. I have to. For Katya's sake. And my own. I want him to know what she must have felt when he put the

374

gun to her, the bastard. I want him to beg my forgiveness for taking her away. For taking her life from her when she was so young. How could he do it?"

Tears of fury and frustration leak from his eyes.

"She had everything to live for, Lauren. We both did. He could have helped us."

He sighs, deeply, twice, and she senses that his rage is spent for now. Physically, he cannot continue without giving himself a heart attack. She sits next to him and holds him, trying to calm him. She does not know how she can go on with this story, although there is more to say. But can she really leave the next part for later?

"I miss her so much, Lauren," he whispers. "My poor Katyushka. What a way to die."

She takes these last words as some kind of sign that she must go through with the rest of it immediately. Checking that he is calmer, she leaves the room, and returns within a minute, feeling weighted down by the small, light suitcase that she is holding in her hands. She comes to where he sits and places it before him.

"Do you recognise this?"

He shakes his head.

"Misha says they gave him no choice but to kill her; and that she gave him no choice by confiding in him. But he says he's been consumed with guilt ever since…"

His voice is fierce. "He could have helped her. He could have escaped with her. He was our *friend*, Lauren."

"I know."

"I'm glad I didn't come with you. I would have killed him myself."

"I know. But if it's any consolation to you, he's been drinking himself to death for years now. Trying to forget what he did, I think. He's dying. He has a few months left at the most. I think that's what made him give me this."

She picks up the case, gently, rests it on her knees, and watches as realisation crosses his features. There is a shadow thrown over his face, as if the inner pain he feels is somehow being reflected darkly back through his skin.

"It's not hers?" he whispers, nodding at the case.

"Yes."

He reaches out for it, hands shaking, and she hands it over, placing it gently on his lap.

"She had it with her when she… She was all packed to try and get out. He told her he was taking her to a safe house."

The click of the catch opening sounds deafening in the quiet of the room. Alexander slowly lifts the lid. On top of a small pile of clothes is a photograph in a tarnished silver frame. He picks it up and looks at it. Then he sets it down on the table before Lauren.

"Her parents. Your grandparents."

She resists the impulse to take it and examine it well. There will be time for that later. She looks respectfully at the photograph, but then watches her uncle closely. In his hand he has a yellowed envelope that has been lying, sealed, just beneath the frame.

"She gave Misha that letter," Lauren says. "To give you in

case anything should happen to her. He put it away after he…
after she died and never looked at the case since. He says he
couldn't stand to see it, and couldn't bring himself to throw
it away. He said that keeping it in his house, knowing it was
lying there, was his punishment these last decades."

"There is no punishment hard enough for him," Alexander
says savagely. He holds the letter, passing his fingers over it,
caressing it, a look of such seriousness and sorrow on his face
that Lauren can hardly stand to watch him. Then, at last, he
lifts it and hands it to her.

"Shall we keep it for later?" she asks. "You've been through
too much already tonight."

"Please open it," he says. He is right, she feels that. How
could either of them carry on without finishing this tonight?
She gently pulls open the envelope and slides the thin paper
out. It crackles slightly as she unfolds it. Then she hands it
back to him.

"It's in Russian," she says, redundantly.

He nods, and begins to read.

My darling Sasha

*I am on my way to you. My heart is so light at the thought
of starting this journey towards our new life together, I have to
force myself to remember you will only be reading this if I never
reach you.*

*I love you more than I knew I was able to love anyone or
anything. Please remember this always – I don't worry that you
will ever forget, but I am afraid that you might come to doubt it*

because of everything you have so recently found out about me. You know now that I have spent most of my life working against the system that killed my parents. I used to think it was a life of such honour and nobility. But I have had enough of it. Enough of being driven by revenge and pain. That is why I am so happy that we have decided to try and get away from here. Outside, we can tell the truth about our country, about my parents. We can say it all, loudly, without fear of being silenced.

You opened up my eyes and made me see a world that is worth living in. You have made me love life. I never did before. What a gift to be given – three years of discovering that the world can be an exhilarating place to be in. No matter what happens, I will always be grateful to you for that.

Which brings me to the point of this letter. If something has happened to me, Sasha, don't let it ruin your life. Carry on well, as though we were with you. I say "we", my darling, because I have just found out I am pregnant. I wanted this to be the first news I told you when we meet again, so forgive me for not confiding it before you left. I am so full of hope for our new baby. I will always admire my parents, but their politics left me an orphan – it was a terrible childhood, and I will not put our baby through it, if there is a chance we can get out of here and live together in freedom. All I really wanted to say was I love you, and adore you. More than anything, I live to be with you again. But if that does not happen, I rely on you to live the life we dreamed of on my behalf.

Yours always

Katya

She thinks he has finished reading, but she cannot be sure. She is holding her breath, reluctant to make any sound or movement at all in that room. The fire crackles like distant gunfire in the stillness around them. His eyes have stopped reading, but his head is still down. Something is about to happen, she can feel it, but just as she makes a move towards him, he makes a sound, an utterance that is beyond the human or even animal, a noise that seems to have been ripped out of the very centre of him. The letter falls back into the suitcase, and his hands are lifting the clothes inside, lifting them up, and he is crushing the cloth and garments to his face, sobbing and trying to inhale the scent of his dead wife at the same time. He is rocking back and forth, his hands still clinging to the clothes, his arms drawn up around his head and ears, as though seeking protection. The sounds he is making are new to her, and are sounds that she never wants to hear again – a distillation of sorrow, pure sadness and a deep raging that she cannot begin to reach. She sits, paralysed, on the edge of her chair. She cannot touch him or comfort him at this moment, so she just waits, helpless, and watches her uncle disintegrate before her.

CHAPTER TWENTY TWO
SOUTH BOSTON 1960

THE SMELL OF FISH – even the pickled fish that they stock – makes Yuri's wife dizzy, she says. All that vinegar, she complains, evaporating into the air around her head. Yuri and Alexander laugh about it, and tease her. Today, her complaining is defiant and loud, a challenge to her husband to listen. Yuri picks up a whole fillet of pickled herring, and chases her around the shop with it. Around the central table piled with candles and cans, past the sweet counter, and behind the cheeses and meats. She runs from him, screaming and laughing at the same time, finally gaining the front door and throwing it open with such force that the shop bell rings for ten whole seconds. She disappears down the street, and will probably not come back for two hours, because they know she will simply keep running, and go to see her friend Lulu, who works at the hairdresser's on the next block.

Yuri comes back into the shop from the street where he

has been watching her go, and he smiles. Alexander opens the big wooden barrel for him to put back the fish.

"Why do you torment her like that?" he asks.

"It's good for her. Anyway, she likes it. Women like a strong man, who gives them some trouble."

"Chasing her with a pickled herring?"

"Whatever," Yuri says, shrugging. "She likes it. And it gives her an excuse to run away from her own shop, which she doesn't like, and sit and gossip with her friends."

It is true that she prefers not to be tied to the shop. She is young and restless, and of little real help to Yuri, and he seems to have recognised this fact long ago and has stopped trying to change her. And so he is even more grateful for Alexander. His brother-in-law is conscientious and clean, and works hard. He is, Yuri thinks, always keen to prove himself an asset, and eager not to be thought a burden to them, as if such a thing would be possible from his sister's husband. His dead sister's husband. Yuri wipes down his counter tops, and thinks about the day he arrived at their door. Yuri had known at once that this man whom he had never met, had loved his sister Katya well. He had understood immediately the depth of Alexander's love because beyond his brother-in-law's polite words, and earnest tone, and uncomplicated appearance, were his eyes, and when you looked into those eyes you saw the clear, unseeing eyes of a dead man. Alexander, he realized at once, was a man for whom everything was now over.

In the months following his defection, Alexander had been fully investigated, interrogated and finally, congratulated by the American government. He had his papers, and he had declined the offer, the pressure, of continuing work with the government, and he was then free to continue on with his new life, except that he did not have one. Yuri had happily fed him and clothed him and he also put him to work immediately in the shop, for if Alexander, despite his anguish, were willing to continue in the outward forms of living, Yuri decided that he would help him as much as possible. In truth he is grateful to Alexander for loving his sister. In the midst of his own grief at her death, he is relieved that she found happiness and love, even for such a short time. She was always a sensitive child, she had always felt everything deeply, and she suffered terribly after their parents' deaths. Yuri has always felt guilty for leaving her completely alone. He had been handed an opportunity to get out of the Soviet Union by travelling out with the circus, but he had hesitated to take it because there was a place for only one person, and she would have to stay. Katya, though, had encouraged him, even pushed him to go.

"In this place, Yuri," she had told him, "If you get a chance to do what you want, you must take it."

He remembers leaving her at her workplace that day, after she had said this to him, and he had hurried away, for he was late for work himself. He remembers he had found her gloves in his pocket as he ran, and he went back to give them to her, and then he found her crying alone, outside, crying over the fact of him going. She had only doubled her encouragement after that, and he had faltered, hating to leave her alone, but he had taken his chance in the end. Now, he welcomes this chance that has been so unexpectedly thrown at him, to make amends to her by caring for her husband.

The two men stop talking to each other and begin chatting to customers; there are now two in the shop. An old lady is buying bread from Yuri, complaining that the crust hurts her teeth.

"Are you sure you want it then, Mrs Davis?" he asks, his tone teasing.

"Of course. It hurts, but it strengthens my teeth. Anything that hurts you must be good for you, right?"

Not necessarily, thinks Alexander. He opens the barrel of fish for the other customer to look at. The vapours of vinegar and salt and the sea rise up and spread through the room. Your wife is right, Yuri, he thinks, while he waits for his customer to decide; the vinegar is strong. The man asks for a pound of the herring, and Alexander reaches in and pulls the fish out. Across the room, Mrs Davis is asking why they don't have cakes and pies.

"Alexander!" calls Yuri. "Why don't we have cakes and pies?"

Alexander shakes his head. "We don't make them."

Yuri is enjoying teasing the old lady. "Alexander! Why don't we make them?"

Alexander replaces the lid on the barrel, and places the wrapped fish onto the scales. Then he scribbles down the cost and the weight with a pencil on some waxed paper, and multiplies them, underlining twice the price that he arrives at.

"I don't know," he says, and his tone has lost the bantering edge that it had. Yuri looks up at him. "I don't know," he repeats thoughtfully. "Perhaps I should try."

"You like to cook, Sasha?" Yuri asks, placing the chosen loaf in the bag that the old lady is holding out for him.

Alexander shrugs. "I used to. Though, what did we have there to cook with?"

"Don't remind me."

Yuri goes to the door and holds it open for the old woman, and follows her out, where he stands looking at his fruit and vegetable displays, set up on trestle tables against the windows.

"These plums will have to go," he calls in. "After today."

Alexander follows him out and catches the plum that his brother-in-law tosses to him. They both bite into the fruit, soft and overripe, and they lean forward as they eat, so that the juice will not fall onto their shirts or shoes.

"They are not bad," Alexander tells him. "Just soft."

"They can't be sold."

"No, but they can be cooked."

Yuri laughs, but watches his brother-in-law closely. "My God, were you serious?"

"Yes."

"Another thing my wife will love you for," smiles Yuri. Alexander looks at the plums, and waits for Yuri to explain. "Not only do you keep her out of the shop, but now you want to keep her out of the kitchen."

"She hates cooking, Yuri."

"I know. So, whatever ideas you have swimming around in that head of yours, go ahead and try them out. I won't stop you, and God knows, she won't. And if any of it is any good, we can sell it."

"Good," says Alexander. "Can I take them now?" he asks, pointing at the plums.

"When we close, Sasha, when we close. We may still sell some, you know."

Yuri pats him on the back, and the two men walk back inside. Good, thinks Yuri to himself, watching Alexander walk briskly ahead of him. Something else to occupy his time, he thinks, and a good chance on top that we will get better food to eat.

It is two hours since they have all finished supper. Bowls of steaming vegetable soup and lots of thickly buttered bread. It is the first time that Alexander has gone into the kitchen to help his sister-in-law prepare the evening meal. She was disconcerted at first by his presence, but soon reconciled herself to it when he showed her how quickly and willingly he could chop the vegetables. He stirred, and tasted and added salt and herbs, persuading her to go and wash her hair, while he looked after the dinner. His soup was a great success, and Yuri ate three bowls and secretly congratulated himself on his latest suggestion.

The house is quiet now. Yuri is reading beneath a weak lamp in the living room, with the wireless providing a low hum of dance music in the background. His wife has gone to bed. Alexander still sits in the kitchen, a cookbook open before him, and a bowl of flour and butter by his side. He frowns as he reads, and then abruptly stands up and plunges his hands into the bowl. He works the pieces of butter into the flour, lifting it up high above the bowl and letting it fall. He rubs and sifts with his fingers, again and again and again until he has before him a bowl full of fine crumbs. He consults the book once more, and then goes to the sink and fills a large spoon with cold water. He carries it back, carefully, to the bowl and pours it in gently. Again he repeats the movement, knowing full well he could easily take the bowl to the sink, but somehow enjoying the extra steps, the extra effort, the concentration required to carry back the full spoon without losing a drop. Then he cracks an egg, and puts his hands once more into the bowl, turning and binding and pulling together. With some innate instinct he does not handle the dough much, but lightly rolls it out and places it into a buttered flan dish, which he fills with heavy, dried beans, and places into the oven. He goes out to the living room, where Yuri looks at him from over the top of his book.

"Are you all right, Sasha?"

"Fine. I'm baking."

Yuri looks back down at his book and shakes his head. "He works, he cooks, he bakes. It will be a lucky woman that marries you!"

Even as he finishes this last remark, he feels the pain emanating from the man standing before him. Yuri frowns. "Sorry, Sasha, I didn't think…"

Alexander stops him with a raised hand, for he wishes that he did not feel such a light-hearted comment so deeply, and he hates to make himself into an object of pity.

"I have to go back to the kitchen," he tells Yuri, his tone now deliberately ironic. "My plums are waiting for me."

From the refrigerator he takes another bowl, filled with the fruit, which he washes, then halves and sprinkles with sugar and a little cinnamon. He removes the pastry from the oven, pouring out the beans, and places the soft fruit into the cooked case with care, piling up the layers. Over the top he lays some extra lengths of dough, like a latticework, and brushes it with milk, and sprinkles the whole pie with sugar. Pulling open the oven, he slides it in, and then stands watching the closed door as though expecting some sign. He turns his head towards the light that comes from Yuri's lamp, and as he watches, the lamp clicks off, and he hears the sound of his brother-in-law rising heavily from his chair. Yuri's shadow falls into the kitchen, outlined against the soft light streaming in from the streetlamp outside.

"I'm going to bed."

Alexander nods. "Goodnight, Yuri."

Yuri smiles at him and turns. "Goodnight, Sasha. Sleep well."

Alexander sits at the table, his chair slightly to one side, so that the streak of yellow light from the street falls next to him and not across him. He listens to the distant noises of the city night. Cars passing on the main street to the side of them, a siren fading in the distance. He hears some footfalls echoing up from the street below, and a woman's low, soothing voice, reading aloud he thinks, in the apartment next to theirs. That voice somehow sharpens the dull ache that is always in his heart. He turns his head away, trying not to hear it, listening instead to the throb of the oven, baking the pie. But the voice is unrelenting, soft and musical, and he cannot block it out, nor does he now want to. He waits for a few minutes, listening hard, sitting with his head in his hands. The weight of his head seems huge to him now, and slowly, he lowers it onto the kitchen table, so that his ear and cheek are resting on the warm grain of the wood. The pain of listening to that low, light voice is fine and excruciating, and just when he thinks he cannot bear it a moment longer, he makes himself visualise her too, this unknown neighbour talking through the walls. He sees her, dark-haired and slim, like Katya, and in his mind she is reading a story to her baby, and the child he has invented is a miniature of her, long-lashed and beautiful, and already asleep. Now he imagines her turning out the lamp, and closing the door with a gentle click, and walking softly into her own bedroom where someone she loves is waiting for her. Alexander stands up quickly, for his stomach is turning and he feels he might vomit. He wants to cry, but he has cried so much in the past months that he feels all dried up inside, as though there is nothing left to weep out. A couple of lengths of pacing in the kitchen begins to calm him, and he stops at the oven door and edges it open to look at the pie. It looks moist and delicious, and he nods and closes the door, and sits back down at the table. The woman's voice is gone now, vanished away like an hallucination, leaving only the sound of late night traffic, and he is thankful for it.

"What do you mean, there are no more?" The woman stands, hands out in disbelief, staring at Yuri. He shrugs.

"We are sold out, Mrs Sachs," he says.

The woman fingers her pearl necklace and taps a polished heel. She is most unhappy.

"I've been coming here every week for two months," she says. "That salmon is my signature dish; how can I have my friends over tonight without my salmon?"

Her reasoning seems flawless to her own ears, but it makes Alexander smile from the back of the shop.

"Perhaps for next week, you'd like to reserve some?" asks Yuri.

"Next week?! I need it now, not next week!"

Yuri looks to Alexander, his face contorted with uncertainty. He hates to be faced with anyone shouting, which is why his wife gets away with anything she likes so long as she raises her voice. Alexander comes out from behind his counter.

"I apologise, Mrs Sachs. We had a smaller delivery of salmon today, and I couldn't…"

"It's you?"

"I beg your pardon?"

"Who makes the fish?"

"I make all the food, yes."

Mrs Sachs has lost her angry demeanour, and is filled

with interest now that she is faced with the man who can produce meals a hundred times more inviting than her own. She regards him for a moment as he stands there in his white apron. She takes in his short, dark hair, a damp curl sticking to his wide forehead, his shadowed jaw and his huge brown eyes. He is not overly tall, but his leanness and erect posture give him a length of bone most unlike her husband's meagre stoop. She puts a hand to her wavy red hair and smiles.

"My," she says. "And all this time I thought a woman was producing all this food. I can't imagine."

Alexander smiles briefly, and looks down at the counter, where a brisket of beef lies, ready for trimming and tying.

"What am I going to do about tonight's dinner?" she asks, a slight sigh in her tone. He turns and meets her look, and she touches her top lip nervously.

"There is a fishmonger on the next block," he says. "You can get the salmon there. If you like, I will write down the recipe for you. I can explain how..."

"I don't cook," she says, with finality.

"Ah," replies Alexander. He is tired, and tempted to frown and hurry the woman out of the shop, but he tries to keep his temper. "Then I have a new dish, which you may like. It is made with chicken, and has a cream and chive sauce..."

"Cream?"

He nods.

"With chicken?"

"Yes."

"We're Jewish. No mixing meat and dairy."

"I see." Alexander smiles politely, and excuses himself.

"What if I ask you to cook the meal – the salmon, I mean – deliver it to my house, and prepare it to be served?"

Alexander stops short, and glances at Yuri, who shrugs.

"Now?"

"Right now."

"It would cost too much," says Alexander.

"For who?" Mrs Sachs laughs. "You name the price, and I'll pay it."

And so he begins. Three and a half hours that pass in a blur, but a happy, adrenalin-packed blur, and that culminate in a three course meal for eight people, prepared, cooled and packed. He makes the drive in Yuri's shuddering red Chevrolet to the lower end of Beacon Hill, a different city from the one he lives in, and he twists and turns up and down the steep streets, by the quiet light, soft as butter, of old, ornate street lamps, until he finds the Sachs' house. He gets out and knocks, and enquires to check that he is at the right place. Then he unloads all the boxes and dishes, which are covered over with crisp aluminium foil and heavy plates, and he carries them straight into the kitchen by the back entrance. Mrs Sachs and her housekeeper are there, one in a black cocktail dress, the other in a grey uniform.

"Wonderful!" Mrs Sachs cries. "Here," she says. "If you lay it all out here, on this table, and just show Mrs Monks what goes with what."

She disappears through a swinging door, and as the

door opens, Alexander can hear laughter dying in a distant room.

"The sauce," he says, looking at the housekeeper. "It needs heating."

The woman looks into the bowl and evaluates the amount of sauce. She reaches up to a rack of saucepans above their heads and takes one down.

"A very gentle heat. It shouldn't be hot, just warmed through."

She nods and turns to the stove while Alexander unwraps the pieces of fish, and the dessert. As he does so he glances about the kitchen, at the rows and rows of pans floating above him – pans for every kind of kitchen work. The serving dishes, white with ornate gilded patterns around the edges, every single piece matching. Rows of utensils, shining silver under the lights, so many gleaming rows that he would not know what to do with most of them.

He bursts into the apartment with more life in him than Yuri has ever seen.

"How was it?"

"Wonderful."

Yuri smiles and folds up his newspaper. "She likes you. Mrs. Sachs."

Alexander ignores the comment. "I like this work, Yuri."

"You cook every day in the shop."

"Yes, but tonight, I decided a whole menu, and arranged it all on the most beautiful dishes, and she let me stay and make

SHAMIM SARIF

sure that everything was heated properly, and served well. It was like having those people in my own house."

"If only you had a house like that! Good. I am happy that you are happy."

"She asked me to do it again. Next Saturday."

Yuri nods approvingly. "You know, you can start a good business this way."

"*We* can."

"No, Sasha, not me. I have enough to do. You can do the work for this one, and take the profits!"

Which is why Yuri wonders, three months later, why he should be up to his armpits in onions and garlic. True, his bank account is better than it has ever been, but what a price he pays! On days like this he goes to bed still reeking of the pungent bulbs – all the milk and lemon juice and soap in the world will not help him – and his wife refuses to touch him. Or to let him go near her. Alexander should be doing this job, Yuri thinks; he sleeps alone. No-one will care what he smells like.

He leans forward and watches his brother-in-law through narrowed eyes, as he works in the kitchen. He sees the hands and fingers and eyes working in perfect harmony, producing dishes that Yuri gets to sample every night, and he knows that he is chopping the onions because he cannot do what Alexander is doing.

The cook looks up. "Did you get the fresh herbs?"

Yuri sighs and wipes away a burning tear. "Bradshaw is

394

laughing at me. I asked him for fresh rosemary, and he said, who uses it fresh? We have it dried, lots of it…"

"He can get it if he wants to. He finds the fruit and vegetables that we need, why not the herbs? Someone somewhere is growing them to dry them."

"Not here. It's not warm enough."

"Yuri!"

"Okay, okay. I'll tell him again tomorrow. You are too fussy. It will make your business harder to run."

"It will make the difference between our business and everyone else's."

"No-one else is doing this!"

Alexander laughs. "But they will. And we have to be far ahead of them when they do."

Yuri shakes his head, but inwardly he is smiling. It's a good thing you made it to the States, Alexander, he thinks to himself. This way of thinking would have been wasted at home. With a sidelong glance he watches his brother-in-law at work, and Alexander knows that he is being watched, but he chooses to feign a lack of awareness. When Yuri least expects it, Alexander's eyes dart up and catch him, and Yuri smiles and looks away, although he has nothing to be embarrassed about. When he looks back, Alexander is still watching him, intently.

"You know, just then…"

"What?"

"You looked just like Katya. With your head down, and your eyes…"

"I'm her brother," Yuri shrugs, and he continues with his work, but he is pleased. It is the first time that Alexander has voluntarily mentioned her since he arrived. It must be a good sign, Yuri decides. A sign that he is getting over it a bit. For no reason except that he feels suddenly light-hearted and happy, he looks up, and lobs a clove of garlic over at Alexander. Alexander sees it coming, watches the clove's short arc through the air, and with a deft swipe of his sharp knife, he halves it before it falls. Yuri laughs, and Alexander bows, sticks the tip of his knife into the wooden chopping board, and goes to clean his hands.

CHAPTER TWENTY THREE
BOSTON

THERE CAN BE NO SLEEP FOR ALEXANDER that night, or for many nights to come. The sheer force of emotion has drained him physically, leaving him feeling knotted and yet shapeless, as though his muscles and nerves are slack with exhaustion. Lauren takes him up to his bedroom, switches on his reading lamp, brings him water and tea, and he is aware of her moving around him, but his heart and mind are filled with nothing but Katya and Misha. Much later, in the weak light that just precedes dawn, he persuades Lauren to go to bed. She is red-eyed from sleeplessness, travel-weary. Reluctantly, she leaves him for a few hours, and she sleeps at once, a blank dreamless slumber, and when she wakes, jet-lagged, she forces herself to step immediately under a hot, reviving shower, so that she can get back to her uncle as quickly as possible.

She finds him in the kitchen, sitting at the table. Or rather, he is slumped in his chair. She feels a small pain in her heart to see him like this. He does not even look up when she comes in, and when she walks around the table to sit across from him, she realises that he has fallen asleep. She watches him for a moment. He looks old now, already, in a way she has never seen before, and the change has happened only hours after she has told him what she learned. Or perhaps it happened in moments. His hair seems lank, despite being short; his eyes and mouth are pursed and his skin is dry and grey.

He opens his eyes and gives her a fair attempt at a smile.

"How are you?" he asks.

"Worried about you."

She gets up and hugs him, then moves around the kitchen preparing tea and toast. He is watching her; at least his eyes are following her around the room, but his mind is elsewhere, filling up again with the hundreds of questions that he has thought of during the night, the questions that he has been waiting here to ask her.

"I need to know everything, Lauren," he says. "About how he killed her."

To his dismay, he feels the tears rising to his eyes again. Just saying those words brings back a grief that surrounds him like subtly suffocating fumes.

She nods. "I'll tell you whatever I know."

She is so grateful to Melissa, so pleased that she came with her to Moscow. Not only did she catch hold of Misha before he left the hotel, but after she broke through his silence and got him to talk, she ensured that they heard as much detail as he could possibly provide. While Lauren herself sat hardly speaking, overwhelmed with the sheer fact of what he had done, Melissa had simply gone on questioning him with delicacy and intelligence. Lauren had watched her legally trained mind working to fill in as many details as she could, to clarify every nuance and suggestion, to sift the reality of what had happened back then from any wishful thinking on Misha's part, to ensure that every last, bitter drop was wrung from his memory. Later she had told Lauren that her subtle interrogation was done partly to satisfy herself that Misha was telling the truth, but mostly to ensure that when they came back home, they would be able to give Alexander as much of the story as they possibly could.

"What do you want to know?" Lauren asks gently.

"I want to know how she died. Exactly. How did he betray her, what did they say to each other, how did he do it? *How could he have done it?*"

So she tells him the story of Katya's final hours, as Misha had told it, and she also fills in the details that led up to it. How Misha had been caught by the KGB and he and his family threatened. That he had agreed to give up the names of other American spies in return for his life. That he said he had intended to protect Katya, until she came and asked him for help.

"Do you think that's true?"

"Who knows for sure? Maybe that's how he lives with himself. Pretends he really would have protected her. Blaming her for coming to him for help."

"Why didn't he just help her? Why tell them?"

"He said they were watching and listening to his every move. Just by contacting him, Katya threw suspicion on herself, and then, they were watching them when they met that day. She had her suitcase with her, it was too obvious. He felt he had no choice."

Alexander has to grip his cup to stop his hand shaking. He feels incandescent, glowing inside, as if there is a fire burning in his stomach which is lit by pure rage.

"And then?" he says, and his teeth are clenched.

"And they told him to get rid of her, and followed him when he went back for her. She saw them just before the end, and she tried to persuade him to make a run for it. She tried everything to convince him." Her voice drops. "She even told him about the baby."

"Our baby…" he whispers, and he puts a hand over his eyes. She clears dishes for a few minutes, waiting until he is ready for her to continue. There is a loud bang behind her, and she turns to see his fist crashing to the table again.

"He could have run with her," he says, and his voice is loud. "He could have tried. They could have caught them, probably they would have, but my God, was it better to have stayed and lived whatever sham of a life he's lived for the last thirty years? He could have tried to save her, and get out himself. He could have made it out and lived together with us…"

"That's the other thing."

He looks up at her, waiting.

"One of the last things he admitted was that he loved Katya."

At his core, he understands the full implication of this statement at once, but there is something in his mind which prevents him from acknowledging it. The betrayal so far, all the revelations, have been so spectacular that he almost wills this one to be a mistake.

"He was her best friend," he says, with exaggerated calm. "He should have loved her."

She hesitates. "No, I mean he was in love with her."

He looks at Lauren, sadly, helplessly.

"He'd always loved her, for years. And I think watching you and Katya together, so happy, drove him crazy."

Alexander is thinking back – there are so many years to cross, so many later memories to push through – to any time when he could ever have had the slightest clue that Misha was in love with Katya. He can recall many vague situations. Words, gestures, glances, smiles, that come to his mind. Misha was always physically demonstrative with both of them, but perhaps Alexander had never wanted to consider the fact that his hugs and friendly teasing of his wife hid a deeper passion. He cannot pick out details – this part of his past is so far away and his memory is simply not good enough – but somehow, all of this revelation about Misha is not quite as surprising as it should be. Just as Katya's confession of her betrayal had allowed him to feel a certain, parallel reality clicking into place, even as it shocked him.

"Why didn't he go after her himself?"

"Because she never wanted him. She just wasn't

interested, and he wouldn't chase any woman. They chased him, apparently."

Alexander nods his assent.

"She was never interested in anyone except for you, and he hated that. He tried to keep her on track, to push her to marry you just to spy on you, but all the time she was falling more and more in love with you, and turning away from the work he had trained her to do, that she had always wanted to do. After you got married, she refused to do it any more, and he ended up having to blackmail her into it."

"She told me she had been blackmailed, but I never knew it was *him*."

"Yes. He had made her steal papers from you when you first met, and he held that over her. She was so scared she'd lose you that it worked, for a while anyway. But he never counted on her loving you enough to confess everything. It drove him crazy that any man could have this effect on her, especially when it wasn't him. He resented you horribly by the time you defected. There was something she said to him, in the last moments, he can't even remember what exactly, something about you, and he felt again how much she adored you, and he says he just felt a blind rage, and it helped him to… to do it."

Alexander is crying again, silently, except for a slight choking noise. She feels she should stop speaking, but there is one more thing that she hasn't told him, that she knows must be said.

"Her last words were about you, Uncle Alex. She said 'I love you, Sasha.' That was the last thing he heard her say."

Her own eyes are so full that her uncle is a blur to her for a moment. She grips his hand, and feels him shuddering. His tears are falling in round drops onto the bare wood of the table where they sit, heavy and pooled, as though they will never soak away.

After a week, Lauren calls the doctor. During this time, Alexander has been in his bed; he has hardly eaten and hardly spoken. The doctor's tests, as much as Alexander will allow them, show him to be healthy. Lauren sees the doctor out, and goes back upstairs with some soup. Her uncle is sleeping again, has been sleeping most of the days. She hears him sometimes at night, padding about the house. She sits on the edge of the bed and strokes his head. Then she shakes him gently awake, and offers him the soup.

"Thank you," he says, and he sits up.

"Why don't you go and freshen up, and then come downstairs and eat with me?"

"Okay." He nods, and gets out of the bed. Pleased with herself, she carries the soup downstairs, and hears him running the shower. But when, forty minutes later, he has not joined her, she runs back up again to find that he is back in bed, asleep. He has changed his pyjamas and combed his damp hair, but has not bothered to shave. With a sigh she checks her watch. She will wake him again in an hour and try to get him to eat.

"And Estelle? Where is she through all this?" Lauren asks. She is walking with Melissa towards the car, on their way out to dinner.

"In Concord. Not far. She's always loved the little inn there, and that's where she's been staying."

"Does your father know?"

"Sure. She's been calling him now and then to check in." Melissa gives a wry smile. "She can't even leave him properly."

"Are you sure about that? What if she does leave? What if he ends up losing her?"

"That's the risk he's always taken, I guess. How long can you treat someone off-handedly and get away with it? Maybe forever."

"Maybe not," replies Lauren sharply.

Melissa knows that her father misses her mother, but his routines of living are so defined, and involve Estelle so little, that he can continue practising them with very little disruption. Melissa has been buying for him the type of cold food that needs little preparation – she knows that eventually, when he becomes hungry enough, he will remember to come out to the kitchen and eat it. She has felt a chill, standing there in the deserted kitchen of the silent apartment, her father sequestered in his study, unable to reach out for her mother, or even to say anything about what is occurring to his daughter. During the time she was growing up, her father's path always struck her as containing an element of nobility – that devotion to his books, to vast study, to the delineating of original thought; the passion that was not circumscribed in any way, even by wife and family. But in the last few days, it has appeared to her as a cold, self-absorbed existence, filled with a kind of ultimate loneliness. Perhaps that is simply her own projection, and something of which he is not even aware, but nevertheless the sense of it lies strongly within her, and she finds that she dislikes it intensely.

Lauren gets into the car.

"Can you do me a favour?" she asks. "Call up Uncle Alex and get him back into working on this deal with you."

"I hate to push him on that after what he's been through. The deal will wait."

Lauren is grateful for this, for she knows Melissa has been working closely with her uncle just before the trip to Moscow and is impatient to complete this sale – but she is also wondering if a reminder of his other life, his working life, would not be a kind of relief to Alexander at this point.

"He's becoming more and more depressed. I just think it could help. Even a short meeting, here and there."

"He probably needs more time. But if you want me to, I'll try."

"Please," says Lauren. "He'll be reluctant at first. You'll have to be aggressive about it. Pushy, even."

"Pushy? Moi?" smiles Melissa. Lauren leans over to kiss her.

"I know. Hard to imagine," she says dryly. "But give it your best shot."

Alexander has always wondered whether leaving the Soviet Union with that delegation, leaving Katya behind to try and follow him, was the greatest mistake of his life. He cannot be sure, no-one can about such things, because he can never know for certain what the alternative outcome would have been, what would have happened had he stayed. Would they both have been captured and killed, or imprisoned? Would she have been tortured? Would Katya have somehow pulled Misha over to their side and would they have escaped together? The possibilities, likely or unlikely, unfold themselves in his overwrought imagination, forming ever-lengthening, tangled strands. What he does know is that he would have liked to have been there with her, would have felt less helpless, more able to try and protect her from harm. To be in America was not simply to be in a separate country than the Soviet Union; rather it was like being in another universe. There could be no contact, no communication, no news, nothing. Just silence, and then smuggled information filtering slowly and unreliably outwards. Such isolation he felt when he learned of her death; not only was she gone, but there was no detail, no body for him to grieve over and nobody to tell him the terrible story of what had happened. Until now.

Over the years he has imagined countless deaths for her. In his mind he has watched her lose her life over and over and over again, in different ways, all of them violent, all of them terrifying. He has been haunted by her last moments, even though he has never known what they were. The most bearable versions of this sickening torture that he has put himself through show her death to be quick. A surprising bullet that she did not know was coming. The idea that she might be aware, caught, tortured – that she would have to wait, knowing what was going to happen to her is intolerable to him, and yet he has forced himself to tolerate it, day after day, year after year. But now he knows. He knows the details of those last, long minutes, and the idea of it, of Misha, and of Katya's misery and fear is all he dreams of now, and what he thinks of most often when he is awake.

He spends long hours in the night sitting in the dark under the cool gaze of Katya's portrait. It is a refinement of the agony for him to think about these things while he sees her face right before him, and her eyes looking into his. It makes the pain almost unendurable, but not quite; for in the end, he is able to sit there, enduring it. He talks to her sometimes, always reverting to the Russian language that he has not used for so many years, and after a while he begins to hear her reply to him, and her replies are always kind, and well thought out. It is as if he has trained himself to think and feel as she would, so that he can have some semblance of the dialogue that he has craved for so long. He begs her forgiveness and she accepts his plea, but then he remembers her letter, that last, beautiful letter, and he knows that she does not want his apologies. He knows every word by heart, knows the curve and fall of the letters that her hand wrote; he has traced the lines with his eyes and fingers so many times that he cannot remember ever not knowing the words. There is much in that letter that has made him cry over what she gave up and what she lost — *I am so full of hope for our new baby… I live to be with you again…* But there is also enough within it to begin to remind him during these dark, silent days and nights that she wrote it for a reason. For him to keep and to live by if she were to fail in her attempt to reach him. It is harder for him to recall and consider these parts: *we can tell the truth about our country… I rely on you to live the life we dreamed of.*

Has he lived that life well? He tells her, during the nights that pass, of everything he has done with his business. How he has built a career from cooking and food, from the things that he always loved and was good at. How he has set up foundations to help others to do the same thing. That he is as a father to Lauren, and how proud of her he is and how happy. It has been a good, full life, but he is conscious now that he has always avoided Katya's death and the reasons for it. He has tried to keep everything that happened to her, and everything associated with their old lives at a distance. He has not told the truth. He has not lied, but he has never been prepared to face up to the reality of the world he came from and to speak about it openly and widely. Rather he has kept quietly within him that void where Katya should have been. That this void exists and has always existed is simply the case, as far as he has always known. For forty years he has assumed it to be an unchangeable fact, like the relentless spinning of the earth. But now for the first time, in the light of his wife's words, he begins to understand that he has not continued the work she was so driven to do, and he begins to consider whether she would be happy to see his heart still sealed off and guilty and unspoken, so many years later.

He is far from ready to return to work. In truth, his business, and its sale mean comparatively little to him at this time, and he tells Melissa this directly and honestly. He cannot imagine a time in the near future when he will feel able to think of it; and so he suggests that she continue working out a deal with Lauren, and to Lauren he repeats the same thing, assuring her that his finance officers and directors will help her.

"What do you think?" Lauren asks Melissa.

"I think, forget about it."

"You don't want the company any more?"

"Oh, I want it all right," Melissa tells her "But in any negotiation, I will eat you alive. And the directors. You won't get a good deal."

Lauren cannot help but smile. "So why not just give me a fair deal? It's up to you."

Melissa tries to explain. Her business success up until now has been based on making a series of deals which were weighted in her favour, so that the risk was always lower than usual. Throughout it all she has always prided herself on never taking anyone for a ride. She has always been upfront about the deal she requires, and if the other side accepts it, at least they know what they're signing. This preamble confuses Lauren somewhat.

"Why would anyone sign a deal that was bad for them?"

"I'm not saying bad, just not great."

"Whatever. Why would they?"

"Usually desperation. A company might be on the verge of bankruptcy for example, so they need to sell fast. Occasionally it can be ignorance. Someone might not recognise that you're offering below the odds."

Melissa watches Lauren's face. Her reaction is uncertain, but has a definite edge of distaste to it. For that is what I do, Melissa thinks. Something that is distasteful; at least it feels that way to her here and now, with Lauren.

"Anyway," she continues. "I don't want to work like that any more. I don't think it's wrong, necessarily, but I want to try something new. I think maybe it would be nice to look at a company as a business to build and grow, instead of a stack of pieces that can be dismantled and sold for more than the sum of the parts. And in this case, because you both are insisting on things like the charity stuff, there is really no other way to do it."

Lauren looks relieved. "Good. Then we can work this thing out, right?"

"No. We can talk about scenarios. Especially how we can keep the philanthropy going, without me losing too much of my margins. Maybe you or Alexander should maintain a stake. I'm not sure. But we'll talk. And then we'll wait. When your uncle is ready to do this, or when he appoints someone as good as he is to advise you, then we'll complete." Melissa smiles. "I have no intention of giving you a bad deal, Lauren. But this is business, and I don't ever want you to wonder one day if you really did get the best deal. I don't want what happens here to get between us personally. I'd rather lose the company."

It is perhaps the least romantic declaration Lauren has ever heard in her life, but she knows it represents a huge step forward for Melissa, in every way.

"Thank you," Lauren tells her, and she smiles.

The courtyard feels surprisingly familiar and comforting. He had assumed that the many weeks that he has been away, and the violent emotional storms that he has been through would have made his old offices and the business that he is preparing to sell seem alien and unimportant to him. Alexander pauses and looks up at the glass and steel structures that rise up from the paved slabs, up at the windows that used to be his, the boardroom from which he did so much of his work. A glance at his watch propels him forward, to his meeting with Melissa, and he strides into the building and up to the banks of elevators.

"Glad you could make it," Melissa says, when he knocks on the open door of the boardroom, and she takes the hand that he holds out, but also leans to kiss him on the cheek.

"It's good to be back," he says, without thinking. It is an automatic, unconsidered reply, but he finds to his surprise, that it is suddenly true. The hum of conversations and computers, the relaxed air of the staff – he has missed all this, at least a little, and it is good, after all, to be out of the house and thinking of something else.

His afternoon passes quickly, for Melissa has piled up an agenda for him that leaves no room for more than a snatched cup of coffee along the way. But the progress they make is good, and to his relief, he comes to the end of the day with the realisation that he has not thought about Katya for much of the time.

"What's next?" he asks Melissa, as they leave another meeting.

"Nothing. Home time," she replies.

He smiles. "And tell me, have you ever gone home at five thirty?"

She shrugs. "Not that I can remember, but then I'm hardly your role model." She walks with him to the exit. "Go on home," she says. "If you feel like it, I'd love to meet you back here tomorrow. But only if you're up for it."

"What sort of time?" he asks, stepping into the glass elevator.

"Since you ask, nine sharp," she says, with a smile, and the doors close.

He follows the same routine the next day, and the next, and when he leaves for the week on Friday evening, he stops and breathes deeply of the cool courtyard air. There are a lot of people walking purposefully past him, and around him, hurrying home for the weekend. He wonders if any of them see that the fading light has a crispness about it, a patina of life that hints at the coming springtime. He stops under the huge tree that dominates the centre of the paved area, and notes the sticky, ripe buds that are already clinging to its upper branches.

"It looked a lot of different the last time we were here, didn't it?"

He turns immediately to the bench behind him. Estelle's eyes hold a mischievous smile, a familiar look that he has tried hard to forget. They look at each other for a long moment. He is collecting himself, trying to repress the unseemly crashing of his heart inside his chest. When at last he takes the few steps towards her, she shifts over on the bench and waits for him to sit down. Now that he is so close to her, she finds she cannot quite look at his eyes. Not just yet.

"Are you waiting for Melissa?"

She shakes her head, then gives him a quick glance.

"I'm flattered," he says, finally.

"Do you wish I hadn't come?"

"Of course not. I just didn't expect it. Didn't dare to expect it."

The emotion in his voice settles over her residual fears like a soft, warm blanket, easing them away so that she feels able to speak.

"I was wrong to have pushed you away that evening," she says. "I didn't want to – I guess I felt I had to." She waits, unsure of how to formulate her next sentences, hoping that he will fill in the gaps with questions that will guide her towards what she wants to say. But he remains silent, his brown eyes fixed on a point just before them.

She wants to touch him, just the sleeve of his coat, or the top of his hand, or the back of his neck, which even at this age has the slim, shorn look of a little boy's. But she does not dare. Instead, she leans over to her handbag and takes out a sheaf of paper, and offers it to him. He takes it, and then holds onto her hand. To her chagrin, she blushes suddenly.

"The first few chapters."

"Is it about Katya?"

"Yes and no."

"Because I don't know if I can read it just yet," he says. "If it is."

"Well, I started out with her, but then I had a slight problem; I didn't know a thing about the places I was trying to describe. Oh, and half my plot line was missing."

"So what did you write about?"

"Well, I thought about the characters and story that I knew best. And so, we have the following scenario. Picture it. A mature woman – I hate to say old – who has always lived a safe and easy life. Who has been married for nearly thirty years, and who believes that marriage is for life, because there are such things between her and her husband as loyalty and respect, if not the attention and care she would have wanted."

"I see."

"But then, this woman meets someone. Someone who she loves to be with and who maybe sees in her more than there is. And there's another character, you see, though I'm not sure how to bring her in yet. This character is my Katya. Someone whose story proves interesting and then inspirational to my main character."

"Why inspirational?"

"Because in her young life, she has always lived for her passions and ideals and beliefs, no matter what the risks might be for doing that."

He feels his eyes moisten, but with a breath, he controls the tears.

"How does your story end?" he asks at last.

"That's the thing. I'm not completely sure. But I think the old lady gets up the courage to live life in the end. I really do."

Standing up, he offers her his hand, and together they walk across the courtyard and to the main road. They join the line for a cab and he turns to her. His face is handsome and stern and kind as he stands there watching her. She feels lost suddenly, and a moment of panic crosses her face.

"Tell me what you feel, Estelle."

She laughs nervously. "It's a lot easier to talk about my characters."

But he will not let her go so easily. His eyes hold her down until she looks away. Perhaps he is challenging her to show that courage that she just talked about. She swallows and looks up at him again.

"While I was away I began to realise that I would never see you again. That my life would just continue the way it had before – except that I've changed. And that's the problem, you see. I don't want my life to be the same as it has been. And I began to understand that – God help me – even with good blood pressure and low cholesterol, I can only have a very limited number of years left on this earth. And I don't want to spend them away from you."

He takes a deep breath, to try and slow his heart – he wonders how many more shocks it can take.

"What about your husband?" he asks, finally.

"I'm not sure," she says. In her mind she has envisioned packing up, walking out, not returning, but the vision is one

415

of too much brutality and harshness. "I would have to ask you to bear with me for a while."

"Yes, I will," he says quickly.

"Really?"

"Yes."

She looks at him, a weight of compassion in her face. "Melissa told me you've had a hard few weeks."

"Yes."

"I'm sorry."

"Don't be. It was time for everything to come out. But it just brought it all back, with such force. What she gave up for me, what she and I both lost."

Estelle only nods, for she cannot speak just now. She does not know whether it is tiredness, excitement, relief or uncertainty, but she feels tears in her eyes. Despite her best efforts, a rogue droplet escapes from the edge of her eye and runs over her cheek. His hand reaches up to brush it away.

It is late, perhaps one o'clock in the morning. To be able to sit in her uncle's living room, wrapped in a thick darkness that is scattered away only here and there by the last flickers of the fire, seems luxurious to Lauren, like being swathed in the softest velvet. She has waited until Alexander is asleep before methodically turning out all the lights downstairs. Her head begins to feel heavier as she watches the dying flames, and before she should fall asleep, she rouses herself and goes over to the cloth-draped easel that stands at the other end of the room. She lifts the cloth away, and glances at the beginnings of

Estelle's portrait. She can see little of it in the dim light. Lifting it down, she leans it against a second sketch that outlines the features of her uncle. Then she wraps the cloth around both.

She watched them both tonight at dinner, closely. In Alexander she saw a new softness and peace, a relaxation of the features. And in Estelle, she sensed a more determined look in the blue eyes, which previously had only masked her inner feelings with irony and laughter. Or perhaps she merely imagined these changes – had wished for them so much that she read them into the faces before her. In any event, she is tired. She does not want to paint for a while, and maybe the time off that she takes will allow those developments to occur that she wants to see in her two latest subjects. Wandering back to the fireplace, she looks up at Katya's portrait. The shadows cast onto her face by the glowing embers mean that her eyes and mouth are barely visible. How would her aunt have changed, had she been given the chance? Lauren looks at the painting, trying in her mind to re-work the familiar features so that age and experience cause their alterations. But she cannot – the choices that her aunt may have made, the way her character could have developed are too varied to be pinned down so easily. Lauren closes her eyes, but beneath the lids that burn from lack of sleep, the image of Katya still lies, clear and bright. She pushes down the last embers of the fire with the poker, and turns to leave the room.

"Good night Katya," she says. "Good night."

Also by Shamim Sarif...

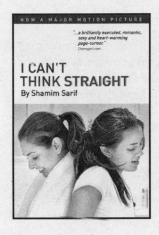

I CAN'T THINK STRAIGHT

Exploring the themes of self-discovery and tradition-breaking, the acclaimed novel *I Can't Think Straight* is award-winning author Shamim Sarif's third novel. Including behind-the-scenes photos from the movie, the book follows the journey of Tala, Leyla and their families in a touching and often humorous narrative.

**Available from
www.enlightenment-productions.com,
Amazon.com and other retailers.**

ACCLAIM FOR *I CAN'T THINK STRAIGHT*

"…a brilliantly executed, romantic, sexy, and heart-warming page-turner… the work of an amazingly talented writer and one that is a refreshing and immensely enjoyable read that leaves you smiling. The only thing to not like about the book is that it had to end…"
– Cherrygrrl.com

"Each character in the story is wonderfully complex and endearing… Sarif evokes an atmosphere so diverse and inviting, each page is something to be savored. Sarif's descriptions are beautifully crafted; delicate, seductive and enthralling, they make *I Can't Think Straight* a sheer joy to read from start to finish."
– GracetheSpot.com

THE WORLD UNSEEN

Shamim Sarif's first novel took the
publishing world by storm and went
on to win the Pendleton May First
Novel Award and the prestigious
Betty Trask Award, garnering
huge critical acclaim for its delicate
portrayal of 1950's South Africa.

**Available from
www.enlightenment-productions.com,
Amazon.com and other retailers.**

ACCLAIM FOR *THE WORLD UNSEEN*

"It is an impressive debut. Sarif's story brings together the
descriptive power of the novelist with the screenwriter's
mastery of dialogue."
– *The Times*

"I read *The World Unseen* at a gulp, so entrancing is its style, so
complete its tale of love and betrayal, and so accurate its depiction
of the physical, social and political scene…"
– *Johannesburg Star*, Book of the Week

SHAMIM SARIF is a multi-award-winning novelist, screenwriter and film director. She has written and directed films of three of her novels – *I Can't Think Straight*, *The World Unseen*, and most recently, *Despite the Falling Snow*. She lives in London with her wife, film producer Hanan Kattan, and their two children.